and metaphorical, external and internal, and her tug-of-war with the forces driving her down a dark path makes for tantalizing reading. A fascinating examination of destiny, responsibility, and how choices shape a person." —*Publishers Weekly*, starred review

"Rich in detail and full of gore and blood, this dark novel will satisfy *Game of Thrones* fans." —*School Library Journal*

"Readers will appreciate the sweeping fantasy saga lifted from East Asian dynasties and endearing characters that are beautifully rendered." —*Kirkus Reviews*

"Readers will be drawn into the lush, fully realized world of Feng Lu and be intrigued by the sinister forces that awaken within and around Xifeng." —*The Bulletin of the Center for Children's Books*

"Dark, lush, and intense, *Forest of a Thousand Lanterns* draws you into a world filled with mystery and intrigue. . . . A stunning debut!" —**Cindy Pon**, author of *Want* and *Serpentine*

"An enchanting debut with a powerful and ambitious lead." —**Zoraida Córdova**, award-winning author of *Labyrinth Lost*

"Magnetic, seductive, and alluring, Dao's *Forest of a Thousand Lanterns* is a lush, captivating read." —**S. Jae-Jones**, *New York Times* bestselling author of *Wintersong*

"Equal parts lush and devastating, this is a tale that will grab you by the throat." —**Roshani Chokshi**, *New York Times* bestselling author of *The Star-Touched Queen*

"*Forest of a Thousand Lanterns* is dark and seductive; beware, this tale will

draw you deeper into the forest than you want to go. Disturbingly good."
—**Stacey Lee**, award-winning author of *Outrun the Moon*

"Beautiful, lush, and stunningly intricate, *Forest of a Thousand Lanterns* is this year's must-read fantasy!"
—**Sandhya Menon**, *New York Times* bestselling author of *When Dimple Met Rishi*

"*Forest of a Thousand Lanterns* is a stunning debut, a sort of inside-out fairy tale where beauty is a weapon, ambition is armor, and the empire is the battlefield. Xifeng doesn't ask for what she wants—she takes it. This book is dangerous; you should read it."
—**Jodi Meadows**, *New York Times* bestselling coauthor of *My Lady Jane*

KINGDOM
of the
BLAZING
PHOENIX

ALSO BY JULIE C. DAO

Forest of a Thousand Lanterns

KINGDOM

of the

BLAZING

PHOENIX

JULIE C. DAO

Philomel Books

PHILOMEL BOOKS
an imprint of Penguin Random House LLC
375 Hudson Street, New York, NY 10014

Library of Congress Cataloging-in-Publication Data is available upon request.
Printed in the United States of America.
ISBN 9781524738327
1 3 5 7 9 10 8 6 4 2

Edited by Jill Santopolo and Brian Geffen.
Design by Jennifer Chung.
Text set in Fairfield LT Std.

To Lam and Tuan, legendary warriors,
and to Tamar Rydzinski,
for whose company on this quest
I am forever grateful

KINGDOM OF THE BLAZING PHOENIX
CAST OF CHARACTERS

THE MONASTERY

- **Amah**, *Jade's nursemaid* (ah-MAH)
- **Abbess Lin**, *leader of the monastery*
- **Auntie Ang**, *a monk*
- **Auntie Tan**, *a monk*
- **Empress Lihua**, *former Empress of Feng Lu and Jade's mother* (lee-HWA)

JOURNEY TO THE PALACE

- **Wren**, *granddaughter of Amah and employee of the Imperial kitchens*
- **Tengaru**, *guardians of the Great Forest* (teng-GAR-roo)
- **Tung**, *teahouse owner*
- **Ning**, *Tung's employee and former acquaintance of the Empress* (neeng)

THE PALACE
ROYALS

- **Empress Xifeng**, *Empress of Feng Lu and Jade's stepmother* (SHE-fung)
- **Emperor Jun**, *Emperor of Feng Lu and Jade's father* (jhoon)

COURT LADIES AND FAMILY

- **Lady Tran,** *a noblewoman and former friend of Empress Lihua*
- **Hana,** *lady-in-waiting to the Empress and sister-in-law of Lady Tran* (hah-nah)
- **Minh,** *son of Hana and nephew of Lady Tran* (min)

EUNUCHS

- **Kang,** *Xifeng's faithful eunuch companion* (kong)
- **Pei,** *a eunuch faithful to Emperor Jun* (pay)

OTHER CHARACTERS

- **Shiro,** *former Ambassador of Kamatsu and cousin of Hana* (shee-ro)
- **Koichi,** *Shiro's son* (ko-eee-chee)
- **Lord Tanaka,** *a nobleman of Kamatsu* (tah-nah-kah)
- **Gao,** *current Imperial Physician*
- **Bohai,** *former Imperial Physician* (BO-hi)

THE QUEST

- **Ming,** *a former soldier*
- **Fu,** *the ghost who haunts Ming*
- **The Crimson Queen,** *leader of the Crimson Army*
- **Sparrow,** *a lieutenant of the Crimson Army*

THE DRAGON LORDS' WORLD

- **Feng Lu,** *the continent* (fung loo)
- **The Dragon King,** Lord of the Forest

Dominion: Kingdom of the Great Forest

Element: Wood

- **Lord of the Sea**

  Dominion: Kingdom of the Boundless Sea / Kamatsu
  (kah-maht-soo)

  Element: Water

- **Lord of the Desert**

  Dominion: Kingdom of the Shifting Sands / Surjalana
  (SOOR-jah-LAH-nah)

  Element: Fire

- **Lord of the Four Winds**

  Dominion: Kingdom of the Four Winds / Dagovad
  (DAH-go-VAHD)

  Element: Metal

- **Lord of the Grasslands**

  Dominion: Kingdom of the Sacred Grasslands

  Element: Earth

1

The messenger came at dawn, riding up to the gates with a scroll in his hand.

Jade tensed as his looming black-robed figure emerged from the wintry forest mists, thinking at once of the bandits who had tried to attack the monastery three nights ago. They had been hungry and desperate enough to attempt to rob the monks of what little they had, and even after Abbess Lin had chased them away, the women lived in fear that they would return. Jade tightened her grip on her bucket of animal feed, wondering if it would be heavy enough to disarm him so she could sound the alarm.

But her fear turned into curiosity as the man approached. Not only was he by himself, but he rode an elegant black horse and his robes were trimmed with gold.

Auntie Ang hurried past with a lantern in her hand, breath emerging in the frigid air, her glance at Jade both reassuring and apprehensive as she approached him. "May I help you, sir?"

"I have two letters to deliver. One is for the abbess," he told her in a deep, strident voice, passing the scroll through the gate. "She will know for whom the other is meant."

The middle-aged monk accepted the missive, her eyes widening at something she saw upon it. "My goodness. This is from . . ."

Jade craned her neck. In the dim lantern light, she could see only a large black circle on the thick roll of paper. There could be nothing shocking in a seal. Abbess Lin had an entire shelf of rusty-red wax sticks in her quarters for correspondence.

But the messenger seemed to understand Auntie Ang's awe. "See that it is delivered immediately." As the monk bowed and left, the man caught sight of Jade standing in the shadows and went still. Even his horse held its breath; the little columns of smoke puffing from its nostrils disappeared. Something gold gleamed on his chest, an emblem that looked strangely familiar. It was clear he served someone of great importance.

Jade tried to remember her manners, but couldn't find her voice and bowed instead. In one fluid motion, the messenger swung off his horse and returned the bow, much more deeply than hers. He wore a black hood that hid all but his eyes. "Princess," he murmured, before climbing back on his horse and disappearing once more into the trees.

Princess.

Now, there was a word she knew well.

There was often a princess in the children's tales Amah still insisted on telling her, even though she was almost eighteen. It was a word meant for old stories and faded texts, a word that belonged to the outside world. It lived in the shaded leaves and branches of the Great Forest. It did not fit into her life, into the rough robes she wore or the sound of the morning's first gong, waking the monks for prayer and meditation.

Jade pressed her face against the gate, watching the treetops shiver in the icy wind. Everything outside the monastery, from prowling bandits to cold-eyed messengers, seemed like a realm apart she was content to know only through Amah's fables. She let out a slow sigh, wrapping her fingers around the bars that protected her.

Still, the coming of the messenger and the word he had uttered unnerved her.

Princess.

It was as though the Great Forest had reached through the gates with branches like eager hands . . . as though that other world had, at last, found her.

2

Jade shut the door on the winter morning, puffing warmth into her cupped hands, and walked down a narrow corridor to the sleeping quarters. None of the rooms had doors. The floors and walls were of heavy stone, each with a small window set high above one or two straw pallets. Abbess Lin discouraged all ornamentation except flowers, with which Jade readily decorated her chamber in warmer months. When the frost came, however, she had to improvise.

Amah looked up when she entered, and clucked disapprovingly at the snow-kissed branches in her hands. "We have enough weeds already, little mouse."

"They were so lovely, I couldn't help it." Jade placed them in a jar, then bent to kiss the old woman's wrinkled cheek. "And don't you think I'm too old for that silly nickname?"

"Don't slouch. No woman in your family ever walked with anything but a straight back. And you'll be my little mouse whether you're seventeen or seventy."

The nursemaid looked at her so fondly, Jade couldn't find it in her heart to argue. She straightened obediently, pulling her shoulders back and her chin up. "You'll hurt your eyes sewing this early with so little light. Is it something for my birthday, perhaps?"

"Never you mind." Amah hastily folded the blue-green brocade into a wooden chest in the corner. This chest had always been a source of wonder to Jade. It held bits and pieces of finery from a forgotten time—scraps of silk and embroidery and foreign lace—that Amah took care to hide from Abbess Lin, who forbade worldly riches of any kind. Whenever Jade asked about the items, her elderly nursemaid would only say they were treasures she was saving.

For me, Jade decided, watching Amah fuss over the lock. *Though I haven't the faintest idea what I might do with them.*

Tufts of coarse white hair trembled on the old woman's head as it jerked this way and that, scanning the room for untidiness. She resembled a chicken more than ever today, Jade thought affectionately. "Fifteen years we've lived here," Amah confessed, "and I'm still skittish as a schoolboy when inspection day comes around."

Jade giggled. "Auntie Tan will be merciful, I think. Though I fear," she added, as the gong struck once more, "if we get in trouble, it will be for coming late to meditation."

"I'm getting too old to kneel for an hour, morning and night," Amah grumbled.

"We could ask Abbess Lin for a stool, but it will depend upon her mood." Jade thought of the scroll that had arrived that morning. Auntie Ang had recognized the seal, that was certain, but it hadn't been clear from her astonishment whether it might be good or bad news.

The abbess didn't give anything away when they entered the meditation room. A small, birdlike woman in her forties, Abbess Lin had the gift of authority. When she inclined her head to signal Jade and Amah to take their places, they obeyed, forgetting all about the stool.

Jade sensed a ripple of awareness through the ten other women as she knelt beside Amah. Even after all these years and the friendships she had formed, Jade still stood out among them: the youngest, and the only one, aside from Amah, whose head had not been shaved. *Still not one of them,* she thought, tucking her braid beneath her tunic. *Still not home at home.*

Years ago, she had begged Abbess Lin to let her become a full monk and finally belong to the women she considered family. The abbess had refused, not unkindly. "You are with us, but you will never be one of us. Be patient, my child. You are meant for another life."

Now, Jade closed her eyes and fell into the soothing rhythm of her own breath, as she had done every morning for as long as she could remember. *Inhale, exhale.* The silence and stillness were absolute, except for Amah's occasional fidgeting beside her. She envisioned the room around them, the one they used in winter when it was too cold to sit outdoors: pale stone walls, mats of woven straw for their knees, daylight streaming in through narrow windows.

Once, many years ago, she had asked Auntie Ang what she meditated about.

"You don't meditate *about* something," the monk had replied, amused. "You simply meditate. You let go and clear your mind of thought. You just *be*."

But no matter how hard Jade tried, images insisted on dancing behind her lids. Perhaps it was part of the reason why Abbess Lin wouldn't accept her as a monk: Jade lacked the patience, selflessness, and detachment necessary. For her, meditating was like trying to catch raindrops. She could put out hundreds of bowls to collect the water, but there would always be some that escaped and soaked into the soil of her mind. Today, it was the messenger and his quiet, solemn *Princess* that kept intruding on her thoughts.

Jade knew who she was. She knew it in the way that she knew the desert was hot and the ocean vast: through hearsay, never with her own eyes and ears and heart. Amah reminded her constantly: "You are the daughter of Her Imperial Majesty, Empress Lihua, a descendant of the Dragon King." Lihua had died many years ago, but Amah told Jade so many stories of the former Empress's kind and beautiful spirit that Jade felt as close to her mother as though she still lived. That part was easy: loving and revering her.

It was the other part she had trouble with. She wondered what her mother would think if she could see Jade now—a girl who would gladly give up her family and her name to be a monk.

Empress Lihua would always be part of her, but that outside world would not. She was a girl, after all, and as meaningful to her father as an old shoe. Emperor Jun had tossed his three-year-old daughter into the monastery after taking a new Empress. Out of sight, out of mind, because Jade wasn't the son he'd craved. Instead of fading over time, the bitterness of that truth had lingered on like a shadow. She had lived fifteen years as a humble penitent, her true identity kept secret from all but Amah and Abbess Lin, and she had worked as hard as any other monk for bed and bread, untouched by that old life.

So why, now, did a stranger recognize her for who she was?

The hour passed in a disquieting haze, and then the gong rang for the morning meal.

"Finally. I thought my bones were going to grow into the floor," Amah wheezed as Jade helped her stand. "Looks like we'll have to wait a bit longer to eat, though."

Abbess Lin stood waiting for them by the door. Neither Jade nor Amah were tall, but they both towered over her. "Would you join me in my quarters? I have news that concerns you both." Without awaiting a response, she walked down the corridor, her footsteps nearly silent.

Jade expected her nursemaid to make a joke, as she always did, but instead the lines on the old woman's forehead deepened as they followed the abbess.

Abbess Lin's quarters were large, but every bit as austere as the rest of the monastery. A single table of weathered wood stood surrounded by a few old chairs. The woman gestured for Jade and Amah to sit down, then pulled out the scroll that had been delivered earlier. In the daylight, Jade clearly saw the seal that had stunned Auntie Ang. Whereas most seals were red, this was of onyx-black wax and depicted a dragon with something curved within its talons.

"Do you know to whom this emblem belongs?" Abbess Lin asked Jade.

"Yes, Abbess. It looks like the Emperor's Imperial seal." But as she peered at it, Jade realized the dragon's talons contained a serpent with many forked tongues. She glanced at Amah, whose thin lips turned down. "But the dragon should be holding a forest, and not a snake."

It made Jade think of an afternoon many years ago. She had been swimming in the stream where the monks did their washing, splashing and ignoring Amah's scolding. A snake had watched her with vigilant ruby eyes from outside the gates, its slender poisonous body as black and still as the night. She wouldn't have seen it had it not been for the tongue darting in and out of its fanged mouth. It had slithered away as she ran screaming to Amah, and for years afterward she had dreamed of its watchful gaze like two drops of blood in the dark.

"Correct. This is the Empress's new seal. She has written to me."

Abbess Lin paused, then looked Jade directly in the eyes. "And to you."

Jade felt the same tug of foreboding as the abbess handed her a thin scroll that had been folded inside the larger one. The world *had* found her, after all. Amah's blue-veined hands twisted in her lap, but she said nothing as Jade broke the black seal and unrolled the crisp paper.

The calligraphy of an accomplished scholar met her eye. Each sprawling character swept across the page with bold, unyielding confidence. "'Your Imperial Highness,'" Jade read aloud, continuing through a list of honorifics and titles she hadn't even known she possessed. "'And my own dear stepdaughter, jewel of His Imperial Majesty's court . . .'"

Amah let out a cough that sounded suspiciously like a snort.

"'I hope this missive finds you in good health. In the letters from your esteemed guardian to His Majesty over the years, you are by all reports a paragon of grace and integrity, and everything the Emperor has dreamed of in a daughter.'" Jade glanced at the aforementioned guardian. Amah seemed to be struggling to keep her eyes from rolling heavenward. "'I regret the time and the distance that have separated us. It is a failing I take upon my own humble self, and I beg your forgiveness. Many duties have occupied my attention, but I can no longer deny the great wish of my heart: to meet you at last, and claim you as my own.'"

Abbess Lin shifted in her chair, a slight frown marring her usual placidity.

"'Your revered father, Emperor Jun, wishes to hold a banquet in honor of your eighteenth birthday. I have sent a palanquin for you that shall come in two days, and you will be with your loving family again as soon as the gods will it. The Great Forest will rejoice, and the lanterns will shine for you like stars welcoming back the moon. I am, forever and always, your loving stepmother, Xifeng.'" Jade ran her trembling fingers over the beautiful name. The characters gave the impression of having been woven into the paper, rather than inked.

Amah fidgeted in her chair, lips still twitching with words Jade knew she longed to say but would not in the abbess's presence. "She does write beautifully, doesn't she?" she said at last.

Jade touched the phrase *claim you as my own.* "I don't understand. Why does the Empress want me with her now, after all these years?"

"You are the heir to the empire, as she and the Emperor have no other living children," Abbess Lin said. "None of His Majesty's stepsons, your half brothers, survived."

Over the years, Jade had heard much about Lihua's three sons with her first husband. The youngest had died of illness. The second had been captured on a mission overseas, and although his eldest brother, the courageous Crown Prince, had sailed into enemy territory to rescue him, the attempt had been in vain. Both were reported dead, but whereas the younger man's head had been returned to Emperor Jun, the Crown Prince's body had never been recovered.

"But that's impossible," Jade protested. "I can't go, Abbess. I thought I would . . . I hoped to still persuade you to let me take the vows one day."

"You've been a joy to us these many years," the woman said in a gentle voice, "but you are meant for a different role in this life."

Jade lowered the letter to her lap, a sensation of cold spreading through her chest as she imagined the gates yawning open, releasing her from the monastery's warm, snug embrace. The forest, enchanting from a distance, became a woodland of cold mists that were full of watchful, unfriendly eyes and a large and looming sky, ready to consume her.

"*This* is the role I want. I love our life," she said, struggling to keep her voice calm. "You taught me yourself that we are closest to the gods in quiet prayer, and we do so much good here."

"This could be an even greater opportunity for you to do good." Abbess Lin folded her hands. "We all thought the Emperor would father sons to inherit his crown, but fate had different plans. His Majesty's health is declining, and it's natural for him to want his only child at court."

Jade looked resentfully at Xifeng's signature. "Then why didn't he write to me himself?"

"He might have been too ill to do so." Abbess Lin's eyes darted to Amah, who muttered something darkly. "Regardless, you must prepare yourself for the journey."

The letter fluttered, forgotten, to Jade's feet. Everything she had ever known was coming to an end. She would trade her garden, her books, and her quiet reflections for a palace full of eyes and whispers—torn from the family she wanted and flung toward the one that had never wanted her. But Emperor Jun and his wife were her true family, and it was her duty to go.

"I understand," she heard herself say.

Abbess Lin nodded approvingly. "We have valued your company, my dear, but the monastery has become a shield for you. Perhaps this summons comes at an auspicious time. That world," she said, gesturing to the snow-blanketed forest, "is where you truly belong."

"Does she have a choice? That letter is a command, however much it is framed as a courteous invitation," Amah spat, her jaw working. "Let us make no mistake about that."

"Come." Jade stood as the abbess's disapproving gaze swiveled to Amah. She slipped a hand beneath her nursemaid's elbow before the old woman could say anything else indiscreet about the Empress.

"We will eat, if the abbess will excuse us. I can hear your stomach rumbling."

Abbess Lin waved a hand in dismissal. "Ensure that you eat too, child, to gain strength for the journey. After all," the woman added with a faint smile, "your stepmother is calling you home."

The gates opened the next afternoon, welcoming poor families who came each week for a hot meal donated by patrons of the monastery. The villagers lived on the woodlands' edge, on the border between the Great Forest and the Sacred Grasslands, and Jade always looked forward to their arrival. At every meal, she would chat with the village elder, who was the only person aside from Amah and Abbess Lin who knew her true identity.

She bowed low before him. Though the old man greeted her with the same smile he had given her for fifteen years, today his eyes in their nest of wrinkles held concern. "Amah told me everything. You are to leave us, then."

The monks moved around them, spooning steaming white rice into the villagers' bowls.

"I can't imagine my life away from here . . . and you," Jade said. "Sitting with you as I might with an honored grandfather, listening to stories about your village and the people who pass by on the trade route. It's through you and Amah that I know the world."

The elder twinkled at her. "It was an honor when Amah asked me years ago if I would help her see to your education. That astute woman always suspected the Emperor would summon you one day, and she prepared you accordingly, even as she embraced your humble upbringing."

"But she never breathed a word," Jade said, stunned. "I assumed she educated me because it was what she had done for my mother and grandmother, and that *you* taught me because you saw how I loved learning."

"Literature, history, and politics are not taught to most girls, even those with quick minds like yours. We had our reasons."

Memories flashed through Jade's mind: Amah teaching her to walk gracefully, to keep her chin high and sit with a straight back as she learned calligraphy; basking in the elder's pride as she recited the history of the Dragon Lords, the gods who had created Feng Lu in friendship and abandoned it after a rift in their alliance; listening to Amah describe the exported goods of each kingdom—lumber from the Great Forest, pearls and jade from Kamatsu, precious metals from Dagovad, rice and grains from the Grasslands, skins of desert animals from Surjalana.

All these years, Amah and the elder had not been indulging an eager student.

They had been training an empress.

"Still," the elder continued, "you must see the world for yourself and meet your true teachers: life and experience. Never in my hundred years have I been close to the Imperial Palace, and now you will experience it in all of its grandeur and beauty."

"But this monastery is in my blood. I can do good work here, training as Auntie Tan's apprentice in herbal medicines and healing." Jade nodded at the white-haired monk, who had stopped nearby to hand a young mother a tonic for her baby. "Your lessons paint a broken world of greed and corruption of which I want no part. I have no ambition for a throne. My father valued the *idea* of unborn sons more than he valued me, and his wife calls me back now only because they have no other options. All of a sudden, they care that I exist."

"Fifteen years in the monastery have not erased that worldly resentment of yours. I don't blame you for your bitterness," the elder added when Jade bowed her head, "but you cannot be a monk if you are unable to detach yourself from it, my dear. Haven't the monks taught you compassion? To put other lives before your own?"

She looked up, alarmed. "Yes, of course."

"And you said, just now, that you want to do some good?"

"Yes, I do."

He gestured to the people around them. "Observe these men, women, and children. See how their clothes hang from their bones and how sunken their cheeks are. Ours is not the only suffering village. You know this. All these years, you've heard me tell you that the empire is full of hungry babies, of women who go without food so their little ones can eat, of men who work until their backs break but still cannot afford a bowl of broth."

She took his frail hand in her strong, sun-browned ones, aching at the sorrow in his voice.

"Feng Lu is dying," the old man murmured, "rotting from the core. There is no more time for beauty, for music, for closing one's eyes and feeling the clouds drift overhead. The heart and soul is being drained from this world, Jade, and its people feel the pain first." Despite the milky film covering his pupils, she saw a ghost of his old vitality in his stern gaze. "Through Empress Lihua, you are a descendant of the Dragon King, the god of gods. His blood does not run through Their Majesties as it does through you. They do not feel this devastation, and they will not fix it."

There is no one left but me. The truth settled into Jade's gut like a stone as she and the elder sat in silence, listening to men speaking in low voices, chopsticks scraping against wooden bowls, and the rustling of the monks' robes as they moved around.

"Strange to see the two of you so quiet," Amah said, coming over. "Usually you're talking nonstop about the radish tax in Kamatsu or the court policies of the king of Dagovad."

"We've been talking of what I owe my father and stepmother," Jade explained, and her nursemaid's lips twisted with disdain.

"Xifeng isn't fit to scrub the floor your mother walked upon."

The elder clucked his tongue. "Have a care, my friend. People have been imprisoned for saying less. Not for nothing is she called the Empress of a Hundred Thousand Eyes and Ears. Her soldiers are everywhere, watching and listening, and even the people are encouraged to turn in friends for speaking against her. They are richly rewarded with clothes and food if they do."

"Be that as it may, venerable one," the old woman answered tartly, "she has no business ordering *Jade* about. Not when her crown truly belongs to Jade."

"Hush, please, Amah," Jade pleaded.

Amah had never hidden her feelings about Empress Xifeng from Jade. Almost all of her eighty years of life had been spent as adoring nursemaid and tutor to three generations of the royal family: Lihua's mother, Lihua herself, and now Jade, who Amah considered the last of the line of true Dragon Kings, as Emperor Jun's own blood ties to the throne were weak and diluted. Even so, Jade had no desire to find out what the loyal woman's outspokenness might cost them.

"Marriage is a weaker claim to the throne than being born to a centuries-old lineage," Amah pointed out. "Before her death, your honored mother ensured that you would be next in the line of succession. Xifeng has done nothing but destroy us and send us into ruin."

Jade shook her head. "Taxes and poverty. Revolts and war and secret police. What can *I* possibly do with such hardship and devastation?"

"You will have help and, gods willing, decades ahead in which to learn," the elder said. "Feng Lu yearns for a ruler with a good heart. This world is vast and varied, and sometimes amidst the pain and sorrow, it can be beautiful too. Don't spend your life here, praying instead of living. It is a noble thing to be a monk, but it is not a life for *you*."

Jade pictured the gates opening once more, and the forest breathing her into its dark embrace. "I have no choice but to obey the Empress's summons," she said, though her heart sank as she spoke. "I will stand by my duty to my family and our people."

The elder squeezed her hand. "You will be in my thoughts always."

"And *I* will be with you in the flesh," Amah told her fiercely, "and protect you as I promised Lihua I would. You will have me and a mother who watches over you even in death. The gods know you'll need both of us, walking into Xifeng's court."

After so many years of loving Amah, Jade often felt she could hear the old woman's unspoken thoughts. And she heard them now: *We may never come back out again.*

A chill crept down her spine. "That comforts me. But I wish my mother were here, too."

"So do I, love." The creases deepened on Amah's forehead. "So do I."

4

"You're as restless as a caged tiger today," Amah chided Jade the next afternoon during their daily lessons. "That's twice now you've stopped midsentence to stare outside."

"I'm sorry," Jade said, lowering the volume of Kamatsu poetry as her eyes strayed once more to the window. The wintry sky had already begun to darken over the forest. "But I thought I heard horses. Don't you think the palanquin should have arrived by now?"

"It'll come when it comes, and no amount of fretting will change that," the nursemaid said reasonably, sewing away at the blue-green brocade. "Now, read that poem to me again, and mind your pronunciation this time."

Jade did so, taking care with the lovely, lilting language. "You've never told me where you first learned the Kamatsu tongue," she said, when she had read to Amah's satisfaction.

"Your mother's first husband, Emperor Tai, always had foreign ambassadors at court," the nursemaid explained. "Their women stayed with us in the harem and made it easy to learn about other languages and customs. That education was important. Tell me why."

"We learn about ourselves when we learn about others," Jade said. "We respect different ways of life as food, traditions, and storytelling are shared across borders."

"And won't it be a gesture of courtesy and respect, when you are Empress, to speak to the ministers of Kamatsu in their own language rather than the common tongue?" Amah grinned at her, and Jade couldn't help the sinking feeling in her stomach at the thought of entertaining important diplomats. "Now, the kingdoms of Feng Lu are separate and distinct, but not isolated. They are joined by not only the empire, but a shared history. Explain."

Jade resisted the powerful urge to peer out the window again. "The kingdoms were created by the Dragon Lords, gods who descended from the heavens many ages ago. Each god chose one land: the seas of Kamatsu, the mountains of Dagovad, the Sacred Grasslands, and the deserts of Surjalana. But the greatest of the gods, the Dragon King, chose the forests."

At that moment, Auntie Ang appeared at the door, and her stunned expression sent Jade straight to the window. The chamber Jade and Amah shared faced the gates, where a moment ago, there had been nothing. Now there were twenty men, some on horseback, some hoisting a palanquin on their shoulders, and a few carrying the Emperor's banners. They stood in an eerie, perfect silence, as though they had materialized from the forest mists.

"They've come for us," Jade said, swallowing hard. Her identity could no longer be a secret from the monks or anyone else, not with this grand procession. "We'd better bring our belongings out. Auntie Ang, would you mind notifying the abbess?"

The monk stood for a moment, her mouth moving wordlessly, before hurrying away.

"There's no hiding who you are now," Amah said, chuckling. Then she frowned at the window. "These men can't expect you to depart immediately, without any supper."

"I packed plenty of food for us earlier," Jade reassured her. Somehow, she didn't think these soldiers would be willing to delay, not with the Empress waiting.

The men stood like rigid statues, dressed head to toe in black metal armor that appeared to have been wrought in smoke. Like Xifeng's messenger, they wore black cloth over their faces that covered all but their eyes. Having spent a lifetime among women, Jade was struck by how impossibly large and imposing they seemed. She recognized the Empress's symbol upon their chests, but the flags they bore had the true Imperial Seal: a dragon rampant, holding a forest in its talons.

"This is how royalty travels, then, is it?" Jade said weakly.

"Get used to it," Amah told her.

"They must work for the Empress only, if they're wearing her seal."

"I think we'll find that anyone in His Majesty's employ must be in *Her* Majesty's first."

When they went outside, Abbess Lin was already there with the other monks, speaking to the leader of the soldiers. He towered over her like a great black tree, his icy gaze shifting to Jade as she approached. His body snapped into a sharp bow, which the soldiers behind him echoed as though a single giant hand had bent them all at the spine.

Jade stopped in her tracks, overwhelmed by the show of respect. *I'm just a girl in faded robes,* she thought, and then she glanced at Amah, whose arched brows told her, *You are a princess.* The soldiers straightened, and a taut silence stretched out in which they and the monks watched her. She realized with a start that they were waiting for her to speak first.

"Welcome," she said, her voice shaking. She cleared her throat and forced herself to hold her head high. "Thank you for coming to escort me to the Imperial Palace."

The leader of the soldiers addressed Jade in an odd, clipped voice, as though he did not often speak. "It is our privilege to see you safely through the Great Forest, Your Highness. We intend to bring you before Empress Xifeng in two weeks' time." He gestured to the palanquin, which was made of ivory and covered with heavy scarlet brocade. "Would you step inside?"

Before Jade could respond, approaching hoofbeats thundered, and a square-shouldered figure on a stout gray pony burst out of the forest. The newcomer broke through the line of stiff soldiers and pulled to a stop beside the leader, who scowled at the interruption.

"Thought you'd lost me, did you?" the rider said breathlessly, tugging down warm cloth wrappings to reveal the broad, pink-cheeked features of a young woman. A knot of coarse black hair emerged next, above alert eyes that went straight to Amah. "Hello, Grandmother."

"*Wren?* How . . . when . . ." Amah sputtered. "You should be in the palace kitchens, not gallivanting around the bandit-ridden forest. What are you doing here, reckless girl?"

"When I heard the princess was coming home, I asked if I could join the retinue to bring you back. Not that it mattered whether I got permission. They refused, and I still came." Wren slid to the ground, scanning Jade from head to toe before she gave a halfhearted bow. "Your Highness," she added, her familiar manner freezing into chilly formality.

Jade gave her a friendly nod. "It's a pleasure to meet you. Amah has mentioned you often and shown me all your messages over the years. And please call me Jade."

"Thank you . . . Your Highness." The young woman kept her eyes down, as was proper, but they flickered up as she used the title. If Jade hadn't known better, she might have called it a *glare*. She turned to Amah for help, wondering if Wren felt awkward in her presence.

"Headstrong and disobedient, just like your father when he was alive," the old woman rebuked her granddaughter. "You traveled for two weeks alone with these men for what?"

"To see you, of course, for the first time in fifteen years. I was only five when you left." Wren reached for Amah's hand, and the nursemaid gave it to her with a grudging smile. "And I didn't travel *with* these men. They wouldn't let me. *This one*"—Wren indicated the leader with a careless gesture—"thought they could easily lose me."

Amah laid her free hand on Jade's shoulder, and Wren's eyes followed the movement. "I will scold you properly later," the old woman said. "We shouldn't stand too long in the cold."

The time had come.

Jade turned, her dread as heavy as iron, and looked into the gentle faces of the monks as they stood in a solemn line with their hands clasped. She wondered if she would ever again see these beloved women who had been her friends and teachers. They had welcomed her into their lives, a wayward, unwanted girl, and had taught her all they knew of kindness and compassion. She bowed low to each, murmuring farewell.

But when she stood before Abbess Lin, the woman shook her head. "You do not bow to me, Imperial Princess." She touched Jade's forehead in a sign of quiet well-wishing.

"Thank you," Jade whispered, and then she took in the monastery one last time.

Her gaze swept over everything she had loved: the vegetable garden she helped tend in the summer, the herb room where she and Auntie Tan had dried plants for medicine and tea, the stream in which she had learned to swim. She had left pieces of herself here, and it was slightly comforting to think the monastery might not soon forget her because of it.

She wiped her wet eyes. "I'm ready, Amah."

Wren returned to her horse as Jade and Amah walked through the line of soldiers. Jade felt a cold, trickling dread being this close to them. A strange smell like fire and damp soil emanated from their smoky armor, and they stood so still, they did not resemble real men at all. One of them moved stiffly to hold the brocade curtain so she could step inside the palanquin.

After years of living in stark austerity, the vessel was a vision of richness. It was made of rosewood, with a nest of satin cushions and fur blankets on the wide seat to make their journey comfortable. A window faced the door, also covered by heavy brocade to keep out the chill.

Amah leaned against the pillows, looking content against her own will. The faint light illuminated each of her lines and wrinkles, and Jade thought, with a pang, that her nursemaid had grown old. The two-week journey in cold, cramped quarters would be an ordeal for her. Jade wrapped a soft blanket around the older woman, tucking the ends in, making sure her feet were covered.

"Thank you, little mouse," Amah said wearily, and for once, Jade did not take offense at the silly nickname. She only settled next to her nursemaid as the door shut, surrounding them with dark and quiet, like a cocoon of cushions. It was much warmer than she had expected.

The palanquin shifted as the soldiers heaved it onto their shoulders, then began moving, and Jade peered out the window as they passed through the gates. Beyond the soldiers and their coal-black horses, the monks bowed low in farewell. Jade watched as the monastery and the women—her home, her family—grew smaller and smaller until they vanished.

And then they were out into the world, and the Great Forest swallowed them whole.

5

The palanquin's rocking motion made Jade's stomach uneasy at first. She spent the first few days of travel with her nose out the window, her illness soothed by the icy wind. But by midweek, the side-to-side sway felt familiar and almost comforting, and many times she found herself growing sleepy in the middle of a conversation with Amah.

The retinue stopped three times a day so she and Amah could tend to their bodies' needs and stretch their legs, but Jade sensed that if the soldiers had their way, they wouldn't stop at all. The men fed and watered their horses regularly, but she had yet to see them eat or rest themselves. As it was, she and Amah found the weather so cold and the men so rigid and silent that they took no more time than was needed before hurrying back into the palanquin.

So far, Wren had managed to keep up with the soldiers' fearsome pace. She sometimes joined Jade and Amah when they stepped out for air, and though her manners were above reproach, they were not entirely respectful. More than once, Jade returned to see her joking with Amah, only to resume her coldness when Jade tried to join in.

Jade discovered the reason about five days into their journey. Amah had gone off to relieve herself, and Jade was rummaging through their packed food. She took out a large, cold steamed bun for herself, then began breaking a second bun into small, bite-sized chunks.

"Why are you doing that? Your Highness?" Wren asked, watching her. At twenty, she was tall and stocky, with strong shoulders and calloused hands, and might have passed for a young soldier in armor if she'd had the rigidity of the Empress's men. Jade found it easy to imagine her flouting authority to embark on a dangerous journey through the Great Forest.

"It's for Amah. She's been having trouble with her teeth and can't chew bigger pieces."

"You don't have to do that—I'm here now and she's *my* grandmother. I didn't even know about her teeth." Wren's lips thinned. "I should have been with her all these years to care for her. Anyway, shouldn't princesses eat and sleep in different quarters from their servants?"

"Amah isn't my servant," Jade said, shocked. "And I've shared meals and a room with her my whole life."

The older girl let out a breath through her nose. "How fortunate to have had someone care for you who doesn't even share your blood. *Your Highness.*" She moved away when she heard Amah's slippers crunching toward them.

Jade climbed into the palanquin after Amah, torn between anger and pity. It wasn't her fault Wren had decided to hate her for something she couldn't control. But . . . could she have controlled it? Could she, at any point, have said, *Amah, you should be with your orphaned grandchild and not me?*

As Jade watched the old woman chew tenderly on the torn-up bun, her wispy white hair a cloud around her temples, she knew she never would have. Amah was her guardian, protector, and last link to Lihua. She had always made Jade laugh when she was sad, wrapped her in blankets when she was cold, and healed her hurts with a kiss. She had stepped into Lihua's place, and Jade would never have given that up— even it was the right thing to do.

But who, selfish thing, cared for Wren?

"Will Wren be all right, riding in the cold like that for another week?" she asked Amah.

"She'll be fine—she seems as hearty as a young oak," the old woman said proudly. "Her mother was a weak, dainty thing, but Wren's got my son's strength and stubbornness."

Jade didn't doubt that Wren thought her a *weak, dainty thing*. Flushing, she remembered how Wren had watched her lean against a tree a few days ago, sickened by travel. She had probably been repulsed by the sight of a pampered girl, ill despite sitting against cushions, while Wren herself rode in the winter air night after night at a breakneck pace just to keep up.

She peered out at the canopy of silver branches against the evening sky. Almost a week of uneventful travel and remembering how Empress Lihua had loved these trees made her feel less afraid of the forest. "Did you ever regret being with me instead of with Wren?"

Amah's eyebrows touched her hairline. "What a question, little mouse. It was my duty to be with you. A vow to your mother is never given lightly. But tell me," she said, patting Jade's crestfallen face, "why should duty and love be two different things? I have loved you like my own, as I did your mother before you, and *her* mother. I have seen you all grow into women."

"But we were always other people's children," Jade whispered.

"*My* children, too. Family is not only defined by blood."

The palanquin shifted as the soldiers lifted it onto their shoulders once more. "It doesn't feel right, being carried about," Jade said. "I wish my stepmother had sent horses for us instead."

"If she had, we'd likely arrive in time for your *nineteenth* birthday instead of your eighteenth," Amah joked. "Now, enough chatter. Where did we leave off in our lessons?"

Jade couldn't help smiling. Even this far from the monastery, the nursemaid was bent on keeping up her schooling. "The gods descended to create Feng Lu. To honor their friendship, they each placed a treasure of their land in a shrine in the Mountains of Enlightenment."

"But the friendship didn't last," Amah prompted her.

"No," Jade agreed. "The god of Surjalana, the desert kingdom, resented the Dragon King and shattered their alliance with his jealousy. They removed their relics and returned to the heavens, leaving behind five floundering kingdoms. Eventually, the Great Forest conquered the other lands and formed an empire, naming its ruler Emperor of Feng Lu."

The thought of an empire ruled by *her* family had always felt deeply uncomfortable. She had said as much to Amah and the elder once, and they had smiled indulgently at her idealistic concept of free kingdoms linked by trade and friendship.

"But not every land wishes to belong to the empire," Jade went on. "Kamatsu has made many bids for independence from Emperor Jun."

"Good. Why won't he release them?"

"Power. The more kingdoms in his control, the longer the reach of his arm."

"Perhaps you ought to say *her* control and *her* arm," Amah said darkly. "After all, Xifeng is the one pulling Feng Lu's strings. The continent is falling apart under her rule, and Kamatsu's increasingly aggressive attempts to leave are evidence of that. It won't be long before their sentiments spread to the other kingdoms, if they haven't already."

"And this is the empire I'm meant to inherit," Jade said quietly.

Long after her nursemaid had fallen asleep, she sat awake thinking about Xifeng. Her stepmother sounded like a fiend, but she couldn't help feeling curious about the woman who had risen from peasant to Empress at the age of eighteen. No one, Jade reflected, did that without brains, resourcefulness, and a will of iron. She wondered if Xifeng had ever felt uncertain and hopelessly out of her depth, as Jade did. It was difficult to imagine.

Perhaps I'll ask her for advice.

The thought was so ridiculous that she settled against the cushions, laughing softly so as not to wake Amah, and allowed herself to be lulled into slumber as well. And if she dreamed at all—about the loving mother she had lost, the father who had discarded her, or the stepmother who hoped to claim her—she did not remember any of it.

Jade knew two things about herself: she had always been afraid and fought hard against it, and she had always hated Amah's pet name for her, little mouse, because it suggested timidity.

At six, determined to conquer her fear of the dark, she had sat in the monastery kitchen for an entire sleepless night. At eleven, frustrated by her terror of water, she had begged Auntie Tan to teach her how to swim. At fourteen, she had let a child put a harmless garden snake in her hands. It hadn't changed her mind about serpents, but at least she had met the fear head-on.

Now, with the palace only two days away, Jade decided it was time to face another fear: approaching one of the soldiers. He stood motionless, blank eyes staring, and his eerie manner almost made her return to the palanquin at once, but she forced herself forward. Besides, they weren't alone: Amah sat eating nearby while Wren did some sort of strange exercise in a tree. She hung by her fingers from a thick branch, then bent her arms and lifted her body until her chin was at the level of the branch, repeating the motion over and over.

She wasn't afraid of the soldiers, Jade thought enviously, or anything at all. Courage seemed to come easily to everyone else. She squared her shoulders and went up to the soldier. "Excuse me, how long will it take to arrive at the palace once we're in the Imperial City?"

The odd smell of smoke and soil rose from the soldier as he spoke. "Half an hour, Your Highness. But our orders are to take you to a teahouse first."

"Why?" Jade crossed her arms, hoping she gave the impression of being at ease.

"So you may eat, rest, and be properly dressed to meet Her Imperial Majesty."

She waited, but he offered nothing more, so she sighed and had turned to go back when she noticed a soft glow on her hand. She spread her fingers, spotting the same pearlescent shine on the soldiers' armor. It was everywhere now that night had come: glistening in the tree trunks, the snow, and even Wren's severe knot of hair.

Jade looked up.

Leafless branches stretched like veins across the deepening sky. Set against this encroaching darkness were hundreds of orbs like enormous fireflies nesting in the treetops. They were brilliant white lanterns dangling from the forest canopy, casting their light upon the bleak winter woods, radiant sentinels against the night.

An odd, buoyant feeling rose in Jade's breast, like the urge to laugh.

It didn't make sense, but somehow she felt both comforted and overwhelmed with joy as she basked in the glow.

"Amah," she exclaimed, "there are lanterns in the trees like in my mother's story."

"I know," the old woman said tenderly as Jade came to sit by her.

Wren dropped down from the tree, breathing hard. "I'm not familiar with that story."

"It was my mother's favorite," Jade said as Wren pushed snow with her boot. "There was once a princess who loved a poor musician, but the queen wished her to wed a nobleman, so they decided to elope. The musician would leave a trail of lanterns in the forest, and the princess would follow only the red ones to him. But before he could put the red lanterns up, he was killed, and his blood splattered one of the white ones. The princess thought he had abandoned her and walked in the forest every day, heartbroken. One morning, she found the single red lantern. She heard a bird singing her lover's song on a branch nearby and realized that it was the musician come back to her. When she drank its tears, the princess was transformed into a bird herself and reunited with him for eternity."

They sat looking up at the lights. Each globe hung on the uppermost branches, too high for anyone to climb. And though Jade knew it was only a folktale she was much too old for, she couldn't help feeling disappointed that all the lanterns were white. "Who put them up?"

"No one knows, Your Highness," the leader of the soldiers said stiffly. "They appeared years ago all around the palace and the Imperial City. Empress Xifeng has had them removed many times, but they keep returning and doubling in number."

Amah let out a strangled laugh that she disguised as a cough.

Jade stared. "Doubling? How many are there now?"

"Likely thousands. If it pleases Your Highness," the man said, "we ought to be on our way. We can't keep the Empress waiting."

"Well, you heard the man," Amah said, with an unmistakable smirk of triumph. She lowered her voice as she and Jade walked back to the palanquin. "The lanterns appeared after Lihua's death. On our journey to the monastery, I rode through the Great Forest with their light upon you in my arms. Odd, isn't it, that your mother's tale came true and the usurper Xifeng cannot remove them, try as she might?" She gave the lights a conspiratorial wink. "Lihua is watching over you, my love, and always will be."

Whether that was truth or a mere hope, Jade didn't know, but she felt sure the image of lanterns shimmering in the trees would stay with her long after this night. She glanced at Wren, who stood puffing warmth into her cupped hands. Whatever her feelings toward Jade, she had ridden many long days and nights in the cold.

Jade's stomach twisted. *And perhaps I deserve her jealousy.* "Would you like to take my place in the palanquin?" she called. "I can try riding your pony, if she'll let me."

Wren gaped at her. "Ride in that fancy vessel like a queen? You can't be serious."

Jade couldn't help chuckling at her astonishment. "I don't feel right riding in it either, to tell you the truth. But it's warm and snug."

Wren's eyes grew even rounder. After a long pause, she said, "I'll ride my pony. But thank you for the offer."

"At least take a blanket. We have more than we need." Jade tugged out a thick fur wrap for Wren, then stepped into the palanquin before the other girl could protest.

As the swaying motion began once more, the last conscious image in Jade's mind was the lantern light twinkling at her like a kindly wink.

6

They arrived at the Imperial City gates on a cold, clear morning. The stones on the wide gravel road made a *shh, shh* sound beneath them as Jade peered out, blinking in the sunlight reflecting off the soldiers' armor. She had never seen so many people in one place, pushing wheelbarrows and lugging baskets of goods upon their shoulders. Children ran around shouting, neighbors greeted each other, and farmers led skinny donkeys through the crowd. In fact, Jade noticed that all of the animals were so thin, she could see their ribs.

She watched a mother divide a piece of bread among six children, taking only a morsel for herself. One of the girls dropped her piece, which her brother seized. The girl began crying as the mother yanked the hem of the boy's shabby tunic and shouted at him.

"That was all we had for today, and you ate your sister's share!"

The girl sobbed even more loudly, pressing dirty hands over her tear-streaked little face.

Jade's eyes stung in sympathy as the child's shoulders trembled.

She and the monks had eaten plain meals, but none of them had ever known a day of such cruel hunger. The boy, too, was crying now, for even the extra piece of bread he'd stolen had not been enough.

Amah saw her turn to their small sack of food. "You cannot feed them all, my love. Even if we had more to offer than this."

The palanquin moved swiftly past the family, attracting plenty of attention. Snippets of conversation floated in through the brocade coverings:

"Mama, is that the Empress?"

"Her Majesty travels in a grander litter. That might be a noble lady on her way to court."

"Is she going to marry Emperor Jun?"

Amah's eyes twinkled at Jade's shock. "They think you're a concubine. As though Xifeng would *ever* tolerate that."

The nursemaid had explained the concept to Jade long ago. Poorer men had one wife each, but a wealthy man of high stature might have concubines as well to give him sons and ensure his line continued—a practice Xifeng had long ago done away with at court.

Jade had sympathized with Xifeng. "I would want my husband for myself as well."

"It is not for a woman to decide."

"But Empress Xifeng decided."

"She is not like other women," had been Amah's careful response.

The Imperial gates loomed ahead, and Jade noticed patterns carved into the enormous gold doors: dunes of sand, a mountain range shaped like a dragon, a swirling ocean, and grasslands all dwarfed by an immense forest. Soldiers teemed in front, armed to the teeth.

Three long objects hung from the watchtowers with thick black rope, dangling just above the entrance to the Imperial City. Jade bit down a scream when she realized what they were: corpses in ragged clothing, their arms and legs limp, heads lolling and eye-holes staring sightlessly out at the crowd. One of them was a young woman who didn't appear much older than Jade.

"What did they do to deserve such a terrible fate?" she demanded.

"Perhaps they stole food, or spoke out against Xifeng. It could be as simple as that."

Jade squeezed her lids shut at Amah's grim response, but she could still see the bodies in her mind. Men's voices sounded as the soldiers spoke to the guards, and then they entered the bustling city. Jade had wanted to gaze out, imagining an eighteen-year-old Xifeng seeing it for the first time, but found she could not. She kept picturing the dead woman, her rags fluttering in the winter wind.

The palanquin stopped in front of a large, elegant teahouse with a façade of red lacquered wood. It rose a dozen floors high, its roof so wide, it touched those of the neighboring buildings. When the soldiers opened the door, the chilly air carried the smell of smoke, cooking meat, lantern oil, and sandalwood incense. The place was deserted, despite its well-kept grandeur.

The leader of the soldiers bowed to Jade. "Tung, the owner, ensured that the teahouse would be empty today, Your Highness. Her Majesty commanded it to be so for your safety."

"Will any of you eat?" Jade asked, though she knew it was a lost cause.

"We will remain out here to protect you."

"Wren may come in with us, at any rate," Jade said, sighing, and the young woman got off her pony at once, perhaps too hungry to argue. Jade lowered her voice as she spoke to Amah. "I haven't seen any of these men eat or rest in two weeks."

"They *are* resting. And it is right for them not to eat in your presence," her nursemaid explained. "You are above them and will receive treatment they aren't entitled to have."

"But everyone in the monastery was equal and had a share of the food and work."

"We're not in the monastery anymore, dear," Amah pointed out.

Jade caught Wren looking at her strangely as a middle-aged man greeted them. He was short and balding and bowed so low to Jade, his nose nearly touched the floor. She fought the impulse to bow back, though it seemed rude not to. Amah had taught her that outside of the monastery, a princess bowed only to her superiors, including her parents and any brothers.

"Your Imperial Highness, allow me to show you to our warmest table." He ushered them into a large room, his head lowered as he scurried beside Jade.

The teahouse was just as elegant on the inside. Bright wooden beams lined the high ceiling, and bamboo mats lined the walls. On every surface was a blue porcelain vase filled with gray pebbles from which miniature trees grew. A roaring fire stood against one wall, illuminating a dozen long wooden tables flanked by cushioned benches. The air smelled of ginger and pepper, with the undercurrent of cooking meat Jade had detected outside.

Her stomach rumbled as Tung led them to the table nearest the fire. The minute they sat down, an army of servants hurried out from a side door. Two brought a basin of warm, lemon-scented water for Jade to wash her hands in while one poured steaming hot tea. One girl placed lacquered, padded footrests beneath the table as two women swept out and placed bowls of soup on the table. Another girl darted forward, tasted Jade's bowl, and handed her a fresh spoon.

"The Empress has ordered that your food be tasted for your protection," Tung explained.

"I don't want anyone to die of poison on my account," Jade said, stunned, but the man guffawed as though she had made a clever joke.

Most of the servants kept their eyes lowered with respect, but a few of them stared at Jade. She shifted in her seat, knowing they would probably all discuss her in the privacy of the kitchens. One was a plump, round-faced woman of forty or so, who blinked open-mouthed at Jade and scurried off when Tung scowled and barked an order at her.

"So sorry for their rudeness," he said, all smiles again. "I'll have a word with them."

"No need," Jade said, but he excused himself and hurried after the servants.

Amah sniffed. "That peasant could have caught a fly with her mouth. They've never seen a royal before. Likely Tung didn't have much notice that you were coming and had to scrape the bottom of the barrel for last-minute help."

Wren, who had been silent throughout this exchange, had already inhaled her soup, and when Jade tasted it, she understood why. The monks had only ever eaten the plainest broth: nothing more than water with a few slices of onion. But this was a thick, rich soup brimming with silken cubes of tofu, diced scallions, tender slivers of pork, curly black mushrooms, and bamboo shoots. It was both spicy and sweet, and the warmth of it radiated to Jade's toes.

"You must be used to food like this, working in the palace kitchens," she said to Wren, who seemed more relaxed beside the fire. "I'm sure you've prepared the most delicious meals."

"They don't trust me enough to touch the food. I only scrub pots and pans for banquet cooking, since Her Majesty has a celebration almost every week."

"So often?"

Wren shrugged. "Before I left, she held a celebration for some fancy Kamatsu nobleman. The Imperial cook prepared twenty pheasants and a roast boar the size of this table."

Jade thought of the mother who had divided one piece of bread among six children. "Does she ever invite any of the citizens to partake in these lavish feasts?"

Wren gave her another strange look. "No, only nobles and high-ranking diplomats."

The servants flocked out again, bearing tray after tray of steamed dumplings stuffed with shrimp and pork; buns containing every filling imaginable, including ginger beef and chicken; minced pork and onions in crispy wrappers; and a plate overflowing with crunchy, crisp greens, roasted just enough to bring out their color and flavored with a tangy glaze.

"This is a meal made of smaller dishes, Your Highness," Tung explained, coming out to supervise the serving girls. "A tradition along the trade route of Feng Lu. Travelers want light, simple fare with variety, so they can be on their way again." He led the servants back to the kitchen, uttering commands as he went.

Only the round-faced woman remained. She held the teapot aloft as though to pour, but stood motionless with her eyes on Jade. "I'm sorry for staring, Your Highness, but you are very like your mother. There are a few paintings of Empress Lihua left in the city."

Amah scowled at the servant. "Her Highness doesn't wish to be disturbed."

"I'm sorry," the woman repeated, her eyes moving to the kitchen door, "but I wanted so much to meet Her Highness. You can imagine how eagerly I offered to help when Tung was hiring new servers! You see, I knew Empress Xifeng a long time ago."

Amah opened her mouth to rebuke her again, but Jade stopped her, intrigued. "What's your name? And how did you know my stepmother?"

"I am called Ning, Your Highness," the woman answered, her pink face glowing at Jade's interest. "The Empress and I were raised by her aunt. Of course, I haven't seen Her Majesty since she left our village. The path she took was a bit different from mine!" She let out a great laugh.

The other servants came back, so Ning hastily refilled their teacups and hurried off.

Wren lowered her voice as the girls cleared the empty dishes. "Smart people don't often speak of the Empress in the city. You never know if something you say could be misinterpreted."

"A most irritating gossip," Amah grumbled. "She made up that story to impress you."

"But think how fascinating it would be if it *were* true," Jade pointed out. "Ning could be one of the few people left who remember the Empress as a girl. I wonder what she was like."

"Well, you won't have to wonder long," Amah said tartly when Ning returned with a few other servants, bearing fragrant hot cloths for the guests to wash their hands and faces.

"I wish you all the best at the palace, Your Highness," Ning whispered, beaming as she pretended to wipe the table. "Though you must be nervous about all of the disappearances. Just keep your servants about you and you should be safe."

"Disappearances?" Jade echoed.

Ning could not have looked more delighted. "You didn't know?" She paused for dramatic effect, watching Jade's reaction. "They say a dozen women have gone missing from the palace over the past few years. A maid or two at first, then a kitchen wench and some garden workers. Their families were given a tidy settlement and told never to speak of their loved ones again."

"The kitchen girl ran off with a lover," Wren said, frowning.

"That's what they *want* you to think," Ning said eagerly. "But then a visiting minister's wife went next, and then a lady-in-waiting. Those were not so easily explained . . ."

"Ning!" Tung barked, appearing in the doorway. "What do you think you're doing?"

"It's my fault. I kept her here," Jade told him. "I was complimenting your teahouse and asked if she had ever served any distinguished guests."

The owner's face creased into a broad smile at the flattery. "This servant hasn't been here long, Your Highness," he said, giving Ning a look that sent her rushing back to the kitchen, "but you are correct in guessing that we've had many interesting customers . . . though none as honored as your own self, of course. Last week, we had an assassin from the Crimson Army."

Wren's head snapped up. "Here, in this teahouse?"

"The female assassins who supposedly live in the mountains of Dagovad? I thought they were a folktale," Jade said, taken aback, glancing at Amah.

"They're real as life, Your Highness. And there's no need to fret, my young friend," Tung said, grinning at Wren. "The woman was polite, dressed and hooded in black. I suppose being a cold-blooded killer doesn't affect one's good manners."

Wren bristled. "I'm not *fretting*. Was she in full armor? Were her lips painted blood-red?"

"I don't remember, I was so flustered when I saw her crimson sash. I didn't want to give her any reason to kill me, you see."

"Imagine walking around as you please," Wren said dreamily, ignoring him. "*Alone*, dining when you wish and going wherever it suits you because no one would dare take offense."

Amah rolled her eyes. "Better to imagine a good day's work in the kitchens, for that's what you'll do tomorrow, my girl. I hope they'll take you back after running away like this."

Just then, the teahouse door opened.

The leader of the soldiers entered, bowing to Jade, and Tung beamed as he said, "Your ladies-in-waiting must be here, Your Highness. Allow me to show you upstairs so they can prepare you for your first meeting with Empress Xifeng."

7

That afternoon, Jade stepped out of the Tungs' teahouse dressed like a princess. The ladies-in-waiting had scrubbed her with rose-scented oils and dusted some shimmering substance on her eyes and lips. Her hair had been pinned into elaborate knots with shining gold ornaments, and she wore deep ruby brocade with delicate gold piping around the sleeves and collar.

She walked with the attendants trailing her like colorful birds and an honor guard of fifty gold-armored soldiers at attention before her, and felt certain she would wake from this dream soon. She would open her eyes and see her tiny room at the monastery again. She strained her ears for the sound of the gong, for Auntie Ang calling her and Amah to the morning meal.

Instead, Jade heard metal scraping as the Imperial soldiers bowed low and hushed whispers from the crowd of spectators gathering on the street. A gilded two-wheel carriage pulled by four gleaming black horses stood waiting for her. Though it was larger than the palanquin, her attendants moved to a second carriage and the soldiers mounted their steeds, ignoring Wren and Amah. Apparently the men expected them to walk or ride Wren's pony.

"Excuse me," Jade called awkwardly. "Would it be all right if my nursemaid rode with me? There is plenty of room."

One of the soldiers obeyed at once and opened the door for Amah, who grinned as she climbed in. "You have such power now," she said, running an approving eye over Jade's robes. "I'll say this much for that stepmother of yours. She has a good eye for clothing."

Wren pulled her pony alongside the carriage, scrutinizing Jade with her customary sullenness. "You're wearing enough fabric to last you the rest of your life."

"Speak to the princess with respect!" Amah chided her.

The young woman gave a cold bow. "I apologize, Your Highness. I'm a lowly kitchen wench who knows nothing of silks and jewels." She turned her face forward and didn't look at Amah or Jade again as the retinue began moving.

"Don't mind her," the nursemaid began.

But Jade waved the apology away. Wren's rude behavior irritated her, but acknowledging it might only give the older girl satisfaction. *And her jealousy isn't unfounded,* Jade thought, but she pushed aside the stab of guilt. She had too much to occupy her mind, including the fact that a massive crowd had begun to gather to gawk at the honor guard and the ostentatious carriages.

The procession traveled at a stately pace, parting the sea of wagons and livestock, and Jade shrank back against the cushions at the citizens' craning necks and staring eyes.

"They know the princess has returned," Amah said. "No other personage would warrant such an escort to the palace."

Jade wiped her clammy palms on her silks. "What are they saying? Are they angry?"

A steady, rhythmic chant had begun to rise beneath the hubbub of the crowd, becoming a dull roar as the procession progressed. It seemed to be localized to one quarter—an open square in front of a blacksmith's shop. A middle-aged man, his clothing ragged and his arms powerful with muscle, stood on a rock in the square. He led the crowd in the chant, all people dressed in the worn attire of poor farm folk. They stood proudly, fists clenched at their sides.

"Free the children! Let them go!" they shouted over and over, the words harsh, furious.

"What's happening?" Jade asked Wren, alarmed. On her gray pony, the other girl had a better vantage point.

"They're protesting child labor," Wren answered, pointing at the blacksmith's shop, where several men continued hammering away as though nothing had happened. But every so often, they wiped their faces and darted wary glances at the Imperial soldiers passing by.

Jade shook her head, confused, but then she saw them: small, thin figures scurrying about in rags and barefoot despite the cold. Two boys no older than twelve held a large piece of bronze steady as a man shaped it, wincing each time sparks flew at them from his hammer. A girl of six or seven, who coughed as she swept ashes, stopped to stare at Jade's carriage until a man poked her in the back, hard, and said something sharp. Other children ran all around her, carrying heavy bricks and tools, their wan faces smudged with soot.

"Orphans, or children whose parents couldn't afford to pay taxes," Wren said. "They're lucky to be out in open air. Some are shut up in warehouses, breathing in toxic dyes for silks."

"Lucky?" Jade sputtered, horrified.

Behind them, the chant grew louder. "Free the children! Let them go!"

The protesters' leader, whose eyes were fixed on the royal procession, bellowed, "All hail the princess! All hail the *true* queen!" The crowd echoed him, magnifying the power of his words twentyfold up and down the avenue.

"How can they oppose Xifeng in such a public way?" Amah demanded, horrified.

Wren leaned her head inside the carriage window, her face intent. "Stay down."

In one smooth motion, the nursemaid pulled Jade onto the floor, her face taut with anxiety. A moment later, Jade understood why. Several members of the honor guard and the Empress's black-clad soldiers broke away from the parade, moving with seamless precision. The protesters raised their fists, which weren't clenched in anger as she had thought. They were holding large, heavy rocks, brandished at the soldiers' faces in self-defense.

"The people support you," Amah whispered. "They won't hurt us if they can help it. But I'm afraid we'll get caught in a cross fire."

All at once, the carriage stopped and a soldier barked gruff commands. The rest of the gold-armored men on horseback formed a tight circle around the carriage, spears facing out. Jade could not see beyond them, but she heard everything: the protesters screaming, the soldiers roaring. Horses whinnied and a shattering sound came, then moans and the running of many feet.

And through it all, the chant went on and on, fainter, but just as defiant.

"Free the children! Let them go!"

"All hail the princess! All hail the *true* queen!"

A female voice shrieked, "Where are the women? Where have they gone?"

"Why have they disappeared? What has the false queen done with them?" a man yelled.

Ning's words about the missing women came back to Jade. Were these foolhardy people accusing the *Empress* without proof when a mere whisper was cause for execution? She leaned against Amah, seeing again in her mind the corpses on the city walls.

Over the commotion, a soldier boomed: "Proceed!"

The gold-armored men turned crisply without breaking rank and rode aside the carriage in perfect formation as it continued down the avenue, moving at a brisker pace.

Jade gripped the edge of the window. She saw teeming crowds and flashing spears, and, inexplicably, several citizens attacking their own kind—or so it appeared. One such man accepted a sword from the soldiers and wielded it with a sure hand, swinging it at others.

A soldier disguised as a villager, she realized, watching more men in peasant garb wield Imperial weapons with too much confidence. At the monastery, the elder had told her and Amah of hearsay from travelers passing through his village: that Empress Xifeng employed a coalition of secret police, Imperial soldiers who dressed as commoners to hear what people said about her.

But before Jade could see much more, the carriage pulled away from the chaotic scene, with Wren keeping pace beside it. Jade helped Amah back onto the seat and wrapped her arms tightly around her. "Are you all right?" she asked her nursemaid.

The old woman shook, but it was not from fear. "Imbeciles," she seethed. "What did they think would happen? That they could speak their minds, fling rocks at palace soldiers to defend themselves, and escape? Gambling with their own lives, for nothing!"

Wren's eyes blazed. "Was it for nothing, I wonder?"

"Don't get any ideas into that foolish mind of yours!" her grandmother snapped. "It is all very romantic until Xifeng has your head roasting on the end of a spit."

"Please calm yourself," Jade begged her. "It will do no good to make yourself ill."

They sped on for another quarter of an hour. At last, they passed through the palace's gilded gates, which slammed behind them. Amah exhaled as Jade surveyed their surroundings, her heart still racing from the chaotic scene.

The palace looked like something from one of her nursemaid's fables. Gold roofs gleamed above immense buildings connected by elegant covered bridges. Heavily armored soldiers stood all around the great stone courtyard, as did nobles in resplendent silks. They bowed low as the carriage pulled to a stop.

Jade's breath caught in her throat as she realized that all this pomp and splendor was for *her*. She sank against the cushions when some of the courtiers tried to catch sight of her.

"Home again," Amah said, looking a bit calmer as she feasted her eyes on the spectacle before them. "It doesn't seem to have changed since Lihua was here, and yet . . ."

"I wish Mother were with me."

The nursemaid squeezed her hand. "She always is, dear one."

Jade breathed in and out slowly, her eyes closed, trying to conjure up some image to quell her anxiety. Somehow, it was the lanterns in the Great Forest that appeared in her mind, with their cheerful white glow, so like the ones she pictured whenever she heard her mother's beloved folktale. She felt her shoulders relaxing as the carriage door opened.

The courtiers bowed when Jade stepped out, and kept their chins lowered even when they straightened. Still, she felt curious eyes on her that dropped when she met them. Not a single person spoke, out of deference. She swallowed, wondering if they expected her to say something.

A large, bald man moved to the front of the crowd. He appeared to be about forty, with gleaming eyes and an air of command. Brown silk cascaded around his broad body, standing out from the nobles' colorful attire. For one heart-stopping moment, Jade wondered if he was her father. She had never thought of what to say to Emperor Jun when they met.

Relief flooded her when he bowed, which His Majesty would certainly not have done. "Welcome to the palace, Your Highness. The Empress is eager to see you again," he said.

Jade knew from his high-pitched voice that he was a eunuch, a person who had been deprived of his physical manhood as a child. Amah had explained that they were the only males allowed to guard the harem. The man's tone was courteous and friendly, but from his keen, intelligent appraisal of her, Jade suspected he was not someone to be crossed.

"I am Kang," he said. "The Empress entrusted me with the task of bringing you to her."

"It is a pleasure to meet you, Kang," Jade said, recalling what Amah had taught her of the hierarchy of the palace. Most high-ranking eunuchs possessed the honorific of *Master*, but it was not a princess's duty to use it. "I would be honored to come with you."

The eunuch glanced at the ladies-in-waiting, then at Amah and

Wren. "Your attendants may accompany you, but your other servants can bring your belongings to your quarters."

"They're not my servants," Jade said quickly. "Wren may leave whenever she prefers, but Amah is family, and I'd like her to accompany me. That is, if it's all right."

Kang blinked at her. "Of course, whatever Your Highness wishes. Did you have a pleasant journey?" he asked, leading them up the steps.

"We did, thank you." Jade's mind raced for something clever and appropriate, what Amah called the *little talk* of the court. She had not practiced it much, for the monks had never wasted words. "The Great Forest was beautiful, and I wish we could have spent more time there."

The eunuch gave a trilling laugh. "You're like your mother. She, too, loved the forest. She gave me employment in her household when I was a boy, and I maintain it even today."

"For a different Empress," Jade said without thinking, then blushed.

But Kang didn't seem offended by the implication that he had betrayed Lihua. "I serve Empress Xifeng now, it's true," he said as they entered an imposing edifice with gold doors. "This is the main hall of the Emperor, where banquets and functions are held. The royal gardens are just beyond, but they're much lovelier in the spring, of course."

The guards bowed low, their chests parallel to the ground. Jade wondered if she would ever get used to people behaving this way for her.

She placed a hand on Amah's shoulder for comfort as they walked. The palace was so magnificent that it was almost frightening, and she felt homesick for the monastery's simplicity at the sight of the painted ceilings and jade-embedded pillars. She guessed Abbess Lin was leading the monks in meditation right now, before their simple afternoon meal.

"Will I see His Majesty today?" she asked Kang.

"The Empress will bring you to see him, but I'm afraid your visit won't be long. His Majesty has a fever, but Gao, the Imperial physician, will have him feeling better in no time."

"Gao?" Amah echoed. "What happened to Bohai?"

Kang's eyes swept over the old woman before he addressed Jade. "Your Highness may remember Bohai, who served your mother, Empress Lihua, years ago. He was deemed unfit after endangering Empress Xifeng's life several times and failing to save the baby boys she lost in pregnancy."

"He was dismissed?" Jade asked.

"Executed," Kang said with a tight smile. "Since Gao came on, Empress Xifeng has had her longest pregnancy yet. It was not successful, but we have high hopes for another."

Hope blossomed in Jade's chest. She had assumed this summons meant she would certainly take the throne, but if Xifeng was still trying for a son, Jade might be free after all. But the hope faded as quickly as it had come. Even if her stepmother had a boy, they would still find a use for Jade. Her studies on history and politics had shown countless royal daughters being married off for lands, goods, and even armies.

They had brought her this far. They would not let her go so easily.

She saw now how hopelessly naïve she had been to think she could ever be left in peace.

"Your Highness, is everything all right?" Kang asked.

Jade blinked, realizing they had stopped. A set of onyx metal doors stood before them with coiling serpents etched into the frame, their inlaid ruby eyes leering at visitors. "I'm sorry," she said, searching wildly about her for an excuse. "I was lost in thought about . . . why some of the soldiers are in black armor and others in gold."

"The gold-armored soldiers belong to the Emperor's army, and the black are in Her Majesty's service," he explained. "Now, if you'll come this way, the Empress is just beyond."

They entered a vast chamber of black marble, offset by cascades of deep red flowers. Each blossom was in the shape of a heart, dripping a tinier petal. Amah pressed close to her as they approached two black thrones, raised on a platform with stairs covered in rich scarlet rugs.

A woman reclined in the larger throne, her legs crossed beneath yards of fiery orange silk. She leaned to one side, a slender hand tipped with sharp nail guards dangling over the arm of the other throne. She gazed out the window, the soft light bathing her delicate profile, and turned her head upon hearing their footsteps.

Jade felt her throat go dry.

To hear of Empress Xifeng was to hear of her beauty, but everything Jade had been told had been an understatement. The woman looked like a mythical being, a goddess from a legend, all moon-glow skin and blood-red lips. She wore no crown, opting instead for fresh flowers that bloomed like frost against her jet-black hair, and the simplicity suited her to perfection.

Her tilting, long-lashed eyes narrowed at the newcomers, and her mouth opened to show teeth like pearls. She straightened girlishly in her seat like a child caught slouching.

"Approach, my daughter," she said.

8

Though Jade had never seen or heard the ocean, she thought Xifeng's voice might sound like the sea—gentle beneath the wind, but hiding wild, untamed depths below the surface. This, then, was the woman who had risen from poverty to hold Feng Lu in her grasp and of whom people feared to speak, though frightened rumors slipped out like gasps for air.

Jade bowed low, and though courtesy would have her avert her eyes, she could not tear them from her stepmother. Xifeng was like the art in the palace corridors—incandescently flawless, made to draw the eye. This was a woman meant to be admired.

"I'm happy to see you at last, my dear," Xifeng said, her eyes shining as she descended. She lifted Jade's chin with one hand, her sharp nail guards brushing against Jade's neck.

Jade was surprised to find that they were the same height, having thought her stepmother would be tall and imposing. Up close, the Empress's skin was flawless. Her eyes angled bewitchingly at the corners, and every movement she made exuded grace. Jade found it hard to believe the woman hadn't been born noble, emerging from the womb with godlike elegance.

Xifeng's shoulders relaxed as she finished surveying Jade. "You're the image of Lihua. I see her nose and cheekbones and sweetness in you," she said, her tone affectionate and not at all imperious. "And you have your father's mouth—there are lines of determination here and here. But those wide eyes are all your own, Jade of the Great Forest. Yes, indeed," she added softly, as though speaking to herself, "quite a striking girl you have grown to be."

Jade blushed, unused to such praise. "Your Majesty is too kind."

"You don't think I'm being truthful?"

"I've never given much thought to beauty."

The woman's scarlet mouth curved. "I said you were striking, not beautiful."

"Not at all like you, Your Majesty," Jade agreed, and Xifeng's smile broadened, almost wolfishly. "But the monks taught me that a person's true beauty lies in their deeds."

The Empress's countenance flickered, like a mask slipping. "I'm impressed. I never thought any woman could be free from vanity, but I suppose your being kept away from the world has much to do with it. I take responsibility for that." She took Jade's hand, her face shadowed with regret. "Much took place when you were young. Your mother and half brothers had passed on, and there was discord when Emperor Jun married me. It wasn't safe for a princess to be at court. So he sent you away for your protection and I accepted his decision, as I always do." Xifeng's sooty lashes fanned against her cheek, the image of an obedient wife.

Image *is the very word*, Jade thought. The summons had been written in Xifeng's hand, and the soldiers' armor bore Xifeng's seal. The woman could have easily persuaded His Majesty to keep Jade. *But she didn't. She let him get rid of me.*

"I knew sending you away was wise," the Empress said. "You would be safe and given a humble upbringing. But I always hoped to bring you home. The world being what it is, and as occupied as I've been since your father first became ill, there wasn't an opportunity until now."

"It's true that I was safe with the monks, Your Majesty," Jade said slowly. "But I did wish many times that I could know my father better. And you."

The Empress's eyes moved to hers. There was something off-putting about her gaze, as though another person stared out from under that perfect mask. "It must have been hard for you, my dear, but the important thing is that you've come back to us."

Jade forced a smile as the woman slipped an arm through hers, steering her back toward the doors. Kang, Amah, and the attendants followed as they walked.

"I have endured much sorrow, Jade. The gods have not seen fit to bless me with children. But I am a determined woman." Xifeng lowered her voice with a conspiratorial smile. "I never accept failure. I found a new physician, and my hopes for a baby have never been higher. Still, I deemed it prudent to bring you home. We must never make assumptions where Feng Lu's future is concerned, and it is time you learned more about your role as Emperor Jun's only child and heir."

Jade blinked in surprise. "Thank you for being forthright with me."

The Empress patted her arm. "We'll have to find first-class tutors for you. I suppose your education in poetry, literature, calligraphy, and such has been of a rudimentary quality."

"On the contrary, Your Majesty, Amah's schooling was excellent."

Xifeng turned to the old woman. "I remember you. You nursed all of the royal children."

Amah gave the slightest bow she could without provoking offense. "I was nursemaid and tutor to Empress Lihua and her mother before her as well," she said proudly. "I saw the Empress married twice and witnessed the births of all four of her children."

"Much that occurred before my time." Xifeng led them down another ornate corridor and glanced at Jade. "It was your mother's first husband, Emperor Tai, who elevated your father. When Jun first came to court, he was a nobleman of no importance except for a droplet of blood he shared with Tai and Lihua. But Tai saw something in him. He named Jun regent, because the three princes were too young to rule, and when Tai died, your father took over."

"Did you know my mother well?" Jade asked.

"I was your age when I first came here, and Lihua was very kind to me," her stepmother answered. "I was motherless and drawn to her. I loved her, in fact."

Jade glanced sharply at her, but Xifeng's profile betrayed no emotion. *If you loved my mother, how came my father to notice you? When did you decide, together, to betray her?*

A powerful wave of resentment overtook her as she studied the woman who wore her mother's jewels and walked her mother's halls. No matter what Xifeng said, she had seized Lihua's place. No one could truly love another while wanting her life at the same time.

Jade suddenly realized the Empress was watching her with a small smile, as though she'd heard everything Jade was thinking. "And my love for Lihua is why I'm determined to spoil her daughter," Xifeng said. "I've planned an opulent birthday banquet for you, with food and music and dancing. The eunuchs have been working on a play, have they not, Kang?"

"They've been rehearsing day and night, Your Majesty, and even the ladies-in-waiting have a surprise dance for the entertainment." The eunuch took a painted fan from his robes and fluttered it before his face, his wrist twirling to demonstrate.

"Goodness," Xifeng said brightly.

Jade imagined tables groaning with food while children starved in the city. "Please, that isn't necessary," she told the Empress. "To be with you and His Majesty is all I dare ask."

Xifeng waved away her protests. "Lihua would have wanted us to throw you a celebration worthy of a princess. Now, come. Your father is waiting to see you in his quarters."

She strolled through a pair of marble doors inlaid with mother-of-pearl and emerald. Dozens of guards stood along the darkened corridor within, but though they protected Emperor Jun's apartments, they all wore the black armor of Xifeng's private soldiers.

The moment had come. Jade had envisioned meeting her father many times during the journey, but now that it was about to happen, she felt a sudden powerful urge to run. What would he be like? Would he be kind and indulgent? Would he apologize for throwing her away?

She might have felt amused at her own absurd fantasies if she hadn't been so anxious.

Amah's arm went around her. "Strength of the dragon," she whispered. "Fire of the phoenix."

The room they entered was the most lavish yet, but Jade saw it all in a haze. The brocade curtains, ornate metal lanterns, and gleaming furniture blurred around one point of focus: a huge gold silk bed where the Emperor of Feng Lu lay propped up on pillows. Half a dozen eunuchs and maids on either side straightened their spines upon the Empress's arrival.

Whatever image Jade had drawn of her father in her mind, it was not of a dazed man with a sickly pallor. His shrunken build suggested he had not left his bed for some time. His head, which had apparently been shaved to hide the thinness of his hair, shone in the light like a frail, newly hatched egg. He was not yet fifty, but already wore the exhaustion of a much older man.

His unfocused eyes rested blearily on his wife as she bowed and fussed over his covers.

"Enough, Xifeng," Emperor Jun said in a petulant voice, swatting her away with a trembling hand. "You make me quite dizzy. I am as comfortable as I will ever be."

"Certainly, my love," she responded, but she made sure to smooth his pillow and straighten his blankets for a good long minute afterward. His weak attempts to push her away were no more than flies buzzing about her head. "Your comfort is the chief care of my life."

"I had something to say. I thought of it all morning, but now it has slipped from me."

"You'll remember it before long," Xifeng said soothingly, like a mother to a fretful child.

"My father's ministers told me I had the finest mind of any boy, sharp as a blade with an excellent memory. But I forget so many things now." His hands scuttled helplessly over the blankets. "Can you tell me why that might be?"

Jade watched with growing distaste as he continued whining while Xifeng bustled around him in her overbearing way. The scene did nothing to recommend her father to her or quell the irritation she felt upon seeing him being coddled, while out in the world his people suffered. But mingled with her annoyance was pity, too, for he looked truly ill.

Amah had described him as full of life and intelligence. Looking at him now, Jade could scarcely fathom what old Emperor Tai had once seen in him. His condition would explain why Xifeng had to take so much upon herself, but such a man had the best physicians and medicines available—he was no peasant wasting away without care.

"How did he come to be so ill, Your Majesty?" Jade asked, disturbed.

"It has come on gradually for fifteen years," Xifeng said sadly. "He was forgetful at first, neglecting to attend councils or greet distinguished guests. Then he began to complain of headaches and stomach ailments, and to sleep all the time and lose interest in everything."

Jade moved forward tentatively, looking at the sickly face on the pillow. "Hasn't the physician been able to find any helpful tonic? Auntie Tan, one of the monks I lived with, and I found an herbal remedy that helped a village woman with low spirits."

"We sent for medicines from across the continent, but your father grew worse. He had fevers and visions, shivering one moment, perspiring the next. He would lie in a stupor for weeks at a time. I hate to have you see him like this." The Empress gave a heavy sigh.

A thick, unpleasant smell rose from the bed as Jade took another step forward, studying the Emperor's shrunken musculature and the green-yellow cast of his skin. "Has anyone tried to get him outside? Exercise might do him a bit of good."

"In the condition he's in?" Xifeng asked incredulously.

"What sort of food does he eat each day? Is his diet too rich?" Jade persisted. In helping Auntie Tan, she had seen much illness among the villagers, but none so bad as this. It bothered her, the idea that a king with every luxury should suffer so greatly. It didn't make sense.

Xifeng dropped the Emperor's hand and turned slowly. "What are you trying to say, Jade? You suppose that I haven't thought of everything you suggest?"

Jade's stomach dropped at the expression on her stepmother's face. It was like fire on branches, ready to blaze up with one gust of wind. The woman in the throne room had been merry and girlish, but this was a different person, one few had crossed and survived to tell the tale. "I'm sorry. I—I didn't mean to insinuate that, Your Majesty," she said hastily.

"I have done *everything* in my power to make him well again. Do you think if I could, I wouldn't bring him back to full health at once?" Xifeng had the ability to speak in a soft tone that carried through the room in the same way as another person shouting.

Jade bowed her head, her cheeks hot. "I only wanted to help, Your Majesty. I beg your forgiveness. It was not my intention to offend you," she said, though her mind raced at the Empress's defensiveness. Again, the sense of unease, of having been lied to, crept through her.

Xifeng's expression softened. "Forgive *me*, my child. Of course you're right to worry about your father, and my own concern has made me sharp and discourteous."

The Emperor suddenly spoke in a triumphant voice, interrupting the awkward moment. "I wish to attend the council on Kamatsu tomorrow. That was what I wished to say to you! I need to be there, Xifeng, and hear what they propose in this bid for independence."

"Of course, my honored husband." The Empress pointed at a pale, nervous eunuch with a large mole on his nose. "Where is the extra dose of medicine I ordered? It should have been here an hour ago, to calm His Majesty before the princess arrived."

The eunuch gave a shaky bow. "I will go inquire, Your Majesty."

"If you can't be back in five minutes, don't bother coming back." The poor man scurried away as Xifeng's gaze swept to Jade. "Come meet your father, darling."

Jade obeyed, holding her breath against the powerful smell of decay. Sweat gleamed on Emperor Jun's forehead as he turned to look at her without recognition in his bloodshot eyes. Perhaps he had forgotten he even had a daughter. "Your Majesty," she said, her mouth dry.

"Who are you?" Jun wheezed.

"My love," Xifeng said, exasperated, "I told you our daughter, Princess Jade, was coming today. She's joined us for her birthday. Do you not recall?"

Jade watched the Emperor clutch feebly at the covers, wondering why she had been so nervous about seeing him. Perhaps she had been afraid he would change her mind. Perhaps, after what he had done, she had feared that he would make her love him. "I am honored to be in your presence, Your Majesty," she said stiffly.

"Jade," Emperor Jun repeated, shaking his head. "Jade."

"I'm so sorry," Xifeng whispered to Jade. "Perhaps if we . . ."

"Lihua."

They both stared at the Emperor in shock. He had spoken the name more clearly than any other word he had uttered thus far. He looked straight at his daughter, and for the first time, Jade could see a hint of the old vigor and handsomeness Amah had mentioned.

Emperor Jun lifted a limp hand, but Jade did not take it. "You're Lihua's daughter. She longed for you and risked her life to have you, though Bohai told her not to. Where is Bohai?"

"You mean Gao, my love," Xifeng corrected him.

"No, I mean Bohai." The Emperor struggled to sit up. "He told her it was dangerous to try for a daughter at her age, but she desperately wanted a girl. I remember that."

"Be still, Your Majesty. You are too weak to sit up." The Empress pushed him back in place, and he didn't have the will to fight her. The fretful confusion reappeared on his face as he leaned against the sweat-soaked pillow, panting with exertion.

"Lihua named her daughter Jade," he said. "I wonder what became of her."

"You just spoke to her, husband. Don't you remember?" Xifeng asked.

Once more, Emperor Jun's eyes met Jade's and she trembled at his recognition, at the only time in memory her father had ever truly looked at her. "Jade, my only child," he mumbled, his expression clearing once again. "How you've grown. Is it really you?"

"Yes, Your Majesty." She swallowed hard. She saw such sorrow and regret and joy on his face . . . He lifted his hand again. At an encouraging nod from Xifeng, Jade took it, feeling each brittle bone in his fingers as her earlier irritation vanished. There was pain embedded in his skin, and the press of his hand held desperation.

He coughed. "I want to speak to my daughter. Leave us, all of you. Xifeng, please."

In his frightened eyes, Jade saw no Emperor, but a severely ill man who had been secluded for nearly two decades in this stuffy chamber. Jade noticed her stepmother watching her with the intensity of a bird of prey.

At that moment, the anxious eunuch hurried back into the room. A boy scurried after him, carrying a gold vessel shaped like a swan.

Xifeng brightened. "Of course you'll want to speak to Jade more when you're feeling better," she said, touching her husband's thin shoulder. "But you should take your medicine now, Your Majesty, and perhaps soon we three will dine together."

"I want to speak to my daughter," Jun wheezed. "Jade . . . I must . . ."

The Empress beckoned the boy forward. Slowly, he uncovered the vessel to reveal coils of steam and a ladle. The medicine smelled of pungent wet earth, like the rancid soil of a swamp.

Jade bit her lip, struggling for the right words as Xifeng picked up the ladle, her mouth set in an intent line. "Your Majesty, surely my father can take his medicine and I can stay a bit longer? With your permission?" she asked, in as deferential a tone as she could muster.

"I'm afraid that's not possible. The medicine makes him drowsy, and he has had enough excitement for one day." The Empress lifted the ladle to her husband's lips, ensuring that every drop went down his throat. "Kang will see you to your chamber. We'll dine tomorrow after you've been introduced to more of my court. I have business tonight." She glanced up at Jade with a little smile, as though daring her to argue.

But Jade's protest died on her lips. She could not risk angering her stepmother again, not when so many questions needed answering. "Yes, of course, Your Majesty."

"Good. Until tomorrow, my dear," her stepmother said warmly.

Kang ushered her and Amah to the door, but Jade couldn't help peering back over her shoulder.

Xifeng was still bent over the Emperor. His head lolled to one side, and though his muscles seemed more relaxed, one blue-veined hand still stretched toward his daughter. His white lips formed a name, but to whom it belonged was lost as the Empress's faceless, black-armored soldiers shut the mother-of-pearl doors securely behind Jade.

9

Despite Xifeng's promise, three days passed without Jade seeing her or the Emperor. Her stepmother sent a note explaining that urgent business detained her. In addition to the protests cropping up around the city, the king of the Sacred Grasslands—who had always been a loyal subject—seemed to have gone rogue after Kamatsu's continued bids for independence. Rumors of a planned uprising against Xifeng were swirling . . . but she didn't wish to bore Jade with the details.

"She brought me home to learn about my future, as the Emperor's only heir," Jade fumed. "I may not have wanted this throne, but I should be at these meetings with her."

Amah sat sewing on a persimmon silk sofa. "She still believes she'll bear a son, as we heard the other day. It seems you're here as a pawn—she just doesn't know what she wants to use you for yet. She summoned you here to keep you close, not to give you her empire."

Jade tried to pace, but her movements were restricted by the elaborate silks she wore. The attendants had dressed her to meet some noble-women who would pay her a visit today. "There's something wrong here," she said. "I don't believe everything that could be done for my father *has* been done. I think I'll have the Imperial physician call on me."

"Is that wise? You saw how angry Xifeng got when you started asking her questions."

"I'll have to think of some excuse. A headache, perhaps."

Amah quirked an eyebrow. "Does this concern for your father mean you've forgiven him?"

"Forgiveness has nothing to do with it. The Emperor has no one left to care for him, not with all of the servants and soldiers being under Xifeng's control." Jade bit her lip. "And I doubt anyone has investigated those disappearances. The protesters suggested that Xifeng is responsible. But what could she have done with the missing women?"

"You're asking too many questions," the nursemaid warned. "Be careful not to annoy Xifeng more or you may never learn the answers."

Despite the chill, Jade slid open one of the bamboo window panels. On such an overcast day, the lanterns glittered even more brightly in the Great Forest. "We came to the palace for a reason. If nothing is being done about my father or the missing women, then the task must fall to me." She looked at Amah. "My father never summoned me, but what if he *did* need me here? What if the Empress kept us apart?"

A tap sounded on the door of Jade's apartments. It slid open and Wren stepped inside, her face suspicious. "You sent for me, Your Highness?"

"Please come in. Amah, meet my new chief attendant." Jade couldn't help giggling at the identical expressions of bewilderment on their faces. "Well, I can't keep borrowing my stepmother's ladies, can I? I need my own handmaiden to help dress me and do my hair."

Wren stared blankly at her. "I only know how to scrub pots. Is this a joke?"

"Partially," Jade said, waving her to the seat beside Amah. "I know you hate working in the kitchens, and I thought this would solve two problems at once: get you away from the dirty pots, and give you more time with your grandmother. You'd be my handmaiden in name only. I can take care of myself, and you won't have to do anything at all."

There was a long silence.

"So it's pity, then?" Wren asked.

Jade's heart sank. "No, of course not . . ."

Wren leapt to her feet, her face reddening. "You thought it would be charming to play a princess rescuing a peasant! To elevate a lowly kitchen wench out of charity!"

"That is *not* what I . . ."

"Well, Your Highness," Wren said, her voice dripping with disdain, "perhaps you ought to realize that I was born to scrub dirty dishes, just as my grandmother was born to care for you. Instead of for me, her granddaughter by blood."

"Wren!" Amah cried.

"As for the rest of my family, my grandfather served in the stables and my father polished weapons," Wren continued, ignoring the old woman. "My brother, who taught me how to use a sword, was born to be a foot soldier and die in *your* brother's failed overseas mission. We may be servants, but we still deserve dignity. We deserve to live without pity from patronizing royals."

Her topknot quivered as she spoke, exactly as Amah's hair did when she was angry. It was this that saved Jade from firing back, for she had been growing more and more furious.

"I'm sorry that you are always ready to believe the worst of me and that you blame me for your family's servitude," Jade said evenly. "I made this offer because of the reason you just mentioned—that because of me, you lost years with the only family you have left."

Wren stared at her, panting.

"I knew this wouldn't make up for the time you've lost with your grandmother," Jade said. "Nothing ever could, though it was *her* choice to raise me because she promised my mother she would. Still, I wanted to make things right with you, and this was the only way I knew how, so forgive me for its inelegance."

Some of the color drained from the young woman's face. "I . . . you . . ."

"Have you ever heard the advice *listen before you speak*?" Amah asked her tartly. "Did you know the princess could have you executed for the way you raged at her just now?"

"There will be no executions," Jade said quickly. She ran a hand over her hot forehead, wishing she had never suggested the idea. "I'm not offended if you decline my offer, Wren. Please feel free to return to the kitchens."

"So this wasn't charity?" Wren asked, her voice very soft.

"No."

"You were only trying to make amends."

"Yes."

They stared at each other.

Wren tugged at the hem of her worn tunic, shifting her weight from one foot to the other. "I . . . I would like to accept your offer, Your Highness. I'm sorry, I didn't mean to . . ." She took a deep breath and bent at the waist, lower than she had ever bowed to Jade. "Thank you. I would like this chance to spend more time with my grandmother," she added gruffly.

Jade could have laughed from relief. "And you understand you're my handmaiden in title only? That you don't have to do anything you don't wish to do?"

Wren bowed again, her mouth downturned with shame. "Thank you, but I don't like to be idle. I'll be happy to do any tasks you require. Will you let me know?"

"I will," Jade promised.

Amah began to scold the moment the young woman sat down, looking awkward and out of place among the flowered cushions.

Footsteps sounded on the walkway outside. Jade practically ran to the door with relief and admitted three noblewomen who fluttered in like graceful butterflies. The first was a short, pleasant-faced woman in her fifties, her features framed in wrinkles and laugh lines. She wore dark rose silk with two strips of pure white satin encircling each arm. Jade watched in surprise as Amah rose with her hands outstretched to this woman.

"My dear Lady Tran," the nursemaid cried, delighted.

The two women bowed formally to each other before embracing.

"It has been too long, Auntie. I wondered how you and the princess fared all these years." Lady Tran bowed to Jade, then presented her daughters, Plum and Peony, who might have been fourteen and fifteen. "Your Highness, I was friends with your honored mother almost all my life. I still wear the gift she gave me when I first became her lady-in-waiting." She touched a pendant of pale green jade that hung around her neck, her kind eyes crinkling at Jade.

"I'm glad my mother had such a loyal friend," Jade said warmly.

"Lady Tran's family comes from the Sacred Grasslands like ours," Amah told Wren. "It's a custom to wear jade pendants for good luck, and it was just like Empress Lihua to honor that."

Lady Tran nodded. "She was one of the few who ever showed such respect. There's never a good time to hail from the Grasslands, especially not when the king may be building an army against Her Majesty. Many at court are prejudiced against my land," she explained, seeing Jade's puzzlement. "They believe the Great Forest to be superior and more cultured. Some openly ignore my daughters and me because of our origins."

"How absurd," Jade said. "Haven't royal and noble families intermarried for centuries?"

"It's easy to look down on a small farming kingdom, I suppose," Lady Tran replied. "I'm proud of my roots, but don't tell Master Kang. He thinks the Empress too kind for inviting my family to Your Highness's birthday banquet."

"If Kang has anything to say about a dear friend of my mother, he can speak to me."

The maids began serving tea once the other noblewomen joined them. Most of the ladies were merry and educated, and ranged in age from twenty to fifty. Whenever Jade turned to speak to one of them, she felt the intense appraisal of the others. No doubt they all wondered how a girl raised so humbly would do as a princess.

The monks had been learned women, but with so many hours devoted to prayer, they had seldom wasted words. The court ladies, however, danced from one topic to the next.

"What do you think of the palace so far?" a lady in pink asked Jade.

"It's different from what I'm used to," she admitted. "I thought I would be shown to a comfortable room, not an entire floor in the same building as Her Majesty's apartments."

The women laughed.

"You've had a simple upbringing, Princess," another woman remarked. "Do you think court life will soon spoil you?"

"Yes, if the attached bathhouse has anything to say about it. The system of ropes is ingenious," Jade said, recalling the hot bath the maids had prepared that morning by hauling buckets of boiling water up to the second floor. "I've only ever bathed in a stream."

"Goodness. Wasn't it cold?"

"Not in the summer. Amah always had trouble getting me back out. I wish I could say that was only in my childhood, but I seem to recall it happening just a few months ago."

The noblewomen giggled again.

The conversation turned to one of the ladies' sisters, who was married to a Dagovadian noble and had just inherited a vast mountain estate from his father. Jade took the opportunity to ask Lady Tran, in an undertone, if she had known these women for long.

"Some of the married women, yes. They live at court, as I do, when their husbands have business. As for the younger ladies who serve as the Empress's attendants, they never stay longer than a year," Lady Tran whispered. "Her Majesty likes to change them frequently."

Jade pondered this strange and isolating practice. Xifeng likely did so to keep anyone from getting too close to her, either out of a lack of trust or a need for self-protection.

At that moment, a small boy burst into the apartments, pursued by two out-of-breath eunuchs. He kept one arm behind him and hugged Lady Tran's legs with the other, goggling at the women.

"My humblest apologies, Your Highness," Lady Tran said, embarrassed. She frowned at the eunuchs. "It seems my nephew cannot be kept from me."

"What's your name, little one?" Jade asked kindly, bending down to the boy, who hid his chubby cheeks against his aunt's legs. "He's shy, isn't he?"

"Answer the princess when she speaks to you," Lady Tran coaxed him.

He peeked out at her with one eye. "Minh."

"What have you got there behind your back? Will you show me?" Jade asked.

"The little sycophant is starting at a young age," a lady said with coy amusement. "He's brought a present with which to win your favor, Princess."

Minh toddled toward Jade. "It's a noodle," he said, and whipped his hand out to reveal a slender black snake writhing between his fingers. Red eyes glittered at Jade, matching a forked tongue. The old memory came flooding back in a rush: splashing in the stream inside the monastery gates, meeting the eyes that watched her like blood drops, and screaming for Amah.

Jade cried out and fell back as the noblewomen emitted piercing shrieks, jumping up from their seats and running to the edges of the room.

Startled by the commotion, the child dropped the snake and began to cry. The animal lay still for a moment, stunned, then slithered toward the sofa. The women screamed again, and Plum and Peony hopped onto a low table, hugging each other and crying. Wren ran to help the breathless eunuchs as they tried to seize the snake. One of the men finally caught hold of it as it was crawling beneath the furniture.

"Why would you bring that into the princess's apartments?" Lady Tran scolded the boy, who was sobbing into her silks. "You frightened her half to death."

"It's all right—there's no need to upset him further." Jade shivered at the sight of the wriggling serpent. "Would you please take it outside?"

The eunuch obeyed, and the ladies uttered cries of relief, some fanning themselves.

"It's all right," Jade repeated to the child, though her heart still beat like a frantic drum. "I'm not angry with you, Minh. Don't cry anymore." He peeked at her with one wet eye and quieted as she rubbed his back.

Lady Tran pushed her nephew toward the other eunuch. "See that he does not disturb Her Highness again. I apologize, Princess. He's been acting up, what with his mother gone."

"Yes, when *is* Hana coming back?" one of the women asked.

"Soon, I'm sure," Lady Tran answered curtly.

It wasn't until later, when the ladies took their leave, that the woman in pink shared the gossip with Jade. "Poor Lady Tran. Her husband *and* her brother died of illness, and now her brother's wife has disappeared. She's had to care for the child herself. There is no one left!"

Pity swelled in Jade's heart for the boy. The deaths in Lady Tran's family would explain the white armbands sewn onto her tunic, for mourning. "Minh's mother is gone? Where?"

"No one knows, Your Highness. Hana was always flighty. She likely ran off with a soldier or got tired of her crying son. Wherever she is, the Empress isn't pleased about it, because a lot of women have left the palace without permission lately."

Jade watched the lady go uneasily. She did not join in Amah and Wren's excited chatter about the escaped snake, for one word was echoing over and over in her mind.

Disappeared.

10

A few days later, Wren came into the sitting room where Jade sat reading by the window. With her rigid topknot and military stance, the young woman appeared more like a bodyguard than a handmaiden. "The Imperial physician will be here in half an hour, Your Highness."

"Thank you," Jade said shyly. Though Wren had been nothing but civil and helpful since accepting the position, a remnant of awkwardness still lingered between them. "Don't feel like you have to stay if you have something more important to do."

Wren arched an eyebrow. "Like what?"

"I don't know. Dangling from trees, pulling yourself up on railings, carrying heavy buckets of water." Jade shrugged helplessly.

The older girl's lips quirked. "You forgot running in the underground tunnels, where no one can see me except an occasional guard."

"Is that something your brother taught you, too?"

Wren's tentative smile dissolved. "Yes."

"I always wished for a brother I could grow up with," Jade said wistfully. "It was lonely, with only sticks and rocks and flowers to play with."

Wren frowned. "I thought you had the best toys. Carved puppets and miniature teapots."

Jade couldn't help chuckling. "I grew up in a monastery, remember? Abbess Lin discouraged luxury, and besides, no one knew who I was. Amah kept it a secret so I would be treated the same as everyone else." Another pang of homesickness knifed through her gut. Back home, Auntie Tan would be drying herbs and making tonics without Jade to help, and the other monks would feed the animals and do other tasks that had been Jade's. Even the thought of her and Amah's little room, bare and silent now, hurt. "Have you ever felt like you were born the wrong person? Like you should have been someone other than who you are?"

"Yes," Wren said, with a flicker of surprise.

"I loved the women who raised me and the way they lived, full of faith and compassion. I would have dedicated my life to the monastery if they'd let me. But it was silly to think I could stay there forever." Jade's heart and mind had been on the monastery as she spoke, and she had nearly forgotten Wren's presence. She angled a glance at her, but Wren's face held no scorn.

"It wasn't meant for you."

"It wasn't meant for me." Jade gave her a tentative smile. "So I know what it is to wish for a different life, like you. You would be a soldier, if given a chance?"

"I've wanted to since I was little, but I had to hide it. It was exhausting." Wren mimicked a high voice. "Proper girls don't fight or use swords. Proper girls cannot be warriors."

"What about the Crimson Army?"

"That's my idea of freedom. To protect myself, defend the helpless, and go anywhere in the world I wished, at any time . . ." Wren inhaled, as though the words were air and she could fill her lungs with them. "I'd be in control of my own life. And I wouldn't answer to anyone."

"A kitchen wench who longs to be a warrior, and a princess who wants to be a monk," Jade said, with a rueful shake of her head. "I guess we aren't so different after all."

"I'm sorry. For everything."

"So am I."

They looked at each other, their lips curving into matching smiles.

"Thank you for being here and saving me the grief of having a *real* attendant like Madam Ong," Jade said with a grin. Yesterday, her step-mother had sent one of her sour-faced ladies-in-waiting to serve as Jade's personal handmaiden, but Jade had sent a courteous note of thanks, explaining that she had already filled the position herself. "I need someone I can trust, someone who will be honest with me."

"I'm rather good at being honest," Wren admitted. "You know, I haven't had a thing to do except deliver the occasional message for you."

"Is that a complaint?" Jade joked.

"No complaint," the girl said mildly. "But I wouldn't mind doing more for you, truly."

"All right, then. You can stay while I interrogate Gao."

The Imperial physician arrived shortly with a black medicine case. He was a small, bald man in his sixties, with nervous, watery eyes. He took a seat on the sofa beside Jade while Wren stood at attention behind them. "Your Highness sent for me?" he asked politely.

As Jade described some fake symptoms, he pulled bottles of herbs from his case. "I'm not used to the rich palace food yet," she told him.

"I'm sure it's just indigestion. I know the symptoms—I saw many cases of it among the villagers when I was helping at the monastery."

"Your Highness has experience with medicine?" Gao said, surprised.

"I apprenticed under a monk who taught me much about herbs and healing."

He measured out some dried green leaves and crushed ginger root on a square of paper. "Have your attendants make you tea with this every evening. The ginger should calm the stomach and ease digestion, as you already know."

"I will," she promised. "Is this a remedy you've prescribed for my father?"

Gao glanced up, on his guard at once. "I may have in the past."

"Stomach issues seem to be common everywhere," Jade said conversationally. "I used to help Auntie Tan—the monk who trained me—make salty chicken congee to soothe bellyaches."

"A good and mild dish. It settles the nerves, too, and I always recommend a diet of rice and boiled vegetables for digestive troubles."

"A nutritious diet becomes even more crucial as one gets older, I'm sure, even if one has Emperor Jun's strong constitution and an excellent physician like yourself."

Gao flushed with pleasure, relaxing a bit. "And if one eats a single meal a day, as His Majesty does, one ought to ensure the food is of the highest quality."

"The Emperor eats so little?" Jade asked, blinking at him.

"The Empress believes that too much food makes him poorly. And I agree," the physician added. "His Majesty takes a light midday meal to avoid sleep disturbances."

It seemed Emperor Jun's wasted body could be attributed to

starvation as much as to illness. Jade's hands clenched, but she kept her voice light and cheerful. "I wonder if three light meals wouldn't have the same benefit. Only one can't be enough for a grown man."

Gao's easy manner faded. He removed his spectacles and wiped them with a cloth from his case. "The regimen has seemed beneficial so far, Your Highness."

"Exercise might help, too," Jade persisted. "I've noticed how well I feel after walking outdoors, though of course His Majesty is too weak for that. Still, it might do him some good to move around his room from time to time."

"Never, Your Highness. The Empress feels he would get worse if he did so."

The Empress believes. The Empress feels. Jade wanted to shake the nervous man and shout, *You are the physician, are you not?* Still, she couldn't blame him for wanting to stay alive.

She noticed him wipe sweaty hands on his tunic and took pity on him. But one more question couldn't hurt. "My father takes a certain medicine from a gold ladle. Her Majesty told me how effective it has been. What a testament to your skills!"

Gao closed his medicine case, his face miserable. "I cannot claim credit for it, Princess."

Jade pounced. "Who makes it, then?"

At that moment, the door leading into Jade's interior chambers slid open and Kang appeared, his massive frame filling the doorway. "My apologies. I come with a message from Her Majesty, but perhaps I ought to return later?"

"Good morning, Kang," Jade said, struggling to keep her voice calm. Her eyes cut to the front entrance, securely closed. "We didn't see you come in."

Wren moved forward, watching Kang with sharp eyes as he entered the room. When he held a scroll out to Jade, she snatched it away with a scowl and gave it to Jade herself. "I'll go check on my grandmother," she said pointedly, her gaze never leaving the eunuch as she stepped out, and Jade knew she'd had the same thought—that he had crept past Amah napping in her bed.

"I used the maids' back entrance," Kang told Jade smoothly. "I'm sorry to have surprised you." His eyes had the unsettling habit of darting about—he was always thinking, always watching. And, like Xifeng, he had a way of saying one thing and meaning another.

"I wasn't aware there were multiple exits from my apartments," Jade answered.

"As leader of the Five Tigers, Her Majesty's most trusted eunuchs, I make it my business to know as many passages as possible, both above- and underground. It would be my honor to show you one today, if you'll accompany me to the main palace." He gave her a second, much smaller scroll. "Lady Tran is having tea with a relative and would like you to join them."

"I'd be delighted." Jade glanced over the short, kind message, then broke the black seal on Xifeng's letter. The ink looked barely dry, as though the Empress had written it moments ago, and as Jade read it, she realized her assumption was true. Underneath Xifeng's invitation to dine that night, she urged Jade not to disturb Gao unless absolutely necessary.

The Imperial physician is the most learned man of his profession. I would prefer that his time be spent formulating new remedies for your honored father.

Jade kept her face blank, knowing Kang was watching her reaction. Busy as she was, the Empress of a Hundred Thousand Eyes and Ears still had time to spy on her stepdaughter. But under her anger and disdain, Jade felt a thread of fear, too. The palace suddenly felt too small and her quarters too close to Xifeng's.

"Could you please tell Her Majesty I would be honored to join her this evening?" Jade ran her tense fingers over the lovely script chastising her for bothering Gao. "And if the Empress has anything she would like to speak to me about in the future, please let her know I am but a floor away and ready to receive her gracious presence."

The slightest surprise flashed on Kang's face. "Very good. I will deliver your reply and return to escort you to tea." This time, he made sure to use the main entrance to leave.

Wren returned, still scowling. "Grandmother's sleeping like a baby, but I hate knowing *he* can come in anytime, unseen. I haven't the faintest idea where he slithered in." Her frown deepened when Jade told her what Xifeng's message had said. "He was listening at the door, wherever it is. I'll search for it while you're at tea."

Jade gave a heavy sigh. "I'd appreciate that."

Wren lowered her voice. "That nervous eunuch with the mole returned the message you wrote to the Emperor this morning. That's the fourth note he's brought back. But he mumbled something to me this time. He said to tell you, 'Have patience. Attempt no more.'"

Jade shook her head in disbelief, but upon hearing Kang's footsteps, she wrapped herself in a cloak and met him on the walkway. He had brought five other eunuchs, one of whom had his arms full of silk-enveloped packages. Seeing that someone had already opened the gifts for her, Jade easily spotted a comb, a painted fan, and a bundle of violet satin.

"Tokens from the court ladies who visited the other day. They enjoyed Your Highness's company greatly," Kang explained. "It is the Empress's orders that all offerings be inspected for your protection. Quite routine, like having your food tasted."

Jade wondered if they had also opened all of her notes to her father, for his *protection*. She led the way toward the stairs. "Who is this relative with whom Lady Tran is having tea?"

"Former Ambassador Shiro, who used to be a friend of Her Majesty's," Kang told her, and she did not miss his use of the past tense. "Shiro's cousin Hana married Lady Tran's brother, and their son, Minh, is being raised at court thanks to the Empress's generosity. Her Majesty was kind enough to let Shiro come today and meet with Lady Tran about this sad business."

"How could Hana possibly have gone missing?" Jade asked.

Kang shrugged. "She must have left without permission. It disturbs Her Majesty greatly, since Hana was a lady-in-waiting in high favor. Hana went to bed with the other attendants one night, and the next morning she was gone from the Empress's apartments."

"How strange," Jade murmured.

"I beg Your Highness not to trouble yourself with this. The Empress is doing everything to find Hana and bring her back safely." The eunuch's eyes held a disturbing intensity. "If danger is involved, the last thing Her Majesty would want is to put you at risk."

A threat veiled as a warning, Jade thought.

They approached a grand stone bridge linking the Empress's walkway to the main palace. Jade admired the railing as they walked. Images had been carved into the stone, representing each of Feng Lu's kingdoms: oysters and pearls for Kamatsu, rice flowers for the Grasslands, desert roses for Surjalana, and horses for Dagovad. The central imagery, naturally, was of the Great Forest, with beautiful intertwining trees.

Every few feet along the bridge stood an immense granite statue of a fearsome warrior. Jade counted nine in total. "The warriors of the Dragon Guard," she said, pleased and surprised to recognize them. "The legendary army of the gods. Amah raised me on those ancient texts."

She peered back as they passed one of the stern warriors. The old stories maintained that the Dragon Guard could be summoned in times of great need—but only if the gods deemed that the person who called for their aid was brave and true.

And though she knew it was just another one of Amah's fables, somehow it comforted her to know that these warriors stood there, watching over the Imperial Palace.

11

They entered a magnificent hall flanked by Imperial soldiers in gold armor. It was quiet, save for the hushed voices of men standing outside a room off the corridor.

"Ministers awaiting the start of a council on taxes," Kang murmured to Jade, leading the group through a series of elegant rooms, some smelling pleasantly of beeswax and others with lush carpets that emitted the scent of jasmine with every step. But Jade detected another heady, somehow familiar fragrance she could only describe as smoke-like. "That is the Empress's favored incense, which she orders from a merchant in the Sacred Grasslands. I will send some for your use."

Jade nodded politely, but resolved to tuck away whatever he sent. At the monastery, they had used an incense that smelled like sandalwood in the first flush of spring. *This* was a cloying perfume that made her head swim, like waking from a restless sleep full of odd dreams.

They entered a room with a glorious map covering the far wall. It depicted Feng Lu, with its four mainland kingdoms and the island nation of Kamatsu in shimmering blue, green, and brown inks. The continent had been rendered in painstaking detail, with each tree of the Great Forest carefully outlined and the waves of the ocean embracing tiny ships.

"This was a birthday gift for your mother from His Majesty," Kang explained. "The commission took seven years for a single artist to fulfill."

"It is truly fit for a queen." Somehow Jade felt sure the exquisite map had been a gift of love; no such present could have been bestowed unfeelingly. This revelation pained her all the more, considering the anger she had felt toward Emperor Jun her whole life. "Why is this not kept in the city of women where my mother lived?"

"Her Majesty felt its scale was more appropriate for the main palace chambers."

But Jade suspected that Xifeng didn't like being reminded of the woman she had supplanted. *Even though she walks my mother's halls, lives in my mother's quarters, and rules over my mother's people.* Resentment flared in her breast. Xifeng might be Empress, but there was still an heir of the Dragon King living.

"Kang," she said, struggling to find the right words, "I would like my mother's map to be moved to *my* apartments. It would fit well in the sitting room."

The eunuch regarded her for a moment. "That can be arranged, Your Highness, but I will have to seek Her Majesty's approval first."

"You know best, but I worry about bothering the Empress with such a trifling matter. She wouldn't object to my harmless sentimentality, would she?" Jade asked innocently, though her heart raced at her own boldness. Kang bowed, but she knew Xifeng would likely find a way to refuse this request. Still, it felt satisfying to have stood her ground for this piece of her parents.

"I'll give the order. It won't be a minute." He led the other eunuchs back through the doors, leaving Jade in front of the map.

She exhaled, welcoming the brief solitude, but soon realized it wasn't quiet, for she heard low male voices somewhere very near. Strangely, they seemed to be coming from the painting of a kingfisher. Recognizing the lilting language of Kamatsu, Jade went closer and strained her ears, delighted she could understand the conversation thanks to Amah's teachings.

"I'm certain she would have wanted us to do nothing, and so nothing we will do."

"We cannot let this be swept away like the others." The second man spoke with intensity lacing each clipped word. "I'm sorry to contradict you, Father, but I know Hana better."

Jade had begun to move away, ashamed of eavesdropping, but froze at the name.

A woman spoke with a slight accent. "What do you propose, Koichi?"

"I don't know, Auntie. But everyone knows *she* has something to do with all of the missing women, not just Hana. People are just too afraid to do or say anything about it."

"The protesters in the square last week would disagree with you," the older man spoke.

"The protesters in the square last week are dead."

"Then that should be enough to prove my point. No good can come of speaking against the Empress. And you have no evidence whatso-ever. There could be plausible reasons for each woman. Perhaps they grew tired of life in the palace . . ."

The young man uttered a low laugh of disbelief. "All *twelve* of them? And not all servants, but nobles and ladies-in-waiting, too. I apologize for my disrespect, Father, but Hana was family. *Is* family," he corrected himself. "I will not stand by and—"

"Your Highness." Kang materialized beside Jade, and she jumped. "I see you've found the secret passage I meant to show you. Lady Tran and her guests are in the room just beyond."

"I heard them," Jade admitted, her cheeks hot. She hated Kang's appraising expression, as though he knew exactly what she had been doing. "Please show me through."

He pressed his hands on either side of the kingfisher painting and pushed. Instead of another room, as Jade had expected, the wall opened into a short, enclosed corridor with a high ceiling. Their footsteps echoed as they walked, and noises carried freely from the adjacent room.

Jade wondered uneasily if a similar passage ran alongside her apartments. If so, it wouldn't have been difficult at all for Kang to listen to her conversation with Gao.

"The palace is full of nooks built by your ancestors in case of attack. But with the improvement of protective fortifications over the years, the passages have become mere curiosities." Kang pushed open another wall, which led into a sitting room decorated in shades of green. Three people sitting at a mahogany table rose, astonished, as Kang and Jade emerged from the wall of the room. The eunuch announced Jade's arrival, then bowed low and left, closing the wall behind him. *Perhaps,* Jade thought, disturbed, *he's still standing there listening.*

"I had no idea that was another entrance into this room," Lady Tran said, beaming. "May I introduce Your Highness to former Ambassador Shiro and his son, Koichi?"

For the first time, Jade felt glad she had worn such elaborate clothing, for both Shiro and Koichi were meticulously well dressed in crisp navy silk. Both men stood just below her shoulder, and she realized she had never met anyone of short stature before.

"It's a pleasure to make your acquaintance again, Princess. I say *again*," Shiro said, smiling, "because I saw you a long time ago, when you were just a little one."

The former Ambassador spoke the language of the Great Forest without an accent. He had strong, handsome features, with gray hair sweeping back from deep-set eyes framed by a lattice of wrinkles. He observed her with kind, fatherly interest, and Jade warmed to him at once.

"I'm glad to see you as well, sir."

He placed a hand on his son's shoulder. "Koichi was born the same winter you were."

Jade exchanged shy smiles with the young man, who was the image of his good-looking father, but with jet-black hair and merrier eyes. If she hadn't overheard their conversation, she would not have noticed the small lines of tension around his mouth. They disappeared, at any rate, when his face widened into a friendly grin.

"Father tells me Your Highness and I met and became fast friends when we were three," he said. "It was at a banquet shortly before you left the palace. Your nursemaid told us a story."

"I wish I could remember. What story was it?" Jade asked.

Koichi's eyes crinkled. "Father says it was Empress Lihua's favorite tale, the story of the thousand lanterns, which became one of my favorites as well. I was pleased to find it in a volume of Kamatsu folktales I got as a birthday gift, though the rendition was slightly different."

"You like folktales, then?"

"I won't stop loving them, no matter how old I get. And I'm sure you feel the same."

"I do." Jade's cheeks warmed at her small lie, but she enjoyed the way his eyes shone at her. He didn't have to know how often she complained about being too old for Amah's fables.

Two maids entered the room, bringing piping hot jasmine tea and sweet bean buns.

"I like to think that the story is true," Shiro said, helping himself to a pastry. "What could be more romantic than a man hanging the lanterns for his true love? Especially since we don't know where the real lights in the forest truly came from."

"All we know is that they won't budge." Koichi turned to Jade. "You should have seen the soldiers hoisting each other up in the trees with fishing poles."

Jade couldn't help grinning as she pictured Xifeng's stiff, dignified men struggling to remove the lanterns. "I heard the lights not only returned, but doubled in number," she said, but as the others laughed, she remembered the secret passage and hastily changed the subject. "My birthday banquet is in a few days. Will I see you there, sir?"

Shiro shook his head. "Unfortunately my son and I have business, Your Highness, but everyone in the city has been talking of the event. You must be anticipating it a great deal."

Too late, Jade remembered Kang saying that Shiro *used* to be Xifeng's friend. If the friendship had ended, perhaps the former Ambassador and his son had not even been invited. "Truthfully, the idea of a celebration held in my honor is uncomfortable," she admitted.

"You've had a simple upbringing, which is the best way to raise a child," Shiro said. "When my wife died and I resigned from my position, I was generously offered a home in the palace. But a house in the forest suited my tastes better."

"There's something restful about living among the trees," Jade agreed, thinking longingly of the shaded, green-dappled roof of the monastery in summer.

Koichi shook his head with playful disapproval. "What a pair you are. I can't think of anything I want to do less than settle down to a quiet life before I've had a chance to travel. Give me a month in the desert, another in the mountains, and a year on the Sea of Seven Pearls, warring with pirate kings like in the old fairy stories."

"I think my nursemaid would like you," Jade told him, amused.

"And I *know* I would like her."

Jade turned shyly back to her tea when Koichi grinned at her. He clearly liked walking a fine line between boldness and disrespect, but he balanced it well.

"Has she been good to you, your nursemaid?" Shiro asked.

"I love her like my own grandmother."

He nodded, satisfied. "And how has it been at court? Are you happy here?"

"The palace is wonderful, but there are always so many people watching."

"The princess is very well liked," Lady Tran chimed in. "The ladies who visited her had nothing but the highest praise for her manners and conversation."

"I do agree, Your Highness, about the people watching," Koichi said. "On the rare occasions when my father and I come to court, you'd think no one had ever heard of a dwarf before! That openmouthed gawking!"

"I'm sorry," Jade said, contrite. "I complained without thinking."

The young man waved away her apology. "It's a fact of life, and another reason Father prefers to live away from the palace."

"Have you spent much time with your father, Princess?" Shiro asked.

"Only five minutes. I spent most of my life wondering about him, and now we're under the same roof and I can't see him." Jade gazed into her teacup, feeling the already familiar worry gnawing at her stomach.

"I'm glad, at least, that the Emperor has loyal servants by his side," Lady Tran said reassuringly. "Perhaps you saw Pei when visiting your father? A big, nervous eunuch?"

"The one with the mole on his nose?" Jade asked, remembering how he had scurried out of the room to fetch His Majesty's medicine. *Have patience,* he had told her through Wren when returning all of Jade's notes to her father.

"Shiro and I have known him for years," the woman said. "He is faithful and trustworthy, and will care for His Majesty to the best of his ability. But we will still all pray for the Emperor."

"Thank you." Jade hesitated, then added, "And I will pray for the safe return of Hana. I hope, for your sake and that of her little boy, that she'll be found soon."

The men bowed in thanks. "The Empress kindly allowed Hana's family to be together today, but we shouldn't intrude longer than necessary. We ought to go." Shiro's eyes on Jade were soft. "I hope this isn't too bold, but our home is always open to you, Princess. We live by the southeastern gate, not far from the river. Please call on us if ever you need a friend."

"I'd like that," Jade said gratefully, getting up from her chair as they rose. The thought of Shiro and Koichi leaving made her feel lonely.

"It was a pleasure, Princess," Shiro said. "Until we meet again."

"Until we meet again," she echoed.

12

Jade noticed Xifeng's incense at once when she entered the Empress's apartments that evening. Dozens of tall black sticks burned all around the sumptuous chamber, which was showy and ostentatious, but functional. Neat shelves full of bound volumes of poetry, ink pots, and scrolls lined the walls behind an elegant desk. A smaller map of Feng Lu hung by the window, surrounded by exquisite paintings of birds and flowers inscribed with verses.

For what is the gleam of the sun on bright metal, Jade read on one, *without the strength of its sting?*

Another painting read, *The lion knows not to doubt the mouse, for size does not betray strength.* Jade studied the artwork of a timid mouse sitting on a rope severed by tiny teeth marks, feeling both pleased and surprised. She wondered if Amah had known about this poem; if so, her nickname for Jade—little mouse—was not silly, but rather an affirmation.

"I love beautiful words, as you can see," Xifeng said. Jade turned to see her stepmother watching her from the doorway. "Arranged in the right way, they have the power to make you laugh, cry, or feel. I hear you met former Ambassador Shiro today. Did you like him?"

Jade bowed low to the Empress. "Very much, Your Majesty, and his son, too," she said, blushing a bit. "They chose to remain here instead of returning to Kamatsu after he resigned?"

"Shiro had a difficult relationship with his family back home," Xifeng told her, gliding into the room. "They treated him unkindly because of his height. I haven't known many men who deserved more respect than he does, but his own flesh and blood refused to see that."

Jade tried, and failed, to imagine Amah rejecting her because of her appearance.

"A good man," Xifeng said. "I think well of him, though he doesn't always agree with my methods."

"He dares to disagree with Your Majesty?"

The Empress's laugh held a touch of bitterness. "Shiro has always had a mind of his own, whether he's speaking to a peasant or a king. He has had nothing to do with politics—or with me—these ten years or more." She sank gracefully onto a teal brocade couch, gesturing for Jade to do the same. "I'm sorry we haven't dined together until now. The Kamatsu matter has troubled me greatly, but I won't bore you with the details."

"On the contrary, I'd like to hear more about it," Jade said. "I am ready and willing to learn, as Your Majesty mentioned I would have to."

Xifeng raised an eyebrow. "Do you know much about politics?"

"I've read about the relations between the kingdoms. I know Kamatsu's ministers have fought for independence from the empire for a long time, and that their princess is too young to rule, so her uncle serves as regent in her stead."

The Empress gave a contemptuous sniff. "The regent is weak. He bends like a stalk of grass, and his council is the wind. They're determined to win their bid this time, and if I refuse, it might spark a war we can't afford."

"You're considering their independence, then?"

"I must. But, free or not, they will still pay allegiance to the most powerful crown on Feng Lu," Xifeng said, studying her slender hands. "Fortunately, I have a strong supporter in Lord Tanaka, a rising star in the Kamatsu court. If their kingdom leaves the empire, he will ensure our lasting trade partnership and help me . . . *persuade* the regent whenever I need him to. You'll meet Tanaka at the banquet, and I very much hope the two of you will like each other."

Though the Empress spoke offhandedly, there was no mistaking her meaning. *You're here as a pawn,* Amah had said. *She just doesn't know what she wants to use you for yet.*

Clearly, marriage to Lord Tanaka, Xifeng's puppet in a foreign court, was one of the options for how Jade might be used if the Empress bore a son as she hoped.

"As for that little princess of theirs," Xifeng continued, "I can make an additional match with her for my son, when he is in my belly, and further secure Kamatsu to the Great Forest."

A false promise of independence to Kamatsu, bribing a powerful nobleman with marriage to the princess of the Great Forest, and plotting to use a child not yet conceived—all within the span of a few breaths. Jade's mind whirled at the alarming speed of her stepmother's thoughts.

"Tell me what you think about this matter, then, dear. Since you've such an interest."

From the way Xifeng tilted her head expectantly, Jade knew each word she said would be tested and weighed. "When I was little," she said slowly, "I asked Amah why my family rules over all other kings. She told me that the blood of the Dragon King, the greatest of the gods, gives us the divine right to rule."

Something shifted in Xifeng's face, but she nodded at her to continue.

"But I was never satisfied by that explanation. Simply having the right bloodline and the ability to seize other lands by force doesn't make someone an ideal ruler."

"Yet time and time again, history rewards the people who possess those very qualities," Xifeng pointed out. "You should know that, coming from a line of emperors."

"But as history rewards some, it always punishes others." Jade's mind returned to the protesters and the children, laboring for the blacksmith with their faces covered in ash and soot. "Many people crave change. They want power in their own lives, whether that means standing free of an empire or simply having enough money to buy food."

"Power often comes with unexpected burdens." The Empress lowered her eyes, looking a bit ill. After a long moment, she asked, "Do you believe in destiny?"

Jade hesitated. "I would like to think our decisions can influence our fate."

Xifeng went very still. "We have a choice, then?"

"Yes, I believe we always have a choice."

"How funny," the Empress said quietly. "I think Shiro once told me the same thing."

She made a slight gesture, and several eunuchs, invisible until now, came forth with trays of food and jugs of sweet rice wine. They laid a red silk cloth and bowls of delicate porcelain on the table between

Xifeng and Jade. One of them prepared Jade's plate: pickled duck eggs sliced onto a bed of thick, fragrant noodles in a sweet chili sauce.

"I ordered simpler fare," Xifeng said as the eunuchs bustled around them, "since you were so concerned about His Majesty's diet that you had to speak to Gao about it. I mention it in person to you now because Kang told me my writing a note displeased you."

Jade's stomach twisted at the woman's cold gaze. "Your Majesty . . ."

"You've been busy, haven't you? Worrying about your father, commanding my servants." Xifeng sipped her wine. "By the way, the eunuchs are too busy with the banquet to move Lihua's map. I hope you'll understand."

"I do," Jade said evenly, "and I hope Your Majesty will understand that it's my duty as a daughter to be concerned about my father."

"Of course. But when I tell you I've done everything I can for him, it would be gracious of you to believe me. Not interrogate Gao or disturb your father by trying to send half a dozen messages." Xifeng blinked at her. "You're not eating, darling. Aren't you hungry?"

Jade reluctantly picked up a piece of duck egg, but it tasted like sand in her dry mouth.

"You're a bit difficult to please, aren't you, Princess?" Xifeng's eyes ran over her from head to toe. "You even refused my handmaiden, Madam Ong, and insisted on finding your own."

"I did not mean to offend Your Majesty." Jade had done no wrong and had made every effort to be courteous and respectful, and she was determined not to apologize.

But Xifeng softened as though she had. "I only want you to be happy," she said, draining her cup. The moment it was empty, a eunuch stepped abruptly from the shadows to refill it and she gave a violent start at the sight of him, crying out and dropping the cup. The man prostrated himself on the floor, groveling. "I told you," Xifeng told him in a low, dangerous voice when she had recovered, "*never* to approach unless I call for something. Get out of my sight."

The poor eunuch fled, weeping, and Xifeng leaned her head against a cushion, her pallor heightened and her eyes feverish. Jade stared at her, wondering if the woman had expected to be attacked. "Are you feeling well, Your Majesty?" she ventured. "Should I call someone?"

But at that moment, Kang swept in and spoke softly into the Empress's ear, then handed her a wooden box. When he was gone, she took a few deep, slow breaths.

"I'm all right. I was just startled," she said, giving the box to Jade. "Here, this belonged to your mother and I thought you'd like to have it, though I know it isn't the only present you've received." A slight edge entered her voice. "The noblewomen seem to have taken to you like ducks to water. They were just as infatuated with Lihua."

"They only wished to make me feel welcome," Jade said neutrally, accepting the gift with a bow. She opened it to reveal a hair comb with teeth of pure silver, through which white silk jasmine flowers had been threaded. "Thank you, Your Majesty, this is beautiful."

"The silver was tarnished, so I had Kang polish it with a special tonic." Some of the color returned to Xifeng's cheeks as she smiled, looking for all the world like a doting stepmother. All that had passed—her grievances with Jade, her jealousy over the nobles' gifts, and her frightened reaction—was swept neatly under her mask. "I thought you might wear it to your banquet."

There was something childlike in the Empress's volatility, Jade thought, and the way she dismissed people and went from resentful and vengeful one moment to adoring the next. She obeyed the woman's gesture to kneel, bending her head so her stepmother could slip the comb into her bun. The teeth scraped across her scalp, making the skin tingle.

"I see even more of Lihua in you now," the Empress said in a soft voice, her eyes dark and haunted as she touched Jade's cheek. "Your skin is sun-browned and you have wider eyes, yet you are her image. Has she returned in you to watch over what I do?"

Jade followed uneasily when Xifeng rose and beckoned, leading her down a dark corridor into her inner chambers. The plumes of incense, which were even stronger here, resembled shadowy figures darting out of the rooms toward them. They passed through a curtained doorway into a room with one wall covered in a thick, glimmering sheet of burnished bronze.

"Come admire yourself in my mirror," Xifeng said, standing before its murky depths. In the darkness, her reflection had stark-white skin and lips red as blood.

Next to the Empress, Jade thought she appeared frail and childlike. The incense made her feel dizzy and off-balance, and suddenly she recalled why it smelled familiar: Emperor Jun's medicine, the one Xifeng had ladled into his mouth, had possessed the same scent.

No, it can't be, she reassured herself. The Empress's incense must have been burning in her husband's rooms and Jade had mistaken it for the smell of the liquid. But even as she tried to convince herself, her mind spun with the possible revelation. The thoughts raced in her head, one after the other: her father's imprisonment and severely restricted diet, ensuring his weakness and the immediate absorption of any medications; the physician's fear when he told Jade he didn't make the medicine; and this foul remedy poured down the Emperor's throat.

Jade's heart thundered. Her eyes slid to her stepmother's perfect face in the mirror.

Xifeng is poisoning the Emperor.

Enough to keep him under her control, not to kill him. It would not do to have to marry another man, one who might see through her schemes and keep her from ruling in her own right. As soon as the suspicions materialized, Jade told herself firmly to stop—but they had already taken hold in her mind as strongly as any roots in the Great Forest.

The Empress's eyes met hers. "Well? Do you think you look beautiful?"

"I'm not sure, Your Majesty," Jade said, her head still muddled.

"Taking pride in your appearance is everything. Someone once told me that *this*," Xifeng said, touching her own cheek, "is all we have as women in this world. Beauty is our strength, don't you agree?"

Jade shifted her weight. "I'm not sure I like people looking at me," she admitted, thinking of the court ladies' scrutiny, friendly though it was. "It makes me uncomfortable."

The Empress's hand fell from her face. "Why?"

"They're forming an opinion that has nothing to do with who I am. You, however, are so beautiful, Your Majesty," she added hastily, "that people do not dare presume to know you at all. It makes sense that beauty is your strength."

Xifeng waved a hand. "You didn't offend me. I understand, even if I don't agree." She turned back to her reflection, which was immaculate even though the hollows beneath her eyes were pronounced. "I'm tired. Your banquet is in two days and we should both rest. And, sweet daughter," she added, lips curving as Jade moved at once, eager to go, "a piece of advice. Curiosity is not an attractive quality in a woman, especially at court. Will you remember that?"

She knows, Jade thought, her breath catching as she gave an unsteady bow and stumbled out of the room. Somehow it had grown even more smotheringly hot and oppressive in the dark and smoky apartments, and she had a frightful headache like a band of tightness around her temples.

I am beginning to see now. And she knows it.

13

In the dream, Jade stood in a cavern of stone with a high ceiling and walls of rock. A waterfall raged down into a stream that seemed to boil, coils of heat rising from its surface.

Xifeng, Empress of Feng Lu, sat in this ancient chamber with candles and a pot of the ever-present black incense smoking beside her, the fragrance smelling even more poisonous in the moist, heavy air. Shadows nested under her eyes, and her thin shoulders slumped as she studied a collection of pale yellow objects on the ground.

Like all dreamers, Jade knew she was safe—this was not real, she would not be seen. Yet when she approached to see what her stepmother was studying, Xifeng's head snapped up, nostrils flaring. "Who's there?" she demanded. "I can feel you."

"Your Majesty, there is no one here but you and me," Kang said in the soft, patient tone used to calm a frightened child. He stood nearby, stirring a great black pot that simmered over a dancing fire. The flames illuminated the objects beside him: glass jars of herbs, a bowl of liquid, and a gold bird-shaped vessel with a matching ladle. "Nothing can harm you while I am here."

Xifeng's wary eyes moved to a recess of rock near the base of the waterfall.

Kang followed her gaze. "They're gone now and they won't return," he assured her. "You made certain of that. You destroyed every last woman who stood in your path. The bodies in that pool are a mere reminder that we are all mortal."

"I need no reminder, for those women live on in *here*," the Empress snarled, jabbing a finger at her temple. "They are with me in my dreams. Their faces look back at me in every crowd. They watch me even now, from the shadows of this very room."

Bodies . . .

Nausea clenched Jade's gut as she glanced at the pool. What sort of evil dream was this? Fueled by anger and suspicion, her imagination must have decided to turn Xifeng into a monster.

"The Empress card appears *every* time. I *am* the Empress, I *am* all-powerful! Why do the spirits of magic tell me what I already know?" Xifeng turned back to the objects before her. She touched a flat, polished stone hanging from her neck that shone blue and gold and purple in the light. "And it's still paired with the warrior."

"Wei, too, is gone forever."

"I know that," Xifeng snapped. "Yet his fate is still tied to mine somehow. *How?*"

The yellow objects were slivers of pale, painted wood. Jade grimaced at the disturbing images upon them, some showing men painfully and unnaturally contorted. *Do you believe in destiny?* Xifeng had asked. Perhaps this was an odd method of fortune-telling, but if so, it was one Jade had never known existed. What was it doing in her dream?

"Whatever the cards tell you, the priority is taking better care of yourself, Your Majesty," Kang pleaded. "You need to eat and sleep. Your health is crucial to keeping your throne and bearing sons safely. It's what you owe to he who gave you the crown."

Xifeng's features twisted with anger. "How dare you?" she whispered. "You, who know everything I have endured. I earned the crown. I got myself here and into Jun's path."

"No one denies that, least of all me," Kang soothed her. "But the Serpent God encouraged you and put ideas into your mind. I know him. I lived for years in his dark monastery in the bowels of the desert. My Empress, he is merciless to those who are disloyal."

"What will he do? Keep appearing in my mirror to frighten me? Send his black worms to spy on me?" Xifeng placed a finger on her chin in mock thoughtfulness. "I heard a child caught one that was spying in the gardens. *His Godliness* grows ever careless, and I grow ever *weary*."

"He could turn his eyes to another," Kang said, and her sneer faded. "Have you considered that the Empress card might refer to another? Perhaps the story does not end with you. The Serpent God saw a woman taking the empire, but not who she was."

"He saw *me!*"

"Even the fallen god has his weaknesses." Kang pressed his palms together. "I am saying all this because I worry for you, my friend. I will protect you at all costs and help you keep everything you've worked for, but I beg you to be cautious."

Xifeng took a deep, shuddering breath. "I did everything he wanted me to do and paid my way in hearts, but how many more dead sons must I bear? What in this cursed life of mine is ever certain? I've given up everything, and still my crown is not wholly mine. There are nights I cannot remember my own name, nights in which I see eyes watching me from every wall." The words poured from her in a desperate stream. "And always he makes endless demands. He wants me to build him an army and expand our empire in his name, but with what money? He wants me to eat more hearts to strengthen my resolve, but it's never enough. See how many bodies lie in that pool, how many hearts I've had to consume already?"

Jade stumbled backward and sank to the ground. *Eat more hearts.* Hot bile rose in her throat as the phrase echoed in her head. This was the most evil nightmare she had ever had.

Wake up, she pleaded, but the dark cavern remained in clear focus around her.

"I've grown careless. People are beginning to suspect." Xifeng's thin face looked like that of an old woman and a terrified girl all at once. "I can't shake the feeling that Shiro has always known. He might connect me to Hana. I lost him. I lost Wei. I've lost everyone who ever truly cared about me."

"You haven't lost me," Kang said firmly.

"Somehow I must go on. I must secure the throne. This is my destiny, and at least in *that*, the Serpent God and I agree." Xifeng gazed into the waterfall, clutching a single card in her hand. From where Jade crouched, she could see on it the image of a person on a cliff with one foot over the edge. "His Dark Majesty, once *the creature* inside me. Tell me of the Fool, the mortal enemy whose destiny is entwined with mine. I must destroy her, or she will destroy me."

A loud splash sounded from the pool. The Empress shrieked, startled, and Jade clutched her own pounding heart. Within seconds, a long black snake jumped out of the stream and into the waterfall. A second snake leapt out after it, landing instead on the hard floor of the cavern.

"Ah," Xifeng said bitterly. From the way the woman grew calm at once, Jade realized this was a frequent occurrence. "Another one of my children. Born of the corpses I've created, of pain and darkness from the womb of my deeds. The only children I may ever have."

Jade scuttled backward as the snake slithered toward the Empress. It began to grow, its slimy scales expanding in the candlelight until it became a broad-shouldered man, dressed in the black armor of the Empress's soldiers. Jade gagged, her eyes stinging with tears. *It's only in my mind,* she thought fiercely as the snake-man glided forward on human feet. *It's my fevered imagination trying to explain why the soldiers are so stiff and unnatural.*

"Serve me well," Xifeng told him, and the snake-man gave her a rigid bow and shuffled off. She turned to Kang. "To think I've been searching for the Fool under my nose, and all this time, she was hidden in a monastery exactly where I put her fifteen years ago."

Every muscle, every nerve in Jade's body froze as a shadow moved across the waterfall.

"An impertinent rodent who *still* has a greater claim to the throne. Tell me, Serpent God, Lord of the Shifting Sands," Xifeng breathed, "when I put Jade to sleep beneath the water with the others, will I break my curse? Will I at last bear the son to carry my bloodline?" From within her robes, she pulled out a glittering dagger that she drew across her palm. Blood splattered the cards, and for a long moment, she bent over the images, drawing some meaning from them.

She brought me home not to be used as a pawn, Jade thought, struggling for breath, *but to die. No . . . it's just a nightmare . . .*

Something flickered in the waterfall again: a visage like smoke, all wisps and tendrils like some nightmarish plant had decided to take on a human appearance. The eyes were bottomless black, gleaming above sunken cheeks and a mouth like a hole in soil crawling with white worms.

"Fairest of all," the face rasped in a voice that seemed to come from everywhere.

Xifeng bowed her head in dark prayer. "Her heart will be mine."

The terrible eyes in the waterfall shifted. They looked past Kang and Xifeng and focused directly on Jade, as though they could see her crouching there.

"I knew it! There's someone else here!" the Empress gasped, whirling.

Kang yanked a deadly, saw-edged sword from his robes and brandished it. He whirled and stabbed it wildly in the air. One of his blows went straight into Jade's stomach.

She woke up, dying.

14

"Wake up!" Wren slapped her, hard.

The room spun as Jade sat up, her gut churning. She saw two of everything. She ran to the chamber pot and emptied her stomach, then collapsed on the floor. Her head felt like it had been run through with a knife. Amah's loving, worried face swam across her vision as she felt Wren's sturdy arms lifting her, depositing her in bed. A cool, wet cloth was placed on her head.

"I'm here, little mouse."

"I'm all right," Jade croaked. Her mouth tasted awful. "It was a bad dream."

"This is more than a bad dream." Amah hovered over her, frowning. "Why are you still fully dressed? And what's this dried blood on your neck? There's a line of it behind your ear." Her fingers moved into Jade's hair, touching the silver comb. The movement sent a stabbing pain that radiated down Jade's back, and she cried out.

"Take it out," Wren said, her voice urgent.

"But just touching it hurts her so . . ."

Rough fingers yanked the comb from Jade's scalp, and stars burst in her vision. Then, all at once, the dizziness subsided, leaving behind a sharp, throbbing ache. Wren dropped the comb with a clatter. The tines glistened red with Jade's blood, and a light thread of fragrance coating the silver—the Empress's black incense—wavered in the air.

"Where did you get this?" Amah demanded.

The story poured out of Jade: the dinner with Xifeng, the link between the incense and Emperor Jun's medicine, her terrible headache after leaving the Empress's quarters, how she had lost consciousness upon returning to her own apartments, and the awful dream that had followed.

Wren grew paler with every word. "I have a story of my own. This evening, when you were at dinner, I found the secret door Kang used to get in here without us seeing him. It's tucked behind a painting in the corridor. I don't believe the servants use it or even know about it."

Icy cold prickles, like frozen fingertips, danced up and down Jade's arms.

"The door led to two staircases: one going up to the Empress's rooms and one going down to the underground tunnels," Wren went on. "I know the passageways well, but this was a section I had never seen. The air was thick and hot and damp, and I saw a waterfall in a circular room of rock. There was a hot spring with steam rising from it and a bubbling black pot over a fire beside a golden vessel shaped like a swan."

Sweat trickled down Jade's back. "No, it can't be."

"I couldn't explore more because I heard voices, so I ran back up and piled chairs in front of the secret door." Wren lowered her voice. "The eunuch stood there listening to you and Gao. We must be careful to whisper from now on when we speak of Xifeng."

"Then it wasn't a dream. The cavern and the waterfall were real, the snake soldiers . . ."

And the pool.

Born of the corpses I've created, Xifeng had said. *I paid my way in hearts.*

Jade's stomach boiled as she stumbled out of bed once more, but when she leaned over the chamber pot, she brought nothing up but sour bile. The tight band of pain around her temples intensified as she bent over, breathing hard in sheer panic and revulsion, tears mingling with her saliva. "The Empress is killing people," she whispered as Amah stood behind her and rubbed her back. "She's cutting out their hearts and eating them. Oh gods . . ."

Wren held up a hand. "Wait. No more talking here."

Amah helped Jade out into the sitting room and wrapped blankets around her, then helped Wren stuff cloth into every doorway in the apartments to prevent noise from escaping. Despite these precautions, they sat close together and spoke in an undertone.

The old nursemaid wrapped her trembling arms around Jade. "The protesters in the square were right. None of those women disappeared. They were taken."

"She mentioned Hana. Koichi was right: Xifeng killed his cousin," Jade whispered, her shoulders convulsing. "And Wren, you weren't with us in the Emperor's apartments that day—you had never seen that golden vessel of medicine, and yet you described it *exactly*. Now we know Xifeng has been poisoning my father, too." She shivered at the sight of the bloodstained comb Wren was examining, holding it gingerly by one of its flowers. "She must have poisoned *that* as well, though why it didn't kill me, I don't know."

Even in the dim light, the comb's silver teeth gleamed. Jade leaned into Amah, watching the play of moonlight on the metal as Wren turned it this way and that. It was beautiful, she had to admit, and it had once belonged to her mother—Empress Lihua had worn the same ornament in her hair. She felt a sudden, unreasonable urge to hold out her hand and ask Wren for it back.

"Usurper sorceress!" Amah hissed. "If it's the same poison, it affects you differently than it does the Emperor."

"It's possible she's been giving him a lower dose over many years," Jade said. "And I got a greater dose that went straight into my blood. Cruel, to use an item of my mother's to do it."

The old woman gave her a grim smile. "The fact that it belonged to Lihua might have saved you. Surely Xifeng did not plan to give you a glimpse into her lair."

"The poison hurt me and suppressed my will," Jade said slowly, "but you think the fact that the comb belonged to my mother turned it into a weapon against my enemy?"

"There is more than one type of magic in this world. Not all of it is sorcery."

"Then it protected me." Jade looked excitedly from Amah to Wren, not understanding their grim expressions. The silver teeth seemed to wink at her from Wren's fingers. "Don't you see? This comb may make me ill, but it might be worth the pain if it means finding out more about Xifeng's crimes. And then I can . . ."

"You can't be serious," Wren said, holding the comb away, and Jade realized that both of her hands were outstretched, yearning to feel the weight of it again.

Amah gazed at Jade, her face stern. "You say Xifeng gave her blood to read those strange cards," she said. "And you gave *your* blood before the comb produced its vision. The sort of dark magic that requires a blood price was punishable by death in your grandfather's day."

"I should destroy it," Wren said grimly, seeming ready to crush it beneath her feet.

"Put it in your pocket for now," Amah told her, and as soon as the comb was out of sight, Jade felt the longing dissipate. She sank against Amah, who clucked and held her tighter. "Xifeng is threatened by you, little mouse. She summoned you here to assess your danger to her and your usefulness as a pawn, but by now, she knows she cannot control you. You might just be the mortal enemy she has feared."

"Don't sound too proud, Amah. Impertinence is a death sentence at the palace . . . but it seems I already have that." Jade was silent for a moment. "You once told me an old folktale about a prince whose cruel father exiled him, threatened by his strength and intelligence. But instead of dying on the deserted island, the prince discovered a fruit that grew there, which he called apple, and he taught himself how to cultivate it. He survived and found his hidden purpose, and I must do the same."

Amah chuckled. "And here I thought you only listened to my tales to humor me."

"I've been a coward," Jade said angrily, "content to hide and let someone else do my duty. Abbess Lin was right: I let the monastery become my shield and pretended what was happening in the world had nothing to do with me. But it is my *own* father who has been ill and alone for fifteen years. It is *my* people who suffer. And it is *my* family's throne Xifeng has seized to torture and take innocent lives."

"You say she's eating people," Wren murmured, her face pale with uncharacteristic fear. "Is it worth it to her? What is it all for, really?"

"Freedom, with shackles. Power she could lose at any time." Jade rose shakily and went to the window, picturing her good, gentle mother giving up her place to Xifeng and her weak, pale father, shivering alone in bed. She thought of the corpses hanging from the city walls and the children crying from hunger. "Xifeng must regret what she has done in some small way. No one could do such terrible deeds and not be affected by them—and yet she deserves no pity. The monks taught me that redemption is within the reach of all. They were wrong."

"What do you mean to do?" Wren asked, fierce, intent.

"Fight. I don't know how, but it is *my* duty to end this. There is no one left."

Jade watched the snow falling over the palace gardens, knowing every woman who had come before her had walked there. Every woman in her family had run barefoot on the summer grass, or sipped tea on the terrace, or come to the palace as a young bride full of hope. The walls breathed their deepest wishes and their most ardent dreams, and there was only one person left who could ensure that their legacy had not been in vain.

"I have to get us out of this somehow," Jade said. "I *will* get us out."

Amah left the room and returned with a bundle of blue-green brocade in her arms. "It's time I showed you this. Both of you," she said, shaking out the shimmering folds on which she had painstakingly embroidered chrysanthemum blossoms. "This cloak is what I was working on so often at the monastery, but you weren't ready to see it."

"It's exquisite," Jade uttered, touching the rich material.

"It's the inside I want to show you." Amah flipped the magnificent cloak over and spread it on the floor with the brocade side down.

"This must have taken you *years*," Wren said, kneeling beside Jade.

"Decades," her grandmother corrected her.

All over the gold silk lining of the brocade cloak, Amah had embroidered a secret: a map of Feng Lu, rendered in rich jewel tones and surrounded by a border of pearl-white lanterns. The five kingdoms nestled in a sea of turquoise thread representing the oceans. Symbols and images had been stitched all around the border: moon-colored cranes taking flight, red roses burning in the desert sand, a phoenix rampant in tree branches, a silvery fish, a shining sword of steel.

"Amah," Jade said slowly, "these are all from the stories you've told me. Folktales and fables and legends." Her fingers traced a maiden in a painting, a wolf hiding as a hunter passed by, three princes on a dark quest, a proud warrior with his sword uplifted.

The nursemaid fixed her with a stern eye. "I didn't tell them to keep you a child always, as you believed. I told them because there is a lesson buried in each, and a woman who can think for herself delves beneath the surface. Pulling out the threads of another's story and applying them to your own life is the mark of a *queen*."

Jade held her breath, her eyes moving from the map to Amah's face.

"It's well you've been listening to me," the old woman said. "The power of storytelling lies in the passing on of messages, histories, and *secrets*. Empress Lihua and I worked on this cloak for you before she was even pregnant with you. She knew you would come. She knew you would face a challenge of this magnitude, as the *tengaru* had long foretold you would."

My mortal enemy, Xifeng had said. *The one whose destiny is entwined with mine.*

"The *tengaru*?" Jade repeated. "The horned horse-demon guardians of the forest?"

"They left the earth in the face of darkness, but I am certain another spirit watches over the woodlands." Amah's face was as grave as Jade had ever seen it. "Xifeng has clearly made a decision: you are a threat to her, and she will kill you if you stay. Empress Lihua often went to the *tengaru* clearing to seek counsel in times of trouble, and you must do the same. Nothing can be gained by confronting Xifeng now. You must first arm yourself with answers."

Wren's nostrils flared. "We're leaving the palace, then."

Amah touched her granddaughter's knee tenderly. "I'm glad to hear you say *we*, my dear, for you've anticipated my wish. Your help is needed." She gestured to the map. "The brocade we used to make this cloak has been passed down in your family for generations, Jade, and may have even belonged to the Dragon King himself, greatest of the gods. Xifeng may use blood, pain, and death to work spells for her own benefit, but there is also good magic . . . *protective* magic. Carry this cloak and it will tell you what you need to know: where to go, what to find, whether enemies are following you. This is your mother's command."

"Then I am to go on a journey?" Jade ran her hand over the Great Forest, imagining her mother and Amah bending over these neat stitches, needles working tirelessly, lovingly, for *her*.

"The map will tell you all when it's time." Amah tapped a small body of water stitched in cerulean thread, tucked south of the Imperial Palace. "This is the pond the *tengaru* called the Good Queen's Lake in honor of Empress Lihua. Their sanctuary is not easily found. You will need to navigate through the Great Forest in search of it."

"We'll have the map," Wren said confidently, her muscles tense with excitement. "And I'll bring the biggest blades I can steal. It's lucky one of us knows how to protect herself."

"If that was a jab meant for me," her grandmother said drily, "I accept it as my due."

"And you, Amah?" Jade asked.

The nursemaid hesitated. "If it is my fate to go with you, then I will."

But the thought of leaving Emperor Jun to his wife's mercy soured Jade's new zeal. "We should stay for the birthday banquet, at least," she said, biting her lip. "It would raise too many alarms if we didn't, and I'd like to speak to my father once more before I go. But I don't know how we'll manage to leave when Xifeng is having me watched like a hawk."

"The banquet may actually be your best chance to escape," Amah said. "There will be crowds and music . . . plenty of distraction for Xifeng. It might be easier to slip away then."

Wren clapped a head to her forehead. "That reminds me. Do you remember that nervous eunuch who returned the notes you wrote your father?"

"His name is Pei," Jade said, startled. "Lady Tran told me she and Ambassador Shiro have known him for years and that he's one of my father's most loyal servants."

A satisfied smile crossed Wren's lips. "He delivered a message from the Emperor while you were at dinner. Your father, too, wishes you to trust Pei. I am to give any notes from you to him, or to Lady Tran to give to him, and they'll see that the message gets to His Majesty, if only by mouth. Maybe they could even devise some distraction at the banquet and help us escape."

Jade released a breath. Her father cared about her—ill and exhausted as he was, he cared enough to want to help her. "We leave the palace on the night of the banquet," she said decisively. "I can slip from the room with some excuse and meet the two of you. It won't buy us all the time we need, but I'd rather have a head start before I have my heart cut out."

Amah hissed through her teeth. "Don't even joke about it."

"We'll need food, weapons, servants' clothes, and horses, too," Wren said, furrowing her brow. "We can't go dressed as we are. I can steal supplies and hide them in one of the underground tunnels. And we'll have to find some route other than going through the Imperial City." She snapped her fingers. "We'll go across the river. It's a more direct path into the forest."

Jade reached for Amah's hand. "In two nights," she said, "we vanish before the Empress makes us disappear."

15

On the night of the banquet, a retinue of eunuchs and attendants
came to escort Jade to the main palace. The city of women
looked splendid, with ornate bronze lanterns floating artfully in basins
of rose-scented water and festoons of bright silk on the railings, but
all Jade could think of was Xifeng's lair and the pool filled with her
victims' bodies. Their families would never see them again, and here
the Empress was throwing a celebration as though nothing was wrong.

Jade felt sick to her stomach, knowing escape would endanger everyone helping her: Amah, Wren, Pei, and Lady Tran. As they passed the
statues of the Dragon Guard, the army of the gods, she wished the heavenly warriors would come to life and put a stop to Xifeng then and there.

In the palace, maids hurried forth to collect their wraps. Jade
smoothed her jacket and skirt of deep blue-gray silk, which fluttered
around her like ocean waves. Amah and Wren had dressed her, and
it would be difficult for anyone who didn't know to tell that she wore
plain, undyed cotton clothing underneath.

Xifeng waited outside the banquet hall. The woman Jade had seen in the lair, with her fury and terror, was nowhere to be found. There was only the Empress of Feng Lu, magnificent in red-and-gold silk with chrysanthemums in her hair and the usual mask of benevolence on her face. The difference now was that Jade could see beneath the mask's edges—she had observed the monster underneath and learned the depths of its ferocity and desperation. Those hands had held human hearts; those lips had tasted hot blood. Jade wanted to run, to tear out of this palace of pain and depravity, and yet her feet continued on until they stood face-to-face.

"Here's the guest of honor, and how sweet she looks," Empress Xifeng said in her merry voice. Her eyes darted to Jade's hair, but she made no comment.

Wren had not destroyed the poisoned comb, but had hidden it with their other belongings in the tunnels, in preparation for their escape. None of them had spoken of it again, though Jade noticed both Wren and Amah watching her when they thought she wasn't looking. They needn't have worried, for her longing to use the comb had faded, except at night when she tossed and turned and wondered when her enemy would come to end her.

Jade bowed to that enemy now. "You are the definition of loveliness, Your Majesty," she said, pressing her hands against her sides to hide their shaking. The woman was a demon in human form, a beast wearing a cloak of beauty, and behind that smile she plotted Jade's death.

"You're looking peaked, darling," Xifeng said. "Haven't you been sleeping well?"

"I have, thank you." Jade forced her lips to curve upward.

"No nightmares, I hope?"

She knows. It took every ounce of Jade's willpower to keep her expression neutral at the sly lilt in her voice. *Somehow she knows I was there.* "No nightmares, Your Majesty."

But Xifeng must have sensed something on Jade's face or in her voice, because her smile widened. "Good. Come now, we musn't keep the Emperor waiting," she said, holding out her hand for Jade's. "How cold your fingers are, little one."

Soft, warm light lit the banquet hall as the court bowed to Xifeng, who dispersed dazzling smiles and greetings in a low, charming voice as she led Jade past tables piled high with sumptuous food. The delicious smells only made Jade's stomach churn. *Who will be her next victim after me? Who will join the others in the pool of corpses?*

Jade caught Lady Tran's eye, and they inclined their heads in greeting. No one could know the escape they had planned from that one interaction, but still, Jade's hands grew clammy.

Emperor Jun sat on a throne with thick bamboo beams so that servants could lift and carry him. Someone had dusted him with powder and salve to brighten his skin and make his cheeks pink, but instead of improving him, it only emphasized his pallor. His tired red eyes found Jade and did not leave her as Xifeng turned to address the court.

"Welcome to this banquet in honor of Her Imperial Highness's eighteenth birthday. We *all* wish her health and happiness." The Empress pivoted to Jade, alight with pride and joy. "His Majesty and I are overjoyed to have you with us, dear. Let us dine in your honor."

She clapped her hands, and servants swept in with platters, pitchers, and trays of fruit. She took a seat at Emperor Jun's right hand, leaving the other side to Jade. The Imperial cook appeared with an immense roast pheasant smelling of garlic, ginger, and winter herbs.

"Serve our guest of honor first," Xifeng commanded. "She comes before me tonight. Go on, my child, there's no need to wait. Take what's rightfully yours."

If the words held a double meaning, her stepmother's expression showed no sign. The pheasant meat smelled sweet, as did the vibrant greens. Still, Jade hesitated. "Your Majesty is most generous. But I would prefer not to eat until you have been served as well."

"There is no need for such formality," Xifeng said softly.

Jade pressed her lips together, aware that everyone was waiting for her to take the first bite so they could dine. But something in Xifeng's manner made her feel certain she should not eat the food before her. Someone who tore hearts from victims' bodies would not hesitate to kill the princess before all the court. She picked up her ivory chopsticks, her mind racing for excuses.

Emperor Jun suddenly cleared his throat. "She needs to have it tasted first."

The room went silent.

"The food was tasted beforehand, as it always is," Xifeng told her husband.

"Then have it tasted again. These people are hungry." Emperor Jun lifted his fingers in a feeble display of impatience. "We can never take too many precautions for the Crown Princess."

Jade released the breath she held, and her father's cracked lips lifted slightly. *I too can be defiant,* he seemed to say. Xifeng must have decided against drugging him before this public appearance, for there was such unusual clarity in his gaze that Jade found herself imagining—just for a brief moment—what it might be like if she and he were different people, if she were nothing more than a beloved daughter to this man.

Though the Emperor had spoken, the servants all remained motionless, waiting for Xifeng's command. "Of course, if you wish it," the Empress said carelessly, waving a hand at one of the eunuchs. He hurried forth to taste from Jade's plate, then retreated, and the tension dissipated. The room filled with conversation as the courtiers began to dine.

The knot in Jade's stomach, however, remained. She took a small bite as soft pipa music began to play, feeling relieved when a nobleman in black silk approached to speak to Xifeng.

A eunuch came forth to cut the Emperor's meat into small pieces. "It is chilly on the other side of the stars," he said, very low, and Jade looked up to see Pei. He avoided eye contact with her, but she understood his words—Wren and Amah were safe and ready for departure. Her father had been the one to suggest coding the messages they delivered through Wren.

"Winter lays its frosted veil on the water," the Emperor agreed.

Jade's heart picked up. All the pieces of the plan had been set into motion.

Then, so quietly that only his daughter could hear it, Emperor Jun said, "Your mother was a good woman. I didn't deserve her or do right by her."

Xifeng was engrossed in her conversation, but still Jade did not look at her father as he spoke. She knew Kang would be watching.

"I've done so many things wrong," Emperor Jun whispered. "But now I am doing one thing right. I will, at last, make amends to Lihua."

His words brought unshed tears to Jade's eyes. She had spent so many years resenting and hating the father who had discarded her, but she knew this act of penance might at last lead to forgiveness. She wished she could tell him, but Xifeng turned to them. In the same moment, Jade saw Lady Tran excuse herself to her companions and leave the room.

"Jade, dear," the Empress said, gesturing to the man in black silk, "may I introduce you to Lord Tanaka? This is the talented young man of whom we spoke."

Tanaka. The Kamatsu nobleman Xifeng hoped to use as a puppet against the regent. He appeared to be in his midtwenties, with a distinguished air and elegantly cut clothing, and his features were what Jade would expect of someone loyal to Xifeng: cold and hard. He bowed low to Jade, and she inclined her head stiffly in return.

"I've invited Lord Tanaka to join us. Perhaps there is room beside you?" Xifeng asked.

"It would be my honor," Jade said. "But I hope Lord Tanaka will not be offended, for I must go. You see, I too have a gift for my parents."

Xifeng tipped her head. "For us?"

"Your generosity has so touched me that I wished to return a token of my esteem." Jade rose, pulse thundering in her ears. "Some of Your Majesty's ladies have kindly helped me with the surprise. With your permission?" She made sure to look at the Empress, not her father.

"How can I say no? I love gifts," Xifeng said with a broad smile. "By all means, go."

Jade bowed, feeling many eyes on her as she went out into the crowded corridor. A troupe of Dagovadian acrobats practiced flips in one corner under the guards' suspicious observation, while five women warmed up their voices to a musician tuning his lute. Jade passed a group of eunuchs in theatrical dress before she reached the end of the hall. There, several noblewomen, including Lady Tran and her daughters, stood behind a large folding screen, swapping their silks and satins for pale undyed cotton—exactly what Jade wore under her own clothing.

"Are you ready, Your Highness?" Lady Tran asked, her voice light though her eyes were full of meaning. "We will be the first to perform."

"I'm ready."

"Your Highness, it's kind of you to join us," a younger noblewoman said. "My mother looked askance at the idea of me dancing, but she approved as soon as she heard you would too."

"You told your mother? It was to be a surprise!" her friend scolded her.

Jade removed her clothing as the girls argued. Secrets weren't kept long from Xifeng, not when shared with flighty court ladies. But Pei and Lady Tran had planned for that when suggesting that the nobles dance for Their Majesties—the Empress would expect to see Jade among the performers. What she *wouldn't* expect, Jade prayed, was what would come afterward.

Each dancer received a handful of long, thick scarves of floaty deep gold silk, with which they wrapped their heads, faces, and bodies. When they were finished, Jade knew no one would be able to pick her out from the other dozen women wearing the same outfit. She met Lady Tran's eyes as they all hurried back down the hall and a eunuch announced their arrival.

"Your Imperial Majesties, may I present the noble ladies of the court and Her Imperial Highness, the Crown Princess, in a special performance to wish you health and happiness!"

Lutes and pipas began playing over the courtiers' murmuring as the dancers ran inside. At the high table, Xifeng and the Emperor watched with Kang and Lord Tanaka, but none of them showed any sign of recognizing Jade.

Jade followed the others in the simple dance she had learned over the past two days. They each spun in a circle to the beat of the pipa, then joined hands in smaller circles as the lutes' melody sped up. They twirled, their scarves floating in a golden spiral, and the courtiers cheered with approval. Every few steps ended in a low bow to Xifeng, who beamed at the flattery.

Yes, bask in the worship you think you deserve, Jade thought as the music played faster. The dead would not forget, and neither would she. *Enjoy your numbered days.*

The women gathered in a large circle, each spinning to the music, and then one by one they danced lightly out of the room as the music came to an end. The courtiers roared their approval, and at the head table, a beaming Xifeng rose to applaud with Kang by her side. Jade glanced at Emperor Jun, but did not dare linger as she left the room with the others.

It was the only goodbye she had time for.

Outside, Jade lowered her scarf and a hand took her elbow. "Keep moving and do not look at me," Pei murmured, steering her into a dark sitting room off the corridor. Behind them, Lady Tran loudly corralled the other dancers, distracting them from Jade's absence.

Pei pushed a wall open, revealing a secret passage. "Kang isn't the only one who knows the hiding places of the palace," he said with a brief smile. "Amah and Wren are waiting for you behind the terrace. The river is frozen, and you and the horses must cross as fast as you can."

"Will it hold our weight?" Jade asked, breathless as they descended a stone stairway.

"It likely will, but it may be safer to go on foot and lead the animals. Shiro will meet you on the other side, and I will linger behind to ensure you aren't troubled." Pei lifted a fold of his tunic, showing her a bronze-sheathed sword.

"Pei, I know you're risking your life and I . . ."

He waved away her thanks. "I am loyal to His Imperial Majesty and

Empress Lihua, our true queen. To serve their daughter is a privilege. Do you have sturdy shoes on?" She nodded, glancing at the plain, hardy servant's boots Wren had stolen for her. "Good. We need to run."

The air grew warm and thick as they dashed through the tunnels, passing several doors before alighting upon one that opened to the outside. Jade shivered in the sudden chill as they stepped out beneath the sky. The darkness was absolute. They would be guided only by the light of the moon, which shone faintly on the frozen river and the Great Forest beyond.

Pei made a sound like a nightingale, and Amah and Wren emerged from the shadows, leading Wren's pony with their sacks on its back. The nursemaid threw her arms around Jade. "I will slow you down on the ice, but Pei says there is no other way," she said anxiously.

"Hold on to me," Jade reassured her. "I'll make sure you get across."

"The ice won't break if we go slowly, two by two." Wren set her jaw and wrapped a hand in her pony's mane. "I'll go first. Jade, I entrust my grandmother to your care." She stepped onto the ice, slipping a bit, then coaxed the animal along with her. They walked slowly, gingerly.

The river had appeared small from her window, but Jade saw now how wide it truly was. It took several long, heart-racing moments before Wren and her pony even reached the middle.

"Shiro will take you to safety," Pei told Jade and Amah. "He lives not far from here. Stay with him until morning and do not venture out beneath the moon."

Jade couldn't help hugging him. "Please tell my father I'll return as soon as I can."

Pei bowed. "Wren is on the opposite shore. Come, you may both cross . . ." But he broke off his sentence as a sudden flash of movement and a rustling came from behind them.

Before Jade and Pei had fully registered what was happening, a huge cloaked figure seized Amah and dragged her away with unnatural strength and speed. It disappeared through a door in the stone wall of the terrace, revealing wooden steps going down in faint torchlight.

"Amah!" Jade cried.

"Your Highness, you *must* cross! I will go," Pei called desperately, but Jade ignored him.

She was already at the door, running down, down, down into the dim light. She had no time to hesitate or be afraid, not when it came to Amah. Her lungs felt too shallow to take in enough air as the stairs continued to descend and the heat grew heavier, thick with moisture.

Oh gods, oh gods, let it not be there . . . not in that place . . .

16

Jade quickened her pace, ripping the scarves from her damp neck. The figure moved so quickly, she had already lost sight of it, despite running as fast as she could. She had pursued it without thinking, because no thought was needed: Amah was her grandmother in all but blood, the woman who had raised Jade when she'd had no one.

"Stop!" she screamed, trying not to fall as the passage twisted and the ground sloped downward. She smelled damp earth and heard the sound of rushing water.

Please let it not be there.

But then the cavern of rock appeared with its raging waterfall, just as it had been in Jade's vision. Confronted by the surreality of a place she knew but had never been, she froze halfway down the stone steps, the sights and sounds assaulting her senses: the vicious roar of water, the sulfurous heat beading on her skin, the steam bringing the scent of the Empress's black incense to her nose from where it bubbled poisonously over a fire.

And, in the center of the room, Empress Xifeng stood over a body so damaged, it could not be recognized. Thick blood from a gaping chest wound covered the person's face.

"There you are," Xifeng said softly, regarding Jade on the stairs.

But Jade could not meet her stepmother's gaze, for her eyes—like the rest of her body—seemed unable to move. She stared at the corpse, at the scarlet rivulets pooling around its edges, but her sobs died in her throat when she realized that the dead person wore a maidservant's clothing. Somehow, she forced her knees to move, bringing her down the steps and into the room, where she saw Amah collapsed on a boulder, breathing shallowly. Jade flew over to her nursemaid, whose temple was bleeding from where she had been struck on the head.

Amah's eyes, dazed with pain, focused slowly on Jade. "Oh, my dear," she whispered.

Anger, white-hot, dulled the edges of Jade's terror. She straightened with her nursemaid in her arms and looked Xifeng in the eye. "You want me dead, and here I am," she said, gritting out the words between her teeth. "No one else has to suffer but me."

"You, suffer? What can *you* ever know of suffering?" Xifeng whispered incredulously, her face full of naked, inexpressible hatred.

Shouts rang out on the stairs, where Pei and Kang were locked in a furious stranglehold. Pei could not free his sword, for Kang—the more powerful of the two—had wrenched his arms cruelly behind him. Kang gave Jade a mock bow, his eyes glittering as Pei sagged with pain. He looked different in the dim light—bigger, stronger, with a mouth full of sharp, pointed teeth.

"I'm forever impressed by your knowledge of the secret passages, Kang," Xifeng said. "You got us down here quickly, and here is your reward: a reprieve from your duty as huntsman tonight, while the Fool offers her heart willingly to me." The eunuch bowed, a smirk creasing his monstrous features, as Xifeng nudged the corpse with a toe. "To think, this maid died for nothing. She could have gone on cheerfully scrubbing chamber pots if I had known this morning that I would have Princess Jade's heart. Ah, the cruelty of life and its timing."

"Kill me," Jade told her. "Take my heart. But let Pei and Amah go."

The Empress considered her. "I might, if only so Kang can have fun hunting them down again. It was a clever plan, stepdaughter. Lady Tran devising that dance so you could leave with the scarf over your head. It might have worked if I were unintelligent." She shrugged at Kang in amusement. "Even after all these years, people *still* choose to under-estimate me."

"A grave mistake, Your Majesty," he returned.

"You would think," Xifeng said, punctuating each word with a kick to the maid's body, "my enemies would respect me by now. Pei will be dealt with, my dear. As will your nursemaid, Lady Tran, and everyone still loyal to Lihua." Slowly, she began to advance on Jade and Amah.

Jade tightened her grip on the old woman, pressing Amah's head beneath her chin as Xifeng moved closer. "You will not touch a hair of hers while there is still breath in my body."

"You love her so much?" Xifeng asked, the glee fading from her eyes. In its place was something Jade could not quite name, but she thought it might be disbelief . . . and jealousy. "Someone who doesn't share a drop of your blood?"

"Blood has nothing to do with love. Not that *you* would understand. Not that *you* have ever loved or known what love is." A flicker of pain crossed Xifeng's face, but Jade was too far gone, too furious to take much note. Her chest blazed with anger that had lain dormant for so many years. "You've killed and tortured and lied to keep your throne.

126 JULIE C. DAO

You've subdued my father; you've taken *everything* from me! For all I know, you killed my mother, too."

The Empress reared back. "I had nothing to do with Lihua's death."

"If you ever, for *one* second, contemplated being Empress instead of her," Jade said, her voice rising, "if you ever had your huntsman dirty his hands for you, then you were involved. And my half brothers, my mother's sons? Did you have *nothing* to do with their deaths too?"

Xifeng bared her pointed teeth, and Jade saw that they were stained crimson. Slowly, insolently, the Empress wiped her mouth. "Maybe you should ask your father about them."

"What is that supposed to mean?" Jade demanded.

"It means that every one of us will do what it takes to survive. Don't fool yourself that you wouldn't do the same. When you've lived the life I have and seen the things I've seen, *then* you may judge me. You think you're so pure and good," the Empress said contemptuously. "But now someone you love is in danger. What would you do to save Amah? Would you kill for her? Would you eat a heart, I wonder?"

Jade shook her head. "That's the difference between us. Your choice is pain and violence first, but my choice is to find another way."

"You're eighteen, Jade," Xifeng snarled. "Grow up."

"We always have a choice!" she shouted.

A loud crack, a stinging warmth on her cheek. Jade was sprawled on the ground before she realized her stepmother had darted forward and slapped her.

"There is only destiny," Xifeng said, her teeth gritted, "and those too afraid to seize it."

She turned and nodded to Kang. He dropped Pei, who had lost consciousness from the pain in his arms, and kicked him aside in a motionless heap. Walking over to the dead maid, he dragged her by her hair to the pool and unceremoniously dumped her corpse into the water.

"Now show my prizes to the girl," Xifeng commanded.

Kang advanced on Jade and she tried to scurry backward, but he half lifted, half dragged her, ignoring her shouts and kicks. She pressed her hands over her eyes when he deposited her by the edge of the pool.

"Don't make me force you to look, Princess," he told her. "It will be unpleasant."

"Perhaps you ought to cut her nursemaid's eyes out to help her see," Xifeng suggested.

Jade stifled a sob and peeked into the water with one eye. At first, she saw only the gentle ripples on the pool's surface. And then they cleared, and she saw it all: locks of black hair like fragile seaweed waving in the current. Ghostly white fingers bleached by time. Fragments of robes in diluted jewel tones, worn ragged in the stream. A powerful stench of sulfur and rot rose with the steam, and Jade gagged, covering her mouth.

A dozen corpses lay entombed in the water, all women, all young, most of them beautiful. Some looked more worn than others, as though they had rested there for many years. One caught Jade's eye, her red lips parted, her skin pale, her hair the brown-black of charred wood.

This time, Jade could not fool herself that it was a dream. This time, she knew it was real—the woman with the red lips, *all* of the women, had once lived and loved and breathed in the world above. And Xifeng had taken their hearts from them.

"The hot spring preserves them and keeps them fresh," the Empress said softly. "It helps me remember what they've given me to ensure that I rule, that *my* beauty lasts forever."

Jade sobbed and ran back to Amah, who held her with one arm. "My little mouse," she whispered, fingers scrabbling behind her as though seeking purchase, something solid in all this.

"I summoned you to determine your worth and your danger to me," Xifeng went on. "But I made the same mistake others have made about me. I underestimated you. And I saw something in you . . . a will to fight, a determination to make the world as you think it ought to be. Are you so very different from me as I once was?"

"I am," Jade seethed, "*nothing* like you. I would never have made the choices you made and pretended to be a victim of destiny." She met her stepmother's gaze and thought, for the first time, that she would gladly kill the woman if she had a chance. She imagined dragging that slender body over to the pool of corpses, forcing that beautiful head beneath the water as the woman struggled desperately to breathe . . .

No. I'm not like her. No.

"Not such a little mouse, are you?" Xifeng remarked. "And not as stupid as I thought, either, winning over everyone at court. The eunuchs and ladies worship you as they never have me. Some even call you the rightful heir and rally behind you."

"The people at court don't *worship* me," Jade said coldly. "I'm not a god. I treat them like human beings. You disgust me. It makes me sick to think of the atrocities you've committed in my mother's rightful place."

Xifeng went still. "It's well, then, that I leave no stone unturned. Tonight you die, Jade. Don't fear, I will make up a romantic story about finding you frozen by the river and clasping you to my breast with motherly grief. Perhaps you weren't happy here; perhaps you left your heart behind in the forest with a peasant boy. Ironic," she added, her smile sharpening, "because your heart will remain here with me. But no one needs to know *that* part."

She pulled a glinting dagger from her robes, its blade jagged like teeth.

This is how it ends for me, Jade thought. She prayed Wren had found Shiro and made it to safety, far from this cursed palace. But when she turned to tell Amah goodbye, the nursemaid's expression held no hopelessness or terror. Instead, her mouth was set with anger and defiance.

"If I die, I die fighting. And you will run," Amah whispered, grasping Jade's wrist with surprising strength. "Do you understand me? You run when I tell you to. Do not look back."

"Amah," Jade began, her gut twisting, but the old woman tightened her grip.

"Use the map. Find Wren, find the *tengaru* clearing," the old woman told her fiercely. "Learn what to do, my dear one, my little mouse, daughter of Lihua's heart. Go into the forest and disappear. Your destiny lies elsewhere."

"Please don't ask this of me," Jade begged, shaking uncontrollably. Without Amah, there would be no more songs or stories or memories spoken aloud of Lihua, no one left who knew the depths of her heart. She clung to her, tears blurring her vision. "I can't leave you. I love you."

"And the gods know how I love you," Amah whispered. "But if you truly love me, you will run. Promise me, Jade. We have no time left. *Swear it on your mother's life.*"

Jade felt, rather than heard, Empress Xifeng approach them. The urge to kill the woman for doing this to her—for robbing her of the person she loved most—raged inside her once more. It was so much easier to accept hatred, in that moment, than the knowledge that she would never see Amah again.

Amah gnashed her teeth in frustration. "Do you love me enough to spare me the pain of seeing you killed?"

All at once, like a dam giving way, the hatred broke and a sorrow like ice crept through Jade's body. "I love you," she whispered, feeling each word like a knife, "and I swear on my mother's life that I will run when you tell me to." Amah pressed her lips forcefully to Jade's temple, and then, with one rapid motion, flung her toward the stairs with all her strength.

"Run!" the nursemaid screamed, rising. In the hand that had been scrambling on the ground behind her, the old woman clutched a sharp piece of rock aimed right at Xifeng's face. She charged at the Empress, catching her off-guard, and Xifeng released a scream of abject horror and anguish. Scrambling up the stone steps, Jade felt a thrill of pride at Amah's courage.

But her triumph was short-lived.

Powerful hands grabbed Jade's legs.

She fell face-forward painfully, scraping her chin on the rock as she looked back to see Kang's black eyes narrowed in fury. She kicked him hard in the stomach, but he held on with a viselike grip. Suddenly, he yelled and fell backward down the stairs as Pei, his face still contorted with pain, yanked his bloody sword out of Kang's back and jumped out of the way.

"Kang!" Xifeng shrieked, her face a mess of blood as she struggled with Amah.

The henchman stumbled to his feet, and when Pei's sword lunged at him again, he stopped the blade by grabbing it with his fingers. Blood rained down from his hand as he tore the weapon from Pei with one fearsome tug, flipped it around, and threw it straight at Amah. It slipped in between her ribs and the old woman fell noiselessly, the sharp rock in her hand bouncing away.

A wail of devastation reverberated through the cavern, and it took

Jade a moment to realize it had come from her own lips. She met Pei's eyes for a brief second, and then, heart shattering within her, she kept her promise. She ran up the stairs and through the winding tunnel, leaving them all behind as the memory of Amah's death replayed over and over in her head.

O utside, Jade skirted along the terrace and nearly ran headfirst into Wren.

"Where have you been? Where is my grandmother?" Wren demanded, breathing hard from having backtracked across the river. She took one look at Jade's pinched, tear-streaked face and closed her eyes. "There's no time to grieve now—we *must* cross. Are they coming?"

"I don't know. It can't be long before Xifeng summons the guards."

Wren tugged Jade onto the ice and half dragged, half pushed her with the strength of a draft horse as they staggered across the river. A layer of freshly fallen snow covered its surface, making it even more treacherous. Behind them came hoofbeats and the shouts of men, and ahead of them lay the Great Forest, the thousand lanterns blazing in the dark. Jade let the lights guide her, every panicked breath accompanied by a stab of heartache. With each step she saw Amah again, frail yet fierce, weak yet full of rage, lunging at the Empress in her final act of defiance.

The lion knows not to doubt the mouse, for size does not betray strength.

So many stories and lessons, and Jade had complained and taken them all for granted. She wiped her face furiously, wishing she could lean against Amah's knees once more. This time, she would shut her ungrateful mouth; she would let Amah tell her a hundred tales all at once.

The muscles in Jade's legs were burning by the time they stumbled onto the opposite riverbank, but there was still a wide expanse of snowy hill before the forest. They climbed up the sharp, slippery rocks, Jade doing her best to stay close behind as the snow stung her skin.

"Shiro?" she managed to ask.

"Waiting in the forest. Don't look behind us—it'll slow us down."

The sounds of pursuit grew louder. The frozen river gave a frightful crack and neither girl could resist peering back, despite Wren's warning. Xifeng's men were crossing on horseback, boldly, swiftly, carelessly, holding their bodies with unnatural stiffness.

"Hurry," Wren gasped. "Oh, hurry."

They made it to the top of the hill, Jade's lungs screaming for air, and plunged into the Great Forest. The lanterns dangled high above them, great globes of kindly white light. Jade prayed ceaselessly as they ran through the snow, calling upon the good graces of every Dragon Lord in the heavens. Wren was in better physical form, her body conditioned by exercise, but she was patient whenever Jade tripped. She merely righted her and they continued on.

"This way!" Wren angled them to the right as the ice cracked like thunder behind them. Any minute now, the Empress's soldiers would be in the forest.

Two horses burst from the trees: Wren's gray pony and a black stallion with a rider. At a second glance, Jade realized the stallion carried *two* riders, Koichi in front and Shiro behind, wrapped together in a black cloak. It was a clever trick to make them resemble one large man.

"Hurry!" Shiro shouted, fear etched into his features.

Jade gripped the pony's mane and lifted her foot, feeling Wren's considerable strength as the other girl propelled her onto its back. Wren leapt up behind her and seized the reins, nudging the pony on after Shiro and Koichi's horse. They tore through the woodlands, dodging tree trunks, clumps of snow flying off the branches and stinging their faces.

Xifeng's men were surely in the forest by now, but there was no noise whatsoever. The quiet frightened Jade more, until she heard a great rushing like the waterfall in Xifeng's lair.

"Don't look back!" Wren yelled, but no one listened.

The lantern light intensified, glowing yellow, as they whirled to see what chased them.

A living, coiling black mass poured over the forest floor like hot, poisonous oil. Jade screamed, recognizing the flood for what it was: thousands of slimy black snakes, fat as small tree trunks, slick bodies gleaming. They moved relentlessly forward, heads held high and alert.

But when the serpents entered the shadows between lanterns, Jade saw their images shift into thousands of masked men, crawling after her on the forest floor.

"The lantern light shows their true forms!" she uttered, horrified.

Shiro clenched his jaw. "We can't take the road home now. With the amount of ground they can cover, they'll catch up long before we arrive."

"The bridge in the thousand lanterns story!" Koichi said abruptly, his eyes widening at Jade, but she hadn't any idea what he meant or how it could be important now. "Follow me!"

"I hope you know where you're going!" Wren urged the pony into a gallop, and Jade clung on for dear life. If she fell, the snakes would be upon her before anyone could save her. The sound of the serpents was like torrential rain, like a plague-ridden flood.

"Keep riding!" Koichi shouted. "Bridge ahead!"

He had grown up in this forest, Jade recalled. He knew it well, and in a moment, he was proven right. A slender bridge of light gray wood appeared, curving over a frozen, boulder-filled stream. Koichi and Shiro's stallion leapt onto the bridge, and the gray pony followed.

Within seconds, Xifeng's snake soldiers arrived at the foot of the bridge, stopping on the last bit of snowy earth before it met the gray wood. They gazed up with their hateful ruby eyes.

One of them hissed, a long, red-black split tongue emerging. *"Death comes for Jade of the Great Forest, whether now or later."* It advanced, but no sooner had its body touched the bridge than it burst into the air, flying backward as though it had been flung.

Jade and Wren gaped at each other.

A current of uneasiness rippled through the snakes, and then another tried to slither onto the bridge. It met the same fate, for the moment its scales touched the wood, it was ejected backward as though some invisible person stood there, gripped it by the neck, and threw it.

"They can't cross the bridge," Jade breathed.

Koichi grinned at her. "It's the story of the thousand lanterns. It gave me the idea."

"I don't understand. There wasn't a bridge in that story."

Before he could reply, several snakes gave up on the bridge and began crawling over the frozen stream. But their plan to surround the bridge on the other side was thwarted. Jade noticed them gliding backward fast and hissing in pain, some returning with missing or shredded scales.

"They can't cross the ice, either," Wren exclaimed. "What is this place?"

"I played here when I was a child." Koichi glanced at the retreating snakes. "Come, it's not safe to talk here. If they can speak, they can listen. Let's move on."

"We need to go to the *tengaru* clearing," Jade told Shiro as they nudged their horses off the bridge. "Amah told me I would find answers there. Do you remember where it is?"

He shook his head sadly. "I've never found it again, though not for lack of trying."

A thought occurred to Jade. "Amah's cloak! Wren, which bundle is it in?"

Wren pulled out the brocade and they stopped, the men keeping watch while Jade spread the cloth over the pony's neck. The mere feel of Amah's stitches beneath her hands almost brought Jade to tears, but her grief subsided when she saw the map: the lanterns sewn around the border, which had been pearl-white when Amah showed them the cloak, were now bright red.

"How could this be?" Wren asked, paling.

"This is no ordinary map." Jade peered up at the trees. All of the lanterns were pure white. Quickly, she repeated the tale of the thousand lanterns as she had told it to Amah and Wren on their journey. Understanding dawned on Shiro's face, and he, Wren, and Koichi looked at each with mounting excitement. "The tale is a clue! Amah said storytelling is the passing on of secrets. Suppose my mother left me a trail of red lanterns, just like in the story."

"We need to go back," Koichi said decisively. "I told you, Your Highness, I read another version of that story in a volume of old Kamatsu tales. The tale must have crossed the sea and changed a bit in doing so."

"Tell us," Jade urged him.

"In the version I read, the princess's betrothed chases her lover through the forest. But his men can't cross a magical bridge that appears and saves the lover. It was created by forest spirits who took pity on him," Koichi said. "The story ends the same way, for the betrothed tricks him. 'Come away from that bridge,' he says. 'The princess sent me for you.' After much persuasion, the lover obeys and is killed."

"Koichi," Jade said excitedly, returning the young man's ear-to-ear grin, "you may very well have saved us tonight. Let's return to the bridge. If the musician died near it in the story, the red lantern must be there."

"So what does this mean? That the story is real?" Wren asked doubtfully.

"These woods hold a strange magic," Shiro murmured. "The *tengaru* once rescued my party when we were attacked. I find it almost easy to accept, here, that a story may turn out to be real and our salvation."

"I once asked Amah if her tales were real or just stories. She said, 'Why not both?'" The lanterns sparkled through Jade's tears, recalling the last time Amah had told her about the thousand lanterns. She felt Wren's trembling hand on her shoulder.

"I wish our grandmother were here, too," the young woman said quietly.

Unable to speak, Jade shook out the brocade cloak and wrapped them both in Amah's loving stitches.

The snakes had gone and the bridge was quiet when they returned to it, scanning the treetops. Jade saw the bright spot of red at the same time as Koichi. "There!" they cried in unison. She would have sworn on her life that the single red lantern had not been there earlier, and Koichi agreed.

His eyes met hers in the gloom. "I wonder if the lanterns were listening, waiting for us to put our stories together. Lead the way, Princess. This story belongs to you and Empress Lihua."

After the first lantern, the trail was easy to find. Wren spotted the next one twenty feet away, and then Shiro found the one after that. Warring emotions of fear and sorrow and exhilaration filled Jade's heart. She didn't know if these muddled feelings caused the dizzying, surreal sense of disorientation that came upon her, but it felt like the horses were crossing a greater distance than her mind could comprehend, despite not changing their speed.

In the story, the trail led the princess to the one she loved.

But who waited for Jade? Who was left to care for her?

The trees begin to thin out, and within minutes a great clearing stood before them with an immense crystalline pond, ringed by snow-kissed willows bending their heads into the half-frozen water. "The Good Queen's Lake," Jade whispered. "We've found it."

The *tengaru* sanctuary nestled in the serene echoes of nature, a place of perfect peace and quiet, with only the song of a snow lark and the rippling of water beneath the moon. No snow touched the grass, and the air, too, was mild without the bite of winter. Jade filled her lungs with it, the grief lifting from her shoulders for a moment. It felt like coming home.

Shiro pointed ahead. "The *tengaru* queen lay there, on that island in the pond."

They dismounted and approached the water. The island was flanked by two gray bridges identical to the one in the forest. One led to where they stood and the other arched over the Good Queen's Lake to a gate of silver iron. Within the bars, a single tree shimmered in the moonlight.

It was the strangest, most beautiful place Jade had ever seen, and as untouched by the world outside as the monastery had been. It was hidden, she guessed, by some magic—protected by the same craft that governed the trail of lanterns and had allowed her party to travel so quickly. *I could hide here forever,* she thought, *and Xifeng would never find me.*

She imagined bringing Abbess Lin, the monks, and the village elder here, where they would be protected, build a new monastery, and pretend the world outside didn't exist.

Something enormous moved on the island, breaking into her reverie.

Wren moved forward with a blade in hand, but Jade's feeling of coming home grew stronger as the smell of white jasmine rose from between the trees. She couldn't explain why it did not frighten her— she only knew that the fragrance was both beloved and familiar. She touched Wren's shoulder and moved to the foot of the bridge.

"Hello?" she called tentatively. "I am Jade, daughter of Lihua of the Great Forest."

The movements stopped. In the long quiet that followed, Jade could feel the creature's astonishment. And then it moved again, this time rising until its head stretched above the trees.

A pair of huge gold-flecked eyes peered at them through the drooping branches of the willows, blinking out from the face of an enormous dragon.

18

Amah had taught Jade to revere the dragon beyond all heavenly and earthly entities. But nothing could have prepared her for the sight of the magnificent being.

For one wild, heart-stopping moment, Jade thought that one of the Dragon Lords had descended from the heavens to stand before her. But upon closer observation, she realized this was not a god. For one thing, the dragon had only four claws on each leg where a god would have had five. For another, it seemed gentle and shy, rather than regal and imperious.

To say that the dragon was blue would have done it a disservice. Its body held a hundred different shades from pale frost to deep navy, swirling across its iridescent scales. The long whiskers, curving deerlike antlers, and flared ridge along its back were of sunshine gold, and its lithe body ended in a serpentine tail and moved sinuously like water flowing to its destination.

The dragon regarded Jade with intelligence, but did not speak.

"Are you now the guardian of the Great Forest?" she asked, and it bowed its elegant head, its breath like a summer wind.

"Then the *tengaru* did leave," Shiro said softly. "Honored One, will you allow us to stay tonight? Enemies are on our heels, and the princess has come seeking answers."

The dragon blinked its gentle eyes at him benevolently, then gazed at Jade's cloak.

"You recognize this." Jade spread the brocade on the ground and saw that the embroidered lanterns had changed color again, this time to ocean-blue like the dragon's scales. Briefly, Jade explained to Shiro and Koichi what her nursemaid had told her about the map.

"It shows enemies? How will they appear?" Koichi asked.

"I'm not sure," Jade admitted.

Wren, who had been examining the map closely, gasped. "Wait, look here."

A tree stitched in bright forest-green thread had appeared beside the Good Queen's Lake. They all looked up at the shining silver gates across the pond.

"The *tengaru* told us that was the last apple tree on Feng Lu, which they had guarded for ages, waiting for someone worthy," Shiro recalled. "I was part of the last Imperial envoy to pay respect at the gods' shrine, which once had a ruby apple belonging to the Dragon King."

"Each god gave a treasure that represented his kingdom. The Dragon King must have chosen an apple," Jade said with wonder. Somehow the apple tree, a symbol of the Great Forest, had ended up here after the gods' alliance ended. Thinking of the Serpent God whose jealousy had poisoned that friendship, she told Koichi and Shiro about the poisoned comb and her vision of Xifeng associating with the fallen deity.

Wren's nostrils flared. "He wants Xifeng to build him an army, as if

Feng Lu hasn't already been torn apart enough by war and bloodshed."

"There's an old theory that the gods never took their relics back to the heavens," Shiro said thoughtfully. "They removed them from the shrine, but left them behind on earth. If that is true, the existence of the apple tree fits."

"So does the legend that the one who reunites the relics will bring peace to Feng Lu once more," Koichi said. "Perhaps the apple tree is meant for the same person."

They all turned to Jade.

"It can't be," she said, furrowing her brow. "It's a fable of gods and heroes, and I'm just a girl raised on stories. All I want is to see Xifeng cast down. I want revenge for what she's done to my father . . . and what Kang did to Amah." Painfully, she told Shiro and Koichi of the fate of Hana and the other women. Shiro's lips twisted with grief, and his son touched his shoulder, fighting back tears. "I would have lain in that pool, too, if not for Amah," Jade added.

Wren got up and paced furiously. "Kang is mine. You may have Xifeng, Jade, but he is *mine* for what he did to my grandmother."

"Your Highness, you are Empress Lihua's daughter and a descendant of the Dragon King. The revenge you seek for your family may have more to do with saving Feng Lu than you think," Shiro said, his voice thick with sorrow. "Xifeng can never turn from the darkness now. She was my friend long ago, but I saw her struggling even then. The woman she is now is nothing close to the girl I knew."

"She believes she can't bear a son and secure her throne while I live. She blames me for what she brought upon herself." Jade gazed up at the dragon, whose eyes held mute sympathy. "Whoever unites Feng Lu will be fierce and strong. They'll have to be more like Wren than me."

Wren said a curse word Jade knew Amah would slap her for. "Only someone fierce and strong would run *to* Xifeng as you did. Don't cheapen my grandmother's sacrifice with self-doubt. She didn't give her life for that." She softened her voice. "She wouldn't have done it if she hadn't believed you had a chance."

"Xifeng fears you," Shiro told Jade. "You don't want power, but you still have a greater claim to Feng Lu, and she'll never be sure of the throne until you're dead."

The dragon rose, causing a great wind to rustle the trees, and indicated for Jade to follow with a movement of its head. She obeyed, her mind a whirl of troubled thoughts as the creature led her to the silvery gates, where it stopped and waited for her to enter first.

When Jade stepped inside, she found it impossible to take her eyes from the apple tree.

It was extraordinary at a glance, glowing like a lantern, like no other living thing in the Great Forest. One side had the fragrant pink-and-white buds of springtime, and the other was wreathed in snow. No apples grew on its branches, and when she touched the pale gray trunk, she realized that all of the bridges they had crossed that night had been made from this tree.

Her fingers found strange, curving grooves in the velvety bark. She leaned closer, and her breath snagged in her throat when she recognized the drawings: a maiden in a crane feather cloak, three princes standing in a field of rice, a girl with a fishbone in her hands, a blazing phoenix, and a man picking an apple. The images felt as dear as friends, as beloved as family.

Amah's stories, yet again.

Jade fell to her knees. She felt the doubt melting away, the uncertainty of whether it was *she* for whom the apple tree was meant . . . for here were the tales told by someone who had loved her, etched into the tree of the Dragon King, the god of gods himself.

"Five stories, one for each of the gods and kingdoms," said a soft voice behind her.

Jade whirled to see an elegant woman standing by the gate. The streaks of silver in her jet-black hair gleamed as she approached, moving gracefully in silks of water-blue and sunshine-gold, matching the colors of the dragon.

"Hello, Jade," the woman said.

"Hello, Mother," Jade whispered. Somehow, her lips knew the truth before she did.

She and Empress Lihua were the same height, and even this small kernel of knowledge about the woman she loved without ever truly knowing threatened to break her composure. They even had the same face, though Jade's was a softer, more rounded version. They stood eye to eye, drinking each other in. Up close, the former Empress's body appeared filmy and transparent—a spirit only. Her fingers reached for Jade's cheek and went right through her skin.

"I knew you would come," Empress Lihua said, smiling, and Jade thought she could listen to her voice forever, like a melody played over and over. "I knew you would follow the lanterns here. I would ease your grief for Amah if I could, but only time can do that."

"And her stories, too."

Her mother's eyes sparkled. "Our ancestors believed in testing leaders and determining their worth. In the old days, you could not call yourself a ruler of mankind simply by lusting for power and seizing what you had not earned."

Jade bowed her head. "I never wanted the throne. To me, it is a symbol of greed, a means by which one controls the lives of thousands and calls it *power*. Yet there is such pain and suffering, and it's my duty to reclaim what is ours. I've shirked my responsibilities long enough. But even if I succeed, how can I heal Feng Lu? What can I do to fix such brokenness?"

"Leaders rarely succeed without help, and you will have that," Empress Lihua told her. "Recall that I gave you only one version of the tale of the thousand lanterns. I knew that someone who will come to mean much to you would have the other. Working together in this way will prove essential."

"Essential?"

"For the quest to dethrone Xifeng." The former Empress closed her eyes. "Like Shiro, I knew her when she was a girl and never imagined she would come to this. She has poisoned the empire, and the people are turning against one another, hungry, desperate. This must and *will* end."

It was all almost too much to bear. "She was right, then—our destinies are entwined, hers and mine. And one of us must destroy the other."

"She sees what she sees in her fear and paranoia. We see only what needs to be done," her mother said sternly. "You know the legend of the relics. The one who unites all five will bring peace back to Feng Lu by summoning a powerful heavenly army to their aid."

"The Dragon Guard," Jade breathed. "The warriors of the gods."

Empress Lihua inclined her head. "They are your only hope against Xifeng, the Serpent God, and their snake army, but you must first prove your worth by finding the treasures. Winning the Dragon Guard's allegiance will not only rid Feng Lu of Xifeng's evil, but prove to all beyond a doubt that you are the true and worthy heir."

Somehow, here by this tree carved with Amah's stories, her mother's words did not sound ridiculous, but *right*. "And these tales will help me find the relics?" Jade asked, her pulse picking up as she studied the pale gray bark. "Each relates to a different kingdom and will take me to that treasure. And I will bring them all here, back to the apple tree of the Dragon King?"

"The cloak, too, will guide you, but do not linger. Danger lies behind and ahead, and one of the treasures will be the difference between your life and your death."

Jade walked around the trunk, gazing up into the branches. "The Dragon King's relic must lie elsewhere," she said thoughtfully. "There are no apples here. This tree bears no fruit."

"Still, every inch of this tree is filled with my love for you," Empress Lihua said. "Time is running out, my child. Xifeng's huntsman will not rest until he brings her your heart in a box."

"Xifeng's poisoned comb allowed me to hear her plans," Jade told her. "Amah thought it was because it had once belonged to you." As she spoke, she pictured the gleaming silver teeth, sharp and full of answers, and felt a tug of longing.

"She might not have intended that effect when she gave you the comb, but if she finds out, she might *want* you to use it again. Be wary of magic that pertains to Xifeng, for a weapon against her could easily turn into one against you." She looked tenderly into Jade's eyes. "I know the doubts inside your heart, but destiny is not something from which you can hide. It follows you like your own shadow, and you must turn and acknowledge it."

"Will I find the courage to face it?" Jade whispered.

"You are a daughter of dragons, and courage runs through you like breath and blood," the former Empress said fiercely. "But you must never underestimate your gentle heart. Love and laugh with all the life in you, my cherished Jade, and you will conquer the darkness. If you are ever afraid, if you ever doubt yourself, look around you and there I will be."

Jade took in her mother's face, memorizing by heart the love and pride she saw there. The older woman's eyes glistened with tears, and her mouth trembled with powerful emotion, and this time, when she lifted her hand to Jade's cheek, her fingers made contact with Jade's skin.

"How strange," she said. "My spirit has never taken corporeal form on earth before."

Jade held Empress Lihua's hand tightly in both of hers. "I love you, Mother."

"I love you," Lihua murmured, "more than all the stars in the sky. And I believe in you."

And as her mother spoke, Jade *believed* for the first time. Her resolve was still only a timid, tender bud, but had blossomed nonetheless. Unlike Xifeng, she would not allow her destiny to master her. She would confront it, accept it, and choose it on her own terms. And if she could make it right, if she could become the leader Feng Lu needed, she would fulfill everything her mother and Amah had hoped for. Their deaths would not be in vain. She would find her courage and hold Amah's stories in her heart like a lantern against the dark.

Jade released the older woman's hand and bowed low before her mother and Empress.

When she glanced up, Lihua was gone and she stood alone once more by the apple tree.

19

We're going with you on this quest, of course," Koichi said. He had found a dry spot near the pond and was busy making Shiro comfortable by tucking their cloak around him.

Wren, meanwhile, dangled upside down in a tree, gripping the branch with her legs. Every few seconds, she raised her upper body without using her arms. "Accompanying you goes without saying," she panted, her cheeks bright red. "Empress Lihua said a leader should accept help, and Koichi has to go because he knows more about these *children's stories* than anyone—"

Koichi scowled. "Why do you say *children's stories* with such disdain?"

Wren ignored him. "And I have to go because I'm your handmaiden and an ardent supporter of killing both Xifeng and Kang. Shiro can keep us all in line."

"I will not go," Shiro interjected, "and Koichi shouldn't, either. This one evening of excitement has nearly done me in." The shadows beneath his eyes and the silver in his hair looked more pronounced in the moonlight. "Wren and the princess must travel undetected, and two dwarfs will stand out. Unless you masquerade as a child—"

"I certainly will not!" Koichi said, outraged, until Shiro chuckled. "You see now, Your Highness, where I get my humor."

Jade laughed with them, but her heart ached for Amah as she watched Koichi tuck the cloak around Shiro to keep the older man warm.

"Father," Koichi said, serious now, "I must go with the princess. You heard what she said: the stories are integral to summoning the Dragon Guard. Whether you believe it or not, I do. After that bridge saved us tonight, there is nothing I won't believe anymore."

"I don't ask for your assistance," Jade said gratefully. "But I'd be glad to have it."

"You see? My help is needed." Koichi looked pleadingly at Shiro. "You know I want to travel. I'm not meant to sit at home, especially not when Feng Lu depends on this mission and I can help in some way. I mean no disrespect, but I'll go with or without your blessing."

"You are all I have left, Koichi," Shiro said, his voice breaking.

"I'm a grown man." Koichi touched his father's cheek tenderly. "I've begged for years to journey across the continent and over the sea as you once did. It's best for you to stay here in the peace and solitude you've earned. But that's no life for me—you must see that."

Jade turned away, pained by Shiro's sorrow. The prospect of a journey with Wren and Koichi, however dangerous, had excited her. Selfishly, she hadn't considered at once that their lives would be in danger, too. As the Empress's huntsman, Kang would chase Jade to the end of the world. And if he cut out her heart, he would not spare her companions.

"This is a task I must do," she said. "But it is *my* responsibility alone. I cannot in good faith ask any of you to risk your lives for me."

Wren swung down from the tree. "Well, then, it's a good thing we offered and you didn't ask," she said, in a tart voice very like Amah's. "I will not rest until Kang and Xifeng face the consequences for my grandmother's death."

"And *I* will not rest until I see justice done for my cousin Hana's death," Koichi added.

Shiro shook his head in defeat. "Stubborn like your mother. I could never argue with her, either. Please don't misunderstand, Your Highness," he said to Jade, "and think that I don't support you and what you must do. I'm only a foolish father."

"You are the best of fathers," she said gently.

Koichi clapped his hands together. "That's settled, then. We'll need to go in disguise, of course. I'll be a silk merchant of Kamatsu who has sold all of his goods and is exploring the continent before returning home, accompanied by my wife and our servant."

Jade blushed, but Koichi's twinkling eyes landed on Wren.

"*You* can be my worshipful wife," he told her.

Shiro burst out laughing at the young woman's aghast expression. Jade joined in, though she felt a pang as Koichi craned his neck up at Wren in mock adoration.

"I have never, nor will I *ever*, wish to be anyone's wife and I do not plan to start now, even if it's just pretend," Wren protested, looking profoundly uncomfortable. "Why don't you be Jade's handsome husband and let me be happy on my own?"

"Because, *my dear*," Koichi said, getting into the spirit of things, "it's safer for you to travel as a married woman. And Kang and Xifeng will be searching for a princess, not a servant girl, so that is the perfect disguise for Her Highness."

"Well, that's decided, then." Jade turned her back on them and crouched by Amah's map, feeling a bit hurt that he had chosen to "marry" Wren so quickly.

"Well, I will say it was a clever idea to share a horse and cloak tonight," Shiro told his son. "Xifeng won't be searching for a small man at any rate." He sighed, pulled the cloak to his chin, and promptly fell asleep.

Wren went off in search of berries, and Koichi knelt beside Jade as she studied the brocade cloak. "Are you all right, Your Highness?"

"Jade, please. And I'm tired." She gave him a half smile, which he returned at once. She had never known anyone to smile so readily or with such genuine contentment. She tapped the expanse of green thread representing the Sacred Grasslands. "The map changed again."

Koichi inspected the large embroidered crane that had appeared, its neck arched to the sky, ripples surrounding the foot that touched water. "I know that folktale well," he said. "It was in the same book as the thousand lanterns story."

"How did it go? Perhaps it too is different from the version Amah told me."

"Once upon a time, a farmer found an injured crane by a lake. He took it home to care for it and saved its life, then set it free without expecting a reward. But the next day, he met a lovely woman lost in the rain." He winked at her. "They fell in love, of course, and married. His wife turned out to be a talented weaver, stitching feather cloaks that fetched a great sum, and made the farmer a wealthy man. But she warned him, 'You must never spy on me when I am working, lest you disturb me.' This aroused his suspicions."

"You tell the story as well as Amah did. What happened next?"

"The farmer broke his promise, naturally. He spied one day and saw not his wife weaving, but the crane whose life he had saved, crafting cloaks from its own feathers. When it saw him, it left him forever to spend the rest of his days alone, regretting his broken vow." Koichi raised his eyebrows at her. "Was Amah's version any different?"

"It's the same, except the crane was one of twelve sisters," Jade said. "Sky-maidens, sent from the heavens to reward human goodness. Each had a cloak made of her own feathers that let her shape-shift between woman and crane. Their feathers bestowed magic when given freely, but if taken forcibly from them, they couldn't return home to the skies. That's how Amah's story ended. The farmer refused to relinquish his wife's cloak, so she was trapped on earth as a crane."

Koichi looked at her intently. She had never seen such long, thick lashes on anyone. "Then a crane feather is the relic of the Sacred Grasslands? It's an odd choice for a god, isn't it?"

"That god prided himself on his shape-shifting ability and was also said to be bashful. It makes sense that a method of disguise may have appealed to him. This is the knowledge that comes of being raised by monks," Jade explained, grinning at his surprise. She ran her hand over the embroidered crane. "The map indicates that our destination is Red Lotus Lake."

Koichi furrowed his brow. "Your mother said the stories were important to the quest. Perhaps we'll need to use what we know about the tale and the god to find the crane feather."

She nodded. "Or the lesson of the tale."

He crossed his arms and cupped his chin with one hand in an uncanny imitation of Shiro. "What do you think is the lesson, then?"

Jade giggled at the gravelly voice that should have come from the sleeping ambassador, but instead emerged from his merry-eyed son. "To keep your promises, of course."

"I think you're right, Your Highness."

"Jade," she reminded him.

"Jade."

Her cheeks warmed at the sound of her name on his smiling lips, and she felt both annoyed and grateful when Wren returned at that moment. They told her what they had discussed while they ate the berries and roots she had brought back.

"It *seems* to make sense, but perhaps we should ask the dragon?" she suggested.

"It can't speak," Koichi pointed out.

"But it can understand us and nod, can't it?" Wren glanced at Jade. "Where *is* the dragon, anyway? Did you leave it by the apple tree?"

"It didn't come in with me," Jade said, but when she peered across the pond, the dragon had curved around the apple tree and closed its eyes in slumber. *Right where I left Mother,* she thought, noticing again how its long body rippled in the same colors as Lihua's silks.

Look around you, her mother had said, *and there I will be.*

"There's nothing I won't believe anymore," she murmured, echoing Koichi's words as they all settled down for the night.

But after Koichi lay down near his father, Wren sat up with one of their sacks. "I'm not tired yet," she told Jade. "If we're to travel across the continent in search of these . . . magical *things,* I thought I'd take inventory of what we have to sell for money."

Jade watched, stunned, as Wren pulled out a pile of riches: a silver hairbrush, a tiny hand mirror, three gold rings, a brooch, and a bundle of handkerchiefs of bright yellow silk.

Wren grinned. "I stole most of these from Xifeng when you were all at the banquet, but some came from my grandmother. She was keeping them for you in her wooden trunk. Unless you're attached to them . . ."

"We can sell them," Jade said. Her breath caught when the box containing the poisoned comb slipped out. "We'll keep that, of course. Just in case."

Wren grimaced, but replaced it in the sack with the other items. "Do you think we can do all this?" she asked, waving her hand at Amah's map. "I'm out of my depth. I can't read or write well, and I know nothing about stories."

"It's all strange to me, too, but my mother wouldn't have given me this task if it wasn't important." Jade hugged her knees to her chest. "Maybe Xifeng wasn't always a monster. Maybe she was like us once, scared and hopeful. But we can't let her go on the way she has. And if I die trying to defend my family's honor and Feng Lu, then it's as the gods will it."

They sat in a thoughtful silence for a moment.

"I hated you, you know," Wren said suddenly. She smirked when Jade turned to her. "I blamed you for stealing my grandmother, and for my brother's death because he died on *your* brother's mission. You were easy to blame when I didn't know you." She regarded Jade with her head to one side. "I thought you'd be spoiled and selfish, but you surprised me. You're nothing like a princess. You're respectful and talk to me like I'm your equal . . ."

"And so you are."

Wren pointed at herself. "I'm a kitchen wench, and *you're* the Emperor's daughter, the heir to the empire. Explain how we are equal, Your Highness."

"That's what frustrates me," Jade said. "I'm beginning to understand why Amah and Abbess Lin kept my identity a secret, so people wouldn't treat me any differently. You being you and me being me is nothing more than an accident of birth. I'm just a person. I like steamed bean buns and rainy mornings and walking on grass in my bare feet . . . Why are you laughing?"

"I like all those things too."

"Also," Jade added, "if we're to travel together, you ought not to call me *Your Highness*. In fact, I'd prefer it."

"All right, then." Wren let out a loud sigh. "But I still don't like these disguises. Why can't *I* be a maidservant, too? It would be closer to the truth. We could both be working for the pampered princeling."

Koichi gave a loud snort and rolled over in his sleep, as though he had heard her.

"It would be suspicious for a man to travel with two female servants. And anyway, Koichi wanted to marry *you*, not me," Jade replied, and although she was careful to keep her voice light, she felt Wren's eyes on her. To distract her, Jade tugged the pins from her hair, feeling its warm weight cascade down her back. "Here, add these ornaments to the items we can sell . . . They should fetch a good price. And would you mind cutting my hair?"

Wren stared. "You can't be serious."

"Of course I'm serious."

"I *cannot* cut your hair, Your Highness. Jade."

"I'm not asking you to shave it," Jade said impatiently. "Just make it short, right below my chin, so it's easier for travel. It's too cumbersome for a maidservant on the road."

Wren frowned, but she pulled out her dagger reluctantly and moved to kneel behind Jade. She lifted a hank of hair. "This is your last chance to change your mind."

"I'm not changing my mind."

"But are you *sure* that—"

"Cut the hair already, Wren!"

"Just remember, you ordered me to do this. Don't execute me later for destroying the Imperial hair," Wren grumbled, and she began slicing away. Within five minutes, she had shorn off the majority of Jade's hair in a blunt, uneven line.

Jade swung her newly light head, pleased. "Yes, this will do nicely," she said, then cackled at the sight of Wren sitting on the grass, looking askance at the chunks of thick black hair in her lap. "Come on, we should go to bed too. It will take three weeks to reach Red Lotus Lake, and we'll leave tomorrow at sunrise."

20

Koichi took Shiro home and returned to the clearing by sunrise. "He wanted to say goodbye, but didn't want to delay our departure," he explained, showing them a generous bundle of food and extra bedding his father had insisted he bring back with him.

"Will he be all right by himself?" Jade asked, worried.

"He'll be fine. If Imperial soldiers come, he'll tell them I'm visiting my uncle Hideki in Kamatsu." He grinned at Wren. "Good morning, wife!"

Wren rolled her eyes. "You're enjoying this too much."

"You'll have to play your part better, dear, or people will think our matchmaker made a mistake," Koichi joked. "Or that you're uncomfortable being married to a dwarf."

"What do you take me for?" she sputtered. "I'm uncomfortable with *marriage*, no matter the size of my husband." She made a face when she realized he was teasing her.

"I heard your father's family was unkind to him because of his height," Jade told Koichi.

"They weren't the only ones. Other people have always had a problem with our height, but Father taught me to be proud of who I am." Koichi gestured to his special saddle, which had been designed for his shorter limbs. "We've devised many ways to live comfortably, since it can be difficult. Windows are too high, stairs are hard, and I think one day I may have joint pain like Father. But I'm a hardy sort. You won't regret bringing me along," he added, grinning.

"I know I won't," Jade said.

They left the clearing, having been unable to find the dragon to say goodbye, but Jade told herself one day soon she would return and see it—and perhaps her mother—once more.

They took the northeast road through the Great Forest, the most direct route to the Kingdom of the Sacred Grasslands, for three weeks. With plenty of food, warm clothing, and good company, it often felt more like a journey for pleasure than a mission. But always, Jade remembered the huntsman was searching for her, and plain clothes and shorn hair would not keep him from his ultimate goal: cutting out her heart for Xifeng. She spent more nights awake than Wren and Koichi knew, thinking about her father, helpless and alone, and Amah. Often she had to get up and pace to calm her anger toward Xifeng when it threatened to boil over.

The three of them traveled well together for the most part, with occasional teasing from Koichi and sarcastic remarks from Wren. Koichi had a way of assembling his belongings in a flawlessly neat arrangement that irked Wren to no end. Everything had to be lined up straight and in order of use, and his good shoes—when removed for sleep— had to point exactly west, a fact that both amused and frustrated her. He continued to call her *wife* and *dear*, so as revenge one morning, she scattered his possessions in an untidy heap and flipped his shoes upside down. When he woke, it was the closest to a fit of temper that Jade thought she would ever see in a man of his cheerful disposition.

"Touch my things again and you'll find insects in your bedding," he told Wren crossly, having lately discovered *her* weakness in turn: anything that was small and crawled, which had terrified her ever since a bug crept into her ear when she was a child.

"But *why* must your shoes always point toward the sunset?" Wren pleaded, unable to bear the mystery of it any longer.

"It's not the sunset," Koichi snapped. "They point toward Kamatsu. My father and I do it to honor our homeland." After that, Wren never touched his things again.

They passed numerous trading posts and caravans full of foreign goods as they traveled. Koichi longed to stop, but Jade urged them on, unwilling to talk to more strangers than necessary. Soon, however, she began to realize that avoiding other people would be impossible.

The snow disappeared and the path became flattened grass as they continued south, passing many others: mothers and children wearing rags with rough cloth tied to their feet for shoes, farmers leading thin, hollow-eyed oxen, and exhausted men carrying crude tools for digging wells. Jade noticed one woman carrying a basket of rice as carefully as she would a baby, perhaps for her hungry family; every single grain counted. No one bothered Jade's party, but many of the children stared curiously at Koichi.

The day they emerged at last from the Great Forest, the sun shone bright and the air felt mild enough to shuck their cloaks. A vast sea of yellow-green fields stretched out before them, and the smell of sun-warmed grass made Jade long to roll like a child in the fragrant meadows.

"I have relatives here, but we haven't spoken in years," Wren said when they stopped to eat one day. "My grandparents left on bad terms. They were betraying our kingdom, some relatives said, even though working for the Emperor would pay better than anything here. And they wanted a better life for their grandchildren, so we could be scholars and diplomats' wives. They wanted much more for us."

"Why did you choose to remain servants, then?" Koichi asked. Jade saw that though it was a naïve question from a sheltered upbringing, it was also genuine.

Wren scowled. "Nobody *chooses* to be a servant. We are servants because we have no choice. Opportunity goes to people of greater social status, like you or your father. Do you think it's easy to become an ambassador? They want people with family connections."

Koichi's cheeks turned pink. "I'm sorry. I never thought about that."

"And it's hard to better yourself when so many are prejudiced against Grassland farm folk. Great Forest people look down on us and think we've come there to steal their positions." Wren eyed Koichi. "How did your father get his job, anyway?"

"Through hard work and dedication," Koichi said loftily. After a pause, he added in a quiet voice, "And his family in Kamatsu was noble and in good favor with the king."

"Well, that explains your goose-feather bedding and aversion to squirrel meat," Jade said, trying to lighten the mood, and they laughed. She pulled out the map, deciding it was time to change the subject. "We'll pass through a town tomorrow, and the lake won't be much farther."

"Maybe we could get a hot meal in town," Koichi said hopefully.

"Let's wait and see. A town means more people watching us."

They traveled uneventfully the next day. It was a beautiful kingdom, but they saw from the weary faces of passersby that it was a hard life— an existence of tilling land, raising animals, and selling what little they could at market. From a distance, the farms appeared peaceful and picturesque, but they saw the truth when they drew nearer: the bamboo walls were flimsy, the straw was rotten, and the animals in the pens were so thin, their ribs stuck out from their coats.

A woman collecting threadbare garments from a clothesline did not return Jade's polite nod, but glared at her suspiciously. She bent to touch a small statue beside the door, which had been carved roughly with the features of the Dragon Lord of the Sacred Grasslands. She muttered a few words, as though warding off evil, then went inside and slammed the door.

"She's not being rude. People here have learned not to trust strangers," Wren said quietly.

Within minutes, they saw why.

They heard shouting and wailing from a particularly shabby house, the door of which was thrown open. Two masked soldiers marched out, dragging a man with them.

Jade's mouth went dry when she saw that the soldiers wore Xifeng's seal on their armor. She touched Wren's rigid knee behind her and glanced at Koichi, who gave her a silent nod of agreement. He understood without her having to speak: if they raced past, they would call attention to themselves; if they moved past slowly, they might move on unimpeded.

"Please don't take him," a woman begged, running after the soldiers. She tore a pendant from her neck. It was similar to the jade one Lady Tran wore for luck, except it was made of cheap greenish stone. "Let me pay you with this instead, please."

The soldier shook her hand off. "You knew the law," he said in a flat, emotionless voice. "We warned you that if you didn't pay your taxes, you would pay in some other way."

"Take the pendant, take our house," the woman's husband pleaded. "Take anything but our son. How will we till our farm without him? We won't be able to eat."

Jade couldn't help peeking from the corner of her eye. The man who had been dragged out was no more than a tall boy of fifteen or so. He murmured something to his mother, trying to comfort her, but her sobs grew louder.

A crowd of onlookers gathered around their property, clogging the small road.

"You let that boy go," one of the men told the soldiers. He was a large, broad-shouldered farmer, his skin leathery from the sun. "You already take our homes, our profits, and the clothes off our backs, but you don't take our boys."

His words roused the people behind him.

"Good Grasslands boys belong at home with their families!" shouted another man. "The Great Forest has taken enough from us. We give you a cut of the paltry crops we raise. Why must we pay taxes on what we already give?"

"You let that boy go!"

"Shut up, all of you," a thin, red-faced man cried. "Do you want to swing by the neck from the city gates? Let the soldiers take him and be done with it."

"Yes, it's all very well for *you*," snapped the woman beside him. Her tunic had a strip of dull white cotton sewn onto each sleeve, indicating mourning. "You don't know what it's like to lose a son, and can't be bothered with worrying about other people's children."

"Do you *see* what's happened to us?" asked a wide-eyed mother, clutching her child. "How will anything be accomplished if we fight among ourselves?"

The leathery-skinned farmer who had spoken first stepped forward, so that his nose was only inches away from one of the soldiers' faces. "Take me instead of the boy. I'll wager I'm sturdy and strong enough to perform whatever labor you want him for."

"No, *I'll* go," an elderly man argued. "I've lived my life, and you have children to feed."

"None of us will go!" shouted a bent, white-haired woman. "To think I would live to see a foreign harlot of an Empress trying to control our king and rule over our people without knowing the first thing about us!"

At once, several young men and women surrounded her, protecting her from the soldiers. Several others shouted out, volunteering themselves in place of the boy. Two women wrapped their arms around the distraught mother, holding her as her knees buckled, while her husband sank to the ground, his voice breaking as he called his son's name.

Tears ran down Jade's cheeks at the fervor with which the neighbors tried to defend the family. Their loyalty and generosity in the face of such cruelty tore at her heart. They were all struggling, all scraping together a meager living, and it would have been easy to turn away from another's distress—yet they ferociously stood their ground against the Imperial soldiers. She burned with fury and hollow devastation at the lengths to which her people suffered.

"Isn't there anything we can do to help?" she asked, clenching her fists.

"You could turn yourself in to Xifeng's soldiers," Wren said sourly. "The boy and his family could run while they cut out your heart."

Jade wiped her face. "This can't be allowed to happen."

"It *has* been happening," Wren snapped. "You haven't lived at the palace long. You haven't heard the talk about people being used for slave labor or as target practice for soldiers. For almost twenty years,

Xifeng has painted her empire with the blood of its people. Don't think you've seen anything yet." She spat over the side of the pony with a furious, frustrated jerk of her neck.

As their horses cut through the crowd, two farmers began shouting at each other and punches were thrown as a violent skirmish broke out. Some of the men rushed at the soldiers and were quickly defused. Xifeng's men moved unnaturally fast, and Jade—abandoning all pretense of disinterest as she turned back to watch—could not see them move for the life of her, though several of the people who attacked them collapsed to the ground in agony.

"I wish I could give them something," Koichi said helplessly. Like Jade, he gazed back as the soldiers dragged the boy onto one of their horses.

But Wren faced forward, her expression like stone. "Like what? Are you going to feed them all? Knock on each door and offer them a few berries and roots? There is no immediate help you or *anyone* else can give."

Koichi spun to her, his mouth twisted with fury, but Jade knew the young woman's anger was not directed at them. She reached out and touched his arm lightly. "Wren's right. We have to move on and remember our objective. If we succeed in our quest, we could help them all."

They rode in silence for the rest of the day.

21

They reached the town at sunset. Because of its proximity to the Jeweled Coast along Feng Lu's northernmost border, it was larger and wealthier, full of merchants and sailors from across the sea. Buildings sprang up on either side of a wide, bustling road lined with stands and carts. The smell of spiced meat lingered in the air as people haggled over goods, the vendors shouting louder above the din than everyone else.

"We won't stand out as much as I thought here," Jade told her companions, relieved. "There are too many people and there's too much going on."

A few women stared openly at Koichi as they passed by. "Still, we should be cautious, as you advised," he replied. "We know soldiers are near. We don't need to stop at a teahouse."

"What about buying sweets at that stand, then?" Wren suggested. She jingled a handful of coins they had gotten from selling two of the silk handkerchiefs. "I can get some for us."

"That sounds nice," Koichi said mildly. When she slid off the pony, he and Jade pulled over to the side of a building. "Do you think she's trying to make up for being so rude to us?"

"She didn't mean to be," Jade said, smiling. "And she wasn't angry with *us*."

He sobered. "I know. Seeing what happened is enough to try anyone's patience."

"I can't stop thinking about how they all stood up to the soldiers, knowing the consequences. How they protected that family and offered themselves in place of the boy." Jade closed her eyes. "It breaks my heart to think how much better those people deserve than Xifeng."

"My father told me there were rumors that the king of the Sacred Grasslands planned to revolt against Xifeng and free his kingdom from the empire," Koichi said in a low voice.

"I don't advocate violence, but I'm beginning to see why desperate measures are sometimes necessary," Jade said, sighing. "I used to think the crown was all about greed. But if someone who cared about the people took power . . . could it be a way to help them on a larger scale?"

"I believe that, too."

"Amah always told me I was too idealistic."

"I like idealistic. It means your heart's in the right place." He looked straight at her. "No matter what happens, we're all going to be together in this. You know that, don't you?"

There was such kindness in his eyes that Jade reached for his hand without thinking. Her face burned when she realized what she had done, but when she tried to pull away, he held on tight.

"We're together not just in this quest, but in whatever comes afterward, too. Whatever it takes to make a better world."

"Xifeng will hunt me to the ends of the earth," Jade said softly, "and anyone with me will be in danger, too. Do you understand it's very likely she'll find us?"

"We'll just have to give her hell until then, won't we?"

They watched Wren wait behind a well-dressed, dark-skinned man as he paid for his sweets: lumps of soft, powdery dough, colored pink and green and filled with a sweet rice paste. He gave them to his three small daughters, who squealed and ate them rapturously.

Koichi released Jade's hand. His gaze was not on the sweets stand now, but at the building beside them. She followed his gaze, not understanding, until a breeze ruffled half a dozen hand-inked signs nailed outside the door. A sharp pain formed beneath her breastbone as she recognized her own image, crudely drawn onto the center of each sign above the words:

> *Their Imperial Majesties seek a young woman wanted*
> *for murder.*
>
> *Her Highness Princess Jade of the Great Forest*
> *is believed to be extremely dangerous and*
> *accompanied by another young female*
> *who has joined her in taking the lives of multiple*
> *women in the palace, one of whom was elderly.*
>
> *If you see these criminals, seek out one of Their*
> *Majesties' Imperial Guards immediately.*

Jade turned away, unable to bear her own features leering out at her from the signs.

Koichi shook his head slowly. "Look at the reward at the bottom. That's enough to feed this town for a year. I'll wager many would be desperate enough to kill for it."

Even Wren had seen the signs from where she had been waiting in line. "Your face is *everywhere*," she told Jade, handing her a small sack of the doughy sweets as she swung up behind her. "We'd better go. Your hair is short, but someone might still recognize you."

"And I am attracting entirely too much attention," Koichi muttered as two boys pointed at him. Their mother stared at him before hurrying them along.

They urged their horses on. As relieved as Jade had been to see the crowded town earlier, now it felt as though countless people watched them. She wondered if the soldiers they had seen had put up the signs, or whether Xifeng had sent men in all four directions or had somehow known Jade would pass through here. Jade had been foolish to think they had a head start because the Empress did not know of their quest. *She has sorcery, and the Serpent God . . .*

"Oh, no," Wren groaned.

A large crowd stood ahead, blocking their path. A thin and tremulous female voice rose above the din of harsh male tones.

"You're wrong. How could I be?" she pleaded. "You can't say such things."

"You have the hair," a man sneered. "You have the nose, the skin."

Koichi led them around the periphery of the crowd. The onlookers didn't even spare them a glance, so engrossed were they in whatever drama was playing out.

"You don't understand! You're making empty accusations so you can win that reward!"

"Better be nicer to us," another man said slyly, making Jade's skin crawl. "Or we'll turn you in to Her Majesty's soldiers and have *them* confirm your identity. They're not far from here."

"Take her! It couldn't hurt!" someone in the crowd shouted.

"Will you split the reward with everyone?" another person joked.

"The Empress is already taking our goods and money, and now you want to give her more of our people, too?" jeered a hard-faced old woman in the garb of a servant. "What are you, her newest lackeys? Let's see you slither and hiss, then."

The crowd broke into uneasy titters at her comment.

The sly man hurled a crude, disgusting curse word at the woman. "We'll see who's sneering when I bring home that money. Now move so I can escort Her Highness to the guards."

A lump formed in Jade's throat. "They think that girl is me," she said to Wren, who shook her head fiercely. "I can save her. If we don't do anything . . ."

"Then Xifeng will execute those men for bringing her the wrong girl."

"And you *really* think she'll spare the girl?"

"We do nothing," Wren said firmly.

"Please, *please!*" The girl's words were high pitched with fear. The crowd parted and Jade saw two men gripping her arms. She couldn't be older than thirteen or fourteen, but even Jade had to admit there was a slight resemblance between them: wide eyes under thick brows, broad cheekbones, and a flat nose. The girl might have passed for another daughter of Lihua's. The men steered her directly to where Koichi's and Wren's horses were passing.

One of them, who was about thirty with a cruel, sharp profile, glanced up at Jade. His surprise sent a stab of cold through her. "Another one," he exclaimed, and Jade felt Wren stiffen as he looked between Jade and the sobbing girl in his grasp. "You could be sisters."

Koichi, who had made it to the other side of the crowd, stared back in horror.

"Let her go," Jade said, taking care to speak with a servant's accent.

"Why?" the man's sly friend asked, examining Jade as though she were wares put out for sale. "So you can take her place instead?"

"This new one's skin is too sun-browned," the sharp-faced man told him. "None of those fancy palace ladies ever spend much time outdoors. It's not her."

Wren spoke suddenly in a loud, pompous voice, imitating a court accent. It didn't sound in the least authentic, but it got their attention. "You're correct. She's just an impertinent servant girl. How dare you speak to these men like equals?" she demanded of Jade.

"I'm sorry, Mistress." Jade slouched. "I only wanted them to get out of your way."

Wren let out a snort that would have made Amah proud.

"And I also wanted to save these men's lives," Jade added.

"How's that?" the sharp-faced man asked.

"That girl you have there," Jade said, pointing. "She has rough hands and feet, hardened by work like no princess's would be. Imagine bringing the *wrong* girl before Her Majesty. Do you think the Empress will forgive you for wasting her time?"

The girl looked up tearfully at Jade. The men exchanged glances again, uncertain now, as their grips loosened. The girl scuttled away, her long braid flying behind her.

Wren smacked Jade's head lightly. "Enough chatter, servant! My husband is waiting."

"Husband, eh?" the sly man leered, coming forward to wrap his hand around Wren's leg. "Perhaps he won't mind if you and your little maid have tea with me and . . ."

He didn't have a chance to finish his invitation, because within seconds of Wren realizing that he had touched her, he was sprawled on the ground with three fewer teeth. He covered his bleeding mouth with one hand, stunned, as the onlookers murmured in amusement.

"Touch me again and you'll lose the rest of your teeth," Wren spat. The other man leapt toward her, but in the flash of an eye, she whipped out her dagger and positioned it at the base of his throat, right below the large vein. "Yes? You had something to add?"

He backed away, his palms up, as his friend on the ground spat out bloodied spittle.

"Ride on," Wren snapped, and Jade urged the pony forward.

Koichi nudged his stallion into a gallop and the girls followed, ignoring the jeers of the crowd behind them. They didn't dare turn back to see whether they were being pursued.

The buildings grew sparser and the road led them back into grassy fields once more. They rode on for a quarter of an hour, stopping at last when they felt certain no one was chasing them.

Koichi grinned back at them. "Well done, both of you. Jade's quick thinking saved that girl's life, and Wren, that kick . . ." He imitated her movement with his own leg, knocking out an imaginary man's teeth with fierce concentration, and the girls couldn't help giggling.

"You did well to separate yourself from us," Jade told him. "I'm afraid I drew too much attention to myself and Wren already."

"You did, but I'm glad you saved her," Wren admitted. "I suspect those bullies wouldn't have turned her in, but would have kept her for their own entertainment. I hope she runs far and hides well."

Koichi spotted a place to settle down for the night: a cluster of bushes some distance from the road, on the opposite side of the river. They tied up the horses and arranged their bedding, and Wren pulled out the sweets she had bought. The doughy, bean-filled pastries were slightly flattened but no less delicious or welcome after weeks of nothing but berries and dried meats.

Through some unspoken agreement each night, they always placed their bedding side by side, with Jade in the middle. Neither Wren nor Koichi would hear of any other arrangement. Tonight she curled up to see Koichi nestled on his side, facing her, his eyelids heavy.

He yawned. "What do you think we'll find at Red Lotus Lake? The crane wife?"

"Perhaps her farmer husband and the cloak he stole from her."

"Maybe the crane feather will be waiting there, ready for us to take. As easy as that." His eyes crinkled at her. "Don't worry. Wren and I will be right there with you."

"I know," Jade said, and he laid his warm hand on hers for a brief moment before closing his eyes and drifting off. He looked calm and gentle in sleep, his dimples prominent even at rest. She realized, watching him, that she had grown used to hearing his quiet breathing each night.

And after this journey, what then?

If there is an after.

Jade gazed up at the sky, thinking of the daunting immensity of everything that lay ahead. If they somehow united the Dragon Lords' relics, if they called down the heavenly army to defeat Xifeng—what then? Jade would take the throne, but she and Wren and Koichi would have to part and live their respective lives. They would only be strangers who had once shared a journey together, long ago. The thought of it made her ache with loneliness.

Jade turned to her other side and saw that Wren was still awake, too. "Are you ever afraid of anything?" she asked the older girl.

Wren raised her eyebrows and thinned her lips, and it made her resemble Amah so much that Jade felt an involuntary tug at her heart. "Sometimes. Why?"

"I wish it was easier for me to be brave. I've always had to work hard at it." Jade pulled her blanket up to her chin. "Sitting up every night for weeks to train myself not to be scared of the dark. Learning to swim with Auntie Tan because I was afraid of water."

"It's not just you. We all have to work to be brave."

Jade laughed. "I don't think you've ever *not* been courageous. You inspire me."

"How?" Wren asked, bewildered.

"What you did today," Jade said, searching for the words to explain. "What you do every day. I left the palace with so much doubt, and it didn't go away even after I talked to my mother. How can *I* defeat Xifeng? How can *I* bring the treasures together, summon the Dragon Guard, and be this hero everyone keeps talking about? I kept thinking, *I'm just a girl*."

Wren folded her arm beneath her head, listening.

"There are so many expectations for women and girls," Jade went on. "How to be proper, how to behave. But you push against them. Always. And who said heroes have to be men? Why can't *just* a girl summon the army of the gods? Why can't *just* a girl save an empire?"

"I just want to be myself," Wren said. "I want to live life on my own terms, and I'm tired of people assuming all women are the same, or that we're weak and helpless."

"Can you imagine anyone calling Amah weak and helpless?"

They giggled, remembering the old woman's snorts, sarcastic quips, and warm embraces full of endless, unconditional love.

"Sometimes I think Xifeng's the only one who knows what women are capable of, and that's why she's on that throne. I don't agree with anything she's done," Jade added. "But she believed in herself, and that's what's missing in me. If I don't believe in myself, why should you? Why should my people?"

Wren shrugged. "It takes time. No matter what you think, I've had to work hard to be what you call brave, and I'm still learning about myself all the time. For instance," she added, with a spark of mischief, "I now know that I can pluck feathers off a chicken, which they never let me do in the palace kitchens."

"An honorable skill," Jade said, grinning.

Days ago, Koichi had managed to catch a lost chicken wandering in the grasslands. After much moral struggle, he had agreed to let Wren cook it rather than find its owner, and though the bird had been mostly bones, that supper had been extraordinarily delicious.

"I've learned that I can tell the difference between a berry that will make me vomit and a berry that will make me dead." Wren grinned at her. "And as it turns out, I'm rather skilled at tooth removal, as you saw today."

Jade lifted her hand. "Well, there we are, then: consider this quest halfway done."

22

The following afternoon, the grass grew tall and took on a browner tinge. The soil beneath the horses' hooves turned to fine gold sand, and a raw freshness filled the air, with traces of salt and storm. Close to sunset, a ribbon of aquamarine water appeared, waves crashing against the shore. Jade had never heard anything more beautiful or more lonely than the hollow roaring sound of enough water to hide the world's secrets . . . or consume them entirely.

"We've come to the coast," she said, awed. "That's the Dragon's Shadow Sea."

The road was packed with travelers from all over Feng Lu and lands far beyond. Most had black hair and brown eyes, like Jade and her companions, with skin ranging from golden to russet. But she also saw ebony-skinned merchants and officials and a family of women wrapped in silk scarves, their beautiful dark hair framing rich copper-hued skin.

"I wish I had learned more languages," Jade said wistfully, listening to the women laugh uproariously as they held an animated conversation.

"Father's irritated that I speak the language of the Great Forest better than I do our own. And that it's called the 'common tongue,' " Koichi said. "I suppose that's what happens when one nation conquers the others and expands an empire, so everyone may understand one another."

"It's neither fair nor right, forcing a language upon other kingdoms."

"What will you do when you take the throne, then?"

She hesitated, wondering if he would think her answer silly. "I would give the other kingdoms independence and maintain their alliance through trade and mutual respect. I have no desire to dictate other people's languages, laws, and resources."

"You would dismantle the empire."

"I'm not completely naïve. I know this empire was built on blood and slavery and lives stolen by my ancestors. An empire is about power, and I don't want it. I want prosperity and security for all people." She glanced at him. "The village elder used to tell me it was a fanciful, unrealistic view. But I'm only telling you what is in my heart."

"I think it's about time the Great Forest had a ruler with a heart," Koichi said gravely.

As the sun set and the sky deepened, the crowds began to thin out until there was nothing but miles upon miles of sand and sea surrounding them.

"We should have found Red Lotus Lake by now, don't you think?" Wren asked uneasily. "That's what the map showed this morning. And the road emptied almost too fast."

"I noticed that, too." Jade shivered. The wind off the water was cold without the sun, and she remembered it was winter, though there was no snow along the coast. A caravan passed them going in the opposite direction, and the driver looked at their party curiously when Jade called out to him. "Could you tell us if there are any lakes nearby, sir?"

"There's only one, but you won't find any fish or good water to drink, if that's what you're hoping for. Nothing lives there, not even birds."

Jade and Koichi exchanged glances. "Why is that?" she asked.

"Folks believe the water is poisonous. But I can tell you how to get there if you'd like to see for yourself." He gave them some quick directions, then continued on his way.

"It doesn't sound promising," Wren said skeptically. "If no birds live at this lake, then why are we searching for a crane feather there?"

"We've come this far. We might as well try," Jade decided.

They veered off the road and marched their horses through the tall grass, away from the ocean. Clouds drifted over the moon, blanketing them in darkness, and Jade couldn't help looking around nervously. On flat land, without any trees or shrubs, they would be hard-pressed to find a hiding place if they needed one.

The lake appeared in half an hour's time—a sprawling blackness that smelled of reeds and marsh and soil. An air of death and decay hung over the stagnant water.

"This *can't* be Red Lotus Lake," Koichi said.

Jade dismounted and draped the brocade cloak over some dry grass. Just as she began to scan Amah's map, the clouds moved again and the moon came out. The moment its light touched the water, the place was transformed. Knee-high grass swept downward to a vast and magnificent lake like a shimmering silver mirror, like a shard of sky torn from the heavens and pressed into the earth. It was calm and quiet and dotted with bright crimson lotus flowers. Eleven cranes floated in the heart of the lake, so bright they illuminated the water like lanterns.

Koichi and Wren followed Jade to the water's edge, where the birds fluttered their wings and arched their necks. In the moonlight, slim arms and heads with long, jet-black hair emerged from their pearlescent bodies.

"The sky-maidens," Jade gasped, looking at Koichi with mounting excitement.

He furrowed his brow. "But shouldn't there be twelve of them?"

"The twelfth might be with her husband who broke his promise," Wren suggested, and they both turned to her, delighted. She shrugged. "I'm not one for stories, but I *do* have ears."

Jade laughed, and the women heard her. They danced over the water toward her, bringing a breeze that smelled of fragrant tea and warm grass and sunshine as they drew near. Everything about their forms and figures was reminiscent of the cranes they were: the long, white-feathered cloaks they wore, the graceful movements of their arms, their inquisitive gazes.

"Jade of the Great Forest," one of the maidens said, glancing at the brocade map. "I recognize the mark of the Dragon King on that rich fabric. And I know why you have come: to retrieve our youngest sister's cloak and free her at last."

"Yes," Jade said with a respectful bow, "and I have come to find the relic of the Sacred Grasslands. One of your sister's crane feathers, I think?"

"What good would *one* feather do, Princess?" asked the sky-maiden, amused. "No, the god of the Sacred Grasslands asked us to weave him one of our famous cloaks." She and the others twirled gracefully in the air, the folds of their feather garments rippling. "It was a great honor, and so we twelve sisters each gave twelve feathers to create his treasure for him."

"There's a thirteenth cloak?" Jade asked, surprised.

From the air, the sky-maiden conjured a radiant, pearl-white cloak identical to theirs, except that each feather had been rimmed with gold. "This relic returned to our keeping when the Dragon Lords' alliance shattered. I will give it to you, Jade of the Great Forest, if you free our younger sister." She pointed at an island in the center of Red Lotus Lake, which lay shrouded in silence. A few flowering trees dropped bright petals on the grass. "The ghost of her husband guards the cloak that belongs to her. Without it, she can't return with us to the heavens, and he too is trapped on earth because of it, unable to find peace."

A rowboat appeared on the shore, its oars laid at the ready.

"This sounds simple," Wren said enthusiastically. "We'll go together."

The sky-maiden shook her head. "Only one of you may go."

Jade approached the boat, knowing it had to be her, though the sight of so much water filled her with apprehension. She had learned to swim in the monastery stream, but it had been nowhere as deep or vast as this. She ran a hand over the oars, which had been crafted of thin, lightweight wood.

"I could go," Wren offered. "I'm stronger—I may be able to get there and back faster."

"Thank you, my friend, but this is my task to complete," Jade said, more confidently than she felt.

Koichi contemplated the boat. "It almost seems too easy. We know each relic is linked to a story and a god. And the Grasslands god prided himself on his shape-shifting."

"He was benevolent. He loved to disguise himself and listen to mortals' conversations, by which he would reward people for their integrity." Jade knelt down to examine the rowboat, and that was when she noticed the bundle of white cloth tucked into a corner.

The sky-maiden gave an inscrutable smile. "The task will indeed test your integrity, a quality required in every leader. Convey this bundle to the island, and no matter what you hear, you must *promise* not to look inside until you retrieve our sister's cloak. Do you promise?"

Jade saw the same understanding dawn on Koichi's face.

Just as the farmer promised his crane wife . . . except he broke his vow.

The bundle moved ever so slightly. Jade forced herself to nod, trying not to think of Xifeng's snakes. This task would test her resolve in more ways than one. "Yes. I promise not to look into the bundle until your sister's cloak is in my hands."

"Then you may proceed, Princess."

Wren squeezed Jade's arm and took the brocade map from her. "You can do this."

"When you come back with the cloak, we'll celebrate by eating more roots and berries. We haven't done enough of that yet, really," Koichi joked, trying to make her smile.

"It's a deal." Feeling heartened, Jade stepped into the rowboat and tried to give the impression that she knew what she was doing. The sky-maidens twisted in on themselves until they were once again eleven white cranes, scattering themselves across the water. Jade sat facing Wren and Koichi with the bundle at the far end and pushed off by digging her oars into the sand.

She felt clumsy, but at least the boat was moving in the right direction. She prayed she wouldn't hit any of the cranes as she navigated the water between them.

It took a while to find her rhythm, rotating each oar in the water. Her arms and shoulders began to ache, but the sight of her friends cheering her on kept her going. Every so often, she peered backward at the island. It had seemed close at first, no more than fifty feet from shore, but now, by some strange magic, it was so far away that Jade had to squint to see it. The lake had grown a hundred times in size, stretching so far that she could no longer detect the shore.

The moon disappeared, and it felt quieter and lonelier than ever by herself.

"I can do this," she panted, sweat trickling down her back.

She continued pushing the oars, doing so with too much zeal once and splashing herself.

Slowly. There's no hurry, she imagined Amah telling her, and she felt a rush of longing for the old woman. The sky-maiden had not told her to go quickly, only that she needed to get there.

A baby gurgled.

Jade froze, listening, but there was only silence. Perhaps in her stress, she had imagined the odd sound. She stretched her sore muscles and began rowing again, slowly.

The baby coughed once, then twice.

Jade's eyes moved to the little white bundle, having nearly forgotten that it was there. It was moving again, more insistently, but not enough that she could see what lay inside. Whatever it was seemed to take offense at her silence and let out a furious wail.

The sky-maidens had placed a *baby* inside her boat!

Jade dropped the oars and reached for the bundle. Her fingers almost touched it before she remembered. *You must promise not to look inside.* But surely, the sky-maiden would not have left an infant at Jade's mercy, not when she couldn't give it food or comfort. What sort of cruel trick was this? It seemed like something Xifeng would do.

The baby's wailing faded into a soft, sad cry. Little movements pushed against the cloth, as though its tiny arms were reaching out for its mother.

Jade's heart twisted within her. "Shh, don't cry," she whispered. "Please don't cry."

The baby began wailing again, eagerly, when it heard her speak.

Perhaps it was hungry . . . Perhaps it couldn't breathe properly through the cloth.

Jade wrung her hands, wondering if she could shift the cloth without seeing what lay inside. She turned her head away, just to be safe, and tugged at the bundle a bit. It felt warm. She didn't know where the child's face might be, but it seemed to work, because the crying stopped.

"That's a good baby," she said. She still couldn't see anything the bundle contained.

With a sigh of relief, Jade continued rowing, trying not to mind the baby's sad cries. It sounded just like the tiny village infant she had cuddled while the monks served food to his parents. She remembered his feather-smooth cheeks and rosebud lips, and when she had kissed him, he had gurgled with delight. How helpless humans were when first born.

So must Xifeng have been. It seemed unnatural that such an evil, bloodthirsty woman had ever been innocent. What if this child in Jade's boat grew up to be cruel, too? Someone who lied, schemed, and cheated, and took what wasn't hers and robbed people of their families and lives? It would be so easy to pull back the cloth and peep quickly. To see how this baby might appear.

Jade gritted her teeth and wiped sweat from her forehead, fighting against the impulse. The child began to wail again as though in severe pain, and thrashed inside the bundle. *It can breathe,* she tried to tell herself. Some of the village babies she had looked after had also fussed even when fed and comfortable. Perhaps this one had soiled its rags, but there was nothing she could do about that now. But if it was in pain . . . if something was hurting it . . .

She glanced desperately at the island, which was getting closer at last. "Just a little bit more," she told the child. "We'll be there soon."

And then, from within the blankets, came a violent hissing like a serpent tasting the air, baring its fangs. Jade cried out and threw herself backward. The boat tossed as she braced herself for the snake that was about to emerge from the bundle.

But nothing came out, though the hissing continued, low and dangerous and poisonous.

Gooseflesh rose on her skin. What in the name of heaven was in the boat with her?

Xifeng, she thought.

But this could not be her stepmother's doing—it could not be some terrible trap. The quest had been given to Jade by her mother, and she had followed the map stitched by Amah.

It was too late to turn back now. She had promised the sky-maidens she wouldn't look inside the bundle and she could not—*would* not—break that vow.

The hissing blended in with the baby's whimpering, an unnatural cacophony that raised the hairs on Jade's neck. Were there two beings inside that bundle: a snake *and* a baby? *It's a trick,* she thought, wishing she had cotton to stop her ears. *A test to see if I'll keep my promise.* She rowed like her life depended on it, and at long last, her rowboat hit the island's sandy shore.

Gingerly, she stepped out. "Hello?" she called.

This island was smaller than the one in the *tengaru* clearing, with a few sparse trees growing along the periphery. The moon still hid behind the clouds, and the cranes lay motionless on the water, looking for all the world like what they appeared to be—just drowsy birds.

"Hello?" she repeated.

But she saw no ghost, no feather cloak.

There was only an empty island, a rowboat, and a baby that hissed like a snake.

23

The ghost materialized.

Jade shrieked, her heart leaping into her throat. He was her height, with a bald patch on his head surrounded by tufts of wiry gray hair. He wore clothes of cheap hemp fabric and had a farmer's rough, weathered skin. His outline was filmy and transparent, just as Empress Lihua had been in the *tengaru* clearing.

The man contemplated her with dead eyes. "I know who you are," he said, in a voice as thin and threadbare as his body. "You seek something that is mine. Greedy, aren't you?"

Her mouth opened in surprise. "I am not."

"Anyone who wants a throne wants power."

"Power is the last thing I want," she retorted.

"Liar!" the ghost roared, and Jade jumped. He walked slowly around her, and then passed right through her body like a cold wind. "You can't admit it to yourself, can you? You who profess to be good. You want a crown on your head, power in your hands, and people to believe in you when you cannot believe in yourself."

"It isn't true," she said vehemently.

The ghost gave her a knowing smirk. "Don't deny it. You're just like Xifeng." The name hissed from his lips like a sharp winter wind. "Like mother, like daughter."

"She is *not* my mother!" Jade shouted.

There was a long silence.

"I don't owe you an explanation," she said, struggling for calm. "But I seek the throne because I want Xifeng gone, and there's no one left to stop her from destroying Feng Lu. I can't sit back and watch people suffer because of her. Not when I can help."

The ghost did not say anything.

"Do you think I enjoy wandering far from home, knowing her huntsman could find me at any time?" Jade crossed her arms. "Perhaps it is *you* who are greedy. Weren't you the one who broke your promise not to spy on your wife?"

"I had to know what she was doing."

"She was weaving, like she told you. Why didn't you trust her?"

"I did trust her," he said, affronted. "But I wanted to know what she didn't wish me to see. A loving wife ought to have no secrets from her husband."

"Then you shouldn't have promised her. A loving husband ought to keep his word."

The ghost scowled. "She could have told me the truth and saved us all this trouble."

"She probably hid the secret because she knew how you'd react," Jade said, annoyed by his arrogance. "*You* could have saved us all this trouble by allowing her that small privacy."

"Then you're determined to take my wife's side?"

"I take the side of whoever is reasonable."

The ghost paced back and forth, hateful eyes fixed on hers. His outline seem to thicken and glow with his anger, and when he moved a bit close to her, she felt his sleeve brush her arm. "You've become corporeal," Jade said, forgetting her irritation as she recalled how Empress Lihua had been able to touch her hand. "How is it that spirits can sometimes take form?"

"Through strong human emotions," he snarled. "They keep us shackled to our humanity. Feelings like anger, for instance, or vexation toward an impertinent princess."

From the air, he plucked a cloak that shone so brightly, Jade had to shade her eyes.

"This is what you're after, then, *noble* young woman," the ghost mocked. "This is all you cared about while you let that child suffer in your boat."

Jade whirled with a pang of guilt. In arguing with him, she had forgotten all about the child. As if on cue, the bundle in the rowboat began to move and cry lustily. "The baby was not suffering," she said uncertainly.

"How do you know? Some ruler of Feng Lu you will be, letting a child cry and suffer!"

"It's not a child!" Jade's chest felt cold and tight. "I heard it hissing like a snake."

The ghost pointed to her forehead. "Perhaps you're hearing the snake in *there*, the one *she* put into your mind with that poisoned comb. She's in your blood now."

Jade touched her head where Xifeng's comb had been, horrified. "What do you mean? How do you know about that?"

"I see much from the spirit world," he said smugly. "Her mark on you is clear. You're not so different from her after all, and she knows it—she recognizes it. Do you think she'd feel so threatened if she didn't see her own ruthless determination in you?"

Jade shook her head, feeling his words grip her mind like doubtful fingers. *He's toying with me,* she thought, *weakening my resolve.* But a tremor ran through her hand as the baby wailed. Tonight, she might have sacrificed an innocent life to win the relic of the Sacred Grasslands—and if she had, how was she any different from Xifeng?

The ghost's voice softened. "The only way to be rid of your stepmother is to embrace your good heart. If you are anything like Empress Lihua, you had better see to that baby in pain."

The child's cries weakened, and it gasped as though for air.

Jade took a tentative step toward the rowboat.

"This cloak is the last possession I have of my beloved wife." The ghost stroked the soft feathers. "I will not part with it to a cruel, heartless person. Save that child and perhaps you will show me that you are worthy of earning it."

On the lake beyond the boat, the eleven cranes glided toward them, and all at once Jade recalled that this man had taken the sky-maidens' sister away from them. Even after death, he had kept her cloak, cursing her to never return home with her family. This was not a trustworthy ghost, and Jade herself had made a promise.

In the boat, the snake hissed and the baby gave a piercing shriek before falling silent.

Jade couldn't help releasing a sob. "It's not real. It's only a trick . . ."

"And now you've killed the child in your hesitation, *Xifeng,*" the ghost taunted her, his leer ghastly as he called her by her stepmother's name. "I'll never give you this cloak."

She wiped her eyes, furious yet determined to keep her vow. "You *will* give me the cloak," she spat. "You call me cruel, yet you hold on to a piece of your wife that does not belong to you. *She* is not a possession. She deserves to return home with her sisters, and you had better relinquish that to me now." She held out her hand firmly, proud that it did not shake.

The ghost's eyes darted between her hand and the cranes, who had now come up onto the island with them. They ringed the grass like fierce sentinels, their gazes fixed upon their sister's husband with hatred.

"You've made your wife and her entire family suffer," Jade told him, her voice strong though tears slipped from her eyes. "And what for? You're like a stubborn, overgrown child who wants to prove you were wronged. Well, I think you deserved to lose her. You broke your promise, so don't you dare, don't you *dare* try to shame me for keeping mine."

The ghost's hand trembled on his wife's cloak. His face, so insolent and smug a moment ago, sagged at Jade's words. "I only wanted . . ." He let out a long sigh. "Perhaps you're right. Perhaps you have more integrity than I ever did—or at least a true ruthless streak, letting a snake attack a helpless child like that."

Jade ignored the jab, continuing to hold out her hand.

He smirked, but this time it looked forced. "You've completed the task successfully. Go and see what's inside the bundle, then."

"I am about to lose my patience with you," Jade said coldly, advancing on the ghost. He took a step backward, his sneer vanishing. "You know very well I promised not to look until I retrieved your wife's cloak from you. So thank you for the offer, but I'll take that cloak now."

All of a sudden the ghost laughed, and it was so unexpected, Jade let her hand drop. "You have more mettle than I gave you credit for.

You remind me a bit of my wife." His eyes moved to the feathers in his hand, his face sad.

"It's time to let her go," Jade said gently. "I've lost loved ones, too. But if I could choose between keeping them as prisoners or releasing them as memories, I'd set them free."

The cranes stood watching in silence, their beady black eyes wet.

"Please let go." Jade's hand brushed the ghost's cold fingers as she took the cloak.

From across the lake, there came a twelfth sky-maiden in her human form, beautiful and ethereal as the heavens. She left a trail of lotus blossoms in her wake and bowed low to Jade, accepting her cloak. The ghost stretched out his arms to his wife in longing, but she would not look at him as she draped her long-awaited feathers over her shoulders and was transformed into an elegant white bird. Her sisters gathered around her, their wings spreading with joy.

The ghost watched them with tears in his eyes. "I'm sorry I kept you from them," he whispered. "I'm sorry I refused to give up your cloak and played cruel tricks. Let my spirit go now to its natural rest." As he spoke, the crane that had been his wife moved apart from her sisters, stretching her great wings, and met his eyes.

What he saw in her gaze made the ghost fall to his knees before her. "Thank you for your forgiveness," he murmured. He rose, climbing onto the crane's back, and turned back to Jade as his body took on a wispy form once more. "Sacrifice is sometimes necessary to maintain one's integrity, but you know this already, Princess. Perhaps you're not much like Xifeng after all."

The crane spread her wings once more and took off, soaring for the heavens with the ghost upon her back. One by one, her sisters followed like a swirl of white petals.

The final crane bent her long, slender neck and plucked an object from the air once more: the thirteenth cloak, the treasure the sky-maidens had made for the god who had loved and ruled over the Grasslands. The bird tossed the cloak to Jade and she caught it, surprised to find that it was as light as silk though it was as big as a blanket. Each pearl-white, gold-tipped feather was as long as her arm from her wrist to her elbow.

"Thank you," Jade said, and the crane bowed deeply, returning her gratitude. And then it took flight, shimmering up into the sky, the moon illuminating her wings. Jade watched the reunited sky-maidens until she could no longer tell them apart from the stars.

Carefully, she folded the crane feather cloak into her rowboat and got back in. The bundle of white cloth was still there, but it neither moved nor made a sound.

Jade's fingers trembled as she took hold of one corner and tugged, terrified and heartsick at what she might see within it. But when it came apart, there was nothing within the folds at all.

Only air.

24

Something was wrong in the way Wren and Koichi shouted and waved frantically at her from shore. Jade rowed faster, ignoring the soreness in her arms, and saw Wren boost Koichi onto his horse. The second she reached shore, Wren hauled her out without glancing at the relic.

"Kang is coming," she said curtly. "The map showed us that and told us the next relic is in the desert, so south we go."

There was no time for questions. The girls mounted the pony and raced after Koichi.

"They're coming from the north, from town!" Koichi shouted.

The sky was still pitch-dark as they thundered through the tall grass, avoiding the road. Jade's pulse roared in her ears and she clung on desperately. Her triumph in outwitting the ghost and claiming the first relic faded in the face of reality: Xifeng's huntsman had found them.

The air grew warmer the farther they went from Red Lotus Lake. Jade didn't dare glance back, both for fear of losing her balance and of what she might see. Up ahead, Koichi angled his stallion to the right, taking them inland away from the coast of the Dragon's Shadow Sea.

And then they heard it like a great black storm: the thunder of the Empress's men in pursuit. Jade leaned forward, sweat sliding down her face, praying they would find somewhere to hide before Kang caught up. The grasslands were not so flat here, and grassy dunes began to appear, growing higher and higher the farther they went from the coastline.

"Over here!" Koichi tore over to a large grassy hill, which had a shadowy recess covered with trees and shrubs. "This is the best option we have! We can't outrun them."

The horses huddled together in the dark, remaining as still as their riders as the Empress's men came into view. There were about fifty of them on coal-black horses, masked and armored, and despite their human form, Jade could hear them hissing through the silk over their mouths.

The only unmasked man rode in front between soldiers wielding twisted metal lanterns. His bald head shone in the light as it swiveled, and Jade inhaled sharply at the sight of Kang's cruel mouth and hooded eyes. Gone was the mild-mannered, flattering court eunuch—this was an unearthly warrior, encased in black armor with a ferocious sawedged sword in his hand.

In the dark, Koichi reached for Jade's hand, and her icy fingers gripped his. She tasted fear in her mouth like sour bile, imagining Kang's blade biting into her chest and his roar of triumph as he wrenched her heart from its cage of bone.

The Imperial soldiers stopped thirty feet from the recess where Jade and her companions hid. One sneeze, one cough, one snort from the horses and they would be dead. Worse than dead. Images of Xifeng's pool reappeared behind Jade's eyelids: the silent, heartless women forever locked in time, their chests agape and their hair floating like rotten seaweed.

She could not let Wren and Koichi suffer such a fate. She would march out to Kang this instant and give herself up to save them. And then Wren and Koichi could find Shiro and sail together to Kamatsu, farther from the reaches of the Empress.

Xifeng wanted *her*. They were in danger only because of *her*.

But Jade had a duty to her people, and saving her friends meant forfeiting her mission and failing everyone else. She thought of Xifeng ladling dark poison down the Emperor's throat and of Kang flinging the sword into Amah's frail body. Only the gods knew what else the Empress had been up to in the three weeks Jade had been gone from court—and what else she would destroy in the years to come. Jade clenched her jaw with renewed zeal and anger.

When she opened her eyes, Koichi was watching her without a trace of fear on his handsome face. He squeezed her hand, his gaze full of sympathy and understanding as though he had known exactly what she had been thinking. Jade felt the sudden powerful longing to be close to him, to lean her head against his comforting warmth until the serpents went away.

"They may have continued along the coast," Kang told his men, his tone deep and guttural, the opposite of the high-pitched voice he had used at court. "You, take your men along the shore. You, double back to town. Burn all the buildings if you have to and check the docks to see if any ships have left in haste. The rest of you, come with me. They can't have gone far. Go!"

Hoofbeats roared as the soldiers tore off in different directions and vanished from view.

"Don't move," Wren whispered. "They may be lying in wait."

They sat in agonizing stillness until, like a shroud being lifted from the air, the silence was transformed. It changed from a prowling, wakeful tenseness to the restful quiet of night. Crickets began to sing again in the fields, and the horses exhaled, one by one.

Wren let out a heavy breath and patted her pony, swinging down. "I think they're gone." She glanced at Jade and Koichi's still-joined hands, then away with a little smile. "We may as well sleep here tonight and continue on tomorrow morning."

"But they've found us," Jade said. "They know we came this way. I'm so sorry."

"None of that. Wren and I knew what we were getting into when we came with you." Koichi gave her hand another squeeze before releasing it.

"Agreed. Let's sleep, and tomorrow we'll check the map. The feather cloak, too." Wren paused in the midst of unrolling her bedding to beam at Jade. "I knew you could do it."

And though she was warm and safe, tucked between her friends, sleep evaded Jade for the better part of the night. Every time she closed her eyes, she heard the snake-men hissing. It was a sound she felt sure she would hear for years to come . . . if she had that long to live.

Five Dragon Lords. Five relics to summon an army powerful enough to defend Feng Lu from Xifeng and the Serpent God, who were no doubt amassing their own forces at this very moment. The Empress had already discovered her path, and Jade had only one of five treasures. Could they retrieve even one more before Kang found them again? She didn't want to contemplate the consequences of failure.

At the end of the journey lay her destiny . . . but whether that was victory or the saw-edged blade of Kang's sword remained to be seen.

The next morning, a light dew settled over the grasslands, which showed no sign of the soldiers except patches of trampled grass where their horses had stopped the night before. Wren and Koichi examined the gold-tipped feathers of the crane cloak.

"It's beautiful, but what does it *do*?" Wren asked, puzzled.

After a few long, fruitless moments, Koichi decided to drape the cloak over his shoulders and parade grandly about, saying outrageous things in a court lady's accent. Wren and Jade laughed until their sides hurt, but Jade forced herself to recover quickly.

"I'm sure we'll find out about the feathers sometime," Jade said, spreading out the brocade map before her friends. "Right now, I want to see this new relic Wren mentioned."

"The snakes are gone," Koichi said, surprised. "We saw a whole sea of them in black thread—that was how we suspected Kang was coming. Maybe the map shows them only when they're close enough to be a threat."

"This is what we saw last night." Wren pointed to the expanse of gold silk representing Surjalana, Kingdom of the Shifting Sands. An embroidered rose had appeared in the very center of the desert. "Do you know a tale about a rose?"

"I thought it might be the phoenix story, but what do you think?" Koichi asked Jade.

"I agree. It has to be the burning rose from that fable." Jade folded up the cloak. "We can tell you on the way, Wren. It may take weeks to reach the relic, and we should go now."

Within minutes, they were riding south. They filled their water pouches at a stream and replenished provisions at a trading post, knowing that soon every morsel would count.

"Is this phoenix story better than the crane wife?" Wren asked, when they were traveling at a steady pace. "If I'm going to be listening to children's tales, I want ones full of action."

Jade chuckled. "I can't promise swordfights, but I think you'll like this one. Koichi?"

He cleared his throat. "A long time ago, the animals of the forest lived in peace and prosperity. There was more than enough food, but still the phoenix ate sparingly and hoarded her supply, worried that their good fortune would end. Everyone laughed at her because her frugality showed a lack of trust in the gods' generosity. Does this match Amah's version so far?"

Jade nodded. "Point for point."

"One day, a powerful storm came and devastated the forest. The animals' homes vanished in a day and a night, leaving them with nothing. But then they remembered the phoenix's hoard of food, which would be enough to sustain them all until they were able to forage and rebuild."

"If I were her, I wouldn't give them a morsel," Wren said, affronted. "They mocked her!"

"But she had a generous nature and was perfectly willing to share," Koichi told her. "Unfortunately, the storm had torn apart the forest, and the phoenix could not find where she had hidden the supply. Luckily, in her anxiety, she had prepared for every occasion, including this one. She had placed a trail of pebbles embedded deep in the soil to lead her back to the food."

Jade watched his hands move as he told the story and thought how much Amah would have liked him. *When you tell a tale,* her nursemaid had once said, *tell it respectfully.*

"But while following the trail, the phoenix saw a great wave of rain-soaked earth moving toward her at a terrifying speed," Koichi continued. "The mudslide seized her and she panicked, knowing that when it dried, she would be trapped forever. Struggling made it worse, so she remained still and stretched herself out flat. When she began to rise to the surface, she made small movements to *very slowly* extricate herself. At last, the phoenix escaped the mud and reclaimed her hoard. When the forest grew back, she became the most respected of all birds."

Wren nodded approvingly. "I do like that story. But what's this about a burning rose?"

"The forest spirits, who had been watching the phoenix's struggles, were so impressed by her fortitude that they presented her with a rich gift," Jade explained. "A beautiful red rose had bloomed after the rain. The spirits blessed it so that it would burn forevermore, providing her warmth and comfort, and it also purified water for drinking when dipped into a stream or pond. With this gift, the phoenix was honored beyond all other animals for her resourcefulness."

"The Dragon Lord of Surjalana and the Serpent God are one and the same," Koichi said thoughtfully. "I can see why he chose such a valuable relic, but is there another reason?"

"He brought a rose to the desert," Jade pointed out. "Maybe he liked the idea of a plant blooming in adversity and thought of himself in the same way. He was known for his arrogance and dislike of being inferior, hence his resentment of the Dragon King. He also claimed the world would end in fire, so the rose must have appealed to him in that way."

"And isn't that the story's lesson: *waste not, want not?*" Wren asked, not to be outdone by the others. "Fitting for the desert. You know, I'm beginning to see some value to these stories."

Jade and Koichi laughed at her grudging confession.

"I think you'd like *my* favorite story, too. It's about a legendary warrior named Tu Lam. He was only a man, though," Koichi added cheekily.

Wren grinned and poked Jade, pointing at Koichi. "This one is growing on me more and more."

25

Over the next few days, the grasslands became a swirling sea of yellow sand. There was a frightening loveliness to the desert and the rippling sand dunes contrasting with the hot blue sky. When the wind blew over the land, the entire tawny-brown ocean shifted like the haunches of a great beast, ready to swallow them whole. What plants they saw were rough and rimmed with needles and prickly edges, nothing like the lush fauna of the Great Forest. The dry air sucked the moisture from their noses and throats, and the sun left a stinging red trail on any exposed skin. It was Wren who had the idea of wetting their spare tunics and wrapping them around their heads.

The horses struggled on the soft terrain, so the girls got off frequently to give the pony a rest from their weight. Koichi continued to ride, since he could not walk long distances comfortably, but when they stopped to rest, he made sure to give his stallion the greater share of his water.

Jade took the opportunity to check the map. "We're going in the right direction. But look here—it's changed again! Now there are markings all around the rose."

Wren leaned close to the brocade, her eyes widening. "They're little horses."

"Maybe the Serpent God is growing a garden somewhere that's guarded by tiny four-legged beasts?" Koichi suggested.

Jade laughed. "I hope so, because where there's life, there's water."

But as the week went on, they found precious little to laugh about. They hadn't found so much as a trickle of water, and the air itself was treacherous, undulating in waves above the sand until Jade felt dizzy. The horses' heads, too, hung lower than usual. Whenever they stopped for the evening, Jade and Wren removed their sacks to relieve the animals, even though it meant taking longer to get moving if Xifeng's men reappeared.

The desert was even more beautiful at night, with the moonlight catching sparkles in the sand. But the temperature had the habit of cooling rapidly, and before long, the extra tunics moved from their heads to their bodies. Koichi even made a small fire with a box of sulfur matches he had bought from the trading post.

"We've got enough provisions for another week. We're doing fairly well with desert travel, if truth be told. Even *you* must admit we've learned a lot," he added cheerfully when Wren gave him a look. "We now know to dig holes for our bare feet because the sand is cooler deep down. And we know to shake out our bedding before sleeping."

Wren groaned. "Will you *never* let me forget that incident?"

The previous night, she had woken Jade and Koichi with her screams because a black scorpion had been sitting next to her face. Since then, they had made sure to shake out all of their possessions, from blankets to boots, before using them.

"We also know to spread hot ashes around our sleeping area," Koichi said.

Two evenings earlier, a hairy, speckled gray spider the size of Jade's hand had found its way onto Koichi's blanket. He had frightened both girls with his shouting as he flung the creature off into the night. After that, Jade had drawn a protective circle around them using a straggly, ash-covered plant branch that Koichi had burned. She had done it as a joke, but no unwanted visitors had come near their sleeping area again.

"I *will* say that the desert is better than the palace kitchens," Wren conceded.

"This seems like it would be ideal Crimson Army training ground," Jade said, and Wren grinned at her. Despite her complaints, Wren fared better than either of the others in the harsh environment. She often remarked that she would have run up the sand dunes for exercise if they'd had water to spare.

"So," Wren said, lying down with her arms behind her head, "*when* we complete this quest, Jade will be Empress and I will be a deadly assassin. Koichi, you'll be a pirate king?"

He laughed. "I don't know. I might go into public service like my father."

"So what I want to know is," Wren said casually, "if you're a high-ranking nobleman with money, would it be likely for you to be a royal consort one day?"

Koichi raised an eyebrow. "How did you jump to that?"

"I'm just curious, that's all," Wren said.

Jade caught the sly look Wren angled in her direction. Quickly, she busied herself with brushing off imaginary sand from her bedding, pretending she hadn't seen, although she listened for Koichi's response with all her might.

"I guess it would depend upon the person to whom I'd be consort," he said, after a pause.

Jade peeked at him, but he turned away to poke the fire and changed the subject back to the Crimson Army. As the firelight danced on his profile, she thought again how used she had grown to his presence day and night. She knew his voice, his laugh, and the way his moods shifted in his eyes. But she had no idea whether he knew hers, or if he even cared.

Koichi always had a joke or a cheerful word to say when she was frightened or upset, and he seemed to know what she was thinking without her having to speak. But perhaps he cared for her only in a brotherly sort of way. He probably behaved in the same affectionate, teasing way he did with Wren, and Jade's hopeful, reckless imagination had expanded it.

But he has never touched Wren, she thought. He had taken Jade's hand when Kang had ridden past, and when she had held his in town, he hadn't let go. She remembered her urge to lean her head against his shoulder, and felt her cheeks grow warm.

"Are you all right over there, Jade? You're quiet," Wren commented.

"Just tired," she said, forcing a yawn and rolling onto her back where they couldn't see her face. She thought Koichi might be able to read her expression like one of his books if he saw it now. "We should sleep."

But long after they had put out the fire, she lay awake, remembering the press of Koichi's warm fingers against hers.

There were bones in the sand, bleached white by the sun.

First a skull, then a rib cage, then a pair of legs, picked clean like morbid porcelain.

They saw more and more skeletons as the day went on, and though Koichi tried to make light of it, Jade couldn't help thinking it might be their fate if they didn't find water soon.

Her wish was answered by sunrise, though not in the way she might have expected.

A great rectangular shape of blue-gray appeared on the horizon, fluttering in the hot wind, with a large brown lump in the sand nearby. Jade led her friends out of its direct path; her first thought went to Xifeng and what tricks the Empress might devise to trap her. But as they drew closer, they saw that the blue-gray object was a clumsily constructed tent.

"That's a dead horse," Koichi whispered, pointing at the brown lump. Several large black birds pecked at its carcass, but they squawked and flew off when Jade's party approached.

"Be careful," Jade warned Wren, who slipped off the pony and advanced on the tent with a dagger in each hand. "Someone may be yet inside."

"There might be supplies we can use," Wren answered, and because she turned to speak to them, she did not see the gaunt, hollow-eyed man who had crawled to the tent's opening. When she faced front again, she gave a great shout and pointed her blades at him.

The man looked at her blearily. "I'm going to die anyway. Do you think I care how?"

"Who are you?" she demanded.

"Does it matter?" He gave a dry, hacking cough that shook his whole body. His face was like a skull, the skin drawn back tightly across the bones like transparent fabric.

His sunken cheeks and frailty reminded Jade of her father. She dismounted and knelt beside him with her pouch of water, but he refused it.

"Turn back if you can," he croaked. "Don't go on any farther."

Jade and Wren saw it at the same time: a vicious, horrific knife wound in the man's side, soaking his shirt and pants with dried brown blood. His cracked lips spread in a hideous smile.

"My dearest friend took all of our water, then did this to me and *that* to my wife."

Wren grimaced as she moved the flap of the crude tent, releasing an overripe smell like rotten meat. A woman's corpse lay under a swarming cloud of flies.

"Desperation makes monsters of even the best people." He gazed up at Jade imploringly. "The stone horses aren't worth it. There is no treasure more worthwhile than your own life."

"Stone horses?" Jade repeated, thinking of the embroidered steeds on Amah's map, but he did not elaborate. "Is there anything we can do for you, sir?"

"Dig a hole for my wife and me. Please." His bloodshot eyes moved to the interior of the tent. "There are shovels. Blankets and food. Take it all."

Wren pulled her tunic over her nose and mouth and went inside, returning with her arms full: two blankets, a length of rope, a pair of shovels, and a packet of dried meat.

The man turned away, breaking into another violent fit of grating coughs, and lay still.

Jade placed her hand on his chest, which had stopped rising and falling. "He's dead," she whispered, shutting his eyes gently and uttering a quiet prayer.

Wren bowed her head, then chose one of the shovels and began digging close to the dead horse. Wordlessly, Jade joined her, and Koichi dismounted to put away the supplies.

"There's someone else over there on the ground," he said uneasily, pointing about a hundred feet in the direction they were traveling. "Let me see who it is."

"Be careful," Jade urged him as he walked away. She wiped her forehead and continued digging, helping Wren shift the sand beneath the horse to make a large hole into which it would fall. The light, fine sand was not difficult to lift, but shoveling in the midday sun was hot work.

It seemed a long time before Koichi trudged back, struggling under the weight of several heavy objects. "Far be it from me to take joy in another's misfortune," he said, "but that dead man had four pouches of water. I guess we found out where this couple's *dearest friend* went."

"Thank the gods," Wren moaned, reaching for one of them.

"He died from a vicious snakebite," Koichi said grimly, handing another pouch to Jade. "It appears he paid dearly for his crime."

"Good. One less body we need to bury," Wren spat. "He deserves to have his brains pecked out by the birds for what he did to these poor people."

"There's plenty of room," Jade chided her. "And more birds might attract Kang."

They dug far enough to ensure that the bodies wouldn't be disturbed, and eventually the dead horse sank into the hole, pulled down by its own weight. Koichi helped them gently place the couple inside, and then they rolled a blanket beneath the traitor and dragged him over. The man's leg had swollen to twice its natural size and grown an ugly purple-black from the snakebite. When they had finished their task, they set off again.

Though the water had renewed their spirits, they traveled in silence for the rest of the day, each lost in their own thoughts. Jade pondered what the traitor had hoped to gain by leaving his friends for dead, and what the dying man had said about desperation. Was the Serpent God's rose the treasure of which he had spoken?

"I could never do anything like that to either of you," Koichi said, when Jade brought up the subject that evening. They had stopped in the shadow of a dune to rest. "Even if those stone horses guarded a royal treasury. It's not worth it."

Jade shook her head. "People are desperate. I think it's hard to say what we will or won't do until we're in their shoes. All of us have been fortunate to have had food and shelter."

"When you're poor and starving, and ruled over by an empress who literally thinks of human hearts as food," Wren said, "maybe just the *idea* of treasure will seem worth it."

Jade hugged herself, eyes on the darkening dunes. Every step they took, every hardship they witnessed, stoked the fires of her anger, but over the weeks, it had changed from a sharp, burning outrage into a steady, purposeful wrath. Her destiny was no longer something she plodded toward reluctantly, but was now a means to an end . . . a weapon to vanquish an evil she had never imagined in her darkest dreams. And she would do whatever it took to get there.

She thought again of the poisoned comb hidden in her sack. Her fingers itched for it more often than she cared to admit. A bit of blood, she thought, might be worth seeing what Xifeng was planning. But each time the strange longing seized her, she heard Empress Lihua's warning: *She might want you to use it again.* In the vision, Xifeng had seemed to sense Jade's presence—if she knew of the connection the comb forged between them, she might use that knowledge somehow to trick Jade.

Koichi's shout of excitement broke into Jade's grim contemplation. "Look! There!"

Jade followed his finger to where the desert met the sky in a clash of pink and midnight-blue as the sun set. A few hundred feet ahead, at the bottom of a great slope of sand, stood a cluster of heavy-headed trees full of drooping fruit. Jade rubbed her gritty eyes, but the vision did not vanish in the last light of the sun. Something glimmered between the twisting trunks . . .

"Water!" Wren shrieked. "Is this a trick? Do you see it, too?"

"As clearly as I see you," Koichi said heartily. "I think we've found salvation."

As Wren began to wave her arms and sing and Koichi laughed at her, a ringing came to Jade's ears at the edge of hearing. She looked down at the glittering sand, which began to vibrate, and glanced to the east, where a rising cloud of sand and dust had gathered.

"What is it?" Koichi asked.

And then the sound grew louder: the whinnying of horses, the storm of hooves, the whipping of shadowy cloaks on metal armor. It was the coming of a writhing black storm, and Jade's scream died in her throat, knowing what the thousand lanterns in the Great Forest would reveal: the soldiers' true form, an evil rushing tide of onyx serpents.

She could almost see their glowing red eyes hunting the sands for her, and hear Empress Xifeng's whisper rippling across the black star-burned skies:

Find her, huntsman, and bring her heart to me . . .

"Run," Wren whispered, and then the whisper became a shout. "Run!"

26

They plunged down the dune, the horses rearing their heads. The oasis now felt much too far away as they raced across the sand. Jade clung to the pony's neck, her heart in her throat.

He found us. The thought coiled like a serpent in her stomach. *He found me.*

Kang seemed to have brought the lion's share of the soldiers with him. There was nowhere to hide on this vast, rolling landscape. The oasis would be a dead end, but where else could they go? If they tried to run, it would only be a matter of time before the men caught up.

We have lost. Oh, Mother, Amah, we have lost.

"We can't hide the horses," Koichi said, looking sick when they reached their destination at last. "We'll have to dismount and leave them. It's the only way."

Wren leapt off and hugged her pony. "There must be a better way," she argued. "We won't go far in this desert without them. We'll die for sure . . ."

But there was no time to discuss. They seized what few possessions they could—Jade making sure she had the map and the crane feather cloak—and ran into the trees. It became clear at once that they could not climb the slippery trunks. These were not the trees of the Great Forest, but unfamiliar giants with heavy heads and no low branches.

Koichi whirled, noting the boulders that dotted the ring of trees, while Wren examined the shallow body of water in the center. Though the breeze had died, the crane feathers in Jade's arms lifted of their own will and tickled her nose. She peered down at the cloak. There was more to it than met the eye—of this, she felt certain. Her own words came back to her: *That god prided himself on his shape-shifting ability and was also said to be bashful. It makes sense that a method of disguise may have appealed to him.*

Nothing had happened when they had put on the cloak before. But they had not needed to hide then, and they desperately had to now.

There was no time left to think.

"Hurry, get under this!" Jade squeezed herself and her belongings into a recess between a tree and two boulders. Wren and Koichi crawled in beside her, all knees and elbows and frightened faces as Jade tossed the crane feather cloak over their bodies. It was light despite its thickness and more than big enough to hide the three of them. To their surprise, they could still see out as clearly as though they had nothing over them at all.

"This isn't going to do anything," Wren whispered, her eyes full of panic.

But Jade hushed her as the black flood of serpent-men on horseback poured over the sands and into the oasis. Wren stifled a sob as her faithful gray pony and Koichi's stallion fled, taking off across the desert.

Jade put an arm around the other girl as the soldiers dismounted.

"You three, go after the horses," Kang commanded, and the mere sound of his voice made Jade's stomach clench with terror. "If the girl is not here and is riding away, on your heads be it. The rest of you, search every tree and crevice. Leave no stone unturned."

Three soldiers took off at once. The Empress's huntsman stepped into the ring of trees, standing not twenty feet from Jade and her companions, and swirled a fallen tree branch in the water. The black armor and etched breastplate made him appear massive, cruelly powerful.

Twenty masked men followed him into the oasis. One walked stiffly toward the hidden trio, who cowered beneath the cloak, and studied them for so long that Jade's blood seemed to freeze. *This is it,* she thought, digging her nails into her palm. *We're dead.*

It had been a vain and foolish hope that the cloak would disguise them. She had been thinking like a child, pulling a blanket over her head to hide from monsters in the dark . . .

"What is it?" Kang asked, striding over.

Wren and Koichi tensed as the huntsman's cold gaze ran over them. Jade silently sent up every prayer she could, heart beating so loudly she wondered if Kang could hear it.

"A bird," he said flatly. "What is a crane doing in the desert?"

Jade gaped at Wren and Koichi.

"Look at the size of it. I've never seen one quite so large." Kang crouched down, folding his arms on his bent knee. "The eyes, too, are strange. Almost human, don't you think?"

"Yes, sir," the soldier answered tonelessly.

Kang tipped his head. "And what bird of its kind travels in complete solitude?"

As he crept forward, Jade resisted the urge to pull her leg in closer to her body. Any movement might give them away. Beads of sweat trickled down her back as the huntsman ran his sharp teeth over his bottom lip, studying them without blinking.

And then, as though his words had prompted it, a great rustling sounded in the trees. The soldiers tensed as twelve great white cranes descended, tilting their elegant heads. They calmly went about their business: digging in the sand for insects, drinking water, and settling down to sleep by the trunks. One of them took a small, heavy date from the trees and pecked at it.

The sky-maidens, Jade thought, seeing her own relief and exhilaration on her friends' faces. *They've come to help us.*

"Well, well, well. Nothing but a lost family of cranes." Kang rose, his face twisted with fury. "We're losing ground every second. Some peculiar magic is on the girl's side, and if we lose her, the Empress will behead me herself. To your horses!"

Within seconds, Kang and his soldiers took off, and only when the cloud of dust from their horses' hooves had disappeared did Jade feel safe enough to throw off the feather cloak.

Koichi wiped his forehead, laughing weakly. "I might have known a god wouldn't have chosen an ordinary relic. You saved us, Jade. The cloak disguised us only when we needed it to."

Jade leaned against a tree, her legs too shaky to stand. "Don't speak too soon," she said, clutching her still-racing heart. "We've lost our horses and most of our belongings. We may as well stay here tonight and figure out what to do in the morning."

One of the large white cranes approached and blinked benevolently at Wren, then at Jade. It did not speak, but merely folded its wings and settled itself against a tree.

"Thank you, sky-maidens, for your help tonight," Jade whispered.

The crane blinked again and fell into a gentle slumber, and all around them the other birds dozed in trees and between boulders, as though protecting them. Eventually, Jade and her companions followed suit, driven to exhaustion by their ordeal.

27

The first day was hard, and the second day was harder.

They put one foot in front of the other, each step sinking into the sand so that the simple act of moving forward felt interminable. When the sun beat down in the afternoons, they found weak shadows in which to sit. The mere heat tired them just as much as the walking. They had filled their water pouches in the oasis, but by the third day, their supply was almost gone, as was the pile of dates Wren and Koichi had picked off the trees.

Wren had to force Jade to drink. "Don't be heroic," she said sharply, when Jade told her and Koichi to take what was left. "We need you to survive."

They slept by day and walked at night, but even with the cooler evening temperatures, Jade knew that Koichi was struggling. He never spoke a single word of complaint, but his short legs tired more easily than theirs, and he could not go fast.

On the fourth day, they were down to the last of the rations, and on the fifth day, Jade was sure they would die. The wind had intensified, whipping crystals of sand into their eyes, and more often than not, the dunes seemed to dance and sway before her. She had refused the water too many times, insisting she wasn't thirsty though she could have gladly drunk the entire oasis. Wren and Koichi had to support her as they sat down in the shadow of a dune.

"You two rest," Wren said. "I'll scout the area and see if I can't find something."

"She's strong and brave," Koichi murmured weakly as she strode away. Though Jade knew he hadn't meant it as criticism toward her, she still felt a twinge. Wren and Koichi were suffering in the desert because of her, and she couldn't do anything about it.

She could only lean her dizzy head against her knees, wishing this horrible heat would go away. Every time she opened her eyes, fuzzy black dots danced in her vision, so she shut them and breathed slowly, the air chafing her cracked lips and parched throat. The sun had been a friend to her growing up, but here in this land of vast, blinding gold, it was an enemy. It burned the air and lit the world with shimmering fire, making her mind play awful tricks on her.

For surely, that was not Wren hurrying toward them with a tall, strongly built man whose evil weapons gleamed at his side. He was bald with sun-bronzed skin, and though Jade could not see his features, her mind filled them in: fathomless eyes and a sharp-toothed mouth, long fingers braced on the dagger that would cut her heart out.

"No, not Kang," she moaned.

Koichi's anxious words sounded like they came from far away. "I couldn't wake her."

The man crouched down and Jade struggled feebly, imagining his slow bloodthirsty smile, but neither Wren nor Koichi sounded frightened. They seemed to be answering the man's questions as he lifted Jade in his arms, his deep voice rumbling against her shoulder.

The world swayed and she lost her vision, though she could still hear voices. She let herself go limp, feeling sick to her stomach as a great roaring filled her ears. Later, her sight came back in patchy flashes: the ears and mane of a great white horse, the sky deepening at sunset, and a large pale tent, its fabric flapping in the hot dry wind.

And then she was in blessed cool darkness, with something cold and wet on her forehead and someone pouring water down her throat. She fell into the oblivion of sleep. Days must have passed—she opened her eyes from time to time to see Koichi's or Wren's anxious faces as they lifted her head and gave her water. Had her sun-fevered mind only imagined Kang's presence?

When Jade woke at last, she lay looking up at a ceiling of rough hemp a few shades lighter than the sand. She followed the fabric as it cascaded down to where she lay upon a clean, soft pallet. It was cool and quiet, and she was all alone.

Three other pallets lay on the sand nearby, their blankets neatly folded. The tent was spacious, with a long, low trunk along one wall that served as a table. There were pots for cooking, three crude lanterns and sulfur matches, a pile of clothing arranged on a rough stool, and barrels and sacks she guessed were filled with flour and rice and other grains.

An array of weapons lined the opposite wall, the likes of which she had only ever seen Xifeng's men possess. Jade sat bolt upright, but the dizziness came back in a sickening rush, and she lay down again weakly. Whose home was this, that they should own such ferocious swords and daggers and axes? The metal seemed to wink at her maliciously.

Just then, the tent flap lifted and Wren walked in. At the sight of

Jade, she rushed over with water, clucking like a worried chicken. If Jade closed her eyes, she could almost imagine it was Amah fussing over her.

"How do you feel?" Wren demanded. "You've been sleeping for two whole days."

"I'm better," Jade said, smiling, but the other girl scowled back.

"So stupid, to leave us all the water and insist on not drinking any yourself," she scolded, pressing her hand against Jade's forehead. "Koichi and I were afraid we'd lost you. He hasn't slept once. He's been sitting up with you every night." She lifted a cup to Jade's lips. "We were lucky we found that clean oasis. Ming said most of them are contaminated with animal droppings and he always has to boil his water first to kill what's living in it."

"Ming?" Jade repeated. She sat bolt upright again, fighting the dizziness. "Kang carried me here, didn't he?"

Wren gave her a strange look. "You really aren't very good with heat, are you?" she said good-naturedly. "That wasn't Kang, it was Ming, and he's as different from that evil eunuch as could be, because he saved us that day. He's been living here for ten years."

Jade groaned, lying back down. "Why would anyone live in the desert?"

"Because, young woman," said a gruff, deep voice, "it is a perfectly quiet and habitable place if you know how to take care of yourself."

The stranger stepped into the tent, and now that she saw him properly, Jade had to admit he looked nothing like Xifeng's huntsman. He tied the tent flap to a rope hanging nearby, letting in a ray of sunlight, and crossed his arms, studying her as intently as she did him.

She guessed his age to be about forty. He stood more than a head taller than Wren, and though Jade had thought him bald, she saw now that his jet-black hair was shaved close to his scalp. He was striking in a rough, hardened way, with a strong nose and a wide jawline. His sleeveless tunic bared his arms, revealing faded black markings on his skin.

"You don't need to be frightened. I won't hurt you," he said gently.

Wren grinned. "Captain Ming's going to teach me how to fight."

"I said I'd think about it," he corrected her, amused. "I've never heard of a girl who was interested in such things before. Then again, I've never heard of two girls and a dwarf traveling the desert on foot without any food or water." Jade shrank back under his piercing scrutiny.

Wren patted her shoulder. "It's all right, we can trust him. If he had wanted to turn us in, he would have done it already."

Ming's lips thinned. "I have no interest in dealing with Imperial soldiers. They came a few nights ago, before I even knew you existed. I had a hard time convincing them that I didn't know you, because your runaway horses had wound up at my door."

Wren shouted with laughter at Jade's bewilderment. "It's true! Somehow the smart beasts found Ming when they left us at the oasis. Koichi's outside feeding them."

"Once the soldiers determined I had told the truth, they didn't care a whit for me. And then you showed up after all." Ming regarded Jade. "You seemed to be missed, young woman."

"I was accused of a crime I didn't commit," she said carefully. "I'm running for my life. The Empress cannot let me go."

"No, she's not very good at that, is she?"

Ming crossed the room and scooped a few cups of rice and water into a pot, then lit a fire above some dried plants in the corner. Jade saw a sheathed dagger concealed against his body, hidden beneath one elbow, as he moved. Apparently he armed himself even while at home.

Just then, Koichi came in, and his entire face lit up when he saw

Jade. She hadn't known until then that it was possible to miss someone even while she slept. He hugged her fiercely and she gave in to his embrace, not caring about Wren smirking in the corner. Under the scent of the desert and his perspiration, Jade thought she could somehow smell the pine trees of the Great Forest on him. A great wave of homesickness overtook her.

"I was frantic about you." Koichi pulled away, but kept his hands on her shoulders. "We were lucky Ming found us. We're in your debt, sir, for your kindness."

"I only did what was right. You would all have died," Ming told him. "How came you to be without food, water, or your horses in the desert?"

Koichi hesitated. "We told you. The soldiers scared them away when we were sleeping."

"And how did the soldiers avoid finding *you*? That is one thing you have *not* told me."

There was an uncomfortable silence.

"I could insist on truth as payment for my kindness, as you called it," Ming said.

Jade, Wren, and Koichi exchanged helpless glances, but at that moment, another person came into the tent, and they were saved from an immediate answer. The man who came in was younger and shorter than Ming, but just as broad in the shoulders. His hair was longer and rose up in the middle of his head, sloping back like the feathers of a rooster. But there was something strange about him, for his body wavered in the air like a column of dust. In fact, Jade could see the walls of the tent right through him. She had seen two people like that recently.

The ghost turned, and Jade's heart clenched.

Somehow, he was familiar to her—she felt certain that she knew him, and yet she felt equally certain that they had never met before. He had died young, for he seemed to be in his early twenties. He had an open, likable face with thick brows and a mischievous set to his mouth.

"Aren't you going to introduce me?" the ghost asked Ming.

"This is Fu, my personal nuisance," Ming said grumpily, and Koichi glanced at Jade in amusement as they and the ghost exchanged polite bows.

Jade gazed at the ghost, struggling to frame her statement politely. "You're a . . . that is, you're no longer living."

"It's true," Fu said cheerfully. "I've been dead for a long time, I think."

"You think? You don't know?" Wren asked.

"I have trouble holding on to memories of my life: who I am, where I'm from. Bits and pieces come and go, which is rather inconvenient when you're trying to figure out your purpose in this world so your spirit can pass on to the next." He beamed at Ming, who wore an extremely unamused expression. "I only know I've been following *him* around for years."

"Why Ming, of all people?" Koichi asked.

"Because he's the one who killed me."

Wren stepped away from Ming. "You're haunting a *murderer*?" she asked Fu.

Ming growled. "It wasn't murder. If you're going to tell a story, at least tell the whole of the story, you irritating stone in my shoe."

Fu winked at Jade. "See how lovingly he speaks to me? But he's right, it wasn't murder. He tells me I begged for death and he gave it to me as a mercy. I'm inclined to believe him, aren't you? Someone like him would probably boast about murder."

"I killed him in a swordfight," Ming said loudly. "I'm not ashamed to admit I once fought for money. It put food on the table, and I was good at it. This one came rushing in before a match, pleading with me to free him from assassins who wanted his head. So I did him a favor."

"That's quite a favor for a stranger," Jade said, startled, but Ming did not meet her eyes.

"It was all in a day's work for him, I'm sure." The ghost scratched his head. "I can't recall if my tutors showed me how to use a sword when I was alive."

"But you recall having tutors," Wren pointed out.

"There! That's another scrap of memory that blew into my mind." Fu furrowed his brow, thinking hard, then gave up with a sheepish grin. "See how hard it is to live with me? But how rude of me, talking all about myself when you must be hungry. I can't eat, myself," he added confidingly to Wren, "but I'm sure I had exquisite taste when I was still living."

Ming muttered something under his breath, rolling his eyes, and Jade pressed her lips together to keep from laughing. Koichi and Wren were both grinning openly.

"Yes, I must have had a refined palate," Fu declared. "Too bad it's wasted out here with a man who thinks rattlesnake is fine cuisine."

"A *refined palate* doesn't help one much when it's the difference between living and starving," Ming snapped, crossing his arms over his chest.

"He's a bit sensitive," Fu told Wren, who giggled. "How about you and this young man here come with me, and I'll show you where to gather more kindling? Ming likes it when I make myself somewhat useful." The ghost glanced at Jade. "I'm glad you're feeling better, dear. I thought you'd die and grant me your ghostly company when you first came. I was happy because . . . well, you *see* what I currently have for companionship." He twinkled at Ming, who looked like he would gladly kill him a second time, then floated out of the tent after Wren and Koichi.

Ming turned to Jade. He had uncrossed his arms, but his hands were now braced on his hips. She wondered if he had any stance that wasn't confrontational or defensive. "Well, young lady," he said, "I think we ought to clarify how long you expect to stay here at my expense."

Jade blinked, stunned by his lack of hospitality. "I don't believe we'll be here long, sir. We have somewhere we need to be."

"Is that so? And where in this forsaken desert do you have to be?" But Ming held up a hand before she could respond. "On second thought, don't answer that. I don't want to be involved, and I don't need to know more than I already do. I know who you are, Jade of the Great Forest," he said, not unkindly. "There's no use pretending, not when Imperial soldiers are prowling the sands for a lost princess and two girls show up out of nowhere at my door."

Her heart sank. "Please, Captain Ming, I beg you. If you must turn me in to the Empress, let my friends go—they are innocent and my stepmother wants only *me*."

"What kind of man do you take me for, turning a child like you in to her?" he demanded. "Then again, it doesn't suit me to harbor the runaway heir to a bloodstained empire. There's a price on your head, Princess, and I don't mean coins."

Jade's throat closed. "You want us to leave. You have your own safety to consider, and I understand. You've been more than generous."

"I won't pretend my past is pure and innocent, but I never brought the law upon myself if I could help it, and I don't intend to start now," Ming replied. "I've lived in the shifting sands for a decade with only my horses and that meddlesome ghost for company, and I'm happy to go on that way without the Empress's eye on me. Alive and unbothered."

She looked down at her tightly clasped hands. "The soldiers came to ask you about our horses. Was the Empress's huntsman with them? He's a eunuch, large and bald with cruel eyes."

Ming gave a short, harsh laugh. "That's what he calls himself? Her huntsman?"

"He's hunting for me," Jade said in a quiet voice, and his amusement died at once.

"No. He was not with them." The man turned away, gazing out of the tent flap at the desert, his features relaxed and free of anger.

"We can't ask any more of you than you've already given, sir," Jade said, bowing her head. "I'm grateful for your hospitality, and my friends and I will go."

"I didn't mean right away," Ming said awkwardly. "Stay until you're a bit better, at least. But where do you think you'll go that the Empress can't find you?"

"It's not so much a matter of hiding as it is doing all I can before she finds me."

The man's arms dropped to his sides as he scrutinized her. "You can't be more than eighteen. I might have had a daughter your age by now if my life had gone a different way." The sadness on his face vanished as quickly as it had come. "You're only a child. Do you honestly think you can challenge the Empress?"

He spoke with brutal honesty, not malice. But hearing her own doubts from someone else's mouth was worse than thinking them herself. Jade looked defiantly at him. "If Xifeng wants to destroy me, I intend to meet her with a fight. I've been given a duty, and I will do it while I can. Even if you don't believe in me. Even if *I* don't believe in me, at times."

The hard lines around Ming's mouth softened. "You mean what you say, and you'll do it, too. *That* I believe. But I will say again for your ears: I do not want to risk myself and my peace any more than I must."

"I understand. And thank you." She lay down, dizziness overtaking her once more as she pulled the blanket over herself and turned her back on him.

28

Later that evening, Ming took his horse and rode off across the sands with Fu in tow—a habit the man had, Fu told Jade cheekily, of running from his demons. Jade didn't know exactly what he meant, but she was glad to be alone with Wren and Koichi again.

"We've been looking at the map every day, every time we came in here to check on you," Wren informed her. "No sign of Kang or his snakes. They must have gone farther south."

"We thought we'd get a head start and try to figure out some of the other relics," Koichi said in a brisk, businesslike tone. "There's a sword embroidered over the mountains of Dagovad, and I am *very* eager to find out whether it belongs to Tu Lam."

Jade grinned, feeling a rush of affection for her friends. "Has Wren heard the tale yet?"

"Koichi wanted to wait until you woke up," Wren explained. "He kept building up suspense by telling me what a great warrior Tu Lam was and about all the feats he accomplished."

"There are many tales of his daring adventures, but did you know he was a great cook?" Koichi asked, laughing at Wren's horrified expression.

"Here is a man famed for his swordsmanship," the young woman said indignantly, "and you're going to tell me how nicely he could steam shrimp for his supper?"

Koichi snickered. "His cooking skills led to recognition from the gods themselves. But I think I'll let Jade have the honor of telling this story."

Jade looked at their expectant faces, remembering how Amah had told her this legend: with a hushed, awestruck voice. She adopted her nursemaid's style as she began and couldn't help smiling as she did so—it felt like the old woman was sitting there beside her.

"The god who ruled over Dagovad, Kingdom of the Four Winds, was a great warrior himself," she said. "Of the five Dragon Lords, he was the best swordsman, and he was known for recognizing brilliance in others. In particular, he noticed a Dagovadian nobleman who had three worthy sons. The nobleman couldn't decide which to name his heir, so he set a challenge for them: whichever son brought him the dish he liked best would inherit everything."

Wren gave a soft snort, to show what she thought of that.

"The eldest son brought fish and lobster, the costly fare of the ocean," Jade went. "The second son cooked roasted peacock, the emblem of their house. But the youngest son worked hard alongside their people in the fields, fashioning rice cakes with his own hands. It was this simple, homely dish that won the youngest son his inheritance. Rice was the food of their people and a gift from their lands, and this meal showed it the honor and respect it deserved."

"That youngest son was Tu Lam?" Wren guessed.

Jade nodded. "It was then that Tu Lam first attracted the notice of the god of Dagovad. In addition to his humility, Tu Lam also impressed him with his skillful swordplay. The god gave him a beautiful sword, and the Dragon King himself blessed the blade with his own blood, so that it would always aim true. As a result, the sword's name became Silver Arrow."

"I do like that tale after all," Wren admitted, and they laughed. "So you think Silver Arrow is the relic of Dagovad? Between that and the rose, I know what I would choose."

"It wasn't easy retrieving the feather cloak," Jade said, remembering the wailing bundle in her boat and the mocking, resentful ghost. "I wonder what we'll have to do to prove ourselves worthy of the rose and the sword."

"Father always said to cross bridges only as you come to them," Koichi reassured her. "We will find out in time."

And that time will be soon, Jade thought. She remembered Ming's stern determination; he wasn't a man who would sacrifice the life he had built, not for a strange renegade princess. It would not be long before she and her companions were flung back to the mercy of the desert to survive and find the relic—or perish in the attempt.

Although her friends slumbered deeply, and Ming—who had returned with Fu after an hour or so—was snoring peacefully on his own pallet, Jade found herself tossing and turning with the man's words weighing upon her: *Do you honestly think you can challenge the Empress?*

At last, she gave up and slipped from the tent. The night air felt refreshing on her face as she sat beneath the star-strewn skies, missing Amah. A year ago, on a night like this, she would have been at the monastery, listening to another one of the nursemaid's grand and whimsical tales after evening prayer with the monks.

"What are you doing out here?" Fu asked, drifting out and folding himself on the sand beside her. "You should be inside, getting the rest you need."

Jade brushed a hand over her wet cheeks. "I was thinking about home."

As merry as the ghost had been earlier, his gaze on her now was solemn. "You lost someone you loved. Someone who took care of you, and who is taking care of you even now."

She looked sharply at him, but he had turned away to study the stars. "My nursemaid once told me that spirits linger when they have unfinished business," she said. "I wonder what your purpose is in haunting Ming."

"I don't know. It's not revenge," Fu said thoughtfully. "There were assassins in pursuit and I would have died anyway. But I told him I preferred death at the hands of someone kind and good rather than those of my enemies. That's his account of what happened, anyway."

"But how did you know he was kind and good? He was a stranger to you."

"Was he? I wonder. It's hard for him to have me around, and not just because I love to annoy him," he added, grinning. "My presence reminds him of a past he'd rather forget. He has only ever known pain and loss and the years have been hard on him, so he pushes everyone away. I'm only here because I can't leave. I hope you'll forgive him, young friend."

"So you know he wants me gone," Jade said quietly. "He must have told you who I am."

Fu leaned back on his elbows. "He didn't need to. I can't seem to hold two memories of my former life in my head at once, and yet I knew who you were the moment I saw you."

"Not every spirit has such difficulty remembering," Jade said, thinking of her mother and of the farmer with the crane cloak. "Do you think the way you died had something to do with it? Perhaps you gave up your memories when you gave up your life."

"Anything is possible, but I recognized you right away. How can that be, do you think?"

"Perhaps our destinies are tied together," she suggested.

"As your friends are tied to you. Ming doesn't want to help because you're in danger and so too is everyone associated with you."

Jade leaned her weary head on her knees. "I know it. It weighs on me like stones. But every time I bring up the subject of going on alone, neither of my companions will hear of it." She peered at the ghost. "What would *you* do in my place?"

"Me?" Fu raised a brow. "I would do everything I could to protect them. I would use whatever was in my power to determine the danger, and keep it as far from them as I could."

The poisoned comb.

She closed her eyes, feeling the familiar tug of longing. What was a bit of blood if it meant she could see into Xifeng's plans? If she could find out where Kang had gone, if she could anticipate his next move, it would be worth the risk to keep Wren and Koichi safe. She opened her eyes to see Fu watching her with concern.

"On the way here," she said, changing the subject, "we came across a man who told us about stone horses. Do you know anything about that?"

"He was talking about the maze," Fu answered, surprising her. "About a day's ride west, there's a treacherous expanse of sand, a death trap made of stone horses interlinked. I've seen many adventurers passing by to attempt to claim its treasure of unparalleled value."

The rose, Jade thought, her pulse picking up, *given to the phoenix as a reward for her resourcefulness.* The flower's everlasting warmth and light would be a boon outside of the desert, and its ability to purify water was needed everywhere. The relic of the fire-worshipping Serpent God lay in the center of a death trap. "Why would anyone build such a maze here?"

"It's thought to be the tomb of some ancient king who thought himself grand enough to order a thousand stone horses built in the desert. You are too interested in this," Fu commented, studying her. "I hope you know it would be almost certain death. You would be wandering in the hot sun with no means of escape."

"You said *almost.*"

"I beg your pardon?"

She gave him a weak smile. "You said *almost* certain death. Which means there's a chance of surviving."

"Well, when you fall into a river full of starving alligators, there's always a chance of surviving," he said, laughing. "You're determined to die so soon, then?"

"I could succeed, you know," she said, nettled by his conviction that she would fail.

"You could. Or you could be sentencing your friends to a death by roasting alive."

All at once, the pain of Ming's doubt came rushing back with Fu's cruel joke.

Jade rose to her feet. "I happen to know why you're haunting Ming," she said angrily. "It's because you're the same. Neither of you has any faith. You judge people you don't know and make assumptions that aren't yours to make."

"My dear, I didn't mean . . ." Fu began, but she didn't stay to hear the rest.

She went back inside and sat on her pallet, breathing slowly to calm herself. No one could picture her and Xifeng together without imagining a result in which the Empress crushed her like a beetle. Jade leaned her elbows on her knees and put her head in her hands.

Wren, who had been snoring, gave a little snuffle and Jade looked up. The older girl's face was relaxed, and so was that of Koichi, who was still lying in the same position he had been in when he had stayed up late talking to Jade. She remembered how his words had grown slower and quieter as he fell into slumber. She longed to reach out and touch him, just to see him open his eyes and look at her again.

Anything would be more bearable than seeing them hurt and tortured by the Empress. But they were with her on this quest, and it was like having their blood on her hands already. Like playing her stepmother's game of lives, using people wherever it suited her.

Jade turned away, her heart aching.

She felt for the little wooden box. The teeth of the silver comb gleamed at her. The last time, Xifeng had seemed to sense Jade's presence. And Jade's mother had warned that Xifeng might use this knowledge against her somehow, that deploying this weapon against the Empress might backfire. But it was the only way Jade had to see into her enemy's mind, and if it could help her keep Wren and Koichi safe, then there was nothing more to consider.

Fu was right—it was time to protect them with whatever she had, no matter the risk.

Tell me your secrets, she commanded it.

And then she gave it her blood.

Jade stood in the *tengaru* clearing by the apple tree.

A light wind blew, scattering pink-and-white petals on the grass.

Voices rang out from beside the Good Queen's Lake and she turned, hoping to see the dragon again. It stood on the island with the drooping willows, but it was not alone. A woman gazed up at it, and with her were nine men garbed in black.

Xifeng.

Jade fell back in shock at the sight of her stepmother. There was something sordid, horrifying about the Empress being in the clearing so strongly associated with Jade's mother.

The woman's lips and cheeks were redder than ever, but something was amiss—she looked peaked, feverish. She glanced past the dragon to the apple tree, her restless eyes darting over its branches, and then her gaze fell on Jade. *Not again,* Jade thought, her body freezing, as though by standing motionless she might evade the Empress's further notice. But Xifeng's expression did not change, nor she did acknowledge Jade as she turned back to the dragon.

"It seems I'm still not allowed to go in, even after puzzling out your little riddle," Xifeng told the dragon. "It's not complicated, is it? The secret of the red lanterns begins with that bridge, made from the wood of the apple tree. It's lucky for me I'm so well read."

One of the soldiers behind her stepped forward and bowed. "Your Majesty, the dragon may enter those gates and get to the tree, even if we can't."

"You're right," Xifeng told him. She moved closer to the dragon, which held itself with unnatural stillness. Despite whatever enchantment held it rigid before the Empress, the creature refused to meet her eyes. "Come now, we were friends long ago. You haven't forgotten me so soon, have you, Lihua? Or is that not what you're called anymore?"

The dragon's head drooped.

"But I didn't come here to exchange pleasantries with you. Your daughter has been gone from the palace for quite a long time, and I hoped to find her here." Xifeng clasped her hands before her. "I was grateful that the eunuch Pei's heart, as well as the nursemaid's, both healed my face after the old woman ravaged it, but they weren't enough to satisfy my hunger. I think only the hearts of young women can do that. They are, after all, deeper, unfathomable."

Jade gagged, her fists clenched on the bars of the gate, eyes burning with tears of hate and fury. Her brave, beloved Amah and Emperor Jun's faithful eunuch—both gone, both violated in such a horrible manner. She clenched her fists and imagined tearing a bar from the gate to drive through the Empress's own heart. Let the evil woman know what it was to suffer, to have her life wrenched from her ribs as she had done to all her victims.

"The princess will come back to me," Xifeng said confidently. "I know she will, and I will fulfill my destiny at last. Go on."

The dragon rose shakily on its front legs. It staggered in Jade's direction, and when it came near, she saw that its eyes were clouded and lifeless. A deep, oozing wound gaped from its neck to its belly, splattering blood on the ground as it entered the apple tree enclosure and stumbled past Jade.

No, not blood.

Jade knelt down, her shoulders trembling.

It was water. The dragon was bleeding the ocean, raining its essence upon the grass around the tree. The wound had a scent like noxious soil and dead woods, a smell Jade knew well by now. She whirled to see Xifeng's soldier sheath a cruel sword, its blade coated with a shining black substance—the poison Xifeng had used on Emperor Jun and on the teeth of Jade's comb.

"No," Jade sobbed, hurrying to the dragon. "Be well. Heal yourself."

But she knew there would be no surviving this.

The dragon collapsed, its body curving around the tree trunk. Its beautiful antlered head dropped on the ground with a noise like thunder, and its eyes closed. It lay still, but for the water that still flowed freely from its wound.

Another sob of anguish ripped from Jade's throat. *Xifeng has taken this from me, too,* she thought, her anger returning with such power that it threatened to choke her. She pounded her fists into the grass by the dead dragon, screaming with rage and devastation, envisioning all the ways in which she might make Xifeng pay. Whirling, she ran back to the gate, where the Empress and her men still stood.

No, you are not like Xifeng. You are better than her.

Even as the thought ran through her head, Jade realized that Xifeng was once again looking in her direction. The woman's eyes were not focused on her, but somehow she sensed where Jade stood.

"Come home, sweet child," the Empress said in a low, loving voice that chilled Jade's bones to the marrow, knowing the malice it hid. "I need you."

All of this, everything, Jade realized, *was planned carefully, with the knowledge that I would see it.*

Lihua had been right.

Jade watched, cold and frightened, as Xifeng and her men mounted their horses and rode into the forest, back to the Imperial Palace to lie in wait for the heart of a lost princess. Whatever game she meant to play, whatever she had planned for Jade, had been set into motion.

"Oh, Mother," Jade whispered, her sorrow so vast, she thought she would split apart with the unfathomable pain of it.

A small pond had formed around the tree, submerging the dragon's body and relinquishing it to a watery grave like all of the Empress's other victims. The tree, too, began to change as its roots drank this strange water. The buds shifted and whispered among the leaves.

One branch, in particular, began to tremble.

And as Jade watched, that branch sprouted a single perfect, shining apple, as red as the dragon's blood should have been.

29

"Have you been out here all night?" Ming asked, coming out of the tent the next morning.

"I slept a bit, but I had a bad dream and came out here to sit." Jade rose and rubbed at her temples, soothing the edges of her sharp, pounding headache. She had been violently ill upon waking and had taken just enough time to put away the comb before leaving the tent to suffer until dawn, retching as the pain pierced her skull like daggers. Her nausea had faded after a few hours, but the tight band of discomfort around her forehead persisted.

Ming assumed his usual posture, crossing his arms. "Your friends were cheerful at supper last night, but you were quiet. Was it because of what I said to you about leaving?"

Jade shrugged. "I would feel the same if I were you. You have no obligation toward me."

"Then why did I save your life, knowing who you might be? Why you, of all people?" He began walking to where his three horses were tethered beside Koichi's stallion and Wren's pony, then stopped in his tracks. "Do you believe in destiny?"

"You're the second person to ask me that in a month," Jade told him, startled. She waited for him to ask who the other was, dreading it—as though naming a monster would summon it.

But he did not ask. "I knew someone once who lived only for what the future could bring. Life is such a gift, and when someone squanders it that way, and the future they hoped for never comes—or arrives in an unexpected form—what is there left but regret?"

"That person chose to live that way," she said, watching the play of emotions on his face. "What you call squandering is what they might call living."

"Perhaps." Ming led her over to the horses and patted his black-and-white mare, which blinked large, gentle eyes at Jade. "Fate is still a puzzle to me, even after all these years. What led me here to this empty desert? What led *you* here? If you had left a day late, if I hadn't gone hunting at the exact moment I saw Wren . . . we wouldn't be standing here talking."

The mare pushed her nose into Jade's stomach, sniffing for food. Jade accepted a bundle of hay from Ming and held it out to her, smiling when the horse accepted it with a snuffle.

"She likes you. She can be yours." Ming waved away her protests. "You need your own horse, and it will spare your friend's pony from carrying two riders."

"Thank you, sir, for everything. I'm glad our destinies intertwined, even if you aren't."

Ming studied her. "I woke up when you and Fu were talking last night and heard you ask about the maze. You insist on following this folktale nonsense, then?"

"Folktales aren't nonsense," Jade retorted. The familiar pain ebbed below her heart as she thought of Amah and of her old, quiet life—a life that she now knew would never have been enough. Abbess Lin and the elder had been right. "I used to think of stories as you do—foolish, childish. I took them for granted, not knowing how important their lessons would be."

"Important for what?" He raised a quizzical brow.

"For becoming who I'm meant to be," she said, as her mother's and her nursemaid's loving faces flickered across her memory. "Becoming who my loved ones believed I could be. Someone who is strong and just and tries to do what's right—who doesn't give in to fear. It may take me longer than others to find my courage, but I try to find it just the same."

Ming was silent.

"Everything I know, I learned from stories." Jade glanced at him, expecting to see a scornful expression, but instead she saw inexpressible sadness.

"And everything I know, I learned from living," he said. "You love folktales so much?"

"They're shaping my life as we speak."

He looked at her for a long moment, then gave a chuckle, quiet but genuine. She frowned, confused, until she realized that they were facing each other with the same exact posture. She, too, had adopted his stance of crossed arms, legs slightly apart, head to the side. They might have been father and daughter, to any passerby who didn't know the truth.

"I think I judged you too soon, Jade of the Great Forest. You may be a braver soul than even you know. And you've had to work long and hard to be that way. Who among us hasn't?"

She gazed up at him with surprise and gratitude. "*You've* had to work at being brave? You, who live alone in the desert with scorpions and death?"

Ming chuckled again. "Bravery isn't just about being strong and handy with a sword. Sometimes it's about resolve . . . or deciding whether to face a past you'd rather forget."

She thought she could see memories like ghosts in his eyes, but he did not elaborate.

"You're like me. We both of us grow tougher with time." He reached out and placed a large, warm hand on the top of her head. "Go in and get some food in you, young one."

Obediently, Jade went inside, leaving him alone with his thoughts.

That afternoon, when Ming and Fu had gone off to hunt, Jade told Wren and Koichi what the poisoned comb had shown her. Wren listened, horrified by the knowledge that Xifeng had eaten Amah's heart. She rose with her fists clenched and a face like thunder, and neither Jade nor Koichi doubted that she would have torn Xifeng limb from limb if the Empress had been there.

She paced, muttering obscene curses. Without warning, she whirled on Jade. "Why didn't you tell us you were going to use the comb? Empress Lihua said it might be dangerous."

"You shouldn't have taken so much risk upon yourself alone," Koichi said worriedly. "You said your stepmother seemed to know you were there. She might have wanted you to use the comb and hoped you'd see her killing the dragon."

Jade ran a weary hand over her face. "I know it was stupid and I'm sorry. But now we know the Dragon King's relic—the ruby-red apple— is waiting in the Great Forest. It's the story of the exiled prince and the apple tree. His father, the king, was threatened by him and sent him off to die on a deserted island. But he found the apples that grew there, taught himself to cultivate them, and survived. It's about resourcefulness and courage in the face of hopelessness."

"You shouldn't have taken the risk," Koichi said again.

"If not me, then who?" Jade countered. "It's my task and my fault you're both here."

Wren shook her head angrily. "We're in this together. We *chose* to go with you."

"I know that. But I can't allow you to go on and endanger yourselves for me."

They stared at her in stunned silence. Jade went to the tent flap and stared out at the desert, unable to bear their disappointment and anger.

"I have the crane feather cloak, and three other treasures to find. The Dragon King's tree is where I must unite them and summon the Dragon Guard before Xifeng kills me." Jade turned back to them and winced as the abrupt movement intensified her headache. "There is no choice. I have to succeed. I have to end this. It is *my* quest and burden. The two of you should ride west to Dagovad from here and then to the coast in a matter of weeks. Sail away and be safe."

All through her speech, Wren's face had grown redder and redder. But Jade realized, with a shock, that it wasn't just anger: the young woman was as close to tears as Jade had ever seen her, and in someone so strong and unflappable, it was almost frightening.

"You bite your tongue," Wren seethed. "I don't care that you're a princess, I don't care that I'm your handmaiden—I will speak to you the way you deserve. How can you talk to us like you're already a queen dismissing her servants? Don't we have feelings? Aren't we allowed a say in this, too?" Her fury faded as tears began to fall, one after the other.

"You've treated me like your own sister. You've been kind to me. You've respected me and given me time with my grandmother. And now, after all that, you're asking me to leave you for dead?"

Jade put her shaking arms around Wren, as she had done with Amah so many times. She looked at Koichi over the other girl's trembling head. "I can't imagine my life without either of you anymore," she whispered. "Do you think any of this is easy for me to say? I can't imagine a day where I don't hear you making sarcastic comments at my expense, Wren . . ."

The girl's laugh sounded like a sob.

". . . or see your smile, Koichi, and feel like I'm standing at the hearth of my own home," Jade went on, throwing all caution to the wind. Koichi shook his head, his features twisted with emotion, but she barreled on before either of them could speak. "I learned with Amah and the monks that family can be found, and I remembered it again with both of you."

"Then why are you saying goodbye?" Koichi demanded, his eyes shining with tears.

"Because I need to know you're safe. It's the only way I could live without you. Xifeng killed my mother all over again," Jade said, her voice growing louder to drown out his protests. "She ate Amah's and Pei's hearts out of spite. Pei, who was loyal to my father and helped me *once*. What will she do to *you* when she finds us?"

"So you're going to take away my one chance of avenging my grandmother?" Wren pulled away, her voice low and fierce. "You let us find out for ourselves what Xifeng will do. You owe us the chance to take the consequences of our own actions. We're not children, Jade."

"She ate their hearts!" Jade shouted. "Why won't you understand? If she finds us, she'll ensure I die last. And seeing her torture the two of you will kill me before the huntsman's knife ever stabs into me." She sank to her knees, sobbing, and Koichi knelt before her, putting a gentle hand on either side of her face.

"How do you think *we* would feel if we went away, knowing we'd left you to face the same fate alone?" he asked quietly. "How do you think *I* would feel if I lost you?"

And in his eyes, tender and dark with pain, Jade saw the truth at last: he *did* care for her in the way she did for him. She thought she could fill her lungs just with the way he looked at her. She might even grow wings and fly like a sky-maiden if she tried. "Why?" she whispered.

"Why what?"

"Why did you *really* pretend to marry Wren instead of me?" she asked, running her eyes over his dimples and the furrow between his brows, at the face she knew almost as well as her own. "It wasn't just to keep me safe, was it?"

Koichi stared at her, then began to laugh—a great, jolly, hearty sound that filled the tent. He laughed until his eyes filled with tears of mirth, and Wren joined him.

"What a time for *that* question," he said. "I did pretend to marry her because it was safer for you to disguise yourself as a servant. But also because it was easier with someone I hadn't the slightest intention of loving. No offense, Wren."

Wren waved a hand, blowing her nose loudly into a rag. "None taken."

"And," Koichi added, pressing his forehead against Jade's, "in spite of my father's teachings, and the fact that it was only pretend, I couldn't imagine being someone worthy of you. Who ever heard of a princess choosing a little man for her consort?"

"If you *ever* speak disparagingly of yourself again in my presence," Jade whispered, "I will point your shoes away from Kamatsu every night from then on."

And then—despite Wren being there, despite Ming's imminent return, despite the fact that they were faced with near-certain danger and death—Jade kissed Koichi.

His lips were warm and soft and slightly chapped, and beneath the sound of Wren's joyous laugh, Jade heard the drumming of her own heart.

She hoped to hear that sound for as long as she could keep it going.

30

Wren and Koichi rode by her side when Jade left at dawn on the back of Ming's black-and-white mare. They had been merry at supper the evening before, with Fu turning on his full charm to make amends with Jade, and man and ghost had stood watching as the three headed west at sunrise. Jade wished Ming the peaceful life he deserved. He had said nothing when they thanked him, and she had taken his silence to mean he never expected to see them again.

"I think he likes Fu, no matter what he says about it," Wren declared.

"Does he have a choice?" Koichi asked. He rode next to Jade the whole day, and every now and then, he reached for her hand as though to reassure himself that she was still there.

She relished the warmth of his fingers and the bright enthusiasm in Wren's voice, and thought, *I am blessed.* The gods had seen fit to give her friends who would rather march into danger with her than go into hiding without her. She could not fail easily, not with Wren and Koichi by her side and a resolve that strengthened with each passing day.

And when the maze appeared on the horizon that afternoon, Jade was even more grateful not to be alone. They gazed up in awestruck fascination as they approached. It was a great structure of pale stone, made up of thousands upon thousands of linked horse statues. The wind had been carved into their granite manes, which flowed as they lifted their proud heads to the burning sky. Each statue stood at least ten feet high and three feet wide. They had been built nose to tail, forming a solid wall, and any gaps in between were filled with prickly green brambles, as though the desert plants too conspired against whoever dared enter.

Once inside, there would truly be no escape.

"Gods above us," Koichi said hoarsely, taking it all in.

"It must go on for miles." Jade tipped her head back, and the movement brought on the pounding headache once more. It had insisted on lingering since she had used the comb, fading and intensifying by turns. She winced, pressing her fingers into her temples. "Fu called this place a death trap. We'd better keep our wits about us."

Koichi pointed at a distant section of the maze that rose higher than the rest. "The place was built right on top of the rolling dunes. There will be hills within, and unsteady ground."

Wren rubbed her hands together. "What are we waiting for? There's the entrance."

A large, open space yawned before them where a stone horse should have been. No sooner had they reached it than a low, malevolent hissing reached their ears.

A snake coiled on the far side of the wall of horses. In the shadows, Jade could not determine its color as it slithered sideways, tongue darting from its mouth. After a moment, it glided across the sand and disappeared from view. Jade's horse bucked skittishly at the sight of the serpent, and Jade ran a hand down her flank, soothing her.

Koichi patted his own nervous horse. "Just a desert snake."

"Or a spy for Xifeng," Wren said darkly, exchanging glances with Jade.

Inside the maze, death greeted them at once: a man in rags sat propped up against a stone horse, as though he had been waiting patiently for them. What little flesh remained on his skeleton hung off the brittle, yellowed bones in dry, leathery strips. As they stared, a tiny scorpion crawled out of his gaping eye socket and retreated into his lipless mouth.

"He must be one of those adventurers Fu mentioned," Jade murmured as Wren slid off her pony and approached him. "He came all this way only to die at the entrance."

A worn leather bag lay beside the dead man. Wren nudged it with her foot, but nothing crawled out, so she peeked inside. "It's empty," she said, disappointed. "Maybe it always was. Or someone cleaned it out before we could." Her eyes darted around them.

They stood on a road of sand, wide enough to place three stone horses head to tail across it. It was lined on either side by a wall of statues and lay open to the unforgiving sky, twisting and turning in different directions. The place had a solemn grandeur suitable for the tomb of a forgotten king—morbidly appropriate, Jade thought, to mark death with a maze of death.

"That entrance may be the only way out," she said. "We'll need to leave a trail behind us, as the phoenix did with her hoard of food in the story."

Wren frowned. "We have some dried strips of meat . . ."

"A food trail would get eaten, and we'll need all of our provisions," Koichi pointed out.

"And crane feathers won't work. The cloak is a valuable relic and I don't want to damage it, and feathers would blow away anyway." Jade studied the statues around them. "What about marking the granite in some way?"

Wren whipped out a sharp blade, but the dagger did not even make a dent in the stone.

Jade dismounted and knelt, considering the brambles growing in prickly profusion between the statues. With a small dagger, she gingerly cut at the plants, wincing when the needles pricked her, but managed to extricate a tendril about the length of her hand and place it on the ground. The green of the plant stood out brilliantly against the deep gold of the sand.

"Now, there's an inspired thought," Wren said with approval. "No animals will eat that. We should press it down so the wind doesn't disturb it." She stepped on the tendril and applied weight gently until it had sunk about an inch or two beneath the surface of the sand.

Koichi came to help them gather enough green tendrils to fill the dead adventurer's empty bag. Every now and then, they hissed as the plant's sharp edges bloodied their hands.

"It's too bad they grow back so quickly," Wren said, watching with amazement as one of the branches regenerated itself. "We could have opened a shortcut or an escape route that way."

"But look!" Koichi had sliced into a particularly thick plant and a spurt of clear water had emerged. Cautiously, he tasted a few drops. "I think it's safe to drink!"

"Well done," Jade said, hugging him. "It might be a long time before we get out of here, and a constant supply of water will be a blessing."

They filled their pouches and ensured that the horses' thirst was quenched before walking down the main path of the maze. Every ten steps or so, they pressed a bramble into the sand, leaving a clear and definite trail of green that led them back out of the maze.

A heavy silence hung over the maze like a shroud. It seemed watchful, and Jade did not trust it. Fu had said this place was thought to be a tomb, but she couldn't imagine herself wanting to be buried in the cruel and solitary sands, guarded by statues—she much preferred the forest's verdant shade or the grasslands, where one's memory could keep growing like the springtime.

"The phoenix faced a mudslide in the story," Wren said to Jade as they moved on cautiously. "Do you think there might be something similar here to test you?"

Jade nodded. "Koichi's and Amah's versions of the story matched almost perfectly—the trail of pebbles, the storm, the mudslide. But Amah's tale had the phoenix facing another challenge on her way to reclaim her hoard. The storm in the forest had opened many different paths that tried to trick her into getting lost."

"This story could not have been more appropriate," Koichi said as the path branched into four different directions. He and Wren both turned to Jade. "Which should we take?"

All of the paths looked identical, and Jade saw that one guess would be as good as another. "Let's go west, toward Kamatsu," she suggested, and Koichi's eyes shone at her.

Jade and Wren chose to walk and lead their horses while Koichi rode. The heat felt even more oppressive within the maze, and the statues provided weak shade, if any. They came to another intersection that split into four additional branches, but Jade decided to keep heading west. The sky darkened, bringing the cool relief of night. But the wind had begun to pick up, making a strange howling sound as it moved through the gaps between stone horses. It blew grains of sand into their eyes and noses as it increased to an eerie, mournful pitch.

Koichi tossed the girls extra tunics and wrapped one around his own head. "We should stop soon for the night," he said loudly so they could hear him over the wind.

"I think we'll have to!" Wren called back, for when the path twisted and they turned the corner, they saw a dead end. The path was blocked by three stone horses, placed perpendicularly to the walls on either side so that travelers could not pass.

Jade slumped against her mare, discouraged that they had walked all afternoon on the wrong path. "Let's stop!" she cried, pulling the tunic tighter around her face. Bits of sand scratched her skin as she tugged her belongings down from the mare's back and tossed them to the ground. "We can curl up in the corners of this dead end and cover the horses, too."

But within seconds, the wind grew even stronger and more relentless. A sudden piercing flash of light lit the black sky. The lightning was followed by an enormous clap of thunder that made the animals whinny in fear. Jade covered her ears with her hands, coughing, as great columns of sand began to spin around her, slipping into the folds of her clothing.

"Quiet now! Calm down!" Koichi cried to his stallion, who was bucking and tossing his head despite all his rider's efforts to comfort him.

The wind had whipped up a wall of sand so thick that Jade could barely see her friends through it. "We have to cover the horses' heads, too!" she shouted to Wren, but she could not tell whether the other girl heard her, for something strange happened in the next moment.

A face appeared in the wall of sand, the eyes two gaping holes formed by the tunneling wind. It seemed to Jade—blinking painfully as gritty crystals of sand blew into her eyes—that the face was looking right at her. A vicious gust blew her backward, pressing her with violent force against the dead end. The black-and-white mare whinnied with fright and took off in the opposite direction, galloping back down the path they had traveled.

"Jade, come back!" Koichi roared, and through the raging vortex of sand, Jade saw him riding after the mare. Somehow, in the darkness and confusion, he had thought she was on it.

"No! I'm still here!" she shouted. "Wren, don't go!" Dimly, she saw the other girl fling herself onto the gray pony and race after Koichi.

But no matter how loudly Jade screamed, they did not turn around. *When they catch the mare and realize the truth, they'll come back for me,* Jade told herself. She squinted at the sand wall, but the face had disappeared—surely it had been a figment of her panicked imagination.

A loud clunk sounded as a heavy rock missed Jade's head by a few inches, propelled by the violent wind. She shoved her belongings into the corner and turned her face inward to the stone, wrapping the brocade cloak over her head and body. The gale pushed and prodded her like hands yanking her into the spiraling air. If anything, it had intensified in the last few minutes.

Jade wrapped her arms around the leg of the statue, ignoring the brambles that scratched at her skin. She prayed that Wren and Koichi were safe, and gritted her teeth, holding on to the stone horse for dear life. She had not come this far to die at the whim of nature.

But is it a whim of nature?

A chill slid down Jade's spine as lightning ripped across the sky like a line of angry fire. *This is like the storm in the tale,* she realized, *the one the phoenix survived.*

Suppose the maze was testing her, and had separated her from her friends on purpose?

She clenched her jaw, determined that she too would survive to see another dawn. She was the phoenix, and if she succeeded, a burning rose awaited her as in the tale. That helped her forget, if only for a moment, that she was only a frightened girl all alone in a dead king's tomb.

The sandstorm raged all night, whipping cruel clouds of dust against the statues with a powerful fury. Jade must have fallen into an uneasy slumber, for when she woke—her muscles cramped from having curled up for so long—the wind had died away. She stood up stiffly, her bones creaking in protest. She had never been so glad to see the harsh desert sun again. Despite wrapping herself in the brocade cloak, she was covered from head to toe in sand.

She sagged against one of the stone horses, laughing with relief. "I survived."

Now there was nothing to do but retrace her steps, if the trail had made it through the night. Most of the plant tendrils had been covered with a thick layer of sand, but she could still see specks of green here and there. Seizing her bags, she followed them eagerly, her ears strained for any sound of her friends. She was sure Wren and Koichi had found somewhere to hide and were searching for her even now. She wondered if they had found the poor mare.

A light rustling reached her ears, like the hem of a robe dragging on the ground.

Jade whirled. "Who's there?"

She saw nothing, but gooseflesh rose on her skin. Somehow, she knew with absolute certainty that someone was watching her. *That face in the wall of sand* . . . Jade shivered in spite of the heat, and just as she pivoted on her foot to continue onward, she saw a flash of black coiling, disappearing between the sharp brambles.

"Another snake," she muttered.

She walked on, vigilantly scanning her surroundings, but saw nothing as she returned to the place where the path had first split. There was no sign of Wren and Koichi, and though she could see specks of green in the sand, there were no prints, made by either hooves or human feet.

She knew her friends would never abandon her, yet she felt as keen a despair as though they had. Surely they wouldn't have left the maze without her—perhaps they had gotten lost and wandered down another path, in which case it might take days for her to find them.

Jade wiped her damp forehead, feeling faint with worry. Black dots had begun dancing in her vision again. She knelt and cut the brambles, both to gather more tendrils for the trail and to find water. She placed them in her sack, and her fingers brushed over a familiar object: the wooden box holding Xifeng's poisoned comb. *I'm not alone.* The thought fluttered through her mind, along with a strange relief, but she pushed it away as the edges of her headache returned. It frightened her, the way she couldn't stop thinking about the comb and its answers.

It had been foolish to wear it again, and would be even more so to do it a third time. Who was to say that the connection didn't reveal information about Jade to Xifeng in turn?

She might know I'm here, Jade thought with sudden dread. *The storm last night might have come from her . . .*

The odd rustling noise came again, igniting her rising panic. She leapt to her feet, dagger in hand. "I know you're there!" she shouted. "I know you're following me and I'm not afraid!"

"No, of course not," said Fu. "Why would you be?"

31

"Fu!" Jade cried with mingled exasperation and relief. "What are you doing here? Where's Ming? Did you see Wren and Koichi?"

The ghost studied her. "Let's find you a cool place to rest first," he said anxiously. "You don't look well. Sit down at my feet."

Jade wanted to protest, but the black dots were still dancing in her vision, so she sank to the ground. Though Fu cast no shadow, she was shocked to find soothing, tree-scented shade like that of the Great Forest. She could almost hear the monastery bells ringing. She glanced up in surprise, but his kind eyes revealed nothing.

"Rest, little one," he said. "I will take care of you."

"Tell me what happened."

"Ming had a crisis of conscience. After you left, I had to watch him pace and brood and stare at the tent wall all day, fretting like a hen who had lost three chicks. It was sweet, but rather tiresome. Finally, at sundown, he decided to go after you, so of course I had to come."

"Ming came to help us?" she asked incredulously.

"I've never seen that man ride so fast. We didn't get here until night-fall, and he beat his breast over whether to try to find you in the dark or wait until morning. But then you came tearing out of the maze on the black-and-white mare he gave you, looking terrified."

Jade shook her head. "But I've been in here the whole time."

"I know," Fu said. "I recognized the strangeness of the form at once—it was no person, but a spectre in your shape. There are benefits to no longer being of this world, and one is being able to see trickery where the human eye cannot. Also, if it *had* been you, you would have stopped when you saw Ming. But you didn't, and out of the maze came your friends in pursuit."

Jade stared at him, fear and suspicion rooting in her mind.

"I tried to tell them it was a trick, but they were frightened," Fu went on. "They said there had been a sandstorm in only one section of the maze, because when they left, the night was calm and fine. Still, you kept riding away as though possessed and wouldn't answer them. The young man was particularly upset. They're being led west now, with Ming on their tail."

"I knew they saw something odd," Jade muttered. "The maze was separating us. The maze . . . or *Xifeng*. Suppose she knows everything. Suppose she and the Serpent God have guessed what I'm trying to do."

"Gathering the Dragon Lords' relics to summon their heavenly army?" Fu looked a bit ashamed at her horrified expression. "I listened to what you were thinking . . . only a few times, mind you. It's another benefit to being dead."

Jade gaped at him, wondering if he had heard everything she had thought about Koichi. "*Please* stay out of my head! It's a private place, and it's hard enough knowing whom to trust."

The ghost drew himself up stiffly. "I assure you I'm trustworthy. How could you think otherwise when I've just abandoned the person I've been haunting to protect you?"

He looked so offended that Jade apologized. "So you're haunting *me* now?"

"I believe so. Ming and I haven't been apart for fifteen years, and here I am with someone new." He tried to pat her knee, but his hand went right through it. "All I know is that being with Ming helped me find you. In fact, I think I've been waiting for you all these years. So take heart: I'll be with you every step of the way."

"I don't understand it, but thank you," Jade said, grateful for his company though she sorely missed Wren and Koichi. The fact that Ming had gone with them comforted her a bit. "My objective remains the same: do everything I can until the huntsman finds me. And if Xifeng knows about my quest, time is truly running out. I have to stay ahead of her."

She spread out Amah's brocade map and saw that a new symbol had appeared: a fishbone in glowing cream thread, stitched right beside the rose in the desert.

"Something doesn't make sense?" Fu asked, watching her frown.

"I have the cloak of the grasslands, and I'm searching for the rose of Surjalana," she said. "Koichi believes the sword of Tu Lam is the relic of Dagovad, and the apple has to be the treasure of the Great Forest. Which means this fishbone is the treasure of the god of Kamatsu."

"Why would a god choose a fishbone?"

"Because it grants wishes," Jade said with certainty, missing Koichi more than ever. "It's from a tale about a maiden whose stepmother was jealous of her beauty. Every day, when the girl did her washing in the river, a fish would come and speak to her. It was the spirit of her mother. But the stepmother discovered their friendship and caught and ate the fish. Later that night, as the girl was crying over the fishbone, her mother's spirit reappeared and told her that the bone would grant wishes whenever she recited a certain poem."

The story brought to mind the poisoned comb's last vision: the *tengaru* clearing, and the blue dragon collapsing by the apple tree. Jade pushed the memory away, her heart aching.

"The god of Kamatsu was known for his benevolence, which fits. But I don't understand why a treasure of the Boundless Sea is *here* in the desert, and so close to another relic."

"I have a feeling we're about to find out," Fu told her. "And we should go soon, at any rate. That snake that's been following you is very close."

"Then it *has* been spying on me? If it's a servant of Xifeng, it's only a matter of time before Kang finds us, and the trail of plants will lead him straight to us." Jade groaned, cursing her own lack of foresight as she gathered her possessions with renewed speed.

"You did right. There's only one exit, and we may run into Kang on the way out anyway."

"Thank you—that's comforting," she said wryly, and he beamed at her.

Despite her heightened urgency, they were forced to wander the maze for two more days, running into dead end after dead end. Though there was a chance that the trail might lead Kang to them, Jade continued to scatter the brambles, which helped her recognize when a pair of paths circled, joining together in a meaningless loop and leading her back to the beginning.

"Will we ever come to the end of this maze?" she asked, frustrated.

Perhaps that was the Serpent God's cruel little joke, building a maze from which there would be no escape, so that the spirits of lost adventurers would keep him company—for lost adventurers there were in great number.

Corpses were so common, they no longer startled Jade. Skulls grew on the path like obscene flowers, and great black birds feasted upon what flesh remained. She picked through the dead people's belongings, apologizing to them under her breath as she saved sulfur matches, any dried food that had not gone bad, a small dagger, and dusty but relatively clean tunics.

"What else can you do, besides listening to people's private thoughts?" Jade asked Fu on the third day. She rubbed her neck, which had begun to grow bright red and peel from the sun. "Can you take corporeal form? I met two other ghosts who could whenever they experienced great emotion. It tied them to their humanity, one of them told me."

"Well, I can choose whether to show myself to certain people," Fu responded. "And great emotion, me? Living with Ming? Ha!"

"Fu, why is Ming afraid of the Empress?"

He hesitated. "It's not fear, exactly."

"But he doesn't want her to find him," Jade pointed out.

"Not wanting someone to find you and being afraid of them are two different things."

She sighed as they turned a corner. "I'm not too young or silly to understand, you know. You can tell me what he's . . . oh, no."

Something had taken hold of both her feet; her boots were sinking slowly into the sand. She lifted her right foot, but the movement only submerged her left foot more. The ground began to swallow her like a thirsty beast, drinking her in slowly until she stood with her calves stuck firmly into the wet sand.

"It's quicksand! I can't move!" Jade panicked and bent her knees, but every movement she made only served to help the sand suck her down faster.

Fu's eyes were round with fear. "Drop your bags."

Jade threw her sacks away, heart roaring in her chest. Beads of sweat ran down her face as she struggled in vain to lift her legs. She was now buried up to her knees and could no longer bend them. She wiggled her ankles frantically, but succeeded only in sinking more. She was now low enough to the ground that she could brace herself with her hands on the dry sand around the pit, but even with all her strength, she could not budge an inch. *This can't be how I die,* she thought furiously. *I'll never see Wren again . . . or Koichi . . .*

"Fu, now would be a good time for you to become corporeal," she tried to joke, but her voice came out thin and scared.

"I don't think that would help," he said worriedly, but he reached his hand to her anyway.

Jade grabbed for his fingers, but her hand went right through his. She tried once more, with the same result, and a weighty hopelessness pulled at her with as much strength as the quicksand. "Fu, if we can't do this, if I can't get out . . . would you do something for me?"

"Don't talk like that," he said, shaking his head desperately. "No last words."

"But Wren and Koichi—"

"You will see them again," Fu told her, jaw clenching with fear and determination. He held out his hand again. "Try once more. Come on, little one."

Jade obeyed, and this time she could feel his cold hand in hers. "Oh!" she cried joyfully, but she found at once that he had been right. Even with another person pulling her, she could not move an inch. Her body had pushed aside whatever water was trapped in the ground, and the sand was drying fast, hardening around her legs. She heard a horrid squelching sound as the moisture latched on to her waist.

"Let go, Fu," she said, trying to take deep breaths. "I need to stay calm. Struggling and moving aren't doing anything to help."

The ghost obeyed, his face drawn with anxiety.

"If I don't move, I don't sink. That's one good thing, at least. I won't go in any deeper than my waist." She forced herself to remain motionless, inhaling and exhaling, and closed her eyes. There was intense pressure all around her waist and legs, squeezing at her blood and bones as the sand began to solidify. She tried not to imagine dying here in the burning sun—tried not to envision the rose, waiting at the end of this horrific task . . .

The rose.

In her panic, Jade had forgotten the story. The phoenix had gotten trapped in a mudslide and had flattened herself, lying down to spread her weight. She had remained calm and still.

"Yes!" Fu shouted. "Good thinking!"

"When I get out," she told him, "I will scold you for listening to my thoughts again." Though it terrified her and went against every instinct, she lay down, lowering her back to the sand. She kept her eyes closed, pretending she was resting.

"Don't move," the ghost said encouragingly, standing over her.

Again, though he cast no shadow, Jade felt a coolness like the shade of trees. It soothed and strengthened her, and she lay motionless, though she longed to kick and struggle. Slowly, ever so slowly, her feet began to rise about an inch as the shift in the position of her body allowed water to seep back in slowly, softening the sand.

The phoenix had stayed calm in the story and had made small movements, Jade recalled. Tentatively, she twisted her right ankle an inch to the left, then to the right. It rose a fraction as water flowed into the tiny space made by the movement. Heartened, she did the same with her other ankle with painstaking slowness. Bit by bit, her legs began to rise until the tops of her thighs were again visible above the surface.

She reached her hands out for Fu, who took them, his own cold fingers holding hers tightly.

"You're almost there," he said, his eyes wide with fear and relief. "Kick slowly now."

After an excruciating length of time, another loud squelching noise rang out as Jade pulled her right foot free. With Fu pulling, the rest of her body parted with the pit and she collapsed on dry ground, her shoulders shaking with sobs of relief.

"Thank you, Fu," she said weakly, struggling to her feet and wiping her face with a sand-crusted sleeve. Her heart roared like a festival drum. "I've already wasted so much of our time here. We need to keep going."

"It won't hurt to rest a moment. You did very well," Fu praised her. "You knew what to do . . . unlike them." He pointed to an object sticking out of the sand nearby: the blunt end of a skeleton's arm, poised vertically. Though the bony fingers had long gone with the desert wind, Jade could easily imagine a hand waving for help.

Jade gathered her belongings, taking deep, shuddering breaths as she hugged her sack to her. She felt the sharp edges of the little wooden box pressing into her stomach. But this time, beneath the longing to seek answers from the comb was deep-rooted anger. Xifeng wanted her cowed, frightened, and controlled—Xifeng, who even after destroying Jade's family, seizing the throne, and killing countless victims, still desired Jade's death and Jade's heart to eat.

Perhaps the Empress would think these terrifying near-death episodes—Kang and his men in pursuit, the trek through the desert, the storm, the quicksand—would discourage Jade. Perhaps she believed that the little girl whose first instinct had always been fear would grow into a young woman who still sought to hide.

Fu watched in silence as Jade dug in her bag for the wooden box. She didn't bother opening it. The comb had stopped belonging to Empress Lihua the moment Xifeng's poison had been painted on the teeth. Jade dropped the box on the quicksand where her body had been moments ago, applying careful pressure with her hand until the ground began to swallow it.

"There must be water somewhere underneath this maze," Fu said as the wooden box and its dangerous contents vanished from sight. "It rose up and formed a pit."

"Let's hope there aren't many more," Jade said wearily. This ordeal had tired her more than all her weeks of travel. "So many have died trying to find this rose. We passed a man who had killed his friends so he might enter and take it for his own. What is it all for? Is it worth it?"

The ghost shrugged. "A treasure with those abilities could make a man rich."

"I don't understand these people," she fumed. "They want wealth and power at any cost to themselves or others. Hearts, lives, whatever it takes!"

She led the way, testing the ground every few steps. She and Fu walked in silence, which suited her just fine. Every time she thought of that skeleton's hand or of the traitor who had left his friends for dead, it made her want to kick a statue. Life had been as worthless to them as it was to her stepmother. These people seemed to be forever scrambling up the side of a sand dune, slipping and sliding, pushing others down so that they might rise higher. It disgusted her.

But, she reflected, perhaps among them were people who had hoped to do some good. Perhaps they had been like her, employing drastic measures in the hope of helping others.

Jade felt better after a short nap, washing the grime from her pants and cutting more tendrils for their trail. And later that afternoon, they discovered that the path split in two again.

"Look," Fu said, excited. "We've already gone that way . . . See your plant trail?"

"All of these paths seem to circle and run into one another," she said thoughtfully. "But we haven't gone down *that* one yet."

They took the branch to the right, and each step convinced her that she had at last discovered the correct path. The statues appeared older and more weathered than the ones in the outer sections of the maze. She held her breath as they progressed, exhaling with a rush when a huge courtyard appeared, enclosed by stone horses on three sides. She and Fu cheered to see what lay in the center: a granite platform, from which a bright red rose grew out of a crack on the surface. There was a reverence and a beauty that was at odds with the cruel maze.

Jade fell to her knees, feeling as though she might burst into tears. "Oh, Fu, here we are. I was beginning to think it didn't exist."

"Go on, then!" Fu said heartily. "Take your relic and let us be free of this place."

She rose and stepped onto the platform. The blossom clearly grew through some sort of magic, without rain or soil to help it, and a sudden anxiety seized her at the idea of plucking the unearthly flower. But time was running out; even now, Kang might be coming through the maze.

Jade gritted her teeth and took hold of the thorny stem, tugging it from the stone. It came away easily, settling into her hand like a sword in a warrior's grip.

All at once, a great rumbling sound roared from beneath her.

Without warning, the crack in the platform widened as the two halves split apart, flinging Jade down a winding hole into the bowels of the desert.

32

Jade landed on what felt like shrubs and branches, lying still with the air knocked from her lungs. The hole from which she had fallen felt as distant as a star in the sky. A pinprick of sunlight shone from where she had stood seconds ago on the platform. The light shimmered faintly through the treetops . . .

Treetops?

She sat bolt upright, relieved to see the rose clutched safely in her shaking hand. She had landed on a strange bush with black, pale-veined leaves that left a light, sticky sap on her skin. Above her, the thick, lush leaves of onyx-trunked trees whispered in a hot, damp wind.

She had fallen into some sort of underground jungle.

Jade moved her shoulders and arms slowly, checking for injuries, but the sticky bush and the sack on her back had protected her. She got to her feet, feeling springy soil beneath her boots. The air was so humid, it felt like breathing through a hot, wet cloth pressed over her face.

"Where do you suppose we are?" Fu materialized beside her with his hands on his hips. He surveyed the area with an air of calm curiosity, as though sightseeing for pleasure.

"Did you fall down, too?" Jade asked.

"Certainly not," he said, affronted. "I floated after you quite gracefully."

A low, ambient roar echoed from somewhere nearby, putting Jade on edge at once. The sound brought back memories of blades glinting in firelight, blood on wooden cards, Amah's determination as she leapt at Xifeng, Kang's sword embedded in the nursemaid's side . . .

Jade hugged the rose to her, smelling the powerful, sweet fragrance from its petals.

Damp shrubbery surrounded them, all broken twigs and garish mushrooms and twisted trees. The only light came from pinpricks far above, and yet Jade saw it all clearly: leaves with sap like pungent blood, ferns rimmed with fine needles, worm-eaten branches that resembled withered human arms, and disturbing flowers like mouths screaming in pain. The moist breeze rustled the leaves again, adding to the roaring water. No birds or animals seemed to live here.

Jade felt cold, despite the sickly warmth that made her tunic cling to her skin. "Why have we come here? Do you suppose it's a trap for whoever steals the rose?" she asked, considering the flower, which appeared as fresh and immaculate as though it had just come from a garden. "Isn't it supposed to burn?" The moment she spoke these words, the silky red petals burst into flames. She shrieked and nearly dropped it.

"Careful!" Fu shouted. "Don't set the place on fire."

"It heard me. Stop burning . . . please?" The flames disappeared at once, and Jade gripped the stem, excited. "Fu, this *is* the rose from the story of the phoenix and the storm. We'll have heat and light whenever we need it, and pure water, too. And speaking of water, I think we'll have to follow that sound," she added reluctantly, nodding at the roar of the unseen current.

She slipped the rose into her sack and led the way, hating the sight of the humid, oppressive jungle on instinct. The air smelled like a sordid version of the Great Forest, the pine-like scent edged with poison and soil tinged with a sweetness like rot. The vines and branches grew so thickly, she had to cut a path through them with her dagger. So absorbed was she in her task that the source of the rushing water shocked her when it appeared.

A monstrous black river hurtled through the jungle, the water so wide, they could not see the opposite bank. The current tore through boulders and sliced into the damp soil at their feet, so vicious and angry that it seemed to boil as it passed by them.

It was the type of river made to devour.

A figure knelt by the screaming water, dabbling a hand in as though it were a calm summer stream. The man rose, his thin, frail silhouette too tall to be human.

Every muscle in Jade's body tensed as he turned toward them. She could not see his features; only two long, slender hands, each finger like a stark white bone. Dread poured over her like a bucket of melted snow; she felt it creeping down her neck, chilling her despite the heat.

"Princess." The whisper had to have come from the robed figure, but the sound echoed all around them as though the trees had spoken. "You are welcome here."

Cold sweat slid down Jade's neck as she studied the man's faceless-ness, his skinny hands, and the slow and sinuous way he moved, like a snake through slick grass. "I've waited a long time for what is rightfully mine," he uttered, and this time his voice emanated from the river, the grass, the soil—everywhere except the place from which it should have come. "My patience has not been rewarded. But *you* will change that, Jade of the Great Forest."

He raised a bony hand toward the river, and a great curtain of water rose up from its depths. It faced Jade, swirling viciously, and she saw her own reflection in it as clearly as though it were a still pond or a mirror of tarnished bronze. Her mouth went dry.

The Serpent God. Jade looked straight at Fu as she thought the words.

The ghost's eyes widened. "He can't see me if I don't wish him to," he said in a low voice, "but he might sense my presence."

An air of stagnant decay blanketed the entire jungle, but it seemed strongest near this too-tall figure. Something flashed in the curtain of water, drawing Jade's eye away from him: a regal woman appeared in the depths of the dark mirror, in that waterfall where no reflection should be. The woman turned, but instead of Xifeng, Jade saw her own face. She held a gold crown of blazing phoenix feathers arranged like the rays of the sun, which she placed upon her own head.

"I chose wrong before," the Serpent God went on in his harsh whisper. "I thought *she* would let me win her and be my queen, but she denies all I have given her. She uses my gifts for her own ends, instead of keeping her promise to obey me."

Fu called out sharply, "Princess!"

Jade realized she had been taking step after step, moving closer to the mirror-water as though in a trance. She blinked, shaking off the feeling of dazed disorientation, and noticed for the first time that hard white objects were swirling in the river. After weeks in the desert, she recognized them at once: human bones.

Skeletons torn into tormented slivers tossed in the briny black water.

Clumps of hair still attached to pieces of human scalp clung hopelessly to boulders, and shreds of flesh and sinew and skulls with mouths gaping in eternal screams spiraled in the depths. The crowned woman in the mirror-water moved again, but Jade could not take her eyes from the bones in the flood.

"Heed me, daughter of dragons," the Serpent God commanded. "Watch your destiny take shape. You shall do my bidding as Empress and secure the throne of Feng Lu for me. You will give me armies and land, and in return, I will give you peace. I will give you what no one else can: the freedom to live in safety and seclusion, far from the dangers of the world."

The mirror-water changed to show the lush, gentle trees of the Great Forest, and between its branches, the monastery. Jade's heart compressed with painful longing for the home she had shared with Amah and the women who had loved and raised her. She heard the monks chanting and the bells ringing, and could have wept for the yearning in her soul.

"You never wanted power, I know," the Serpent God murmured. "Reclaim the crown, and when Feng Lu is mine, I will let you hide away, safe and sound."

Jade could not deny that he spoke the deepest wish of her heart. And yet, and yet . . .

Was it still her wish, now that her eyes had opened to the cruelties to which Feng Lu had been subjected? Children laboring, people rioting, soldiers dragging boys away as their mothers wept, women hanging dead-eyed from the gates of the city . . . Was Jade still so eager to hide in an impossible fantasy when, all around her, the legacy of her family crumbled to ashes?

That's what he wants, she thought with rising contempt. *He and Xifeng are the same.*

They wanted power built on the backs of others and an empire fueled by blood.

Unable to control Xifeng, to dominate her will entirely, he thought to try it with Jade—to install her on the throne as his puppet, and through her, to further destroy the continent. She saw in her mind a dark legion of snake soldiers, crawling over Feng Lu until it had strangled the life from its people. And then it would spread across the sea, finding a new continent to infest.

It was a game of life and death, and her only option was to win. Otherwise her family's legacy, Empress Lihua's memory, and all of Feng Lu would come crashing down.

Jade was the last of her clan, and her duty weighed upon her like a cloak of iron.

I choose to win, she thought fiercely.

Because the Serpent God was still watching, she said shakily, "You would give me sanctuary? Peace and quiet, and the freedom to live my life as I choose it?"

"I swear it."

Out of the corner of her eye, Jade saw Fu floating along the riverbank toward a cage of human bones. A turtle the size of a rowboat lay inside, so motionless that she thought it was dead until its dull eyes moved to hers. The defeat and despair in its glance moved her heart to pity. It didn't belong in this dark jungle any more than she herself did.

Slowly, with purpose, the turtle shifted its eyes from hers to a spot in the black river. She followed its gaze and for the first time, she saw a soft glow within the churning depths, so unlike the tortured bones that it seized her focus at once. Everything that had once belonged to a human was tossed about by the waves, but the glowing object remained perfectly still.

It was the second relic, the fishbone of Kamatsu. Jade realized that was why it had been stitched near the rose on Amah's map; all this time, it had been miles below it.

Her chest tightened as she met Fu's eyes. *I have to retrieve the relic without the Serpent God knowing,* she thought, and the ghost's eyes narrowed in understanding and he vanished.

"A peaceful existence is what I would wish," Jade told the Serpent God, knowing he was still watching. She gazed back at the mirror, but her feet were moving slowly toward the water.

The fallen deity's voice became coaxing, intimate. "You will be obedient where the *other* has not. You will raise armies and bring Feng Lu crashing to its knees before me."

Jade continued inching toward the river's edge, making a show of contemplating the mirror as she did so. She slipped her bags from her shoulders and knelt dreamily on the sharp rocks as though compelled. "But you are all-powerful," she said. "Why should a heavenly lord need a weak human like me? I have nothing compared with your strength and knowledge."

"Gods have been absent from the earth for ages," the Serpent God answered. "It is simpler for humans to accept and rally under one of their own, and safer for me to stay here, hidden away, until you have ensured my invincibility. Only then will I step forth."

Jade felt another rush of disdain. Once she had done the work and secured the continent, he would come out and take the credit. She wondered why Xifeng had never realized that, never understood that the Serpent God needed her more than she needed him.

She had, Jade realized. *But she figured it out too late.*

"Feeble human minds must grow used to the idea of one supreme deity," the Serpent God went on. "Won't it be ironic when I seize Feng Lu with an heir whose claim to it is irrefutable? An heir whose veins carry the blood of the *Dragon King,* the upstart who sought to exile me?"

Jade reached for the thorny rose, her eyes on the bilious river. She didn't know if the flower would purify the water long enough for her to get the fishbone, but she had no choice.

Fu, where are you? she thought desperately. *Are you listening?*

"You're not paying attention, child," the Serpent God said, and Jade gave a start. "Don't you want to go home to the monastery, far from the reach of the world?"

A ghostly whisper in her ear: "I will hold him for you."

How? Jade thought, but there was a ferocity in Fu's tone that she had not heard before . . . and a deep undercurrent of human emotion.

"Go!" Fu roared.

Jade sprang into action. "Burn!" she cried, and the rose burst into flames.

Behind her, Fu materialized. Where he had been transparent before, now he became solid, furious, and corporeal as he ran at the hooded figure of the Serpent God.

"You cannot survive long in that water, girl!" the fallen god shrieked, his words pulsing with fury as he raged and pushed. But Fu had somehow created a wall around the deity so that he could not get to Jade. For all of his boasting about power and supremacy, the Serpent God could not fight the defiant spirit. "It will be like poison seeping into your lungs!"

"Hurry, Jade!" Fu shouted, his outline flickering.

Jade stood on the edge of the riverbank, clutching the burning rose. A sickly odor rose off the surface of the water, like meat rotting in the sun.

Mother, Amah, gods above, she thought. *Give me strength.*

And then she dove.

33

The water was freezing when Jade plunged in, but the rose continued to burn, casting a circle of golden light as it warmed the river.
She struggled against the powerful current, past grisly human remains,
but the light of the rose protected her from the whirling thigh bones
and skulls. The river almost felt clean, though it was so littered that she
knew the flower shielded her from the truth. She kicked off against a
boulder with all of her strength.

The fishbone floated in the center of the river, a star stuck in a roiling black sky. Jade swam desperately toward it, fighting as hard as she
could against the current. She was forced to come up for air, but wasted
no time before plunging back down, pushing against boulder after boulder until the treasure of Kamatsu was within reach.

She reached out, preparing to resurface in triumph, but her hand
went through the relic. She tried again, but could not touch it. Panic
rose in her throat. Time was running out; perhaps Fu had lost his hold
on the Serpent God already. *Why* could she not claim it? She had easily

taken the cloak and the rose . . . She had only to keep a promise and survive a desert maze . . .

The story.

In the tale, the maiden's mother had told her how to use the fishbone: to first recite the poem that would make her wishes come true.

> *Bones of my mother*
> *Spirit in a fish*
> *Bestow on me your kindness*
> *And grant me my heart's wish.*

The moment she opened her mouth to speak the verse, Jade's chest tightened, her lungs screaming for air. She kicked up to the surface and gasped for air, hearing the Serpent God and Fu roaring furiously at each other, but she had no time. She murmured the poem to herself above the water, praying it would work before sinking again into the black river. This time, her fingers plucked the fishbone and she kicked off for the surface.

Any elation she might have allowed herself to feel disappeared when she saw what was happening on the riverbank. A rain of jet-black serpents had begun to fall in the jungle, writhing and hissing. Their slender, slippery bodies were even emerging from the mirror-water.

The Serpent God stood with his back to her, arms out while dozens of wriggling, coiling silhouettes climbed up his body and the jungle vomited more serpents with blood-red eyes.

"Jade!" Fu screamed. "Get on!"

He had somehow opened the cage of human bones and was urging the enormous turtle into the water. Jade scrambled onto the riverbank and flung her belongings onto her back, still clutching the rose and fishbone, then dove back into the current. The rushing waves propelled the turtle downstream toward her, hitting her hard and almost knocking the breath from her.

She just managed to throw her bags onto its shell and cling on with all her might. They tore down the cascade, and when the water dipped, she mustered every ounce of strength left to pull herself onto the turtle's back. Fu knelt grimly beside her as she held on, gasping for breath.

Behind them, serpents poured into the river like thick slimy noodles in a poisonous soup, their bodies ejected after her by some force much more powerful than the current.

"What do we do? They're gaining on us!" she shouted.

The turtle lifted its head and spoke in a gravelly voice: "What would you wish for more than anything, Princess?"

"What?" Jade was only half listening, too horrified by the pursuing snakes to be stunned by the turtle's ability to speak. Glints of ruby shone nearer and nearer, and any moment now, the serpents would catch up to them . . . Their fangs flashed in the river . . .

In her hand, the rose still burned with a powerful flame. It had protected her from the whirling bones and the water so black it resembled toxic oil.

Jade pushed up on her hands and knees. Her stomach dropped as the turtle tossed and turned in the racing waters. The Serpent God was now far behind them as the river took a sharp hairpin turn, and she nearly lost her grip on the shell. The right side of her body landed in the water and she struggled to climb back on, her fingers slipping. If she fell into the water now, the snakes would be upon her like so many vultures over a corpse.

The turtle shifted as they took another nauseatingly sharp turn, and she crumpled back onto its shell. "What would you wish for?" it asked again, and all at once she remembered the fishbone. She had recited the poem, she had claimed it, and now it owed her a wish.

"My mother," she whispered, and the whisper became a shout. "And that the fire from this rose will burn every single one of these serpents!"

This time, when she touched the rose to the river, it was like applying fire to oil. The flames exploded and shot backward, blazing a trail of destruction through the sea of snakes.

"Hold on!" Fu cried.

The river dipped sharply, submerging both the turtle and Jade in the heaving water.

Jade's empty stomach churned. "Burn no longer," she whispered, and the rose went out. Tucking her relics away, she sprawled out on her stomach as they roared through the caverns, the smell of death subsiding beneath the acrid smoke. She lay still, pressing her cheek against the cool, damp shell and praying for the sickening, rocking motion to end.

Fu called her name, but it sounded far away, as did the sound of the crashing cascade.

"Daughter."

Jade opened her eyes and found herself, quite impossibly, back in the soft greenery of the Great Forest. She was not on a turtle barreling toward death, but sitting underneath the apple tree in full bloom. The blossoms swayed in a gentle breeze, and beside her was Empress Lihua.

"You wished on the fishbone for me," her mother said, smiling. "But I am with you always, you know that."

Jade reached for Lihua's hand and felt its reassuring warmth in her own. "Xifeng killed you—killed the blue dragon. I saw it die and these roots drank its blood."

"She cannot kill something that will live forever. A mother's love transcends death, and you will find my protection in *every* part of this tree." Empress Lihua glanced at the fishbone in Jade's free hand. The relic glimmered with a rose-gold light as though it were made out of precious stones. "The turtle guardian of that fishbone must be glad to see it in your hands."

"Fu freed the turtle from a prison of bone. The Serpent God must have trapped it there."

Lihua smiled. "Fu always did love animals."

"Only two relics left. One of the Great Forest," Jade said, gazing at the ruby-red apple in the branches above them, "and one of Dagovad." A thought occurred to her. "The Serpent God separated me from my friends in the maze—he created a diversion, a spectre that led them west. This river is carrying us west. Will it bring us to the Kingdom of the Four Winds, to my friends?"

"Anything is possible," Empress Lihua said. "Perhaps you won't be so alone after all."

"I'm not alone, Mother. I have Fu."

Lihua laughed. "That pleases me above all things. Keep him with you and treat my Little Fisherman with respect. It was his nickname . . . and a sister ought to respect her older brother." Her eyes sparkled at Jade's astonishment. "Fu was the eldest of my sons with my first husband. He was the Crown Prince in life, brave and solemn, but secretly loved mischief. The eunuchs had their hands full with him when he was young."

"My brother." The word felt like music on Jade's lips. She'd had *family* with her all this time. "Why were assassins after him? Why did he have to beg Ming to kill him?"

"That is Fu's story to tell. He knew Xifeng when she was a girl, and in fact, he brought her to me. I wonder if lingering in the desert, waiting for you and now watching over you, is his way of making amends for what he unknowingly did."

Jade sat back, reeling from the revelation that Fu had introduced Xifeng to Lihua.

"You will come to understand many things," her mother said. "The most important is that those hungry for power are as flawed as they like to appear strong. But you seek to help others. That is what you would do on the throne."

"All my life, I've thought myself weaker than others. But everyone has to work at being brave, don't they? Day after day, in their own way."

Empress Lihua pressed her lips against Jade's forehead. "Uphold our family's honor, my dear one, and don't give in to those who know nothing of goodness. Promise me on the fishbone, this symbol of a mother's enduring love and protection."

"I promise."

Empress Lihua smiled, and then she and the forest both vanished.

When Jade opened her eyes, she was on the turtle's back once more, racing down the black river with Fu, her brother, by her side.

34

The river had mellowed, though it still flowed steadily, and the stench of death was gone. Jade peered over the turtle shell and saw her reflection in the clear water. Fu leaned over beside her. His features seemed clearer, as though knowing who he was had made him more real to her. He had a strong, compassionate face, and his eyes held all of Lihua's sparkle.

"You weren't with us just now. You were somewhere far away," he said.

"I was in the Great Forest. I spoke to our mother."

Fu gazed at her without surprise. "That's true, isn't it? We are family. I didn't remember until you said it, but that must have been how I could leave Ming for you. After all, it *is* a brother's duty to go with his headstrong sister on her deadly missions."

"No wonder I think you're so infuriating. You're my brother, my family." She laughed, blinking away tears. "I'm so happy, I don't know why I'm crying."

"I'd cry too, if I could. But I'll settle for telling you how proud I am of you."

"Mother said you knew Xifeng when she first came to court." Jade studied him. She could almost see the scraps of memory floating in his brain as he frowned in concentration.

"I had no idea what she would become, or that she would destroy my family. Yes, I remember now," he said slowly. "I thought she would be a good companion for Mother. But even with all her brains and beauty, she had not a stout heart like yours, little sister of mine. Rest now. We've left the Serpent God's realm, though it will be a while before we leave this river."

Jade pillowed her head on her bags. "It's a fitting place for him to hide away, controlling Xifeng from afar. I never thought I would condemn a deity to cowardice."

"He is a coward, but perhaps he's right to be afraid," Fu said. "The other gods waged a great battle against him when he destroyed their alliance ages ago, and he has never forgotten."

"What an army he has built, with all those serpents that came to his aid." Jade shook her head, her eyes on the cavern's ceiling far above them. "He and Xifeng mean to join their forces to overtake the continent, but they're in disagreement. They haven't made their move." She bit her lip. "He tried to tempt and manipulate me as he did her. He showed me the monastery."

"Is that what you want?"

Jade sighed. "I thought so once. But now I see it wouldn't make me any different from him, hiding while people suffer under Xifeng. What has she done to this world of ours?"

"Nothing that *you* cannot fix."

Jade couldn't help smiling. "Do I deserve your confidence in me?"

"It's not just me," her brother answered. "It's Mother, it's the whole of the continent—everyone who utters a secret wish for the Empress's downfall, so that the true sovereign may come forward. The last-born of the house of Dragon Kings. You." He touched Jade's shoulder, his mouth trembling with emotion, and she felt the light pressure of his fingers.

At that moment, the turtle raised its head. "I will stop here and rest," it said, slowing as it moved toward the riverbank, where they found a flat clearing of pale grass, withered from lack of sun. High above them, they saw holes through which sunlight trickled down. Fu stepped onto the shore with his hands behind his back like a traveler in a fascinating new land.

"I wonder how Wren and Koichi are," Jade said, taking a seat on the dry grass, but Fu had wandered off and did not hear her.

"Your friends?" the turtle asked, moving with painstaking slowness to lie beside her. It sighed with relief, its shell shining gray green in the dim light.

Jade nodded. "How did you come to be here from Kamatsu?"

The turtle shut its eyes wearily. "My family and I were journeying home for the freezing months when we discovered that ice had formed early: chunks as big as islands, stretching miles below the water. We had never seen winter come on so quickly. It changed our routes."

"You were lost?"

"We separated to find the best way around the ice, but I went too far. I saw a hollowed tunnel of ice deep below the water and thought it might be a passage to the other side." The turtle opened one rueful liquid eye. "Curiosity is a weakness of mine. No sooner had I entered than a powerful current sucked me in, sweeping me away."

"And the fishbone?"

"The Serpent God, or so he calls himself," the turtle said witheringly, "tore the treasure from my back when he captured me." He released a long, slow breath. "I feel so ill and parched. There is something dreadfully toxic about this water, and it weakens me."

"I'll clean some for you," Jade offered. She found a curved, indented piece of rock and filled it in the river, coaxing flames from the rose to apply to the liquid. At once, the water felt lighter. She held the rock out to the turtle, then repeated the process several more times until the animal had drunk its fill.

"Thank you, child." The turtle eyed her. "You're an odd sort of girl to encounter down here. How did you come to be in the desert?"

She laughed. "It's a long story."

"When you are eight hundred years old like me, you'll realize time is of no matter. I have all the time in the world."

And so Jade told the turtle of her adventures, and of how she had come by the rose and the crane feather cloak. "The fishbone was under your guardianship," she recalled. "Will you allow me to use it for my purposes and then return it to you?"

The turtle shook its head. "It is yours now. It was under my protection only until the right person came to claim it. When the Serpent God pried it from my back, it fell into the river and he could not remove it no matter how hard he tried."

"Perhaps he should try reading more stories," Jade suggested.

The turtle gave a dry, gravelly laugh. "An odd sort of girl," it said again, indulgently, and then it closed its eyes and fell asleep.

For ten days, they floated through the dark world without sun or moon to guide them, the quick and steady current taking them far west. Jade felt a peace she had not known since the monastery, knowing not even Kang would be able to follow them now. Whenever they stopped to rest, she found edible mushrooms and plants to eat, and the turtle told her stories of its native Kamatsu, where it would return once they found a route to the ocean. The tales of the Boundless Sea made Jade feel closer to Koichi than ever.

But underneath her contentment was a lingering unease, a knowledge that this might be the calm before the storm. Sooner or later, they would emerge, she would collect the final two relics, and then confront Xifeng once more . . . in either triumph or death.

One day, the turtle said, "We're underneath the kingdom of Dagovad now."

Jade, who had been listening to Fu tell an amusing story, sat up. "We've gone that far west?" She prayed the spectre had led Wren and Koichi here as well, not anticipating she would be propelled after them. "Will you be able to find a channel to the open sea? To go home?"

"Don't worry about me. I can already taste the salt of Kamatsu from here. But I must find a place to leave you. You'll have to find a way to climb up into the mountains." The turtle glided to the riverbank and waited as Jade clambered off with her possessions, followed by Fu.

Jade bowed low to the turtle. "Thank you for all you've done for us. I wish you a safe journey to Kamatsu and a happy reunion with your family."

"And I wish you luck in your task, Jade of the Great Forest. And Fu of the Great Forest." The turtle's gentle eyes swept over them. "There are challenges ahead of you; that is clear even to me. But you have gone far enough that you cannot back out again."

"I don't want to back out," Jade said. "Not anymore."

"Keep that kind heart beating, for if you wished it, you could light all the world."

She bowed again, accepting the blessing, and watched the turtle drift back into the river. The sight of the current carrying it west, homeward bound, filled her with joy and regret and longing. "Will I ever know what that feels like? Returning to a peaceful life?" she asked Fu.

"Anything is possible," he said. "Come, let's find a way up to the mountains."

Both the cavern and the river had narrowed; where once they had been so wide that Jade could not see the other side, the opposite wall of rock was now close enough to throw a stone at. The shore was long enough for a man to stretch out and sleep without his feet touching the water.

Jade lit the rose and led the way along the water's edge. "I'm glad you left Ming to be with me," she said, drawing strength from Fu's presence. "Do you remember Mother at all?"

"I do," he replied, sounding amazed. "Somehow the memories of her are stronger when I'm near you. She loved white jasmine flowers and miniature trees; she filled her apartments with them. There was one tree with tiny white flowers like lanterns. She was often sad."

"Was my father unkind to her?"

"No. Disinterested, perhaps. He didn't love her the way my father did."

"I don't feel bitter toward Emperor Jun anymore," Jade said thoughtfully. "I was happy at the monastery, but I resented him for throwing me away. I kept thinking he wouldn't have done that if I had been a boy. He wouldn't have discarded *you*, for instance."

Fu's laugh had harsh edges. "Don't be so certain."

"What happened to you?"

It was a long moment before he answered. "I argued with Emperor Jun," he said slowly. "I wanted to rescue my brother, who had been captured on an overseas mission. But Jun refused, at first, to let me go. My youngest brother had died of illness, and if this brother died as well, I would be the Emperor's sole heir. But Jun relented at last, equipping and sending my men and me off like a doting stepfather."

"But you never found our brother."

"He was already dead. A piece of information Jun neglected to tell me." Fu's voice rang with bitterness. "The captors' ship crossed paths with mine on the sea. They were going to the Imperial Palace with my brother's head as proof of his murder, which Jun had demanded of them. The captors attacked and killed every one of my men, but I escaped and found Ming."

A stitch formed in Jade's chest. "The Emperor sent you on a lost cause, knowing you would be killed for nothing? Did Xifeng have anything to do with . . ."

"Xifeng was still Mother's lady-in-waiting. I believe it was entirely Jun's doing."

Emperor Jun's voice echoed through Jade's head: *I've done so many things wrong, but now I am doing one thing right. I will, at last, make amends to Lihua.*

"I was nothing to him," Fu said. "Worse than nothing, because I was another man's son. I tell you this so that you know how emperors play fast and loose with *all* of their children. Son or daughter, prince or princess. We are pawns in their game. That is the way of a ruler."

"No," Jade said, the word reverberating through the cavern. "That is *not* the way. That is not *my* way. Had our mother been ruling Empress, she would have sooner put herself in danger than you or me or our brothers."

"She was thought too gentle to rule, but perhaps they were all wrong," Fu said. "Perhaps gentleness is necessary to temper a ruler's ruthlessness, and not weakness at all."

Though Jade's heart was heavy, she felt a new lightness as she walked, too. As ruler, she would honor the qualities people had loved in Empress Lihua. She would be firm and fair and encourage her people's truths and confessions, which they would give her freely—not because they feared her, but because they respected her enough to want her to know and judge them well.

She didn't know if she would be successful. She didn't care to make grand, empty promises—to herself or to anyone else—that she might be the ruler Feng Lu deserved. But if she ever reached that throne, she would try to be an empress of whom her family might be proud.

Yes, there was time yet to discover what sort of monarch she wished to be.

For if you wished it, you could light all the world.

Jade lifted the rose higher and raised her chin to face the darkness.

35

The following night, Jade found a crack in the rock wall leading to a narrow passage that wandered on for miles, angling upward. For two days, they climbed the winding tunnel slowly, stopping to rest often—or at least, Jade did, while Fu wandered off to explore. The air grew colder the farther they went, and after the desert, the chill seemed to creep into her very bones.

Upon waking on the third day, Jade found that Fu had gone off again. She ate and drank a little, studying the brocade map in the light of the rose. She wished for the thousandth time that Koichi were with her so he could see what had grown in size over the Dagovadian mountains: a slender sword embroidered in gold and silver thread. She knew he would have laughed with delight to recognize Silver Arrow beyond the shadow of a doubt, the great sword of Tu Lam, his favorite legendary warrior.

"I will claim it for you," Jade told him softly, touching the stitched sword.

A pebble fell nearby and she looked up. The little enclave in which she sat was like a landing on the slope, small enough to see into the corners. There was no one.

She folded the map and replaced it in her sack, wondering when Fu would come back.

Another pebble fell.

Once more, Jade scanned her surroundings and saw no one. But as she turned back to her belongings, a heavy cloth slipped over her head. Quick, clever hands went around her throat.

"Don't struggle," a woman warned. "We won't hurt you . . . right now."

Jade stopped thrashing, wondering if her captor held a weapon. Her heart drummed in her chest as she felt herself being lifted to her feet. "Please, my belongings," she begged, her words muffled by the cloth as a tight rope was secured around her wrists.

"We have them. Be silent and walk." Strong hands pushed her onto the sloping path.

What would Fu think when he came back to find her gone? *Can you hear me?* she thought desperately, stumbling. But whether he heard her or not, she had no way of knowing.

"Careful, trespasser. Don't try anything stupid." The woman righted her. The clinking of metal on her person corroborated her words; she must have been armed to the teeth.

Trespasser? Jade's breath came in hot, short bursts, and despair settled like a stone in her stomach. Somehow she had unwittingly wandered into a den of thieves or murderers. Her hands were tied, she couldn't see, and her captor had three of the five Dragon Lords' relics. Even if she escaped, she would be forfeiting the treasures she had endured fire, water, and sand to acquire.

They walked for a lengthy period of time, Jade breathing hard as the slope steepened. Every time she lagged, she felt the menacing handle of a sword pressing into her back. And then, when she thought she could go no farther, the woman turned her roughly to the right, where the rock wall should have been. Instead, there was empty space.

"Watch your feet. There are stairs." The woman lifted Jade's leg behind the knee to find one step, then another.

Jade counted at least a hundred steps in total and found herself gasping for air at the top from the woman's fearsome pace. But when the stranger spoke, she sounded barely out of breath, like it was a climb she made regularly. "I've brought the girl, sister," she announced.

"Remove her hood," another woman responded.

Firelight assaulted Jade's eyes as the cloth was whisked away. She blinked, bewildered by the huge room of stone before her. The ceiling soared above them, and the light of several torches danced on the granite walls. An immense table and chairs stood in one corner, and a man-made corridor led to a room full of sleeping pallets. One wall displayed an array of weaponry, reminding her of Ming's tent in the desert: axes, gilded arrows, swords, daggers, and crossbows gleamed in the dancing firelight.

Her captors were all women dressed in warm, heavy furs. One sat on a high throne carved into the rock, reminding Jade so powerfully of Xifeng that she took a step back.

"You're right to be afraid of the Crimson Queen," sneered the woman who had pushed her up the stairs. She was young, perhaps twenty, but she was not like many females Jade had seen: strongly built despite her diminutive height, with a military stance full of authority and confidence. When she turned her head, Jade saw a vicious red scar on her left cheek.

She's like Wren, Jade realized. *They're all like Wren.*

All around her stood dozens upon dozens of women, strong and proud. Their black hair was cropped short or braided away from their elegant features, and they looked as though they ranged in age from twenty to seventy; Jade saw a white-haired woman who stood with no less power than the rest.

Female warriors. The *Crimson* Queen.

The realization struck Jade like a powerful gust of wind: she had ended up in the lair of the Crimson Army, the assassins of whom Wren had spoken so longingly. Once wives, mothers, daughters, sisters who had been ill treated and downtrodden, they had banded together in the peaks of Dagovad, training relentlessly to take their strength into their own hands and never again be at the mercy of another. They worked for whoever could afford to pay, and lived on the bounty of their kills.

The woman on the throne, the Crimson Queen, might have been in her early forties. Her intelligent eyes glittered above sharp cheekbones, and her hair was cropped just above her jaw. She toyed with a jeweled dagger in her hand, the gems shining blue and red.

Jade looked apprehensively at it, feeling their unfriendly observation, waiting to see what she would do. So she did the first thing that came to mind: she bowed to the Crimson Queen.

The cavern felt heavy in the ensuing silence.

"Why did you do that?" the woman asked.

"You were referred to as the Crimson Queen. I thought it only right to show you respect."

All of the women burst into chilly, mocking laughter, and Jade's cheeks burned red. She must have done exactly the wrong thing.

"These outsiders are quick to kiss your feet when they think you're royal," jeered the girl with the scar, and the others murmured in angry agreement. "She is called the Crimson Queen because she is our respected leader, not because she wears a crown or is some king's chattel."

"I'm sorry," Jade said faintly. She didn't even know why she apologized, since they were going to kill her anyway.

The Crimson Queen came down to meet her. She was shorter than Jade, but the way she held herself indicated that she was stronger and faster than Jade could ever hope to be. Jade forced herself to look back, sensing that it would be unwise to avoid this woman's gaze.

"A young sapling, that's all you are. You have a court accent, but you're too sun-bronzed to be a noblewoman." She scanned Jade's garments. "Your cloth is poor. A handmaiden, perhaps, who runs about in the sun on errands? What were you doing on the banks of the Bone River?"

Jade searched for words, but they did not come.

"Answer the leader when she speaks to you," a woman hissed.

"I am not a handmaiden," Jade said shakily. "I am a traveler. I fell through a hole in the desert into a jungle two weeks east of here. I freed a turtle spirit of Kamatsu from a dark god who had trapped it, escaping with my life and riding upon the turtle's back down the river."

The Crimson Queen studied her even more closely. "You escaped the dark god and lived to tell the tale? There is more to you than meets the eye. What have you found there, Sparrow?"

The girl with the scarred cheek approached with Jade's sack. "Water pouches, dried meat, some mushrooms from the riverbank. And this is a fine cloak fit for a queen," she said, holding up the turquoise brocade. "She told you the truth. No handmaiden is she."

The leader's scrutiny returned to Jade, sharp, appraising.

"Here is another cloak of crane feathers, a fishbone, and a single red rose." Sparrow laughed derisively. "She claims to be a traveler, yet she packs such ridiculous possessions."

"There is a purpose to each of them. Where did you get these items, girl?"

"I found them on my journey," Jade answered.

"You cannot be a servant of the dark god, but there is something about you." The leader's tone hardened like steel. "Do you serve that female viper who calls herself Empress?"

The accusation rankled Jade. "I would rather die before I ever served my enemy," she said through gritted teeth, and the Crimson Queen's eyes glinted with interest.

"*Enemy* is a strong word not even the bravest outsiders use when speaking of Xifeng."

"Nevertheless, it is true. The Empress seeks to kill me, and I was running for my life."

"Xifeng seeks to destroy many people. What is so special about you?" the leader asked.

Jade saw that the women's faces were cold, suspicious; they would know if she was lying. A slash of metal rang out, and quicker than lightning, Sparrow's arm went around her torso and her blade skimmed Jade's neck. Jade felt the steel a heartbeat away from her pulsing veins.

"Who are you?" the Crimson Queen demanded.

"You hesitate too often," Sparrow breathed in Jade's ear. "That's the mark of a liar. What do you think happens to trespassers who also lie?"

"Please," Jade gasped, "with all due respect, I cannot tell my name to all who ask."

The Crimson Queen lifted an eyebrow, intrigued. "A name that requires such care and secrecy. Tell it to us and you may live a bit longer."

Jade closed her eyes as Sparrow's blade pressed harder against her skin. "I am Jade, daughter of Emperor Jun and Empress Lihua of the Great Forest. I am the rightful heir to the throne, and Xifeng wants me dead."

At a movement from her leader, Sparrow stepped away at once. The Crimson Queen came close, scrutinizing Jade. "Princess Jade's body was found at the foot of these mountains last week, slaughtered by agents of the Empress. The girl had been accused of murdering women at court."

Jade stared at her. "A body?"

"Riding a black-and-white mare."

The spectre that led Wren and Koichi west, Jade realized at once. It *had* led them to Dagovad on the back of Ming's horse—but where had her friends gone? "It wasn't my body," she said firmly. "It was part of a cruel trick to separate me from my companions. As for the women I'm to have murdered, the Empress killed them herself. She cut out their hearts and ate them to give her strength through dark magic."

There was a long, shocked silence before the women all began talking at once.

"How do we know we can trust this girl?"

"She could be an imposter, a spy for Xifeng herself!"

"The Empress has long wished for our deaths. Xifeng would do anything to disband us!"

"Quiet, my sisters," the Crimson Queen said. "Who on Feng Lu has not dealt with Xifeng's jealousy, paranoia, and cruelty in some way? She learned from a young age to regard other women as enemies, not as allies and sisters."

"I was raised by a good woman," Jade told her. "I was surrounded by other women who were honest and steadfast, and I will carry their values in my heart until the day I die. I swear to you on my own life: I speak the truth. I have a mission to see through, and if you let me finish it, I will never reveal the secrets of the Crimson Army."

"She knows who we are," Sparrow hissed.

"And so she must know that we kill for money. But perhaps she doesn't know our true objective and for whom we *truly* fight," the leader returned, turning back to Jade. "We defend the defenseless. Women who are thrown from their homes, who are forbidden to find work and thus independence, who starve with their children because they are mere chattel to their men." She gestured to the people standing along the walls. "These women have known suffering. Here, they have found family, purpose, and some semblance of kindness in this world at last. Xifeng would seek to destroy us and to take that away. Can we free you, not knowing who you truly are?"

"I speak the truth," Jade said again. "I would never reveal your secrets."

"Those are mere words." The Crimson Queen paced before the throne. "We believed in Xifeng once. We thought a powerful woman at the helm of an empire would help other women, and we brought our bruises, our battered children, and our ragged souls to her care. But time and time again, she refused to help. She enjoys keeping other women down. Yet when I drew these lost souls together and we grew strong in our sisterhood, only then did she seek the Crimson Army's blind allegiance. When we declined, she threatened to kill us."

Sparrow's teeth gleamed. "You see our position, you who claim to be princess."

"I sense the truth in what you say," the Crimson Queen told Jade, "but servants of Xifeng are clever. If you scurried back to her alive, she would find and destroy us in a matter of days. We are warriors, but even we cannot fight against her sorcery."

"She was blindfolded. She couldn't tell Xifeng where we are," one woman pointed out.

"But she doesn't seem unintelligent," the white-haired warrior retorted. "It wouldn't be hard to remember how to return here."

The Crimson Queen watched Jade for a long moment. Then, with a flick of her wrist, she opened a hidden blade. Jade tensed, but the woman only used the knife to cut the rope binding Jade's hands. "You'll need to prove your identity to us with more than words. If you are the lost princess Xifeng seeks, and the blood of the gods runs in your veins, then you will show us."

36

Jade glanced at the relics, knowing they must seem like a child's silly playthings to these warriors. If she put on the crane feather cloak, they might think she was tricking them. If she let the rose burn, they might think it was a weapon. But the fishbone . . .

"The leftovers of your last meal?" Sparrow said mockingly as Jade reached for it, but the Crimson Queen silenced her.

Jade took a slow, deep breath, and recited:

> *Bones of my mother*
> *Spirit in a fish*
> *Bestow on me your kindness*
> *And grant me my heart's wish.*

She held the fishbone to her heart and wished, with all her might, that she might prove herself to these women and earn their trust. In the long, still silence that followed, the women's derisive snorts turned into gasps and stifled cries. They pressed against the wall to make room for the blue-and-gold dragon that had appeared in the center of the room.

It was only a vision, Jade knew—the essence of the dragon's spirit produced by her wish. But it looked just as she had remembered, down to the golden talons, the graceful antlers, and the translucent water-blue scales. It was as though Xifeng had never harmed it. This time, the dragon spoke in a grave, ancient voice like the wind, yet Jade could hear Lihua's gentle tone, too. The sound drew her close, her heart aching and soaring as she gazed up at the spirit of her mother.

"You called me, cherished daughter, and I answer you," the dragon told her.

The Crimson Queen stood in front of her sisters with her arms held out, protecting them, her eyes wide with awe and apprehension. "Is this some dark sorcery of Xifeng?" she hissed. "You are not proving yourself in the way I asked, *Princess* of the Great Forest."

"I beg your patience," Jade said. If she failed to convince them, they would kill her faster than she could draw her next breath. She bowed low to the dragon. "Benevolent One . . . Mother . . . these warriors think I am a servant of Xifeng. How may I prove the truth to them?"

The dragon looked down at her with soft eyes, then turned to the leader. "Deep in the bowels of this mountain, a monstrous carp lives in a bottomless pool. The carp once dreamed of being a dragon, but the gods saw for it a different purpose: to be the guardian of Silver Arrow, an ancient sword that once belonged to Tu Lam."

Oh, Koichi, if only you were here, Jade thought with a pang. She had known the wonder of living in a story when they had followed Lihua's trail of a thousand lanterns, and wished Koichi could know it too by looking upon the sword of the warrior he revered.

"The bottomless pool exists, and it is something only we know," the

Crimson Queen said, astonished. "But Tu Lam is a mythical hero of fairy tales."

"Would you tell that to the carp? With a few careless words, would you eradicate the very reason for its existence?" The dragon's antlers glinted menacingly. "Tu Lam was the greatest warrior among men. The god of Dagovad bestowed Silver Arrow upon him, and the Dragon King himself gave Tu Lam the honor of commanding his heavenly army."

"The Dragon Guard," Jade whispered, and the Crimson Queen's eyes narrowed at her.

"After Tu Lam's death, Silver Arrow was placed in the Dragon Lords' shrine because no mortal was deemed worthy of carrying that sword. When the alliance broke, the god of Dagovad cast the sword into the bottomless pool, where the carp swallowed it, and there it remains." The dragon regarded the Crimson Army. "If Jade retrieves Silver Arrow, will you acknowledge her place as rightful ruler of Feng Lu? Will you promise your army's allegiance to her service?"

The leader hesitated. "I will have to see this carp to believe what you say. And we do not bow before any humanly crown, not after so many betrayals and hurts."

"I do not expect you to bow before me, but as someone who also wishes to see Xifeng defeated: If I retrieve Silver Arrow, will you fight for our shared cause? Will you join me in the war against her?" Jade gestured to the items before her. "When I have found all five relics, I will summon the Dragon Guard to my aid. But Xifeng will not make it easy to obtain the last treasure in the Great Forest, and I will need a fierce human army at my back as well."

"An army of women?" the Crimson Queen asked sardonically.

"Of warriors united in sisterhood," Jade answered. "Fighters who would die for each other to defend their right to live freely, as they choose."

"But what will happen afterward?" the woman demanded. "Suppose this carp does exist and guards the great Tu Lam's sword. You retrieve the weapon, prove yourself, and we fight Xifeng with you. What comes after that? Will you expect to keep us under your command?"

"I'm not Xifeng," Jade told her. "No one will work for me who does not do so freely. People will choose to be in my service or live unburdened. This would be a job like any other. I will see that you are handsomely rewarded."

"We seek no reward but to see the false Empress cast down," Sparrow spat.

The Crimson Queen met each of her warriors in the eye. Finally, she gave Jade a firm nod. "We agree, as long as you can prove yourself. We will take you to the pool."

"Your blood will summon Silver Arrow. It is done," the dragon told Jade, and vanished. The emptiness it left behind felt immense and much too heavy. Jade let out a long, slow breath as the Crimson Queen moved among her warriors, speaking in a low voice to each. The woman bent her head, listening respectfully to all of them, no matter how young or old.

A filmy silhouette materialized beside Jade: Fu, beaming at her.

How did you find me? she thought, her spirits lifting.

"I've been with you the whole time," Fu said cheerfully. "None but you can see or hear me; I've hidden myself so as not to frighten them and further harm their opinion of you."

The warriors seemed to reach an agreement, and Sparrow approached Jade. "We will blindfold you again, with our leader's apologies," she said, with greater courtesy than before. "We must keep the secrets of our home as best we can. It is part of our code."

"I understand." Jade lowered her head, and the cloth was slipped over it once more.

Sparrow's hands guiding her forward were gentler this time, but Jade felt no less frightened. A monstrous carp awaited her, big enough to swallow a sword in its belly. Suppose it were hungry and simply ate her when she swam in to retrieve the weapon? *I've made it this far,* she told herself. *I can't give up now.*

They walked for an interminable length of time, climbing up and down steps, turning corners, and maneuvering through winding passages. Jade knew that even if she hadn't been hooded, she still couldn't have found her way back. She wondered at the size of the Crimson Army's sprawling quarters. At last, Sparrow guided her to a stop and removed her hood.

They stood in another great cavern, lit only by the assassins' flaming torches. The space was immensely wide, with a low ceiling made of cones of rock, dripping with the damp. In the center of this chamber lay a massive pool, still and silent, that smelled of the ocean's salt.

"We've known of this bottomless pool for a long time," the Crimson Queen said, her glance at Jade more uncertain than severe. "A few of my sisters have attempted to plumb its depths, but I discouraged them after they heard strange sounds, fearing some creature lay waiting within. It seems I may have been right."

"But they didn't see the carp?" Jade asked.

She shook her head. "I suppose it's as the dragon says: your blood summons it. The blood of a descendant of the Dragon King." She held out the blade she had used to cut Jade's bonds.

But Jade remembered the poisoned comb with revulsion. "I will not give my blood that way, for I want nothing to do with that type of sorcery again. If Silver Arrow must be claimed by a descendant of the Dragon King, perhaps this will be enough." As she spoke, she knelt and placed her hand in the water, which was surprisingly warm.

They watched and waited in silence, but nothing happened for a long, tense moment. Jade saw the women's expressions change from expectant to suspicious, and was contemplating asking the Crimson Queen for her blade after all when something began to glow orange in the deep. It brightened as it rose to the surface with the light of a small sun. The women gasped as the source of light emerged: the head of an enormous orange fish, with an eye as big as Jade's entire body.

Who wanders into my dreams?

Jade fell back, startled by the voice in her mind. Perhaps this was how Fu heard *her* thoughts. She kept her hand in the pool, pulse racing as she pondered how to respond. She glanced at the warriors, but from their faces, she saw that they had not heard as she had.

Who wanders into my dreams? the carp repeated.

I am Jade of the Great Forest, she thought, hoping it could hear her. *I am sorry to disturb your slumber, for I have heard of your wondrous dreams and would relieve you of the sword in your belly.*

"What are you waiting for?" the Crimson Queen demanded.

"Please give me a moment," Jade begged her. The carp did not respond for so long that she feared it might refuse. And then it sank below the surface and lifted its head, its massive body pointed toward the ceiling. Its dark red-orange lips parted, and a torrent of water poured into its toothless mouth, revealing a great dive Jade would have to take.

You will have all the air you need inside, the carp told her. *Enter and retrieve your sword, daughter of dragons, for I am weary of protecting it.*

It will be my pleasure, revered guardian, Jade answered.

"Our tolerance does not grow with each second you stall," the

Crimson Queen told her coldly. "Nor will courage come to you, no matter how long you hesitate."

Jade looked into the doubtful faces of the Crimson Army. Fu floated among them, unseen, his nod of encouragement filling her with the conviction she needed. "No, it will not," she agreed, "for courage I already have."

And then she jumped.

Though the water was not cold, Jade shivered upon submerging her body. She took one last look at her brother, filled her lungs with air, and then dove into the carp's mouth, astonished to find that the water inside was even warmer. It felt soft and luxuriant on her skin, and somehow the air infused within it filtered into her nose without bringing water along. She inhaled, relaxing at the wonder of being able to breathe underwater, and swam deeper into the carp's belly.

The fish *was* like a small sun, its body brightening and warming everything within . . . and Jade realized that *everything within* was an entire world.

Entire forests grew inside the carp, the treetops swaying with the rhythm of the water. Small mountains sprang up against the warm tangerine fields of the fish's body, and grasses and vibrant flowers of all kinds bloomed in a joyous, radiant effervescence. All around her swam magnificent fish, large and small, colorful and drab, radiant scales and whiskered faces, the likes of which she had never glimpsed in the world above. Her heart swelled at the beauty of it all as a school of brilliant rose-red fish glided past her.

She wondered how she would ever find Silver Arrow in this immense world. It might take her weeks, months, *years* to fully explore this universe inside the carp.

Jade swam downward, her mind running over the legend of Tu Lam.

She thought of the challenge his father, the Dagovadian nobleman, had laid out for his three sons, a challenge Tu Lam had won with a humble dish of rice to honor his homeland. She skirted the treetops of the forest, her fingers brushing the leaves. The branches were so ethereal, they felt like a dream, like gossamer visions transferring from the carp's mind to her own.

Perhaps that was what this world was: an entire miniature Feng Lu the carp had dreamed up and ruled over, as the dragon it had never become.

But then again, we all have dreams within reach, Jade thought. *We have only to shape them to fit ourselves.*

True, the carp answered.

Impossibly, she smelled fir and pine and elm in the warm sweet water, and in the fragile orange light, it felt like being home again. Any moment now, Amah would call her in for supper and scold her for bringing too many bluebells into their room. A powerful pang of missing overtook her, knowing those days and the woman who had loved her would forever and always remain only in her memory—they never again waited for her in her future.

But Jade's sorrow became joy and surprise when she swam over a section of the forest where a thousand little lanterns hung from the highest branches. The small, pearl-white lights were a perfect imitation of the ones around the Imperial Palace.

The realization struck her at once.

This is the Great Forest in miniature. She quickened her speed and kicked out over the edge of the woodlands to see a great expanse of golden fields, the heavy-headed grasses swaying to music only they could hear. *And these are the Sacred Grasslands.*

The world inside the carp truly *was* a miniature Feng Lu.

With increasing excitement, Jade retraced the journey she, Wren, and Koichi had taken together. She swam over a duplicate of the town they had entered, then the coastal road and Red Lotus Lake. A school of luminescent green fish passed by as she found her way to the golden desert of the carp's dreams, a Surjalana that had never existed except in its ponderous mind. There was no maze of stone horses, but the yellow sands speckled with prickly green brambles made her chuckle ruefully, remembering the trail she had left behind her.

Jade swam in the direction she supposed was west and was rewarded by the sight of a great range of windswept peaks: the Dragon Scale Mountains of Dagovad, Kingdom of the Four Winds and erstwhile home to Tu Lam. The warrior had been born and raised there, and when he had completed his service to the gods as commander of their Dragon Guard, he had begged to have his body returned and buried in the home he had loved so deeply.

She descended, not sure what she ought to be searching for. Silver Arrow might be in some sort of shrine, some special location to honor Tu Lam's greatness, but the only unique feature was what appeared to be an arrangement of rocks on the highest peak.

Not rocks, she realized, swimming faster in her excitement. *Swords.*

A hundred swords had been buried in the mountaintop like a forest of jagged metal. Some were thick and others thin, some long and others short, some with embellished hilts and others plain metalwork. Jade ran her fingers over an embroidered scabbard with exquisite needlework.

One of these had belonged to the honorable Tu Lam. Her task, Jade understood, was to deduce which was the true weapon and bring it back with her to the world from which it had come. She inhaled—still amazed that such a thing was possible in deep water—and thought of everything she knew about the Dragon Lords' favored warrior.

He had been noble, brave, and true. Perhaps a beautiful sword would have suited him.

Jade studied one that had a hilt worked in gold, depicting an elegant flowering tree. She admired the stunning metalwork, but according to the story, peacocks had been the symbol of Tu Lam's house, not trees. Slowly, methodically, she located any weapons with forest or tree imagery and set them aside. That still left about fifty swords.

"Wealth and greatness do not always go hand in hand," Amah had often told her when reciting one of the ballads recounting Tu Lam's epic adventures. "But even when they do, true greatness lies in what a person makes of themselves."

Tu Lam had been a nobleman's son, but he had not revered wealth the way his brothers had. He had been charitable to the poor and lived a humble life despite his high birth. It was one of the reasons why the god of Dagovad had singled him out. And in Amah's stories, Tu Lam had been a man of the mountains, born to rugged peaks and storm-ravaged slopes.

At once, Jade removed the fanciest, most expensive-looking weapons. She put aside any sword wrought in precious metals or embellished with gems, exquisitely embroidered scabbards, and priceless silk tassels. This left her with twelve swords of all shapes, sizes, and qualities.

She laughed, imagining Koichi's beloved face if he knew how close she was standing to Tu Lam's sword. Silver Arrow, the blade that had slain evil, defended justice in the name of the gods, and rescued countless princesses—each more beautiful and ready to marry Tu Lam than the last, according to the old romantic ballads—was near enough to touch.

One weapon caught Jade's eye in particular. It was of broad, plain steel, with a simple hilt. She bent down to examine the floral pattern engraved on the handle. *Sheaves of rice,* she thought, her heart soaring, *to represent the dish Tu Lam brought his father.*

She laid her hands, sure and certain, upon this sword. *How strange that such a beautiful thing was created only to take lives.*

Thus are empires formed and kings crowned, the carp told her. *No great leader becomes great without help.*

Still, I have no love for such a price, Jade thought.

The other swords disappeared as she held Silver Arrow with both hands, feeling its hefty weight like a reassurance. She lingered on the mountaintop, admiring all that lay around her: the shimmering fish, blooming flowers, and fragrant trees around the peaks—a miniature Feng Lu of perfect serenity, dreamed up by a heart as idealistic and innocent as her own. For a brief moment, she allowed herself to imagine hiding here for all time, as she might have done in the monastery. No one would ever find her: not the Serpent God, not Kang, and not even Xifeng.

But somewhere out there, in the true Feng Lu where she had lived and loved and lost, a kingdom waited for its rightful, reluctant queen, and people prayed for a new dawn.

Hiding away was for cowards, and Jade of the Great Forest was no coward.

She could almost feel Lihua's gaze warming her skin and hear Amah's approving whisper as she raised her head far above her, where the carp's mouth opened into that other world.

I will not hide, Jade vowed. *I will never hide again.*

And she began to swim upward.

37

An hour later, Jade sat wrapped in blankets before the fire, sipping hot broth. The women had lifted her from the water and carried her back to their living quarters, and now Fu sat beside her—still invisible to all but Jade—while the others ate and talked quietly around the room. The warriors' gazes darted often to Silver Arrow, propped against Jade's chair.

The Crimson Queen approached with her hands folded behind her back. "As you know, we do not bow to any earthly ruler, and so I will not prostrate myself before you, rightful Empress. But you have my allegiance and that of my women, if you'll accept it."

"I will, with honor and pleasure," Jade said gratefully. "On one condition."

"Name it."

"Do not refer to me as Empress." The title felt every bit as uncomfortable as when she had been called Princess by Xifeng's messenger for the first time. "I have not earned it."

"Yet," Fu added, for her hearing only.

Jade smiled sideways at him. "As I said before," she told the Crimson Queen, "I do not expect your army to serve me longer than agreed. You are all free to go when it is done."

"And you understand that we help you dethrone Xifeng for personal reasons only?"

"I do."

The Crimson Queen's mouth relaxed. She had a strong and lovely face, for all of its harsh angles. "You conducted yourself with bravery tonight. My sisters and I will gladly follow you to destroy the usurper, with whom we have many scores to settle."

"How many of you are there?"

"Two hundred in total. Most of the women you see have recently returned from missions and are awaiting new ones. The others are training elsewhere in the mountains or performing their duties in distant lands." The leader searched Jade's face, as though for judgment. "Blood and death is a price we women pay every day. Why not those who deserve it? We have reclaimed our destinies and are helpless creatures no more. Perhaps murder is not your idea of a respectable profession, but we do the work as we find it."

"I do not presume to judge you," Jade said quietly.

Sparrow addressed the leader. "It's my turn for guard duty over the prisoners, sister. I take my leave."

"Guard duty?" Jade repeated.

"Over those who wander unwittingly into our territory, like yourself . . . though they are not so lucky to possess royal blood as you," Sparrow said with a small smile. "They do, however, cause a great deal more trouble, like that young woman with the remarkable knife-throwing skills. You might have thought she was one of us!"

Several of the warriors tittered.

"She nicked me well." One women swiveled her head so Jade could see the nasty cut along her jawline. "I don't believe for a second that she ever scrubbed pots in the Imperial Palace kitchens or served as a royal handmaiden."

"She's a fiery one," Sparrow agreed, amused. "She told me if I didn't free her at once, she would never do us the favor of joining us."

Jade's heart leapt. "Was she accompanied by a man of short stature?" The women's stunned silence told her everything she needed to know. "Oh, please release them. They are my friends and companions—they left the palace with me and have traveled with me since."

"These are the friends of whom you spoke? The ones led astray?" the Crimson Queen asked, and Jade gave a desperate nod. After a beat, the leader nodded to Sparrow.

Within minutes, Jade flew from her seat to wrap her arms around Wren and Koichi, whose arms had been bound tightly behind their backs. At another nod from the leader, they were cut free to embrace Jade in return. They looked cold and tired, but just as happy to see her.

Wren let go after a moment and moved aside as Koichi held on to Jade, his grin fading. "We abandoned you in the desert," he said regretfully. "I'll never forgive myself for that."

"How could you know? You were tricked," Jade whispered, leaning into his shoulder.

"You are soaked to the bone," he realized, pulling away with concern.

She laughed, drinking in the sight of him. "I have so much to tell you both."

The women finished cutting Ming's bonds and he stepped forward, greeting Jade with his usual gruffness. "It's a pleasure to see you unharmed, though you'd better get under those furs again before you catch your death of cold," he advised, moving toward the fire. He stopped in his tracks when he saw Fu. "Well, there you are. I wondered where you had disappeared off to when I stopped hearing your irritating voice."

"I've missed you, too," the ghost said, grinning broadly.

Upon Jade's request, her companions were fed and wrapped up as warmly as she was herself. She suspected Amah would be proud of the way she told of her adventures, and how all of her listeners—including the Crimson Army—hung on to her every word. To her amusement, each of her friends fixated on a different part of her journey.

Ming was pleased that Jade and Fu had discovered that they were related. "I've always known he was the Crown Prince. Forgive me for selfishly keeping this from you," he said to Jade. "I was afraid if you knew that, you might want to stay and ask questions I wasn't ready to answer. Fu is connected strongly to a past I would rather forget. He did me a great favor in my youth."

Jade waited, but he did not elaborate. "There is no apology needed," she said. "I can't blame you for not wanting me to endanger your peace and safety."

"I used to remind your brother often of who he once was, but it did no good. Everything about his former life slipped right through that sieve of a memory of his," Ming said, and the ghost gave a comical shrug. "If only I knew what a pain he would be as a spirit." They all laughed, even Ming as he spoke.

Wren wore an expression of horrified delight when Jade told them of her trials in the maze. "I wish I had been there. To help you," she added hastily, when they all stared at her, "not just to see the quicksand."

Koichi, of course, was enraptured by Tu Lam's sword and kept admiring it as they talked.

"An entire miniature Feng Lu in the belly of a fish. If only I had been there to watch you reason through the story of Tu Lam," he said, his face wistful. "A hundred swords, you say, and you chose the right one because you knew that folktale well."

"I would have chosen wrong," Wren confessed. "I would have picked a fancy weapon."

Koichi raised an eyebrow. "So you agree now that folktales are important?"

Wren pursed her lips. "I *suppose* they're useful on occasion."

When the laughter had died down, Jade leaned her head against Koichi. He folded one of his blankets around her protectively, even though she already had three. "And now I'd like to hear the story of what happened to all of you after the sandstorm," she said.

Wren's face clouded with the memory. "Koichi and I were frantic about you. There was so much sand swirling about, I couldn't trust my eyes. But I felt certain I had seen you jump on the mare and ride out of the maze, and Koichi told me he had seen the same thing."

"Ming and Fu found us," Koichi said. "Fu tried to warn us that it was a trick, but I was so desperate, I didn't listen. After our conversation, with you wanting to go off on your own to keep Wren and me safe . . . I thought you had changed your mind, or been bewitched, or both."

Wren nodded. "Ming came with us, and we followed you west for two weeks. We lost sight of the mare every now and then, so we'd stop to rest, thinking we had lost you forever. And then we would see you galloping west again."

"It was a true body, not a spirit like Fu," Ming said grimly. "We believe now that it was a corpse, reanimated in your likeness to lure us away from you. Once we reached the mountains, the poor mare collapsed from hunger and exhaustion, having been bewitched by whatever spell had been laid upon it. The body fell at the base of the peaks."

"The Crimson Army thought it was me," Jade said, glancing at the warriors.

Koichi tightened his arms around her. "We feared the worst, but when we came over, we realized Fu had been right and it wasn't you after all. It was awful, knowing we had as good as left you for dead in the desert. It began to snow, so we wandered into the mountains searching for a warm place to rest and plan our next steps. That was when the Crimson Army captured us."

"And kept us alive," Ming added, "thanks to our claiming a connection to you, Jade. And also because of Wren, I think. They were intrigued by her . . . spunk."

Wren smirked. "I was downright rude to them." She turned to the listening warriors, many of whom couldn't hide their amusement. "After having dreamed of joining your ranks for as long as I've been alive, I was upset at the conditions under which we had to meet."

The Crimson Queen's lips twitched, but she said nothing.

"It was a stroke of good fortune that the river carried Fu and me here," Jade said, amazed. "The Serpent God thought to divide us when, in fact, he helped reunite us."

"It was destiny," Ming told her. "And it is our destiny to return home."

"*Our* destiny?" Jade repeated. "Whatever happened to not getting involved? I hope you don't feel obligated to . . ."

"I'm not obligated, but I do owe you an apology for my lack of hospitality," he said. "I have business of my own in the Great Forest. And I overheard you telling Wren and Koichi what you had seen in your nightmare of the dragon—and of *her*, eating your nursemaid's heart. You didn't sound shocked that she had performed such a brutal act."

"Xifeng has done it many times before, to many innocent people," Jade told him quietly.

Ming gazed back at her, but his eyes seemed to see someone else. "I've let it go on for far too long," he murmured. "I, who knew what she might become because of the woman who had raised her. This is my fault as much as anyone's."

"You knew the Empress when she was young?" Wren asked.

But Ming did not answer her, and Jade saw an untold story upon his troubled brow. "I will travel as part of your company, Your Highness," he said, passing a hand over his shadowed eyes. "I had already decided that day in the desert when you left for the maze. I'd be honored to fight for you. You see how long it takes me to find my courage?" His mouth quirked, and Jade smiled back, remembering their conversation.

"I would be glad to have you," she said, and then she turned to Wren and Koichi. "All of you."

"You have the cloak, the rose, the fishbone, and the sword. There's only one treasure left, and then we can reunite the gods' relics," Wren said, leaning forward eagerly as Jade spread the map over her and Koichi's knees. They knew what they would see before they saw it: a single ruby-red apple, stitched over the woodlands.

"We return to the Great Forest," Jade said, and it seemed the weight of her words hung in the air around them. "It's time to collect the fifth and final relic."

"You're walking into a trap," the Crimson Queen said. "Xifeng will be waiting for you."

"There's no help for it, is there? It has to be done." Koichi glanced at Jade. "But how can we be sure the apple is still there? If Xifeng has discovered the purpose of our mission, suppose she destroyed the fruit to ensure that you could never reunite the treasures?"

"In the vision, she rode away before the apple grew," Jade said, thinking. "It's possible she may not know it's there, but even if she does, she can't set foot beyond those gates. No one can, except the dragon . . . and me."

Wren spread her hands with delight. "Then you'll be safe there! Our objective will be to fight off Kang and the soldiers and get you safely through those gates with the other four relics. Once you're inside, it's all over." She cracked her knuckles in anticipation, her face alight.

The Crimson Queen's eyes moved over Wren with interest. "We can disguise Jade as one of us. A guard of four warriors will convey her to the gates while the rest fight. Xifeng doesn't know we have joined forces with Her Highness. She won't bring the entirety of her soldiers."

Ming shook his head slowly. "We can't underestimate her," he advised. "If there's anything I know, it's that she's always thinking two steps ahead. She will be waiting, and she will be prepared. We must anticipate the worst."

"But the number of soldiers she brings doesn't matter," Wren pointed out. "The objective is not to defeat her snake army . . . at least, not right away. We just need to hold them off until Jade can summon the Dragon Guard."

"That, we can do. I'll speak to my generals," the Crimson Queen said, excusing herself.

Left to themselves by the fire, Jade and her friends looked at one another. She could see on their faces all of the emotions that warred in her own breast: fear, anticipation, determination.

"My mother told me that one of the relics will be the difference between life and death," she said. "This is asking quite a lot of all of you."

"You're not asking," Wren said tartly. "And we're not letting you out of our sight again."

Koichi nodded in agreement, his dimples showing prominently.

"Have you ever noticed how each of us represents a kingdom of Feng Lu in some way? Jade is of the Great Forest. Ming lives in Surjalana. My family's roots lie on Kamatsu, and Wren's are in the Grasslands. Fu . . ."

"My body is buried in Dagovad," the ghost said with wonder, glancing at Ming as the memory blossomed on his face. "When I escaped my brother's killers, I persuaded a merchant to take me west to Dagovad. That was where I met you."

"That's right," Ming said, surprised. "I was wandering aimlessly to Dagovad, no longer certain what I wanted from life, and fought for money in the city. Imagine my surprise when the Crown Prince of Feng Lu stumbled into one of my matches."

"You wished to return a favor I had done you," Fu recalled. "What did I do?"

"You gave me a position in the Imperial Army, which I left after a year," Ming said curtly. "And I buried you at the foot of these mountains, as you asked."

Jade regarded each of her beloved companions, thinking that it was odd and fitting. Odd and fitting that, countless ages ago, a broken alliance between Feng Lu's five kingdoms had divided the gods' treasures. And now, a renewed partnership between people with their hearts and spirits rooted in each kingdom would bring the relics back together once more.

She wrapped her fingers in Koichi's and allowed herself the luxury of hope.

38

In two days, the company set out from Dagovad more than a hundred strong. The Crimson Army provided horses and furs, and cloaked Jade and her companions in black like themselves. They traveled swiftly by night, choosing deserted roads and shortcuts the assassins knew well. The women wore translucent masks over their faces to reveal their lips, painted a startling bright red. If Jade hadn't known better, she might have thought they were denizens of Xifeng, so sinister did they appear. But she felt relief every time she recalled they were there for *her*.

Koichi did not leave her side, and his presence relieved her growing anxiety as each step took them closer and closer to home. Too soon, she would have to confront Empress Xifeng.

Jade believed in the Crimson Army, and with four out of the five relics in her possession, no one doubted she would have the ability to summon the Dragon Guard. But if they succeeded, if they cast her stepmother down and took Feng Lu back, what then?

She reeled at the enormity of the responsibilities ahead. There was much more to being a ruler than what Amah's folktales would have her believe. Sitting on the throne would require more than just integrity, like the crane's husband should have had; resourcefulness like the phoenix; faith as in the tale of the fishbone; and humility like Tu Lam. It made her feel small, imagining an entire empire of people wondering what she could possibly do to save them all.

Leaders rarely succeed without help, her mother had told her, and Jade clung to those words like a warm embrace, like a boat on a tumultuous sea.

She would have help. She had the Crimson Army and their fierce principles, Koichi's intellect and bright spirit, Wren's boldness and courage, and Ming's loyalty and strength. And she had Fu, her brother, who stayed close to her with his eyes turned to the north and home—blood though he was only air, family though he was but a lingering spirit. She would have their counsel and guidance, and her own heart to lead her true.

Just the same, she uttered a soft prayer to the Dragon Lords, for at the end of this journey, Xifeng was waiting. And the confrontation, Jade knew, would be the greatest of her life, and perhaps of all time in the history of Feng Lu.

Spring had returned to the Great Forest, with all the beauty of fragrant heavy-headed trees and light dappling the wood. Jade breathed in deeply and thought, *I am home.* But she could not revel in the moment, for the Crimson Army's vigilance was contagious. The women fanned out, splitting into smaller groups as they converged on the stream running through the forest. The sky deepened with sunset and the thousand lanterns shone as Jade realized, with a start, that they had once again reached the bridge in the story. Memories of their escape flooded back: letting go of Amah, crossing the river with Wren, tearing after Koichi and Shiro with the snakes in pursuit.

"No sign of Imperial soldiers," the Crimson Queen said in a low voice, sharp and alert. She and Sparrow led Jade's party, along with ten of her strongest warriors. Several lone scouts zigzagged around the periphery, studying their surroundings. "Do you know the way from here?"

"Yes," Jade said, already spying the first blood-red lantern in the trees.

They retraced the trail to the *tengaru* clearing. Every now and then, a scout appeared and nodded at the Crimson Queen to signal that all was quiet. Jade breathed through the knot in her chest, knowing it could not be long before they detected the presence of soldiers.

In case of an ambush, four assassins would flank her and convey her to the clearing at any cost. No waiting for Wren and Koichi, no looking back. She had promised her friends, who had made her swear on it, despite how painful she found the thought of abandoning them to be.

Jade glanced at them now as they rode together on the black stallion, wrapped in one cloak to disguise Koichi's small form. Koichi sat in front searching for red lanterns while Wren's eyes darted all around the forest, as though she were already a warrior of the Crimson Army.

A low owl's hoot came—the scout's signal. She rode toward them noiselessly. "We found enemy signs," she told the Crimson Queen, and Jade's stomach dropped. "There are strange piles of black twigs scattered all around the perimeter. To what purpose, we don't know."

Jade exchanged glances with Fu. "We're close to the clearing now. It could be a trap."

"It almost certainly is," the Crimson Queen agreed, her sharp features keen as she turned back to the scout. "Have you notified the others?"

"Yes. We have passed the message on."

"And Ming?" Jade asked anxiously. He had decided to ride alone, independent of the Crimson Army, cloaked and disguised as a traveler.

"We were unable to locate him," the scout told her. "He must have taken another path."

"There's no time to worry about him now. We need to execute the plan." Sparrow motioned to her lieutenants, who surrounded Jade at once. "The four of us will bring Jade through the clearing to the gate. She will do what she needs to do, and we will join . . ."

She did not have time to finish her sentence.

A great crackling reverberated through the woodland, echoing from the treetops. And then, one by one, the lanterns fell to the forest floor, knocked down by some unseen force.

"Go!" the Crimson Queen roared.

There was no time to say goodbye to Wren or Koichi as the personal guard steered Jade through the trees, Fu floating close by her side. She gripped her horse's reins, breathless with terror as the lanterns continued falling all around them. Other objects dropped from the trees, too—elongated, slender, and black. One landed on Jade's shoulders and she screamed as the snake's thick, slimy body writhed down her back.

Sparrow leaned over, grabbed the serpent, and flung it viciously at the trunk of a tree without losing rhythm as they charged through the forest, leaving the others behind. But now the rain of snakes had grown so thick and heavy that Jade could not avoid wrestling with a few that had landed on her horse, which bucked and tossed its head in panic. Her entire body shook with revulsion as she pushed their slick bodies onto the ground and tried to calm her mare.

Flames broke out on the forest floor, wild and red and frantic, and the smell of acrid, burning leaves rose toward them. Jade whirled in horror to see the snakes on the ground urging the lanterns toward the many large black bundles: the scattered twigs the scout had mentioned.

But Jade knew them for what they were—monstrous stacks of Xifeng's black incense, which caught fire from the lanterns, sending up huge plumes of toxic smoke. As the flames rose higher and higher, the snakes began to grow, transforming until they stood on two legs as the horrible soldiers in Xifeng's service. The lanterns had revealed their true serpent forms, but the poisonous black clouds returned them to their human shape, armored and armed to the teeth.

"Cover your faces! Keep going!" Sparrow screamed.

Tendrils of fumes clawed into Jade's nostrils and lungs. She coughed, desperately urging her frightened horse on as her chest burned with the poison. The empty *tengaru* clearing lay just ahead. She kept her eyes on the crystalline pond and placed her hand on her sack of relics, to reassure herself that they were still there. Behind them, people shouted and screamed and horses whinnied as swords clanged and the skirmish began.

Jade charged over the first bridge onto the island of willow trees. It was as peaceful and beautiful as she remembered, completely at odds with the blazing devastation in the woodlands. "I can make it from here," she told Sparrow breathlessly. "I'll be safe behind those gates."

The assassin needed no further encouragement. "The gods be with you," she said as she and her women raced off to join in the fight.

Fu looked as unnerved as Jade felt by the peace and quiet of the clearing while fire and pain raged in the woodlands outside. She dismounted inside the enclosure while Fu positioned himself at the gates. She had seen the dragon die in her vision, its water-blue body collapsing and golden eyes fading, but nothing could have prepared her for seeing its corpse in person.

The great creature lay wrapped around the trunk of the tree, submerged beneath the pond Jade knew had bled from its veins. *Oh, Mother,* her heart wept, but she forced herself to focus on the task at hand and empty her sack of treasures. Tendrils of incense scraped her insides, digging for gaps in her resolve. Pungent black smoke hung in the air all around the dragon.

It's here, too, Jade realized, coughing as her lungs struggled against the poison.

Her hands felt slow and awkward, like moving underwater. She laid out the relics shakily: the crane feather cloak, the rose, the fishbone, and the sword of Tu Lam. In this clearing, they glowed with uncanny light. Images of sky and fire flashed in the shining blade of Silver Arrow.

"One last relic," Jade whispered, her mind cloudy.

The fragrance of the apple tree wound its way through the toxic incense like a single pure note in a harsh mess of music. She rose to her feet with effort. A strange, soporific stupor had taken over her muscles, so that each movement felt increasingly slow and exaggerated. The apple blossoms blurred and bled together like water on ink, but one object stood out perfectly: a single red fruit, like a beating heart in a bed of snow-white flowers.

The treasure of the Dragon King, the god of gods.

Jade did not feel the water soaking into her boots as she stepped into the pond and reached for the apple. It came away easily in her hand, fitting perfectly in her palm. Everything else was hazy, but she saw the most minute details of the fruit: the single delicate leaf on the stem, the sheen of pink and gold through the red skin, the gloss of light on its crisp surface.

Her head spun. Her stomach rumbled desperately.

She could already feel the apple's tender skin breaking beneath her teeth, taste the sweet pink nectar as it coated her mouth. This tree had waited here for all the ages of the world, guarded by the *tengaru* and then the dragon. And it had produced one perfect fruit, just for her.

Jade blinked as her surroundings came in and out of focus. The sounds of the battle faded behind her until she heard nothing but her own heartbeat.

Eat, daughter of dragons, the breeze seemed to whisper. *Claim what is yours.*

She lifted the apple to her lips. The fruit smelled intoxicating, like the first clean, cold breath of spring after a long winter—yet there was an undercurrent of black soil and damp caverns that reminded her of the dark world into which she had fallen in the desert.

"Jade!" a faint voice called, and for a split second, Jade's eyes cleared.

"I shouldn't," she gasped, but when she breathed in once more, she returned to her state of fuzzy confusion. Her hand holding the apple moved closer as though another person stood there, gripping her wrist and forcing it toward her mouth.

The apple touched her lips, the flesh smooth and yielding. She could no longer resist.

She bit into the fruit, and it was as sweet and delicious and fragrant as she had imagined. But there was a strangeness to the taste, an underlying tart bitterness like regret. It coiled around her tongue and slithered down her throat. Her lungs tightened and her chest ached as she fell back on the ground, struggling to breathe, the apple slipping from her hand. The branches of the tree seemed to spin above her as she pressed her hands to her neck, choking desperately for air.

Koichi, she thought, as stars danced before her eyes. *Wren.*

Someone called her name again. Jade thrashed on the grass, the fingers of one hand clawing for the apple. She had to unite the relics. If she did not, all of their efforts would have been for nothing. The war would be lost. Xifeng would win and delight in torturing each and every person Jade loved . . .

Her vision went black.

Over the roaring in her ears, she heard a terrified cry: "Jade, no!" It sounded like Fu.

His voice was the last thing Jade heard before she died.

39

Swords clashed. Men and women and horses screamed. Bones and blood and carcasses of black serpents tarnished the pristine grass. As the fires raged and the plumes of incense billowed upward, Koichi leapt off his horse and rolled into the shrubs, shouting to Wren. She crouched beside him, tearing strips off her tunic to wrap around their noses and mouths.

"I lost Jade in all the smoke," he gasped, his words muffled. "Did she make it?"

"Sparrow would have made sure she did." Wren watched avidly as the Crimson Queen speared a man from collarbone to navel, her mouth twisted with hatred, and her lieutenants slashed and stabbed at opponents around her in a perfect dance.

Wren had never heard such music. It called to her, made her blood flow faster and her muscles tense for flight. She had only ever dreamed of battle, of using her rage to fight evil and injustice. Everyone had mocked the little girl swinging blunt swords and handling crossbows twice her size. Everyone kept telling her, "You are a woman, and war is not a place for women."

Yet here she was on a fiery battleground, watching female warriors trade the Imperial soldiers' strikes with fire and ferocity, blow for blow. The Crimson Army moved so fast, she saw only a whirl of swords and daggers and bodies. It sang to her, the power and the vicious beauty of these women—the strength and the fury with which they reclaimed control of their shattered lives and disposed of their enemies.

She pulled out her weapons, ignoring Koichi's hushed warning, and rose to her feet with a blade in each hand. She considered where to begin. Perhaps this soldier ten feet away with his back to her, busy attacking one of the female warriors, would be a good place . . .

Wren waited for the perfect timing, then launched herself at him and embedded her dagger into his neck. He collapsed at once, his body folding in upon itself as a thin stream of smoke emerged from his armor. Within seconds, nothing lay there but a dead serpent.

"Well done," the assassin managed to say, before spinning to clash swords with another Imperial soldier, her long braid swinging behind her.

Wren had no time to study her first kill before another soldier came charging at her. She ducked his blow, but lost her balance and fell to the ground. His arms lifted, ready to bring the blade down, but she executed a move her brother had taught her long ago, sweeping her leg behind his knees forcefully. He collapsed, and she dug her knife straight into his masked face.

Two down.

"Look out!" Koichi shouted.

She spun to see an Imperial soldier racing toward her. Koichi dashed out from the shrub, tripping him. The man executed a neat flip on the ground, rising to his feet, but it was enough time for Wren to stab him through the chest with both weapons.

"Thanks for the warning," she told Koichi breathlessly.

"Let's see if we can get to the clearing and Jade."

Reluctantly, Wren left the battle and followed him. The air was cleaner away from the fighting, where incense hung over the battleground like fog. They scurried along the perimeter as a familiar voice cut through their concentration.

"Well, well, how the lowly have risen. From princess's handmaiden to warrior."

Kang stood apart from the fighting, wearing full black metal armor. Behind him sat a rosewood palanquin covered in red silk, protected by four masked soldiers. Unlike his men, Kang's head was uncovered, and as he gave them a monstrous sneer, Wren could not look away.

He had ridden past them once on their journey, but aside from that, she had only ever seen him at court with a condescending look on his fleshy face. Now, he had been transformed: his eyes had grown larger and the whites had disappeared, leaving only black pupils; his stark-white skin was lined with red veins; and his mouth opened to reveal sharp teeth and a long red tongue.

"You!" Wren shrieked. She lunged forward with her blades, prepared to end the life of the monster that had killed her grandmother, but Koichi gripped her waist with all of his strength.

Kang's sardonic gaze moved to Koichi. "Shiro forgot to mention that his son was a traitor to the crown when we visited him. I'll have to call on him again."

"With any luck, you'll be dead before you disturb my father again," Koichi spat.

"So brave for such a little man," the eunuch said mockingly.

"That's rich," Wren sneered, pointing her blades at him, "coming from someone who styles himself *the Empress's huntsman* but doesn't even ride a horse into battle. I hope they put plenty of satin pillows in that palanquin for you."

"I'll teach you the meaning of respect yet." Quick as a flame, Kang whipped out his sword and held the tip to Wren's neck. The blade caught on her skin and a red-hot line of pain formed across her throat, but she met his gaze without wincing.

"Go on," she taunted him. "Kill me, monster. We'll see how far that gets you when . . ."

"When the Dragon Guard arrives?" the eunuch finished, clucking his tongue at their reactions. "You truly believed Her Imperial Majesty didn't know what you were up to? You prayed we weren't monitoring your every step as you collected the relics?"

Wren bit her tongue, her pulse pounding right below the cool tip of Kang's sword.

"The Empress is more merciful than I am. If it were up to me, I would have killed you at once, but she advised patience. So we waited for your pathetic little ragtag band to gather the treasures, building and building up hope . . . for absolutely nothing."

Wren gave a harsh laugh. "The relics have been found. The Dragon Guard is coming."

The eunuch made a show of looking all around them. "I don't see any heavenly warriors here, do you? Perhaps it's because the princess has fallen into the last trap set for her. The apple, of course." He leered as the color drained from Koichi's face. "The poison made it irresistible to her, and quite deadly too."

Koichi and Wren stared at each other, the same realization striking them both. Jade's vision had shown the dragon dying of a poisoned wound and bleeding out a pool that had watered the tree's roots. If the pool contained the deadly substance, it would have soaked into the trunk, the branches, and then the apple . . .

Without another word, Koichi turned and ran as fast as his legs could carry him. Kang's soldiers made as though to pursue him, but the eunuch shook his head. "Let him see that the princess died before she could *truly* reunite the treasures. The Empress's throne is secure."

"I don't believe you." Wren's gut twisted with terror for the girl she had come to love like a sister. Perhaps Jade hadn't eaten enough of the apple, perhaps Koichi could save her . . .

Kang seemed to sense her thoughts. "The Dragon King's line has ended. No one but the heirs of his blood can enter and retrieve those treasures, so I'm afraid your precious Dragon Guard can never now be summoned." He dug his sword deeper into her throat, and Wren hissed in pain. Suddenly, the sword was slapped away by another blade.

Ming positioned himself in front of Wren. "Step away, eunuch."

Kang's eyes widened in shock. "You!"

"Yes," the former soldier snarled, "me."

"I never thought you'd show yourself here again." Kang opened his mouth to continue, but he fell silent when the palanquin's red silk curtains parted and a woman stepped out.

"I always believed he would, Kang," said Empress Xifeng. Her deep forest-colored robes swirled around her legs as she approached Ming. He pivoted to face her, his muscles tense and his sword clenched in his hand. His blade was close enough to take off her head with one swing.

"Kill her!" Wren screamed. "Kill her, Ming!"

Kang and his soldiers moved forward at once, weapons raised, but

Xifeng held up a hand to stop them. "He won't hurt me," she said in a calm voice, looking up at Ming. "He would never hurt me. Isn't that true, my dear one?"

Wren watched in horror as Ming sheathed his sword, bowed his head, and collapsed to his knees before the Empress. He leaned his face into her hand and closed his eyes.

"Wei," Xifeng said, her voice very low. "The boy who loved me, and the man I will always love."

"Traitor!" Wren bellowed at his back. "You led us to her! You've been working for her all along!" She hurtled toward him, blades at the ready, but Kang seized her upper arm. The touch of her grandmother's murderer was like fire on her skin. Wren twisted in his grip and stabbed her dagger mercilessly deep into the eunuch's bicep. When he let go, roaring with fury, she dug her two blades into either side of his left knee, stabbing sure and strong. He plummeted to the ground, screaming a curse as she pulled back, ready to stab the knife and dagger through his other leg. But he grabbed her foot before she had a chance, and yanked her onto the ground.

Wren fell hard onto her stomach and rolled over, kicking Kang in the mouth with her free leg, her blades slashing wildly as he tried to grab her. One of his hands slipped on the sharp edge of her dagger as he seized it, spurting his thick noxious blood on the ground, but it was enough to pull the weapon from her hand.

It was no matter. She used her free fist to haul back and punch him in the nose with all her strength, feeling some of the bones in her hand crack as she did so. Kang grabbed her by the elbow and wrenched, and Wren was flung onto her side like a rag doll. She dug the knife she still held into his uninjured leg, straight into the meaty part of the calf, but the eunuch was too strong for her. He wrenched that blade away as well and tossed it aside.

Now, free of weapons, Wren attacked him with her fists, legs, and adrenaline only, hatred and vengeance coursing through her veins. He hauled back and slapped her hard across the face, then seized her by the hair and bared her throat beneath his cruel blade.

"Ming!" Wren pleaded, but the soldier and the Empress were walking away together.

"There's no one to help you now, you little witch." Kang lifted the sword, preparing to decapitate her, but the next moment, an arrow the length of Wren's arm pierced his neck. A tremor shook his thick body as he fell backward, and Wren crawled away as a second and a third arrow flew at the eunuch, embedding themselves in his chest and stomach.

Two women garbed in black, lips shining crimson beneath their masks, emerged from the trees and fired their crossbows at Kang. Lying on the ground with arrows piercing his body, the eunuch laughed and laughed, a wild, high-pitched sound that sent chills down Wren's spine.

"No!" Wren shouted as one of the assassins prepared to take the final shot. Kang, his mouth still stretched in a gruesome smile, turned to her. "I want to do the honors."

The warriors lowered their crossbows as Wren picked up the eunuch's sword and brandished it. "Is this what you used to kill my grandmother, monster?"

And despite all of the arrows in his body, Kang lifted his shoulders from the ground to bring his face close to hers. "I used it to slice up her heart for the Empress, too," he whispered.

No sooner had he finished the sentence than Wren swung the sword with both hands like an ax. The eunuch's head rolled across the forest floor and bumped against a tree, his lips still spread in silent mirth. The blood gushed from his neck onto the ground, steaming black, and Wren gave his body a savage kick, then another and another. It took a moment to realize that the violent sobs ringing in the air had come from her own chest.

"He's dead. Let go now," said one of the warriors who had helped her. Wren saw that it was the assassin with the long braided hair. She took the eunuch's sword from Wren and flung it over to his head. "That was for saving my life earlier. You're not half bad with a blade."

"Thank you," Wren managed to say, exchanging a nod with the woman, who ran off to join the battle again with her companion.

She allowed herself one brief moment of grief, leaning against a tree, before gathering her blades and sprinting toward the *tengaru* clearing. When she plunged into the field, she saw two people strolling hand in hand across the grass. She stared in disbelief at Ming and the Empress, talking quietly as though the Imperial soldiers and the Crimson Army weren't felling each other in a mess of blood and fire a hundred feet away from them.

"Ming!" Wren shrieked, furious, but he did not even look in her direction.

I'll deal with him later, she thought, clenching her jaw as she dashed onto the first bridge and across the island. Koichi was bent double by the silver gates, clutching his stomach as though in great pain. She seized his shoulders. "Where are you hurt? What happened?"

"I tried to enter, but I couldn't," he said brokenly, showing her the terrible burns on his skin. "A hot force threw me back out of the gates. Kang wasn't lying, Wren. Jade's gone."

Wren whirled to look inside. A pond surrounded the apple tree, and below the surface, she saw the dragon lying beside a smaller body with a cloud of black hair. Thick roots had wrapped around both corpses, as though the tree had tugged them into the pond. Wren slumped against the gate, shaking with grief and exhaustion. All they had endured. All they had lost.

"I couldn't stop her," Fu groaned. Wren raised her head to see the ghost on the other side of the gate. "I remained here on earth to protect my sister and I failed. I'm sorry, Koichi."

"Fu," Wren uttered, her heart in her throat. "You're inside. The gates let you in."

"I ran in when I saw her bring the apple to her lips."

A wild, rising hope filled her breast. "The gates let you in," she repeated, trying not to scream with frustration. "You're the son of Empress Lihua, a descendant of the Dragon King. You're no longer living, but your spirit is here! You can reunite the relics!"

Koichi looked up, wild eyed. "It's true," he gasped. "Jade said you could take corporeal form when you had strong emotions. You saved her from quicksand and held off the Serpent God in the dark world for her."

"Exactly!" Wren cried.

Understanding bloomed on Fu's face. Without another word, he rushed over to his sister's scattered belongings. Wren could have shouted for joy when his transparent fingers grabbed the crane feather cloak without passing through it. She and Koichi clutched each other, watching as Fu laid the cloak on the ground with the rose, fishbone, and sword of Tu Lam on top.

His mouth sagging with grief, he plucked the apple from beside Jade's body in the pond. The fruit had faded to a dull gray-red, with a perfect circle of white where Jade had bitten into it.

Even this far away, Wren could smell its sweet scent, like a warm spring morning when flowers the color of sun and flame burst in the meadows. She looked at the apple in Fu's hands with a sudden savage hunger and thought she might break down the gates with her bare hands if it meant she could have a bite too. Koichi's hand tightened on her shoulder and she looked away, breathing heavily, the enchantment broken.

"No one could have resisted it," she whispered, and he shook his head grimly.

But the ghost did not seem in the least affected by the apple. Fu carried it over to the relics, the treasures chosen by the gods ages ago to represent their kingdoms and honor their friendship. Integrity, resourcefulness, faith, humility, determination: all the lessons they had sought to teach leaders who followed in their footsteps—all the stories that conveyed their histories and the values they held dearest.

"This is for Jade," Fu whispered.

And he dropped the apple on top of the cloak with the other relics.

40

The world fell away as though behind a muted curtain.

Ming—or Wei, as he had once been called—no longer heard swords clashing as enemy met enemy. He did not see Wren struggling with Kang on the ground, smell the trees of the Great Forest burning in the lantern fire, or feel the plumes of black incense on his skin.

All of his senses, all of him, belonged to Xifeng, the girl with whom he had grown up, the girl he had passionately loved long ago in the village only they could remember.

They walked, hands joined, safe in a world apart from the battlefield. And as she looked at him, her mask fell away, leaving behind someone who looked very young and very tired.

"Wei." Xifeng's lips caressed the name.

He held her hand tightly, afraid it might slip away. "I've never stopped loving you. No matter how many years passed, no matter how many places I roamed or women with whom I tried to fill your place. No one ever lived up to you."

Xifeng's lips, red as the apple that had slipped from Jade's lifeless fingers, curved sadly. "I have never stopped loving *you*. You've always been the only one." She hid her face against his chest as she had done when they were young. Wei rested his head on top of hers, remembering.

"You never loved Emperor Jun."

"That weak husband of mine could no more stir my heart than command the stars. He was nothing. He *is* nothing. Where have you been, love?"

"In the deserts of Surjalana," Wei said, holding her close to him. "Sleeping on the sands beneath the blazing sky."

She looked up with soft eyes. It had been two decades since he had seen her last, but there was not a single line or wrinkle to mar them. "That was where we talked of going," she said, leading him into the *tengaru* clearing. It was as though she had drawn a protective shield around the two of them, and though Wei saw figures darting around, everything was blurred except for the woman on his arm. "Do you remember the first time we came here?"

"You were eighteen and beautiful as the night, and I was hungry to join the Imperial Army. We saw the *tengaru* with Hideki . . . and Shiro." Something about the name brought Wei back to the world outside for a fleeting moment. As they approached the pond, he saw a small man crumpled by the gates of the apple tree enclosure. A familiar-looking girl knelt beside him. But Xifeng turned his chin back to her, and their surroundings fell away once more.

She pointed at the island, still shaded by weeping willows as it had been twenty years before. "The *tengaru* queen lay there, and beyond is the apple tree, which belongs to someone more deserving than me," she said, but the trace of bitterness in her voice vanished when she gazed up at him. "What a life we have lived, Wei of mine, though we lived it apart."

"You've done more than the *tengaru* ever predicted for you," he said, touching her face.

Xifeng's eyes clouded, and she lowered her head under his gaze. The movement was so familiar, it made Wei's breath catch in his throat. How many times had she done that when they were young and in love? The worry on her features, the dip of her chin as though ashamed. Something in his expression had always prompted this.

"You were not with me these twenty years," she said. "But I feel as though you know everything in the way you look at me. You see every woman who turned to me with fear, every shadow in the firelight, every image in the mirror-water. Hearts beating in my hands and blood on my lips, just as my mother taught me all those long years ago."

Wei looked at her in silence.

"No one has ever been able to see me as you did. As you do now." She stood on her toes and pressed her warm, soft lips against his.

"I can't forget the day I left you," Wei said. "I was heartbroken after you had promised yourself to Emperor Jun. But you were crying, and I realized then that you loved me, not him."

"But you left me anyway." For the first time, Xifeng sounded angry. "You left me when I would have raised you high and taken care of you. I would have made something of you and you would never have had to be hungry or lonely. Yes, I can see *that* in you. You languished alone all these years in the desert, when we could have been together. Such a waste."

"You're right, Xifeng."

She went still. "Say my name again," she breathed in a pleading, cajoling tone no one had ever heard the Empress of Feng Lu use. "Please."

"Xifeng," he said, and she kissed him again fiercely, as though she had been starving for decades. They broke apart, gasping, and then their lips met again slowly. "Xifeng," he whispered against her mouth. "I chose to leave you, but you have never left me."

"What a choice that was."

"I've always had a choice. Same as you, and you have it still." Wei held her away from him. "Give up this madness of blood and hearts and ghosts in mirrors. What can the Serpent God give you that I cannot?"

At once, her impassive Empress mask slipped back as surely as if her own fingers had held it there, hiding the girl he had once known. "Don't speak of him."

"Renounce him." Wei gripped her shoulders. It had been years, but that fantasy still consumed him: the thought that by shaking her, he might be able to dislodge her sorceress mother's hold on her. "Give up your crown. It doesn't make you happy, but I can. Even with all your silks and servants, you've suffered as much as I have these twenty years. You've been as alone in the palace as I have in the desert."

Her laugh seemed full of bloodshed and darkness, obsession and madness. "I am never alone, Wei, and never have been. You know that. I'm not as silly and empty-headed as you and my mother liked to think. As *he* likes to think, believing a few empty threats and illusions will coerce me to do his bidding."

Xifeng broke away from Wei and gazed at her flawless reflection in the water.

"I took this path so I could be in control of my own fate, powerful and free. Don't you think I know I lost myself along the way? Don't you think I realized, at long last, that this life comes with the *loss* of freedom, not the winning of it? I have paid a high price."

This argument, too, was familiar. "But you had a choice," Wei insisted.

"Oh, I chose, my love," she said, turning back to him. "I knew I had a choice all along, and I made it. I just didn't choose you."

Even after all these years, her words cut Wei to the quick. He leaned on the railing of the bridge with his head in his hands, but Xifeng forced his face back toward hers.

"I didn't know no other man but you could ever sit by my side. I knew I needed Emperor Jun to take the throne, but I didn't realize how easy he would be to bend to my will. He's just a puppet, Wei. I could take his empire and keep you by my side."

"As another puppet?"

Xifeng blinked at his bitter tone. "As my lover and minister and confidante. Dream of me no more. It is *your* turn to choose. My mother's cards have forever shown the warrior and the Empress together, fates entwined. You've always had a part to play in my destiny."

"Your mother's cards," Wei repeated, the words stirring the dust in his mind.

"You're here now. Play your part in my destiny as you were meant to," she pleaded. "Be with me, if you truly love me. Do you?"

Wei looked deep into Xifeng's eyes. "Yes," he said fervently. "I love you. I always have loved you, and I always will."

And then he tore his sword from its sheath and plunged it into Empress Xifeng's heart.

"I love you," he repeated, tears pouring down his cheeks as he stabbed her again and again. Blood gushed out and stained her green silk robes. "I love you. I love you."

He kept the cards' promise.

He played his part in her destiny.

He ended her dark and brutal reign—took from her what she had taken from so many with neither grief nor conscience. He continued driving the sword through her heart even when she lay still in a pool of her own red-black blood, her sightless gaze on the lanterns of the forest. The little shield she had created around them disappeared, and the clearing came into focus as bloodshed and screaming and clanging weapons assaulted his ears.

"Goodbye," he told her, for the second time in twenty years.

And then Wei left Xifeng—Empress of Feng Lu, love of his life—behind him forever.

41

A great shaking and thundering sounded from deep within the earth. Fu stepped away from the gods' relics, wide eyed as the silver gates around the apple tree began to tremble in a great wind that roared through the *tengaru* clearing.

Koichi pulled Wren onto the safety of the island and they crouched behind a boulder, watching in horror as the wind ripped the gates right out of the soil and flung them away, opening the apple tree enclosure for the first time in countless ages. The sky deepened from blue velvet to ink black as the thousand lanterns flickered in the branches and on the forest floor. Still, the battle raged on, swords clashing and voices adding to the din of thunder.

"Look!" Koichi cried. They saw Ming running out of the clearing, roaring as he charged at Imperial soldiers with renewed fury, gripping a sword and a long lethal dagger in each hand.

Wren detected a splash of green silk where Ming had been standing and saw with a shock that Empress Xifeng lay sprawled on the grass.

The woman had a horrific gaping wound in her chest, and her eyes pointed sightlessly at the roiling black sky. *I must destroy her, or she must destroy me.* Xifeng had believed that of Jade, Wren recalled, but the woman was now dead herself. What would become of Feng Lu with both of them gone?

"Ming didn't betray us after all," Wren said in disbelief. "He loved her and he let her go."

Pain flitted across Koichi's face as he looked back at the apple tree where Jade lay.

The earth's shaking grew increasingly fierce and violent. Rocks scattered and branches snapped from the trees, and at last the battle waned. The fighters looked around them, faces wary and vigilant. Then, all at once, the thousand lanterns shone as blindingly as the sun, illuminating the Great Forest until it was as bright as day.

Wren covered her head with her hands as the sky cracked in two.

The disturbed waters of the pond splashed over her and Koichi, chilling them, and something large descended from the clouds and landed upon the earth. *Four* of them, to be exact.

She dug her fingers into Koichi's arm. "It's them, the Dragon Guard," she choked out.

"No." Fu floated beside them, his eyes on the beings before them. "Not the Dragon Guard, but the gods. They've seen fit to answer this summons themselves."

Four magnificent dragons towered over the clearing, as high as trees and fierce as fire. All of them had five talons on each foot and a serpentine tail that ended in a stream of deep red. Their eyes were bright with otherworldly wisdom and power beneath the two twisting gold antlers upon their kingly heads. Only in the color of their scales did they differ.

The largest, the Dragon King himself, had a body of gleaming pine green like the trees of the Great Forest, while the second was a deep water-blue. The third had scales of fog and smoke, gray as mountains beneath a winter sky, and the last was bright gold like grasslands in summer.

Koichi leaned forward, bowing, and Wren did the same. She trembled at the sight of the gods standing shoulder to shoulder, furious and magnificent as they faced the battlefield.

"When their alliance ended, they pledged to never directly involve themselves with the mortal world again. Why have they come now?" Koichi asked.

"Because the heir of the Dragon King called them," Fu said, his face full of grief. "I helped my sister complete her task, but she brought the relics to the clearing. She proved her worth as a ruler to the gods. And perhaps they wanted to end this, once and for all."

"This?" Wren repeated, but then the wind changed: it became hot and dusty, smelling of vast dunes and days of endless sun.

Glittering grains of desert sand fluttered over the grass, which began to wither and die, turning an arid yellow-gray color where it had been lush moments earlier. The trees that had not yet burned bent their heads, their leaves transforming into the red and gold of autumn though it was only spring. The earth shook once more, and a crevice opened in the ground beneath Empress Xifeng, swallowing her dead body.

A massive, slithering form crawled from the crack: an enormous snake, black as night and five times as long, with a pattern of deep scarlet spots all over its body like a million drops of blood. Its eyes, too, were deep scarlet and full of hatred as it regarded the four dragons in the clearing, and a toxic smell like damp soil and rotten swamp grass hung over it.

"A Dragon Lord who has forfeited his dragon form," Koichi said in a very low voice. "He wanted to be unique and separate himself from the others. And so he became the Serpent God."

"But he's a coward," Wren said. "How dare he show himself to them after everything?"

"The other gods answered our summons and they must have compelled him forth, too. Maybe some magic unites them still, so that when they come forward, *all* of them come."

"If the Serpent God wants Feng Lu," Fu said grimly, "he'll have to fight for it."

The five Dragon Lords regarded one another for a long moment, the first time they had been together since the destruction of their alliance. Wren could not see how the Serpent God could stand against the other four until she realized that the great wind of their arrival had put out the fires in the forest, killing the smoke of Xifeng's incense.

Now, with only the lantern light upon them, the Empress's men regained their true forms as ruby-eyed serpents. The snakes poured into the clearing and piled on top of each other, whirling like a spiraling fog until they formed three massive red-spotted snakes identical to the Serpent God. They joined their master, blurring in and out of focus until it was no longer clear which of the four huge serpents was the true Serpent God. One by one, their mouths opened to reveal a thick forked tongue, a garish imitation of a smile.

Beyond this new battleground, the Crimson Queen and her army stood motionless, looking on. In their posture, Wren saw why: this was not their battle to fight. Not any of theirs.

This last and final battle belonged to the gods.

The four mighty dragons advanced, putting one sharp-taloned foot in front of the other, approaching the four serpents with deadly intention.

"How will they know which is the real Serpent God?" Wren gasped, but Koichi and Fu shook their heads, unable to look away from the scene.

And then the battle began.

The dragons and snakes lunged at each other, their bodies meeting in a colossal crash that shook the foundations of the earth in a deafening roar. Broken branches flew off the trees as the gods hurtled toward each other again and again, every movement rife with hatred and vengeance. Snake scales rained to the ground and dragon blood splattered the trunks of the Great Forest.

Koichi prayed over and over in an undertone, but Wren didn't know how that would help, seeing as the gods were preoccupied.

The largest, forest-green dragon seized a snake with its front talons and flung it against a tree, generating another tremor in the earth. The serpent recovered and plunged forward, sinking two ivory fangs the size of swords into the dragon's shoulder. The very moon shook in the heavens as the dragon roared with pain, blood gushing from its body as it circled the snake.

Beside them, the ocean-blue dragon and another snake were attached in a spinning infinite loop. The dragon's talons were buried in the serpent's neck, and the serpent's jaw was embedded in the dragon's flank. They spun in a painful, frantic whirl until at last, the blue dragon ripped the snake's head off with a mighty scream and threw it into the forest, where it felled a dozen burned trees and lay still, the head rolling away.

As Wren, Koichi, and Fu looked on, the snake's head and body deteriorated into black smoke, vanishing into the air. It wasn't the real Serpent God, but still the victory stirred the four dragons into a greater frenzy as they surrounded the three remaining snakes, teeth bared.

As though in silent agreement, the dragons leapt upon the snake in the middle.

Koichi covered his eyes, but Wren looked on with vengeful delight as they shredded the snake with their talons, sending a haze of blood and black scales down, which also vanished into smoke. The remaining two serpents wasted no time as their comrade died. They leapt into the fray, hissing violently as they sank their fangs into the yellow dragon. One of them, Wren knew, was the Serpent God himself—too angered, too full of hatred to remember his cowardice.

The yellow dragon collapsed, sending a massive shudder through the earth that cracked the bridge. It pinched its eyes shut in pain as blood streamed from its body. Meanwhile, one of the snakes had begun attacking the gray dragon, which slashed and whipped its tail furiously, while the other serpent fended off the talons of the red and blue dragons.

A ferocious scream erupted from the Great Forest. It came from neither dragon nor snake, but from the throat of a man, powerfully built with a blade in each hand, who rushed toward the snake attacking the gray dragon. The serpent had time only to turn its head, startled by this tiny figure running at it, before Ming sliced its head off with three brutal swipes of his weapons. The beast's body shook as the smoke left it and it vanished, leaving only Ming with his bloody sword and dagger still brandished in the air.

"What is he thinking?" Wren hissed. "This isn't his fight!"

But Koichi only looked at the crack in the earth through which Xifeng had disappeared, as though he understood.

In the center of the clearing, the yellow dragon rose painfully on its back legs and joined the other gods in forming a circle around the fourth and final snake—the Serpent God, now without any Imperial soldiers, any shield behind which to hide.

None of the gods spoke. But the snake hissed and the dead

bloodstained grass rustled beneath the dragons' feet, and Wren imagined what they might have said to one another. The loss of their friendship had cut deep enough to sever the ties to the heavens and destroy what they had shared, when once they had walked the earth as brothers and benevolent rulers of Feng Lu.

There was such hurt in the air that it made Wren tremble with the intensity of it. She turned to Koichi, but realized he was gone. Unable to watch the violence or be apart from Jade any longer, he had hurried to the apple tree, now laid bare and ungated.

So it was that Wren, watching Koichi with pity in her heart, did not see the death of the Serpent God. She kept her eyes on her friend's slumped shoulders as he sobbed over the princess who lay beneath the fleecy branches of the tree. It was love and loss that filled her eyes, not the blood or the ravaged tremors of the snake as the dragons devoured it whole.

When Wren turned back to the battlefield, what remained of the Serpent God's body was only a pile of bloody bones, and the four dragons stood sorrowfully facing the direction of the apple tree. She wondered if they mourned the loss of Jade or of the water-blue dragon who had once guarded the tree in their name. Perhaps it was all one and the same.

As one, the four remaining Dragon Lords bowed their heads to the tree. And then the world shook as they burst into the night, parting the stars on their way back to the heavens. The gale they left in their wake swept the thousand lanterns of Lihua's story off the ground and out of the trees. The lights flew up and away into the sky, leaving the Great Forest in complete darkness for the first time in fifteen years.

Their task was complete. They had eradicated the final vestiges of true evil on Feng Lu.

And I played a part. Wren's legs trembled as she walked to where Koichi knelt, stopping to look at the gods' treasures. The rose had now faded, as had the shine of Tu Lam's sword. The cloak looked like a mass of dirty gray feathers, and the fishbone like something that belonged in a pile of trash in the palace kitchens.

The palace kitchens.

Wren's shoulders shook and something bubbled in her throat, inappropriate and yet somehow necessary. She burst into laughter even as tears rained down her cheeks, relief and joy and terror and devastation mingling together, and the disbelief that a year ago, she had been kneeling on the floor of Xifeng's kitchens, scrubbing pots and wishing for a different life.

Ming came toward her, covered in snake blood, as did the Crimson Army.

"It's over," Wren said, gasping for air. Ming placed a hand on her shoulder, his face still full of grief for what he had been forced to do. "It's all over."

42

Dawn broke over the Great Forest and shone its pale light upon the apple tree. Pink streaked through the sky, the only sign of the heavens shattering the night before, and birds sang in the war-ravaged woods. Broken branches and crushed flowers filled the clearing where the battle had raged, but all thoughts lay on the scene before them.

Koichi pulled Jade from the water and laid her upon the grass, his head drooping. He held one of the dead princess's hands and did not look up when Wren came over with Empress Lihua's and Amah's brocade cloak. Quietly, she draped it over Jade's wet body. Ming came too, gathering a branch of rose-gold apple blossoms to lay upon the girl's arms.

Behind them, the Crimson Queen and her warriors dropped to their knees, their right arms folded over their hearts in a sign of respect—not because of her royal blood, but because they had recognized in her what they themselves sought to uphold.

My princess, Koichi thought, *whose love might have brightened my life.*

Jade did not look as though she had passed on in pain or sorrow. There was only peace in the gentle slope of her brows, her sun-warmed cheeks, and her rosy upturned lips. She lay in contentment and joy, for she had loved and been loved. She had known herself, she had made her choices freely, and she had always overcome the fears that plagued her.

Koichi knew *that*, above all, had threatened Xifeng: the strength of the beauty inside Jade, her good and gentle heart, and her determination to right the world as best she could.

And now she was gone.

Xifeng had taken her from them.

A hot tear fell from Koichi's eyes and splashed onto Jade's cheek, and then another, as Fu knelt near his sister with his hands clasped in grief.

"The world must go on without her," the ghost whispered. "But how, when she was the one thing that might have renewed it?"

Grief twisted Ming's features. Some of it, Koichi knew, was for Xifeng. The man had lost someone he loved tonight, too . . . or the memory of her. He had lingered on all these years in the desert, dreaming of a woman who had already gone from him long ago.

And I must do the same, Koichi thought. "Goodbye, Princess. Go with all my love," he whispered, bringing his lips down to meet hers. He kissed her for the last time and squeezed her small, cold hand, as he had done on their journey.

Her fingers twitched in his.

Koichi drew back in shock. He felt them all watching him, full of concern, as he bent over her again. Her skin changed from gray to pink and a light breath emerged from her lips.

Slowly, her eyes opened just as dawn broke over the clearing in its brilliant peach-and-gold glory. "Koichi?" she asked, the name ragged in her throat. She coughed several times, then turned her head and spat a large, ragged piece of red apple onto the grass.

She and Koichi gazed at each other for a long, charged moment, tears cascading down their faces, before he seized her in his arms and kissed her again, deep and fierce. They barely heard the raucous cheering of all who looked on—the Crimson Army's stoic faces brightening, Ming genuinely laughing for the first time in years, and Wren crying with her hands over her face beside an overjoyed Fu.

Though Lihua's thousand lanterns had disappeared, the rays of the sun illuminated the places where the lights had once been. They glowed on the branches where the globes had shone out like beacons watching over the Great Forest and the young woman meant to rule them.

Jade looked around at them, her arms still around Koichi. "I saw my mother and Amah when I died," she told them, her voice hushed with wonder. "They reminded me of the tale of the apple tree, of how an exiled prince discovered one for the first time and survived against all expectations. The Dragon King always taught that hardship shows us who we truly are."

"And from death comes new life," Koichi said, his face glowing with happiness.

Jade looked up at the blooming branches. "When my mother died again as the dragon, her wound bled poison into the tree's roots and tainted the apple. But her love and her protection were in her blood, too, and entered every part of this tree. Your kiss, Koichi, was an act of love that awakened hers, and it was stronger than any poison, hatred, or evil."

The Crimson Army rose and stood before her respectfully as Jade got to her feet, her mother's brocade cloak still wrapped around her wet body.

"We have won, and Xifeng and the Serpent God are no more. My friends and I have traveled through fire and water to bring together the Dragon Lords' relics, and they will hold a place of honor in my halls for as long as the heirs of my blood sit on the throne." Jade looked up at the skies. "I will honor you, lords of heaven, with every beat of my heart and breath in my body. My children will revere your names. We will do our best to repair your shattered world."

Her words stirred the burned and ravaged trees of the clearing. A great and gentle wind rustled through the apple blossoms, showering petals in the air.

"My time here is done. I've accomplished what I was sent back to do," Fu said, his kind face full of joy and contentment, and Jade went to him and put her arms around his solid form. He had not relinquished it since he had reunited the relics. He looked over her head at Ming, calling him by the name Xifeng had used. "Wei, you did me a great favor in life. And in return, I have annoyed you . . . that is, kept your company, these many years."

Wei ran a hand over his wet face, shaking his head and chuckling.

"I must ask yet another favor of you," Fu said. "Please watch over my sister and take your rightful place as the head of her army in the Imperial Palace."

Wei's mouth trembled with emotion as he and the Crown Prince bowed deeply to each other. Then he turned and bowed low to Jade. "I will accept this request of your brother's, Your Imperial Majesty. I will be in your service for as long as you require."

"The Commander of my army," Jade said, looking fondly at him, then turned to Koichi. "I would be honored if you and your father, former Ambassador Shiro, would live with me in the palace and serve as my ministers and trusted advisers." Koichi placed one hand over his heart as he bowed, and her eyes moved from his beloved face to Wren. "What might I do for you, my friend? I would ask you to train under Wei, and perhaps one day become a great war general of mine, if that was what I felt you wanted. But I think your heart lies elsewhere."

"It does, Your Majesty." Wren would have gone on, but Jade held up a hand to stop her.

"You are my sister, and you will never call me anything but 'sister' or Jade. It's what our grandmother would have wanted." Wren's face crumpled as she and Jade threw their arms around each other, heart beating against heart. "No matter where you go, there will always be a place for you in the Imperial Palace. And I don't mean the kitchens," Jade added quickly, and the laughter burst from Wren again, joyous and fulfilled.

"Thank you, my sister," Wren told her, with all her heart in her eyes. She turned to the Crimson Queen and the fierce, courageous women behind her. "I would like nothing better than to join this army of warriors, if they'll have me. I want to live and train in the mountains and be of service to them like I've dreamed all my life."

The Crimson Queen did not hesitate. "More than one of my generals has told me of your prowess with the blade and of your great courage. It will be as you wish," she said, a rare smile crossing her stern features, and the women came forward to welcome Wren as one of their own.

"The hard work has only just begun, my friends, but with your help I am ready to face this new challenge. I'm not afraid," Jade said, standing tall, her shoulders held back proudly. "Not anymore, and never again."

EPILOGUE

Feng Lu struggled on for many long years.

Alliances and friendships had to be rebuilt, the trade route repaired and secured, and the farmlands revitalized after decades of poverty and neglect.

At eighteen years of age, Empress Jade, the last trueborn heir of the Dragon King, knew this well, but did not allow it to frighten her. She learned to call the Imperial Palace home and had every lingering vestige of her stepmother destroyed, ordering Empress Lihua's map of Feng Lu to be moved to her apartments beside the brocade map that had guided her through her wondrous adventures. She insisted on caring for Emperor Jun herself and spent many hours with her ailing father, who never recovered from his years of suffering and tried his best to impart what knowledge and wisdom he had to her. When he passed, Jade grieved him with genuine sorrow.

She gathered a group of ministers with great intellect and insight on how to right her stepmother's wrongs, with former Ambassador Shiro and his son, Koichi, as heads of the royal cabinet. Under her orders, they granted each kingdom its independence and sent envoys and gifts to each ruler, for Empress Jade insisted that no one know the Kingdom of the Great Forest as a supreme power or anything but a neighboring land and ally. She chose to maintain the honorary title of Empress of the Great Forest in name only, as a family tribute.

She pulled from the coffers the gold hoarded by the former Empress and distributed it over the land, strengthening farms and securing the Imperial City, in addition to stationing guards along the great trade route to increase its safety. She sent money to monasteries across the continent, particularly to the one helmed by Abbess Lin, to help them continue to serve the gods faithfully and care for the poor. The world would never be perfect, Jade knew, and change would be slow. But she was determined that Feng Lu would not suffer again during her reign. People recognized in her a shadow of Empress Lihua and rallied eagerly around the young queen, who listened to their concerns as though they were her own and met every challenge with zeal.

And every year, on the anniversary of Empress Jade's birth, the kingdom held a winter celebration in the Great Forest. Children planted trees to replace the ones lost in the Dragon Lords' final battle, and men and women climbed the trunks to dangle a thousand white lanterns on the branches, illuminating the woodlands in honor of the Empress's mother. The cheerful globes of light shone upon the feasting, drinking, and merrymaking in the *tengaru* clearing.

On just such an occasion, five years after the Dragon Lords had eradicated all vestiges of the Serpent God's evil, a young woman with eyes like the stars and a crown of white jasmine flowers in her night-dark hair kissed the man she loved and excused herself. Koichi nodded, his handsome, merry face softening in understanding as Jade left the festivities to walk alone to an apple tree that flourished in the heart of the wood.

New gates had been erected to protect the apple tree and the many seedlings sprouting all around it. Jade gazed at the branches and sleeping buds that would bloom once more in the spring. As she stood paying tribute to those she had loved and lost, she saw on the island in the clearing many ageless eyes watching her from long, angular heads as red as fire. She had only ever heard them described in Amah's stories, these horse-demons, both gentle and fierce by turns, who watched over the Great Forest with love and care. Jade bowed deeply to the *tengaru*, honoring them as guardians of the woodlands, and murmured a prayer of thanks for their return.

Outside, in the midst of the merrymaking, a proud-looking young woman garbed in black gathered all of the children beneath the newly hung lanterns. From her lips, painted crimson, everyone knew she was a member of that fearsome army of women who lived deep in the mountains of Dagovad. But they let their small sons and daughters go to her freely, trustingly, for she was Empress Jade's own heart-sister who returned to the Great Forest for each birthday celebration. And every year, she would tell the rapt children the tale of courageous Empress Jade, and of how that apple tree had taken her life and given it back again, thanks to a mother's powerful love that had transcended even death.

Every so often, Wren would look up in the midst of her storytelling and see Koichi seated beside Wei, grinning approvingly at her newfound appreciation for folktales. She would shrug, smile back, and continue painting with words the glittering lake where the sky-maidens had danced, the sea where a bold young man had fled his captors and found salvation, and the burning, unforgiving sands of the desert where once, a princess who had been lost had found herself again.

Beside the apple tree, Jade closed her eyes, feeling the light of the thousand lanterns on her skin, and thought it was the most beautiful feeling in the whole world.

ACKNOWLEDGMENTS

As surreal as it feels to have one book published, it is nothing compared to having *two* books published! The journey from childhood dream to bookshelf has been an epic quest in and of itself, and I am lucky to have so many wonderful people beside me on this adventure.

I owe the first thanks to my family, most notably: my mom, Mai, for supporting me in everything I do; my brothers, Jonathan and Justin, to whom this book is dedicated and whose Vietnamese given names inspired the great warrior Tu Lam; and my cousins, Hien and Thao Tran, for making it to my *Forest* launch party and buying an ungodly number of copies! I love you all so much!

To my agent, Tamar Rydzinski, whose friendship, enthusiasm, and wisdom I can always rely on: knowing you are there to comfort and advise me gives me so much courage on this often frightening journey. I can't believe it has been three years already! Here's to many, many more together.

My lovely editor, Jill Santopolo, helped me turn a messy manuscript into a book I'm proud of (she transformed a princess into an empress, if you will!). Jill, I am so grateful for your superb attention to detail, your understanding of my vision, and your keen insight into the relationships between my characters. Thanks also go to the kind and fabulous Talia Benamy, whose savvy editorial eye helped polish the story, and to Brian Geffen, beloved friend and mentor and cheerleader, who read an early draft and offered his brilliant ideas (and also many great restaurant recommendations). Most writers consider themselves lucky to have one good editor, but I have been fortunate to have had the three of you!

Thank you to each and every person at Philomel Books and Penguin Young Readers who helped bring my work to life. Katie Quinn, publicist extraordinaire, you expertly handle every question and situation and take good care of me at busy events, and I love you for it! A million thanks to Laurel Robinson, my copyeditor; Jennifer Chung, my interior book designer; and Lindsey Andrews, my cover designer. Much gratitude to Elora Sullivan, who mailed out more stuffed animal snakes than I'm sure she ever expected to in her life, and to Rachel Cone-Gorham, Felicity Vallence, Friya Bankwalla, and all of the magnificent social media, sales, and digital marketing team members who helped shine a spotlight on my books. Thank you to everyone at Listening Library and the Penguin Random House audio team for bringing my story to life in such a beautiful way, especially Julianna Wilson, Christina Rooney, Emily Parliman, and the incredible voice actress Kim Mai Guest, who gave Xifeng such raw, stunning power and aching vulnerability at the same time.

To the teams at Roca Editorial and Roca Juvenil, and to my translator, Scheherezade Surià: I am deeply honored to have *El Bosque de los Mil Farolillos* in your capable hands, and grateful for your support, generosity, and patience as I do my best to recover my high school Spanish!

Thank you to my film agents, Jon Cassir and Sarah Luciano at CAA, for everything you do.

To all of the educators, librarians, and booksellers who have supported my book: I am a writer today because people like yourselves encouraged me and pushed books into my hands when I was little. May you continue to help many a writer grow up to build worlds on the page. To all of the bloggers who took photos of my books and left reviews: your enthusiasm fills my grateful heart. Special thanks to Mish of Chasing Faerytales, my #FOTLFriday hostess with the mostest; Anissa of FairyLoot, who put together a gorgeous book box for *Forest*; and three of the sweetest bloggers I know: Alexa from Alexa Loves Books, Kristin from Super Space Chick, and Brittany from Brittany's Book Rambles.

Giant cookies, coffees, and hugs to Melody Marshall, Marisa Hopkins, N. K. Traver, and C. B. Lee for their fantastic notes on the early drafts of *Kingdom*. Thank you also to my friend Lola Alessi for reading an early draft! You all enrich my stories and my life, and I am forever grateful for you ladies.

Thank you to my ultra-supportive community of writer friends. Alison Green Myers, the most generous of friends, invited me to the workshop that changed my outlook on public speaking and introduced me to great people, including Aram Kim and Cindy Rankin. Thank you to my superstar Lucky 13s: Kevin van Whye, Kati Gardner, Rebecca Caprara, Jessica Rubinkowski, Mara Fitzgerald, Austin Gilkeson, Jordan Villegas, and Heather Kaczynski; I look forward to the day all of our books sit together on my shelves! Much love and gratitude to Stephanie Garber, Tracey Neithercott, Axie Oh, Peter Bognanni, and Tochi Onyebuchi, for commiserating with me, bolstering my spirits, and making me laugh when I need it. Thanks also go to Veronika Carter, David Alles, Kenneth Bechtel, Naima Dennis, Becky Clark, Pam Harris, and everyone in the office. I love you all!

As an Asian-American woman, I stand on the shoulders of literary giants who made it possible for my books to enter the world. Thank you in particular to Marie Lu and Cindy Pon, who have given this newbie the warmest, kindest welcome imaginable and inspired me to pay it forward.

Thank you to Joe Hisaishi, whose breathtaking music inspired every page of *Kingdom*.

And to all writers and dreamers, especially teens who don't have the support they need: please keep filling those pages and believing in their worth. I want to read *your* acknowledgments one day.

Julie C. Dao (www.juliedao.com) is a proud Vietnamese-American who was born in upstate New York. She studied medicine in college, but came to realize blood and needles were her Kryptonite. By day, she worked in science news and research; by night, she wrote books about heroines unafraid to fight for their dreams, which inspired her to follow her passion of becoming a published author. *Forest of a Thousand Lanterns* was her debut novel. Julie lives in New England.

Follow her on Twitter @jules_writes.